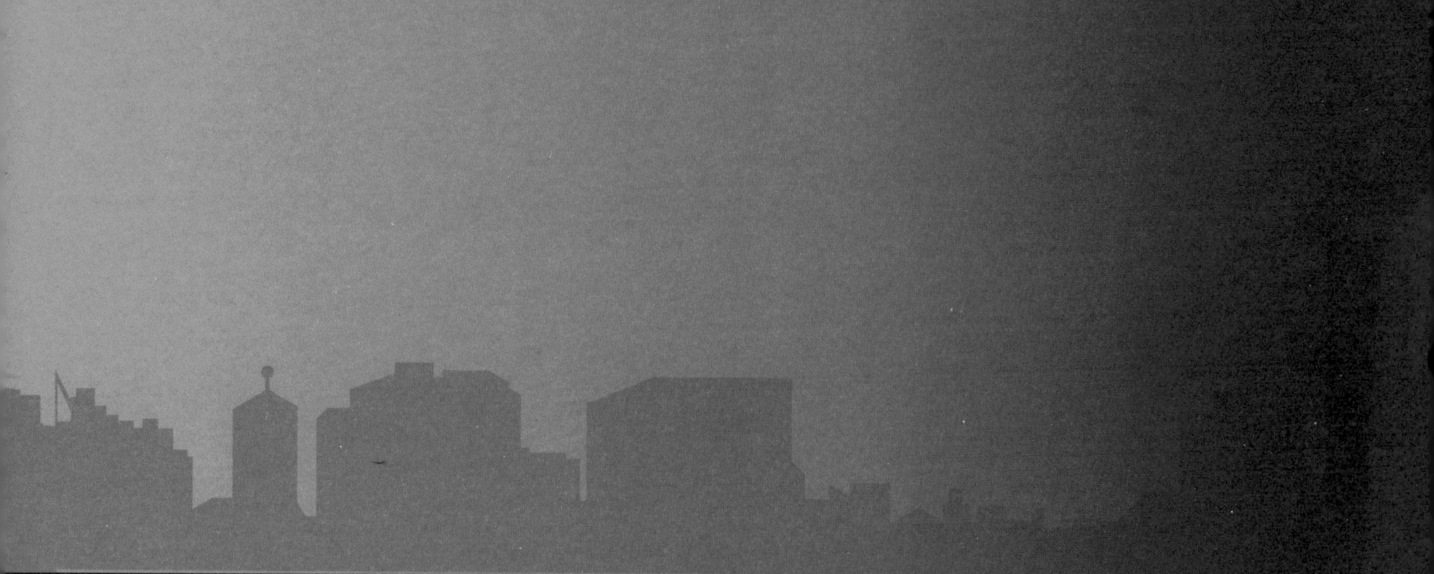

DC

WONDER WOMAN™

5-MINUTE STORIES

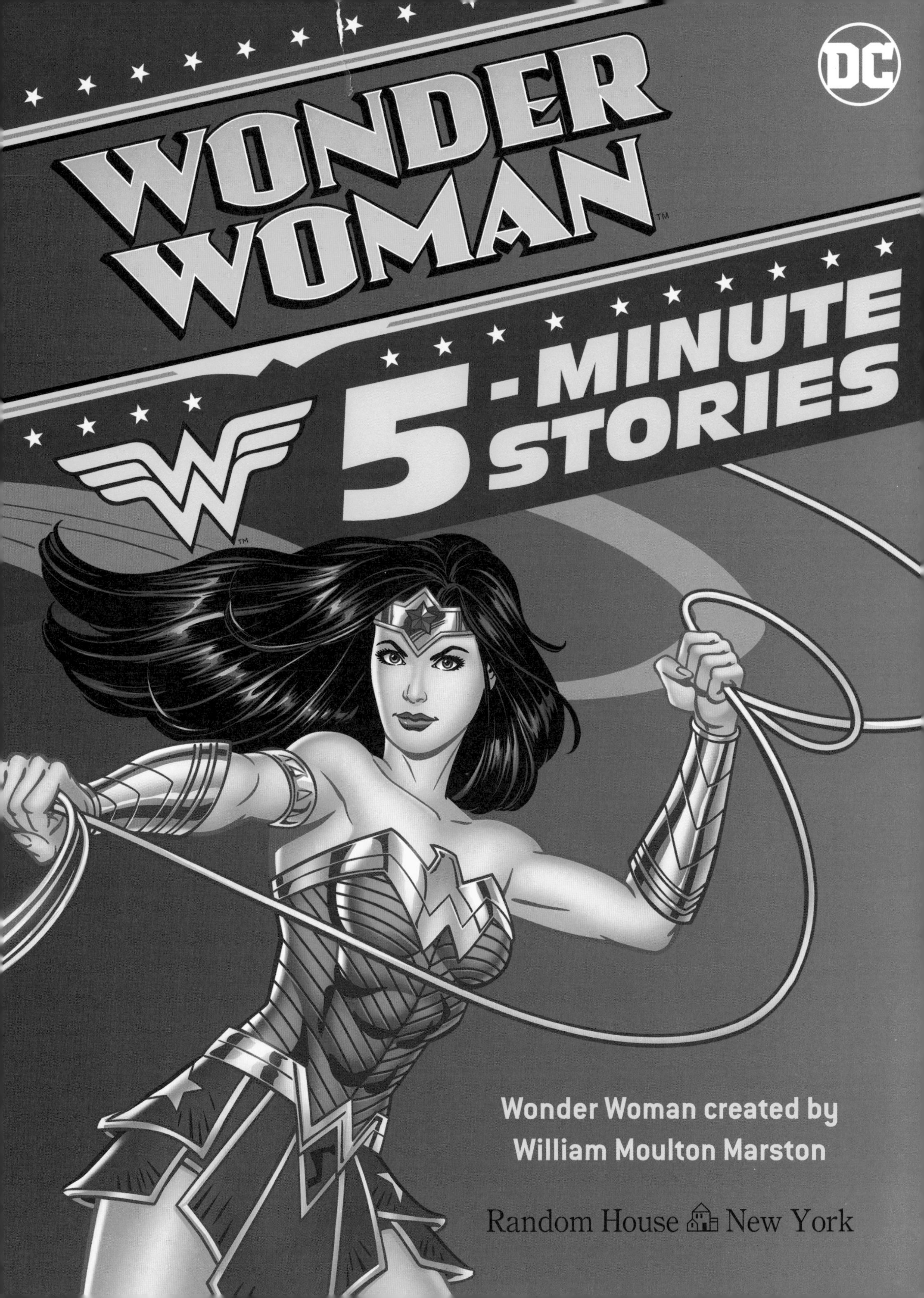

Wonder Woman created by
William Moulton Marston

Random House New York

S0080257

All rights reserved.

Published in the United States by Random House Children's Books, a division of Penguin Random House LLC,
1745 Broadway, New York, NY 10019, and in Canada by Penguin Random House Canada Limited, Toronto.
Random House and the colophon are registered trademarks of Penguin Random House LLC.

The artwork that appears herein was originally published in *Wonder Woman: I Am Wonder Woman*, © 2010 by DC
Comics; *Justice League: The Mightiest Magic*, © 2015 by DC Comics; *Wonder Woman: The Mermaid of Paradise
Island*, © 2015 by DC Comics; *Wonder Woman: Cheetah Chase*, © 2015 by DC Comics; *Wonder Woman: Wonder
Warrior of Troy*, © 2015 by DC Comics; *Justice League: Super-Villains United*, © 2016 by DC Comics; *Wonder
Woman: Big Trouble*, © 2016 by DC Comics; and *Wonder Woman: Maze of Magic*, © 2017 by DC Comics.

rhcbooks.com

ISBN 978-0-593-12354-6 (trade) — ISBN 978-0-593-12355-3 (ebook)

MANUFACTURED IN CHINA

10 9 8 7 6 5 4 3 2 1

CONTENTS

WONDER WOMAN

Brought to life by the power of the Greek gods on the island of Themyscira, Princess Diana has the wisdom of Athena, the speed of Hermes, the strength of Hercules, and the compassion of Aphrodite.

As an Amazon, she is a mighty warrior, but she has come to the world of humankind to fight for truth, justice, and equality for people everywhere.

THE AMAZON WARRIOR

Queen Hippolyta was the wise and just ruler of a group of warrior women known as the Amazons. They lived on a hidden island called Themyscira. It was so beautiful that they sometimes called it Paradise Island. She had a daughter named Diana.

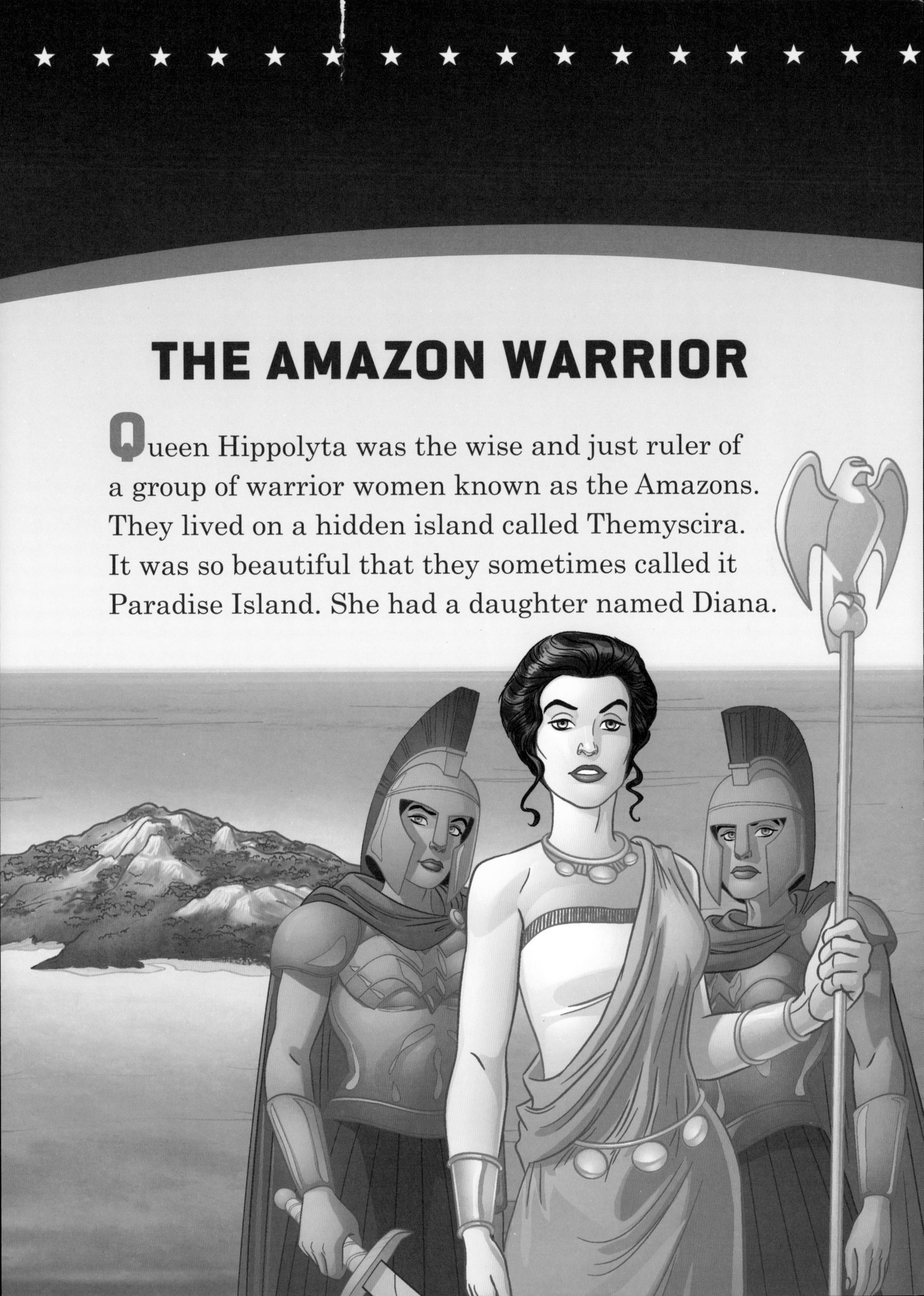

One day, the mysterious and powerful Greek gods visited Hippolyta and warned her that many dangers would soon threaten the world.

"To fight against these threats and keep humankind safe," the gods told her, "you must send a single warrior out into the world—the best and mightiest of the Amazons."

All the Amazons were mighty warriors, so Queen Hippolyta thought long and hard about how to pick the finest and most capable of her people.

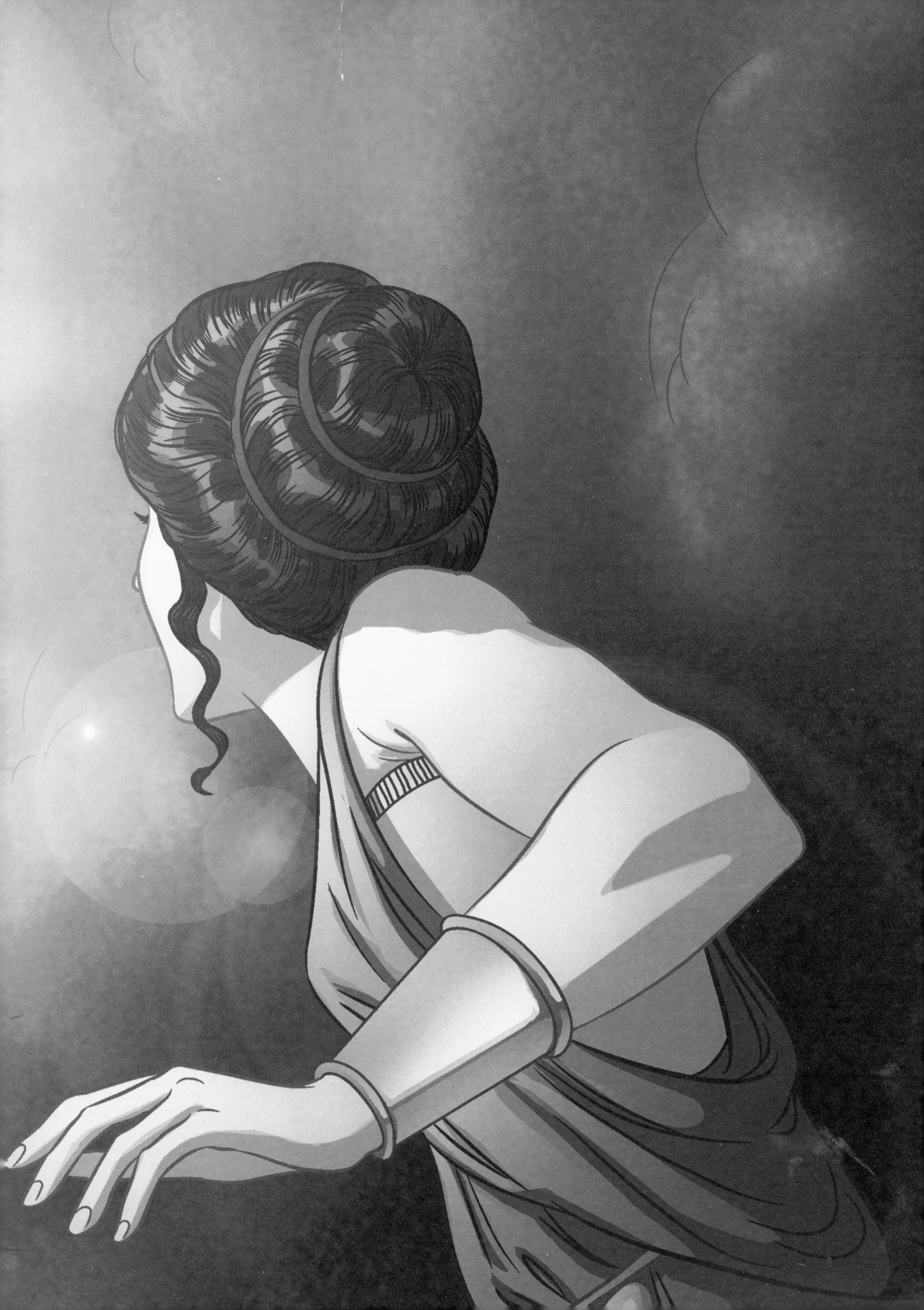

The queen came to a decision and made an announcement. She had decided to hold a great contest. "We will find out who among you is truly the strongest, fastest, and smartest of all the Amazons," Hippolyta declared.

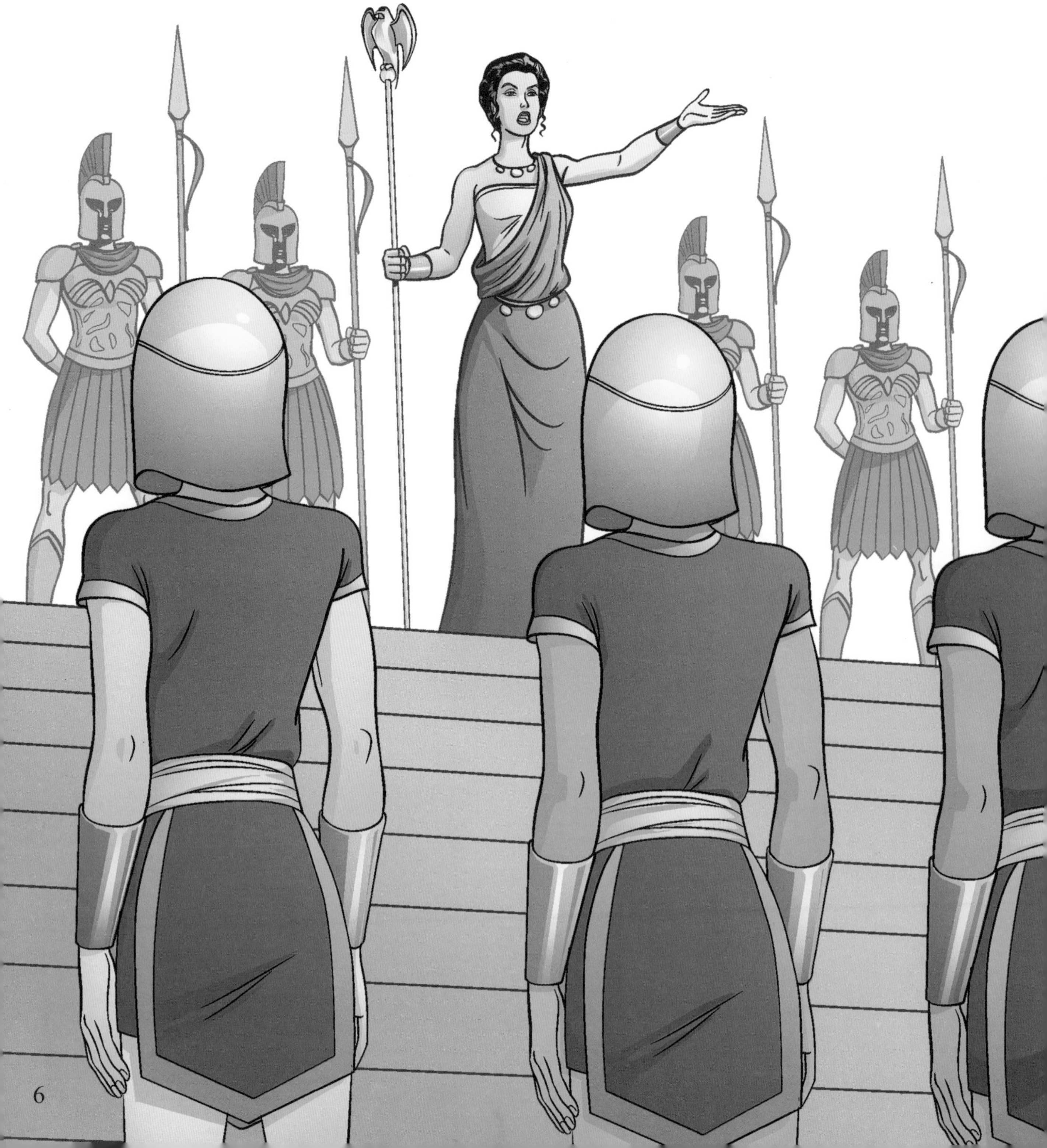

When Diana heard that the winner of the contest would go to the outside world, she became determined to win. She was a princess, but she had no desire to be queen. She wanted to explore the world and help its people.

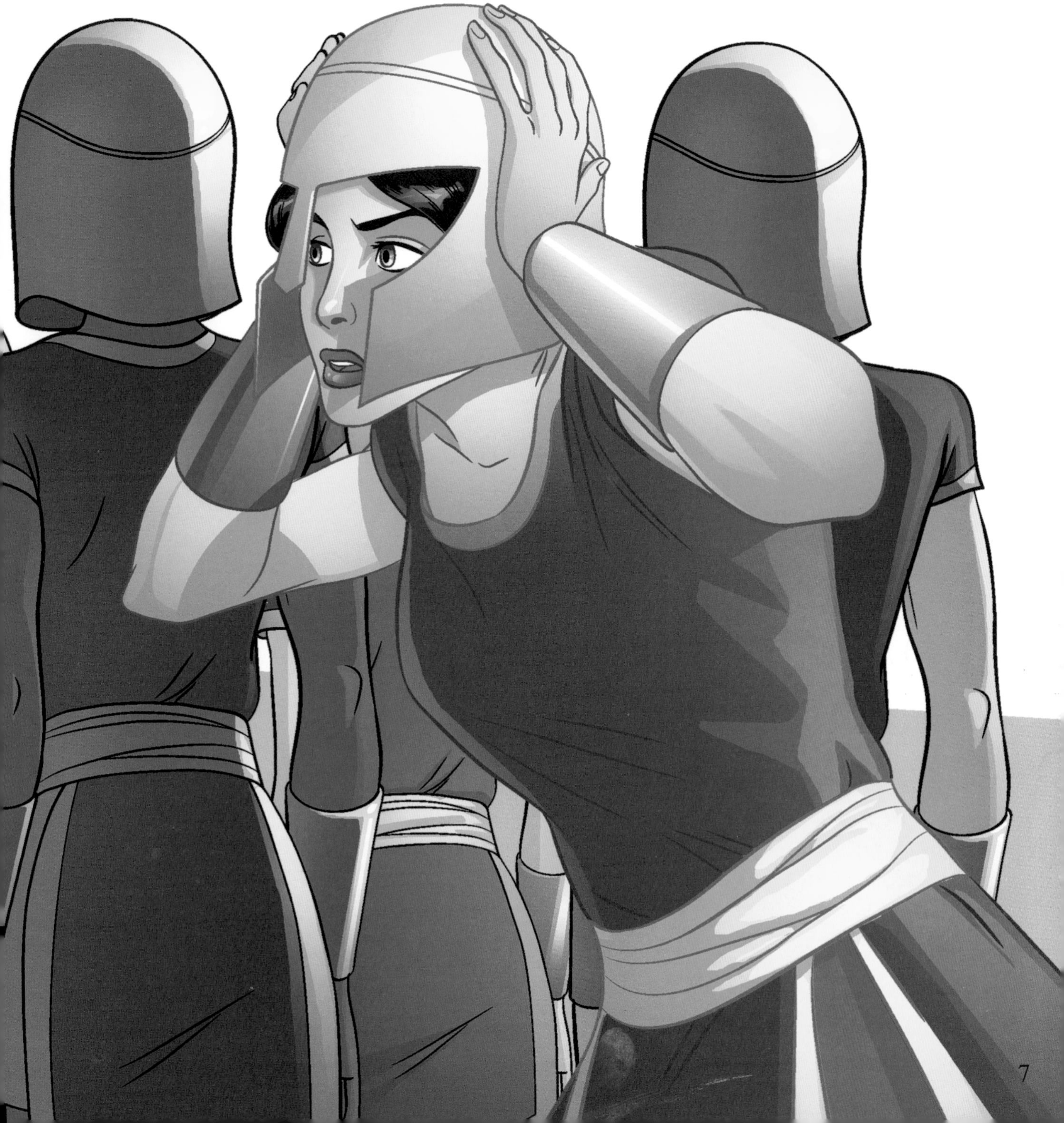

Wearing a helmet to hide her face, Diana entered the contest in secret. In the archery event, her arrows hit the bull's-eye again and again. In the races, she always finished first.

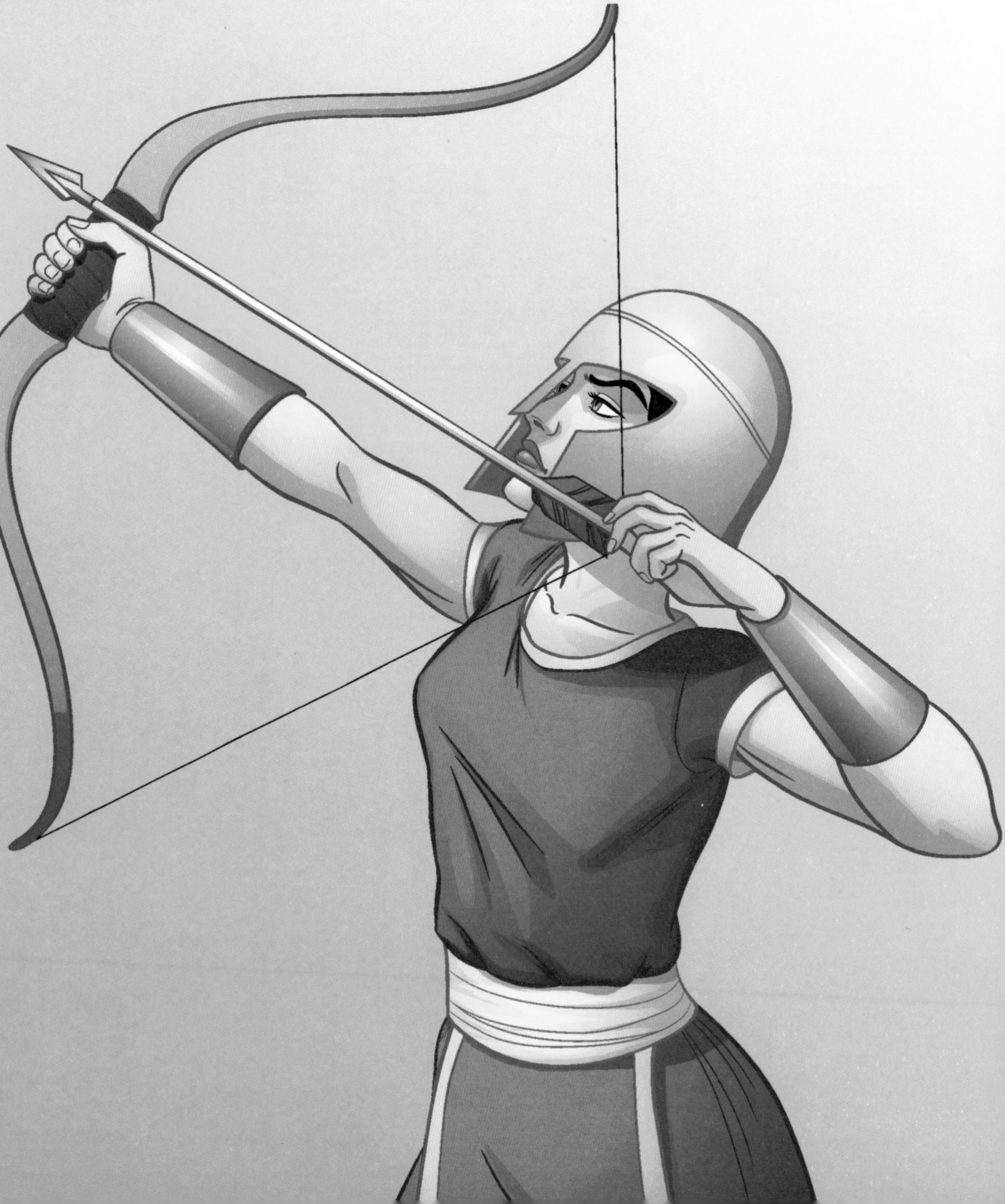

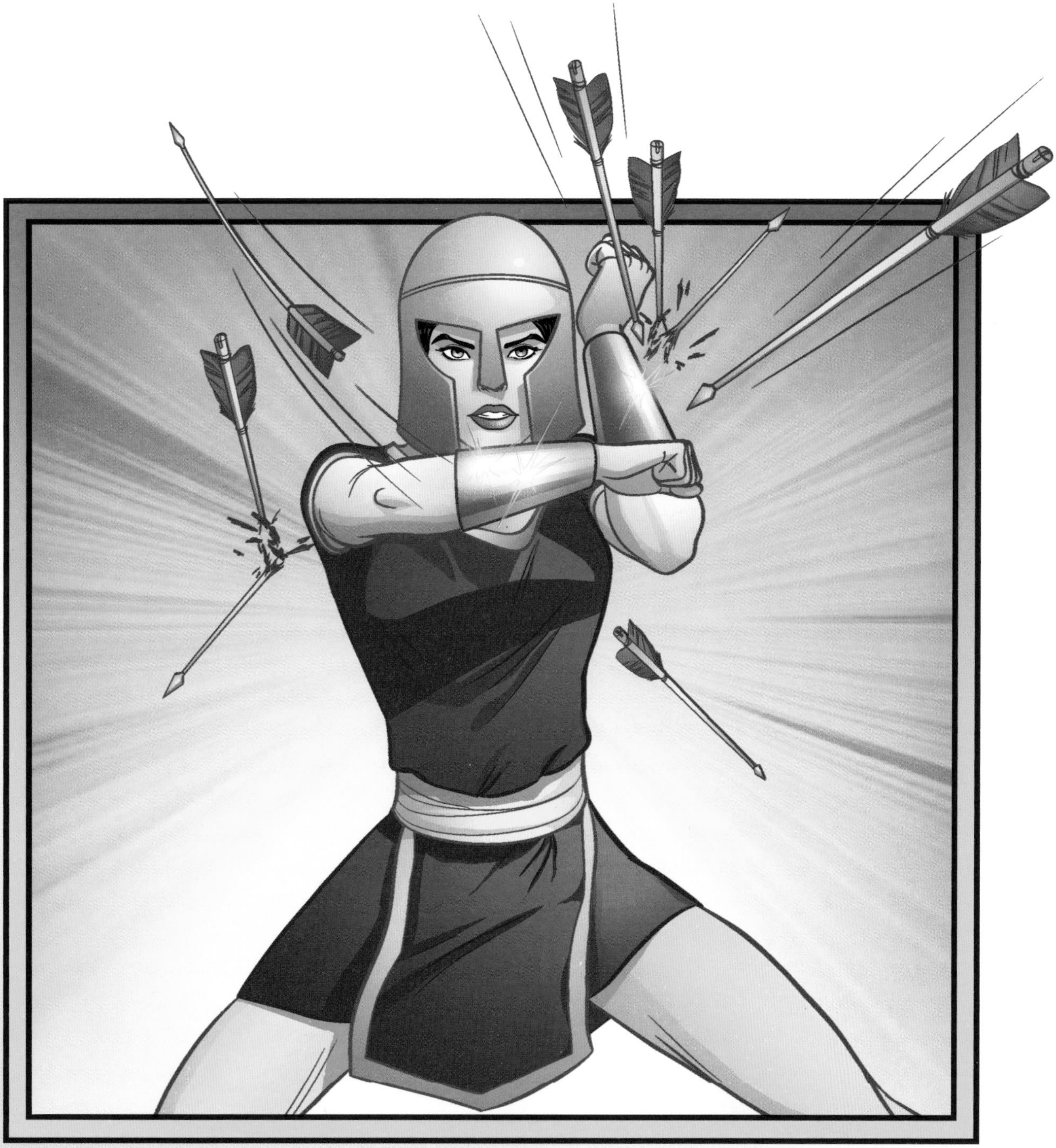

And with a pair of unbreakable bracelets on her wrists, Diana proved that her reflexes were faster than everyone else's. She blocked every arrow and projectile that was shot at her. She was a wonder to behold!

Diana also beat her opponents in the hand-to-hand combat and sword challenges. At last, Hippolyta proclaimed that the mysterious contestant was the champion.

When Diana removed her helmet, the queen was shocked to see that the winner was her own daughter.

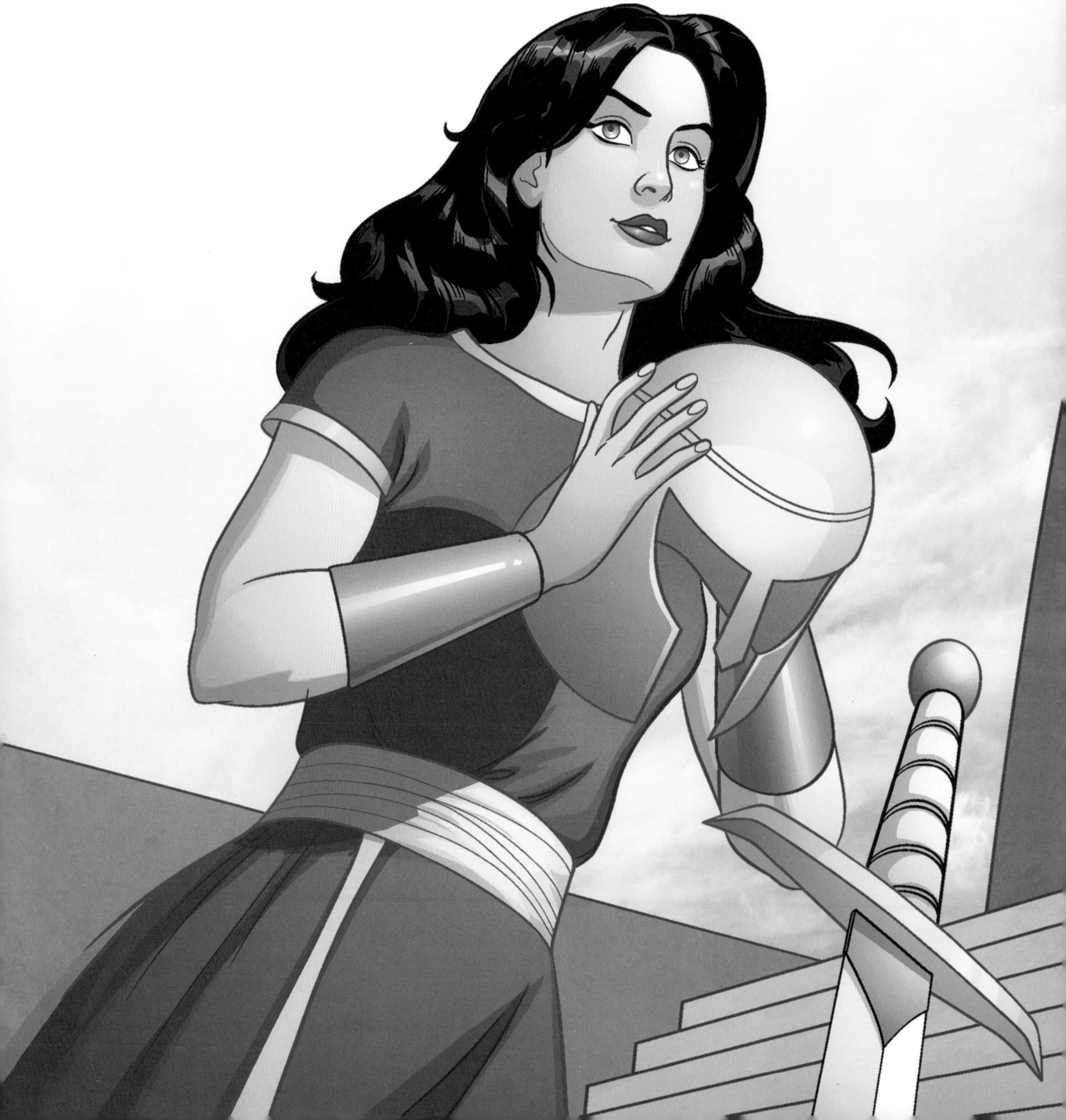

"You have earned this honor with your natural talent and skill," her mother said. "You shall go out into the world as a warrior and a symbol of justice. You have made me proud."

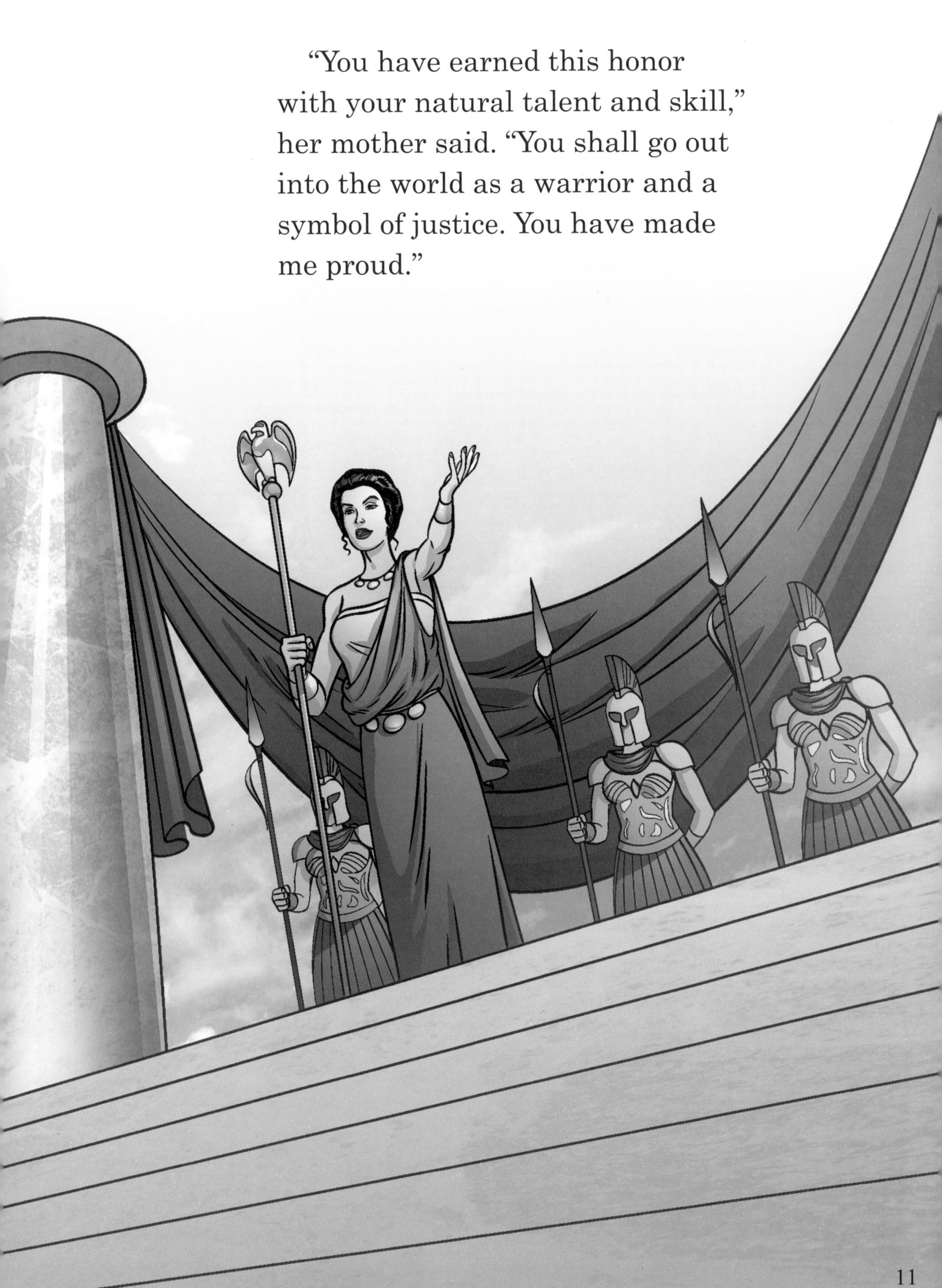

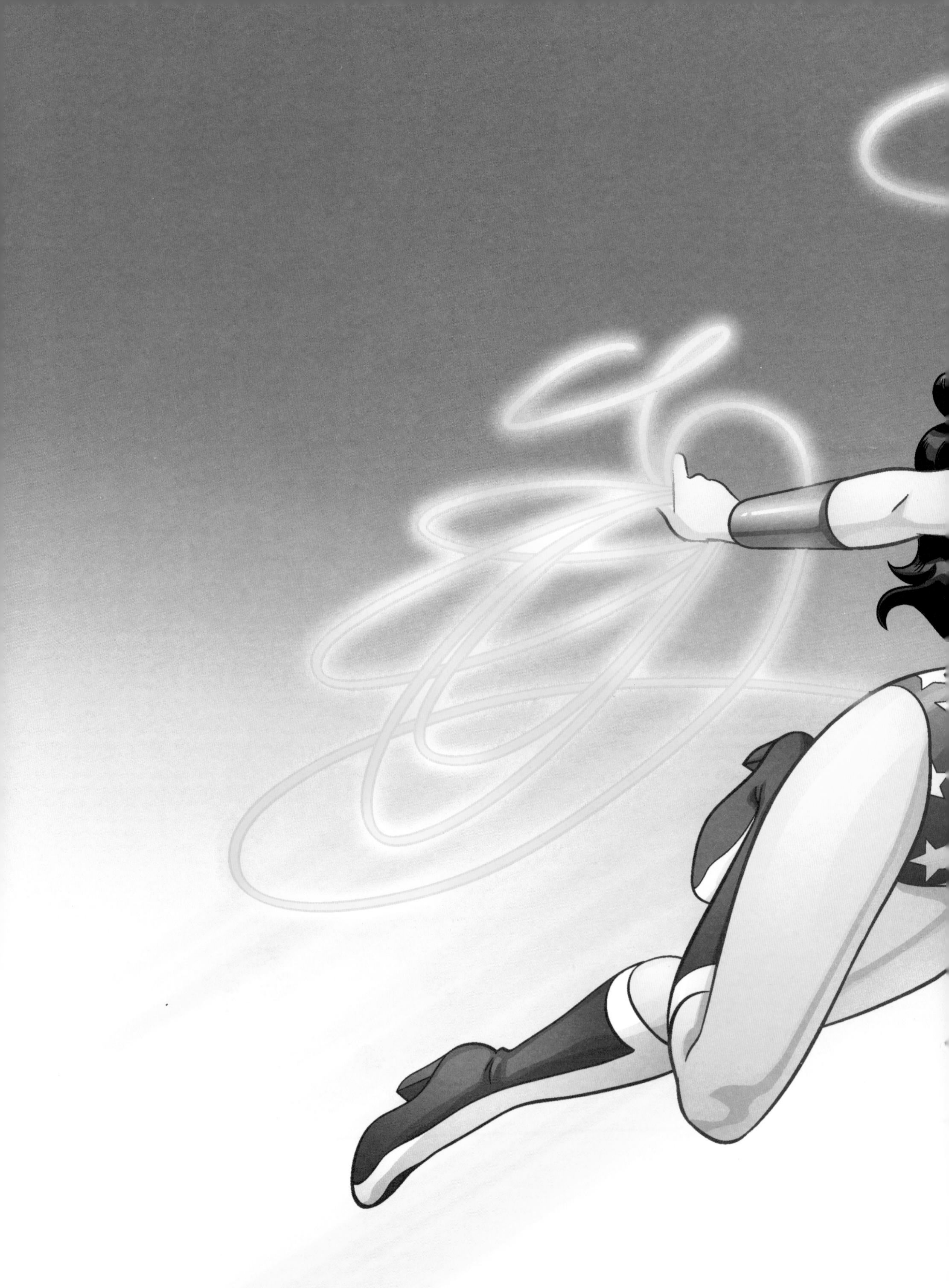

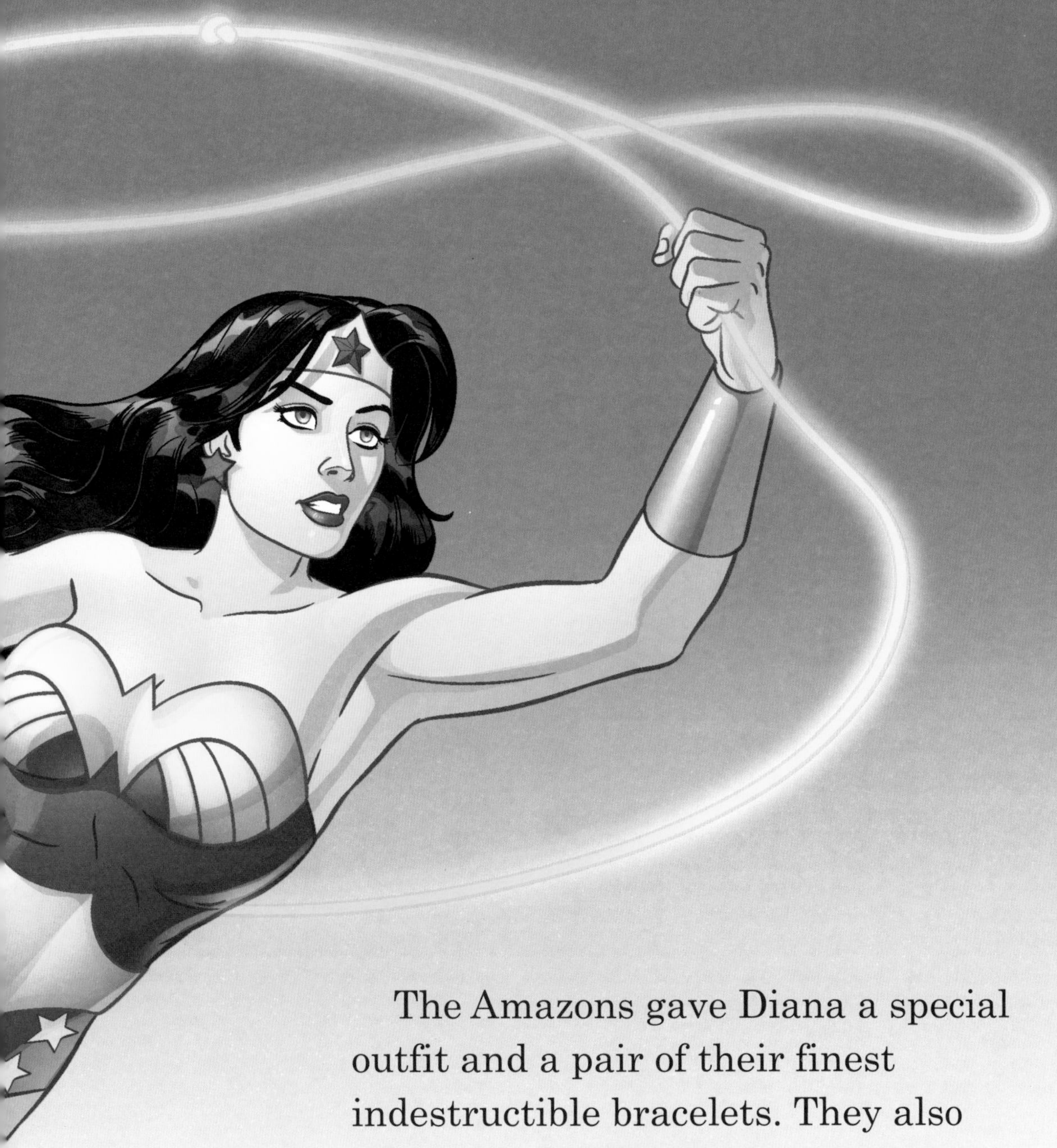

The Amazons gave Diana a special outfit and a pair of their finest indestructible bracelets. They also gave her an unbreakable magic lasso called the Lasso of Truth. When the lasso was wrapped around someone, that person was forced to tell the truth. And the gods gave Diana the ability to fly and talk to animals.

To protect her true identity, she decided to call herself Wonder Woman.

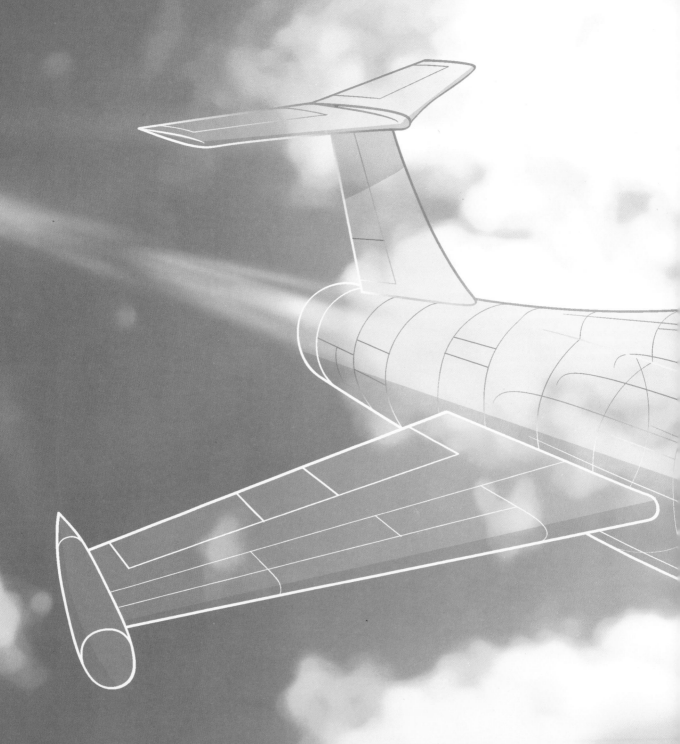

Diana left Paradise Island in a special airplane called the Invisible Jet. The jet was completely undetectable and would prove to be handy during rescue missions.

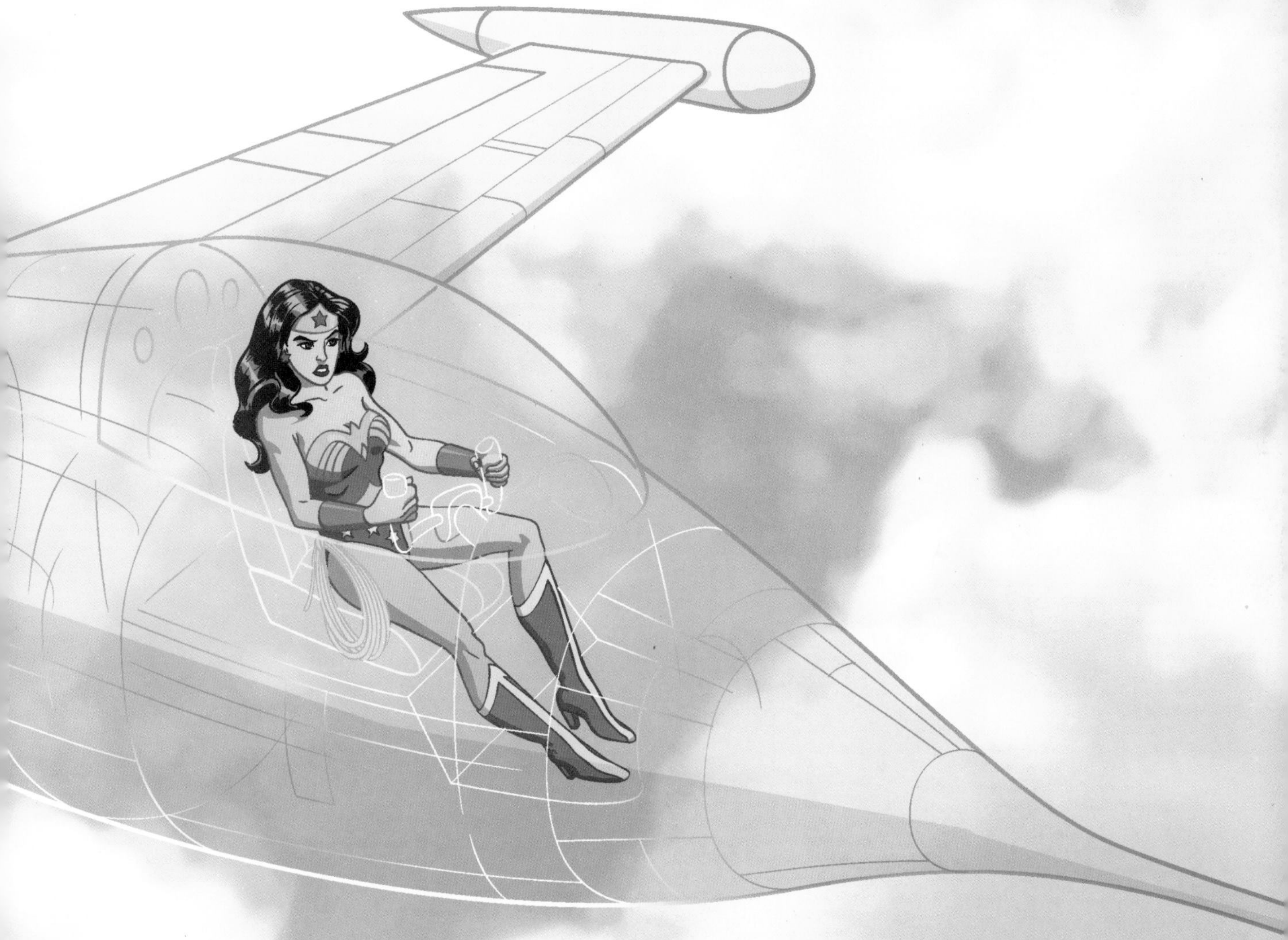

Under the name Diana Prince, she got a job at a top-secret government agency. From there she was able to spot trouble anywhere in the world!

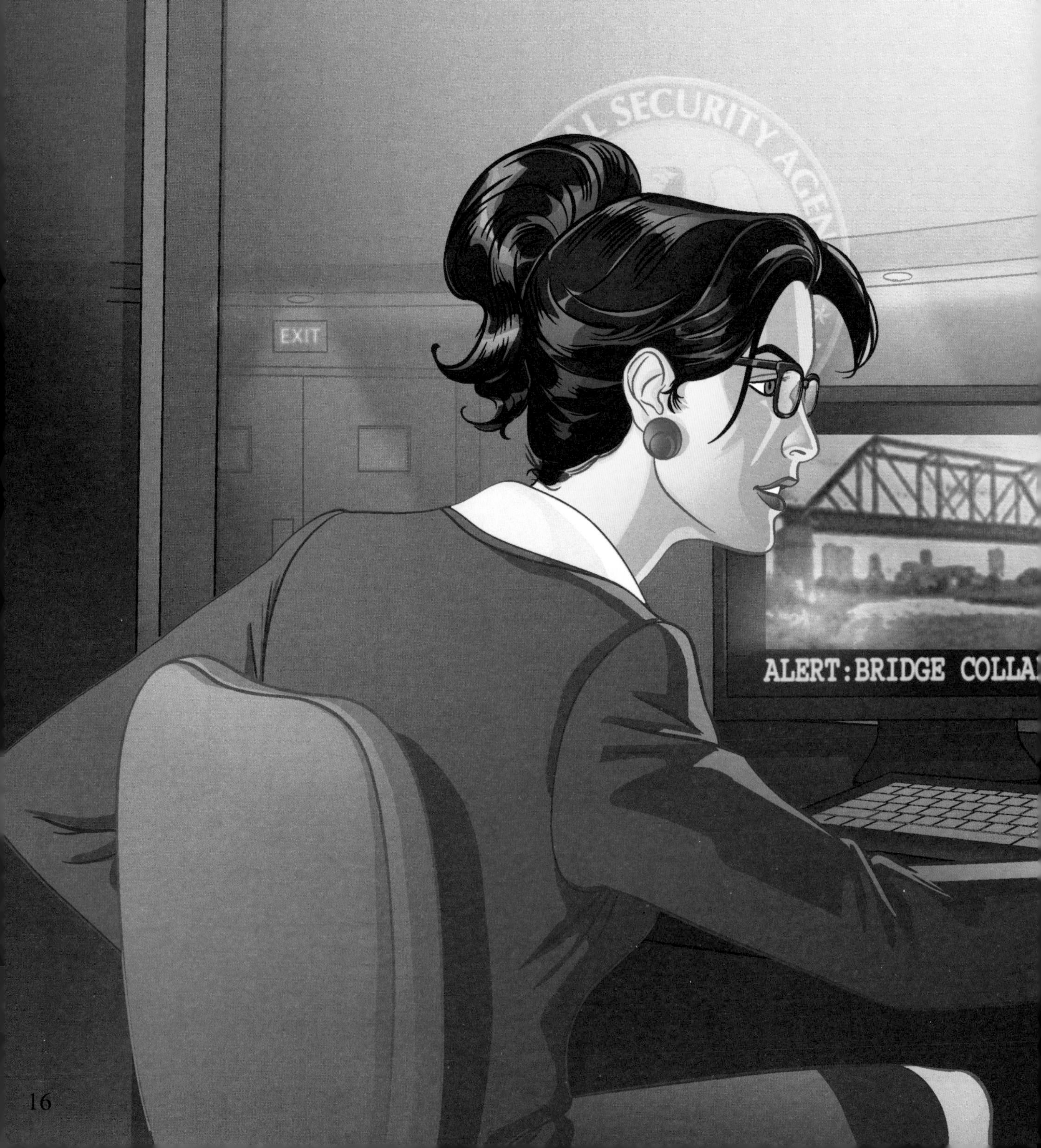
SECURITY
EXIT
ALERT:BRIDGE COLLA

And when the trouble was big enough, or when people needed help . . .

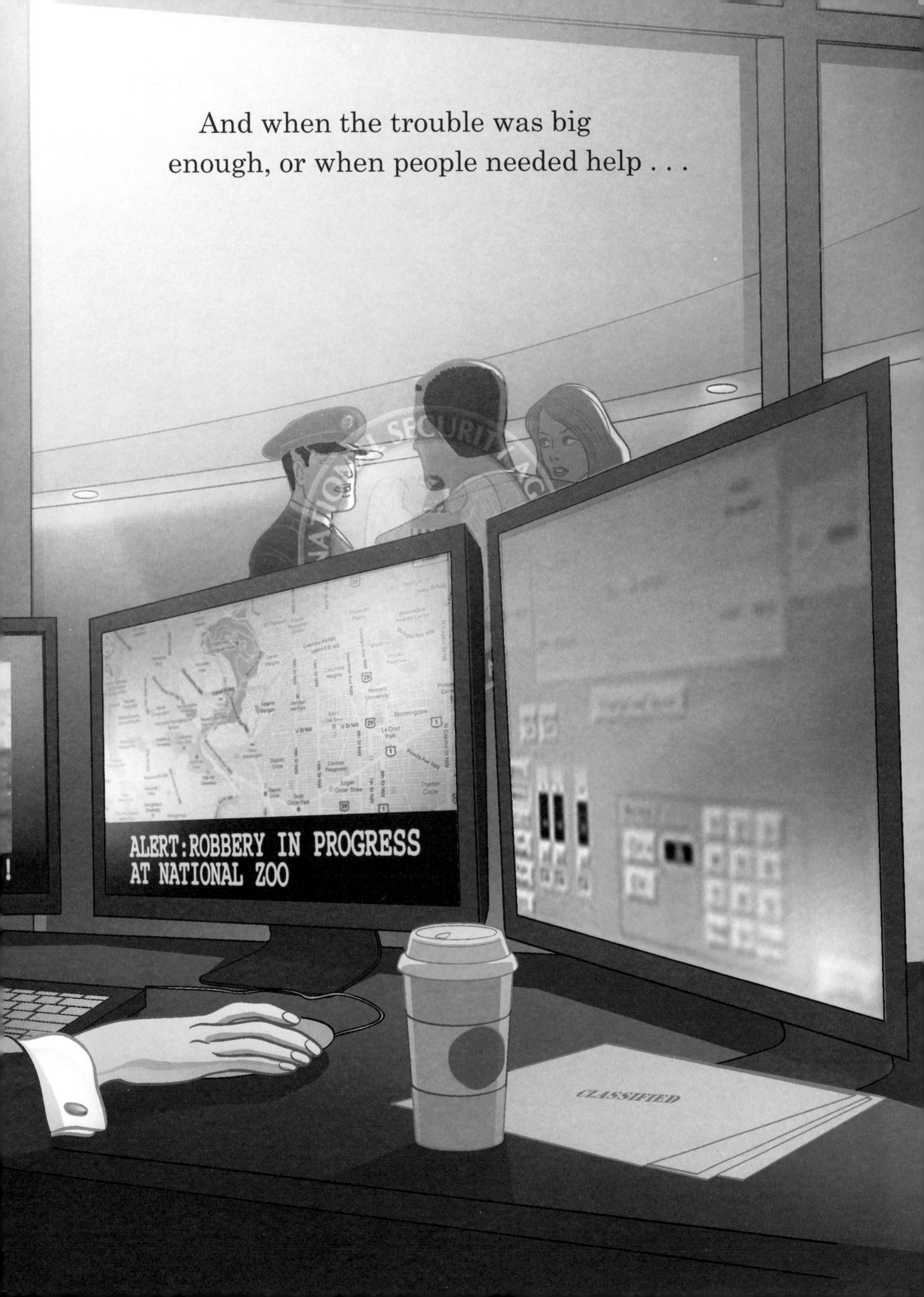
ALERT:ROBBERY IN PROGRESS
AT NATIONAL ZOO
CLASSIFIED

. . . she would change into

Wonder Woman!

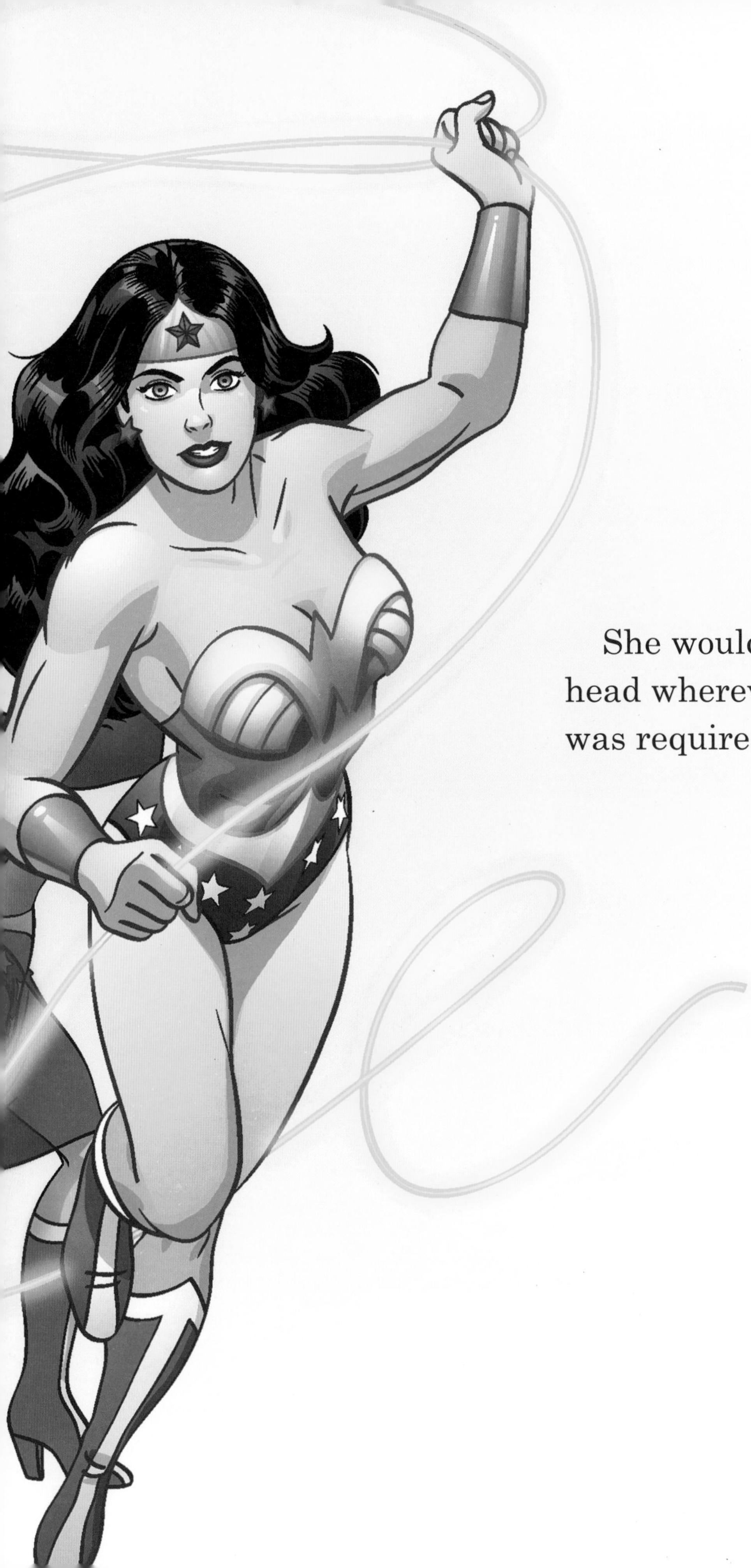

She would immediately head wherever her help was required.

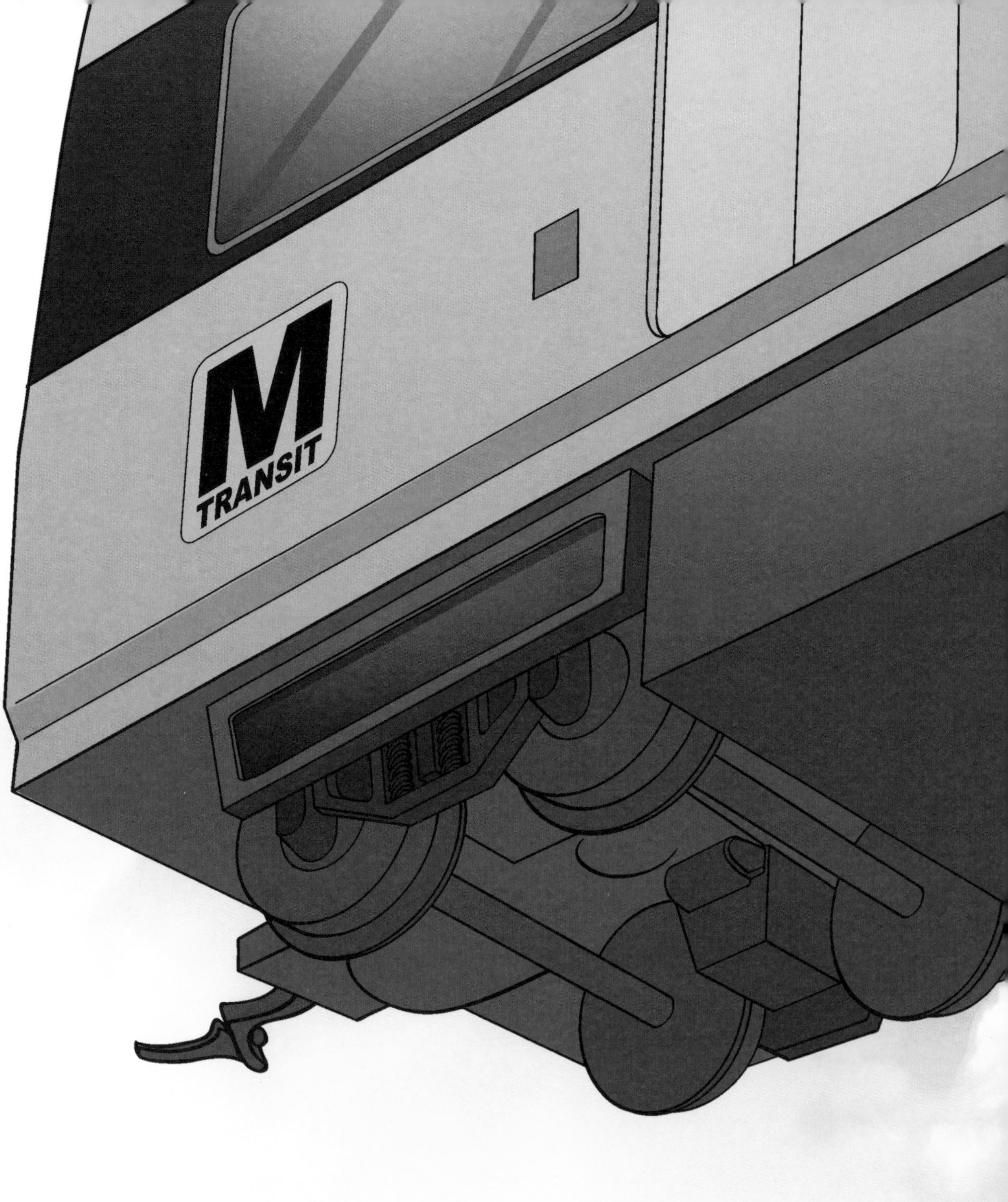
M
TRANSIT

Wonder Woman's super-strength and ability to fly helped her rescue people. When a bridge collapsed during one mission, she reached a train just before it fell into the river. She lifted the train and flew it to safety!

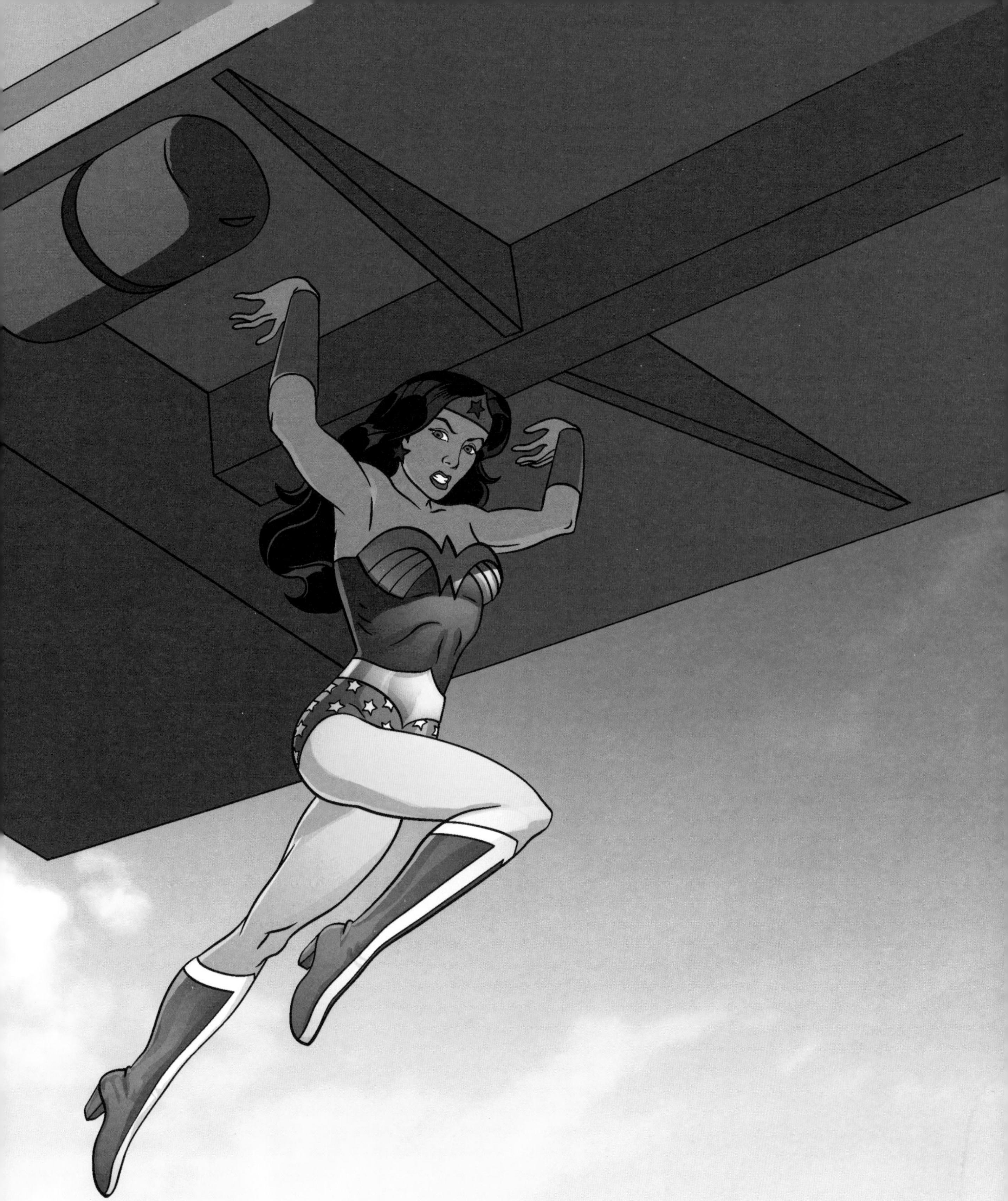

"Don't worry," she told the people on board. "I'll have you on the ground in no time!"

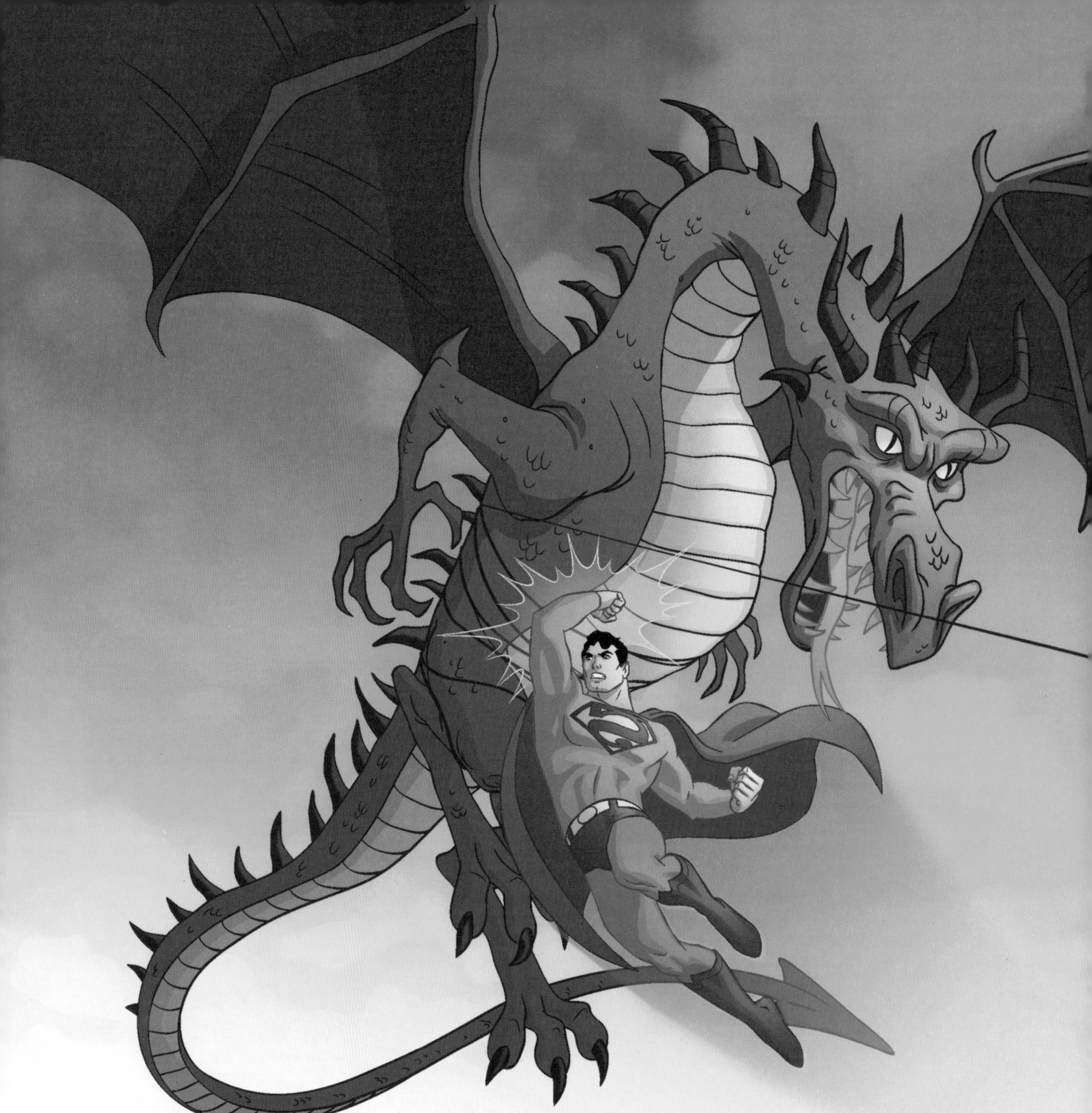

Wonder Woman has made friends with the world's other super heroes. When threats are too much for any one hero to handle, they combine their might to save the day.

And when the trouble is *really* big, heroes like Batman and Superman know just who to call. . . .

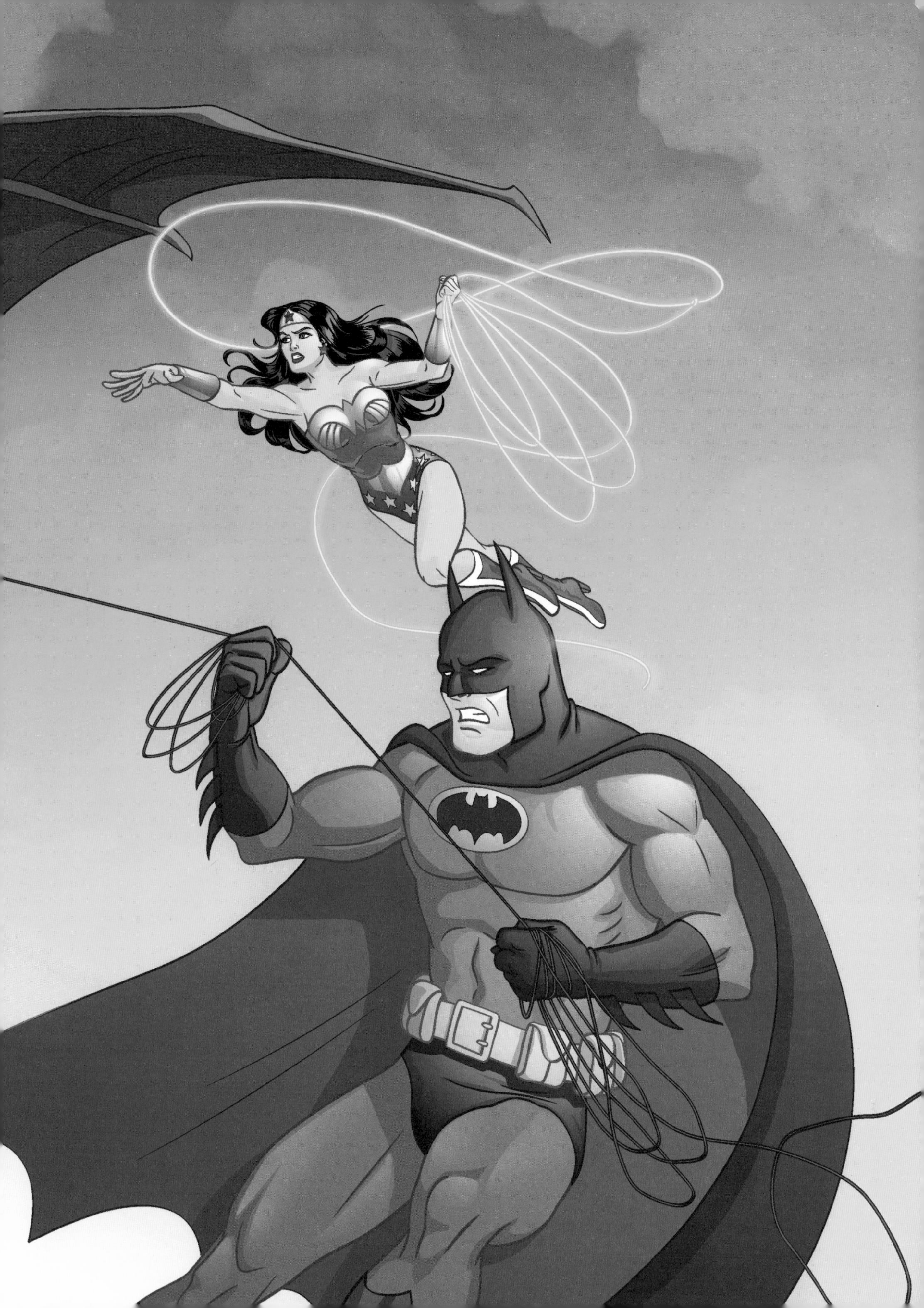

Wonder Woman!

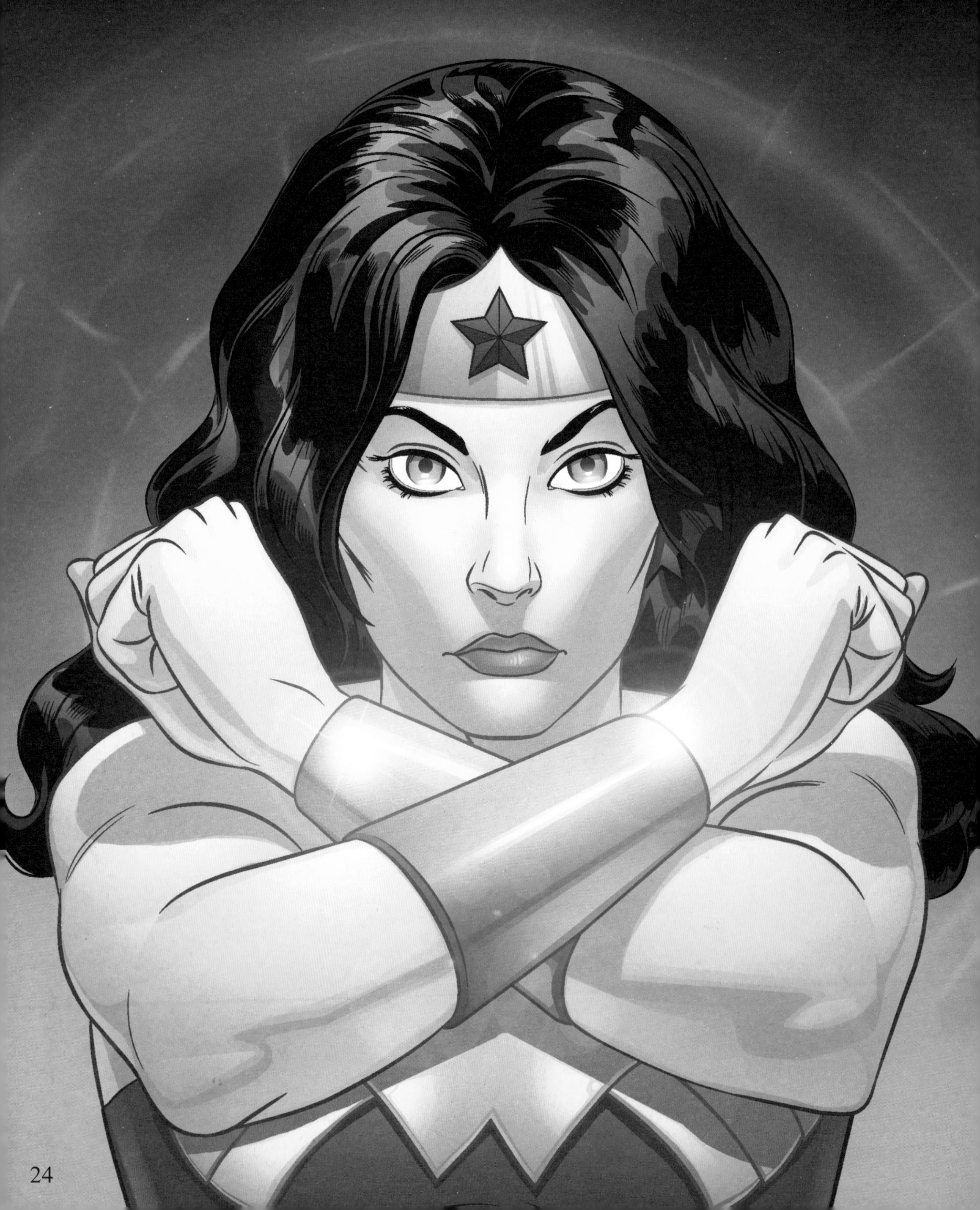

BATTLE IN THE PAST

Ares, the Greek god of war, was one of the few immortals Wonder Woman did not get along with. So it was no surprise when she heard he was causing trouble on the island of Troy. When she arrived, she found several tourists tied up and in danger.

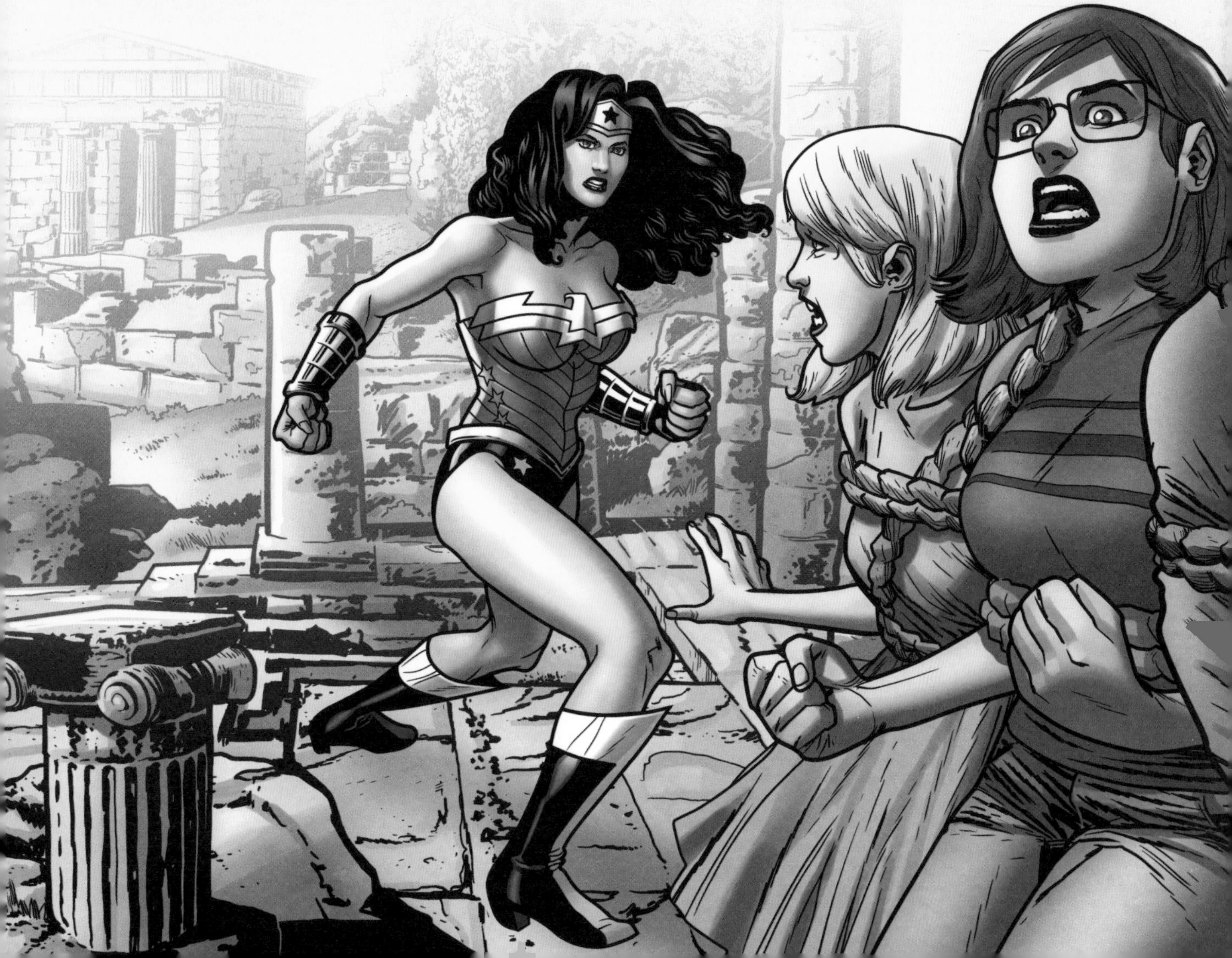

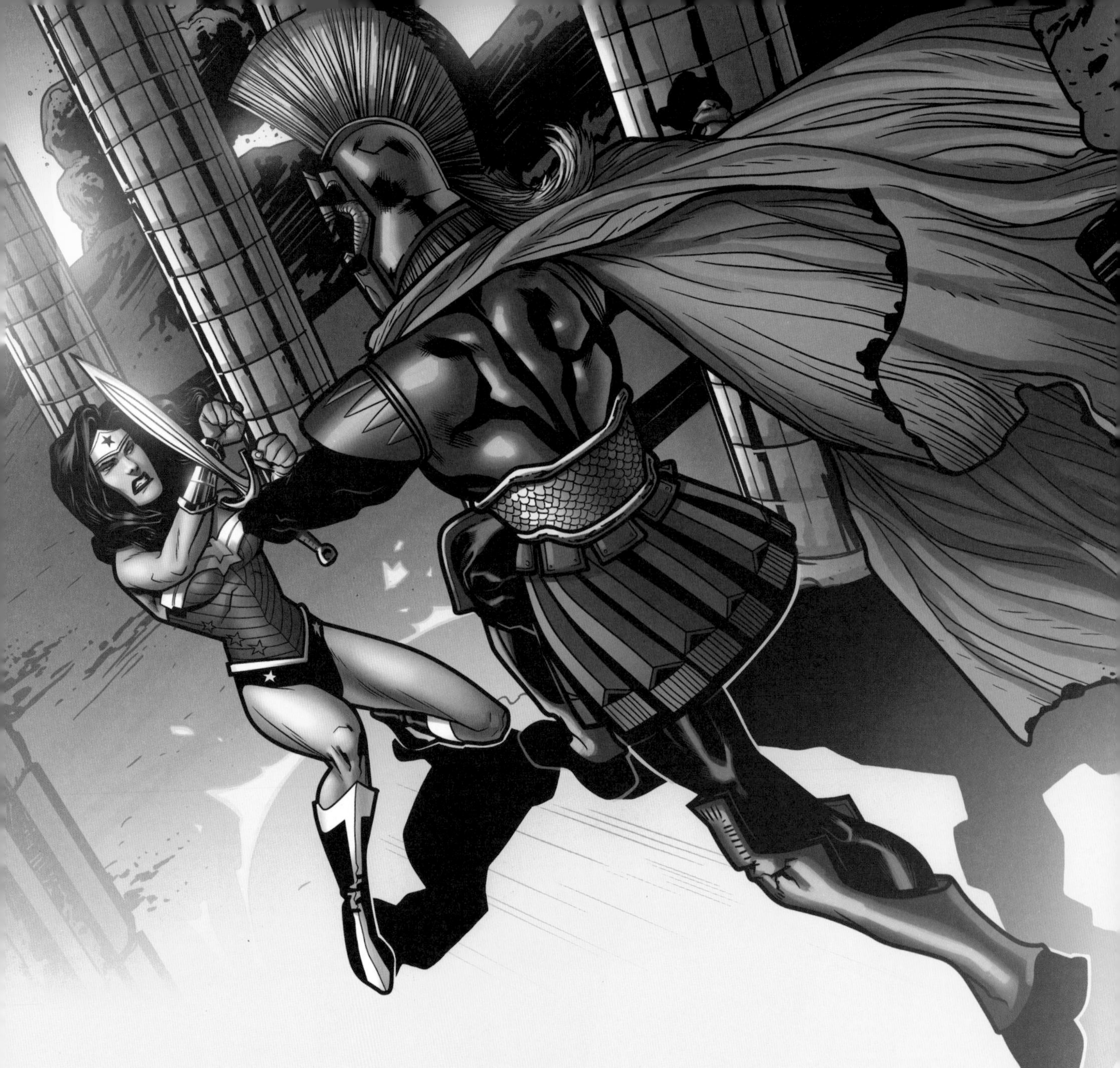

"Let them go," Wonder Woman commanded, sensing Aries's presence. Ares laughed as he appeared before her.

"They were only bait to get you here," he bellowed. He swung his sword at Wonder Woman, but she blocked the blow with her indestructible bracelets.

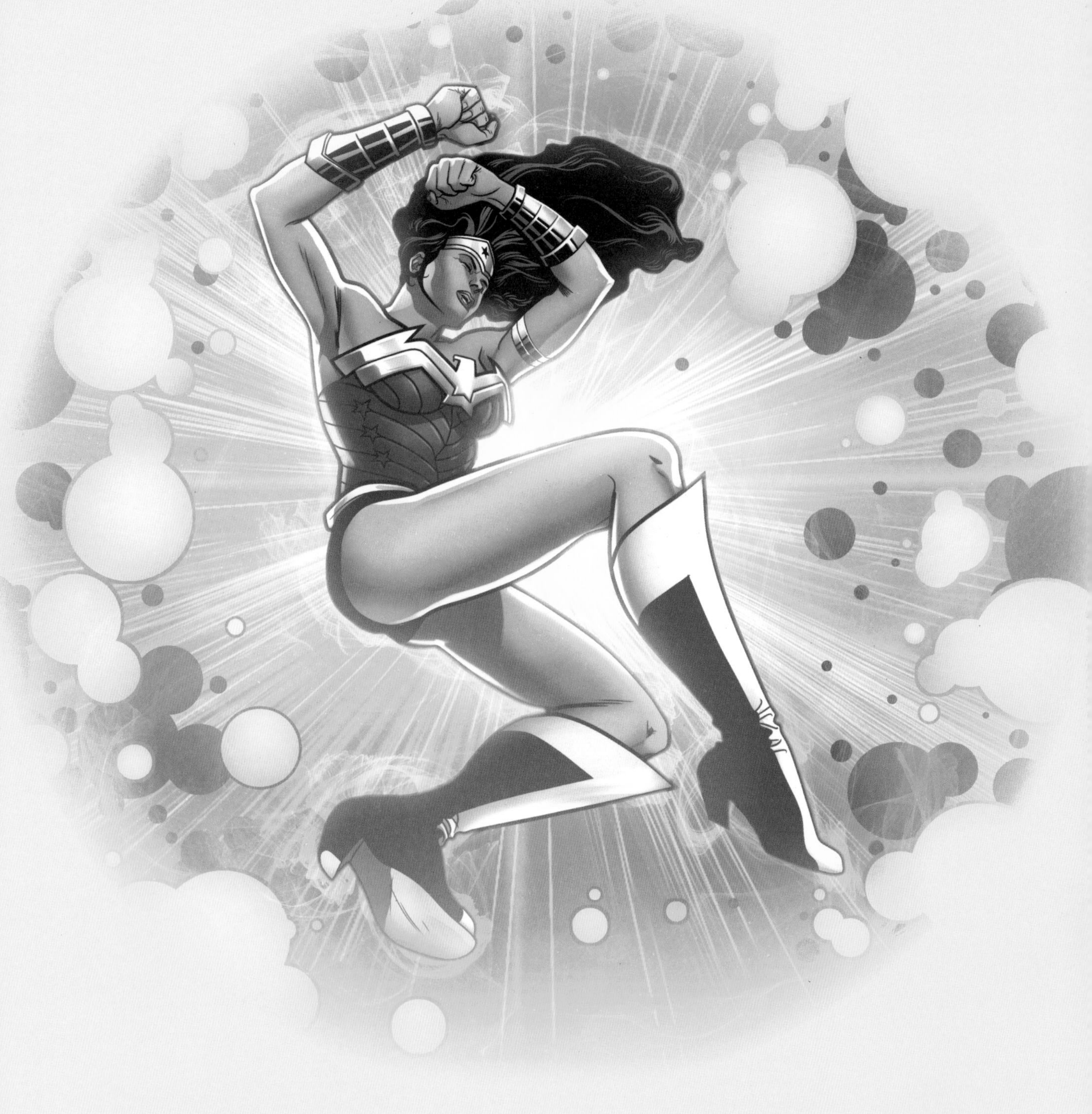

Suddenly, with a wave of Ares's hand, there was a blinding flash of light. Wonder Woman knew he was using some kind of powerful magic, but she wasn't sure what it was for.

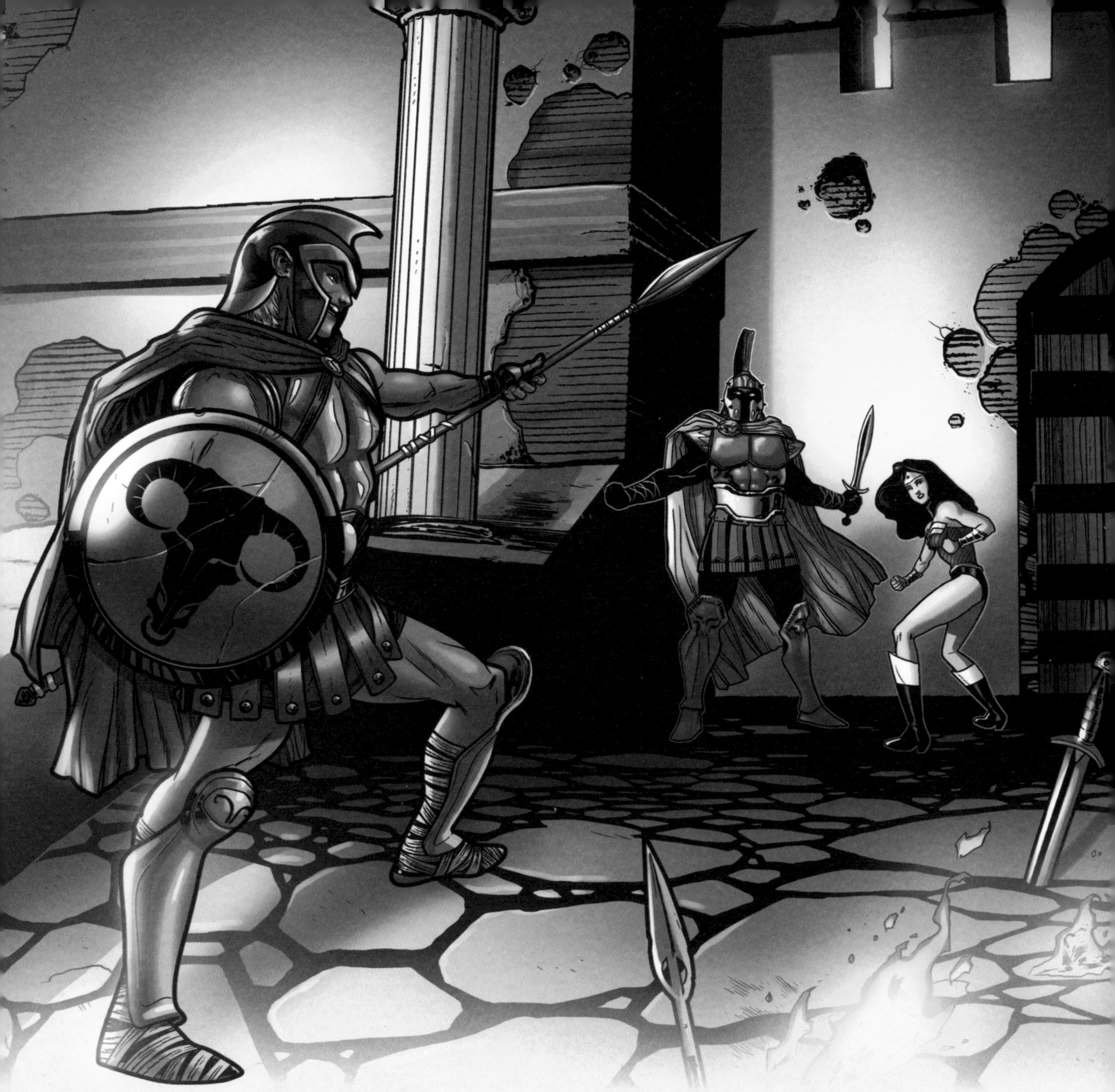

When her vision cleared, Wonder Woman found herself standing in the same place as before, but it was somehow different. Very different.

A man in ancient Greek armor hailed them. “Welcome, warriors. I see that you have come to join the battle!”

“What battle?” asked Wonder Woman.

Before the warrior could answer, a powerful female soldier raced up and attacked him. Their swords and shields clattered and clanged.

"Please stop this senseless fighting," Wonder Woman said to the clashing warriors.

"The sound of war is music to my ears," Ares roared. He seemed as pleased by the battle as the hero was horrified by it.

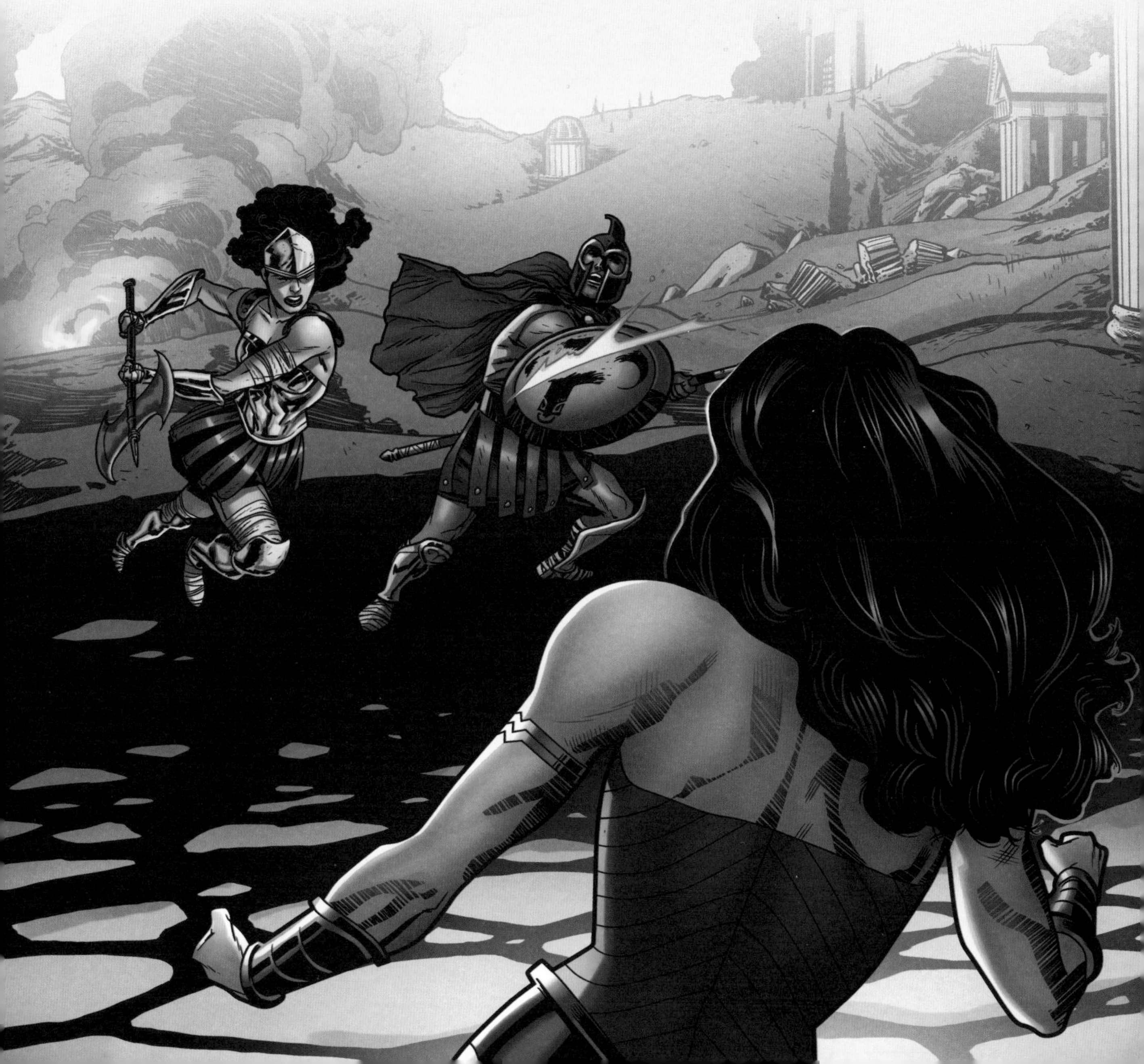

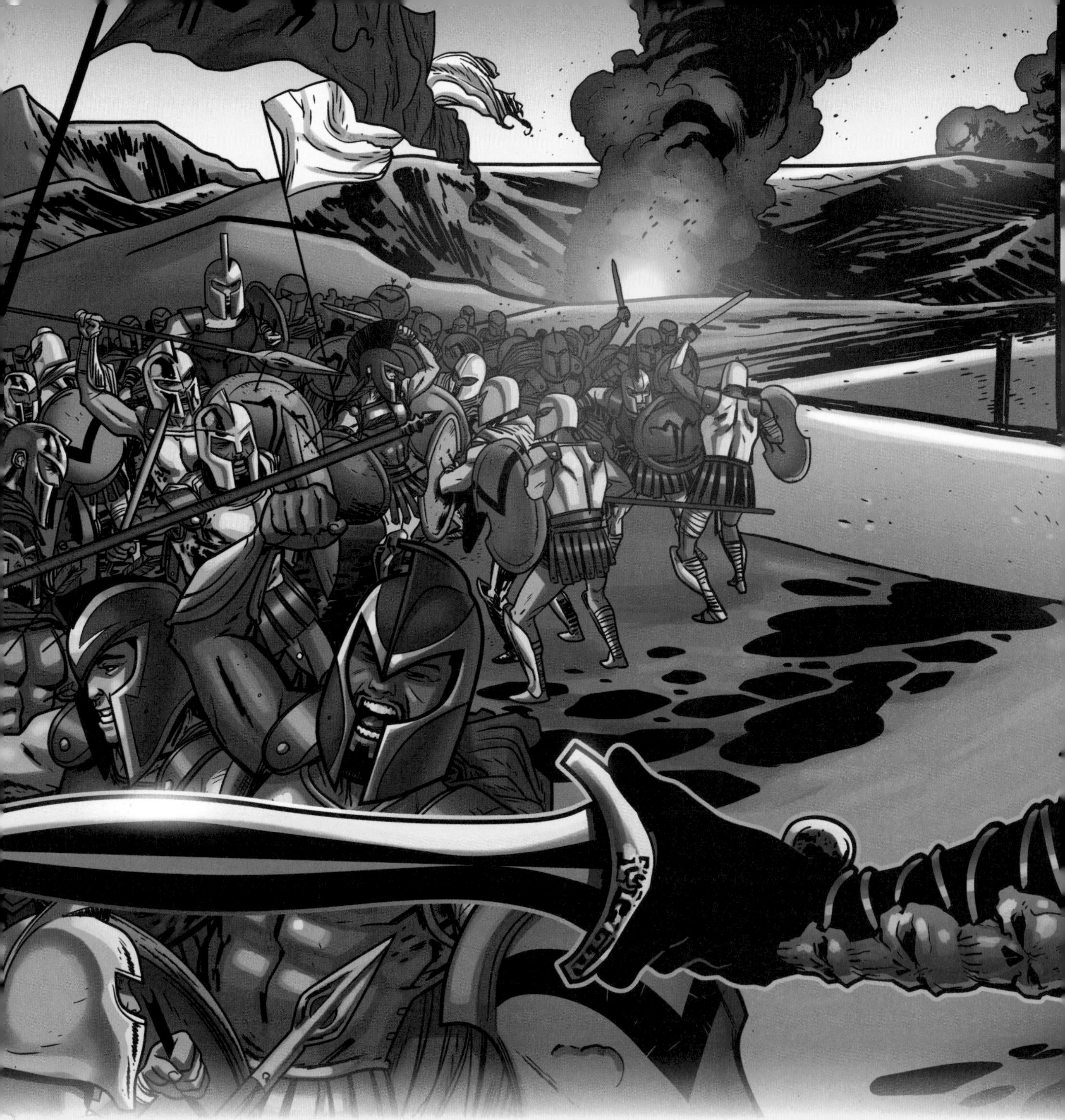

The Greek god laughed again, more cruelly this time. "I have brought you to witness the famous battle between Greece and Troy."

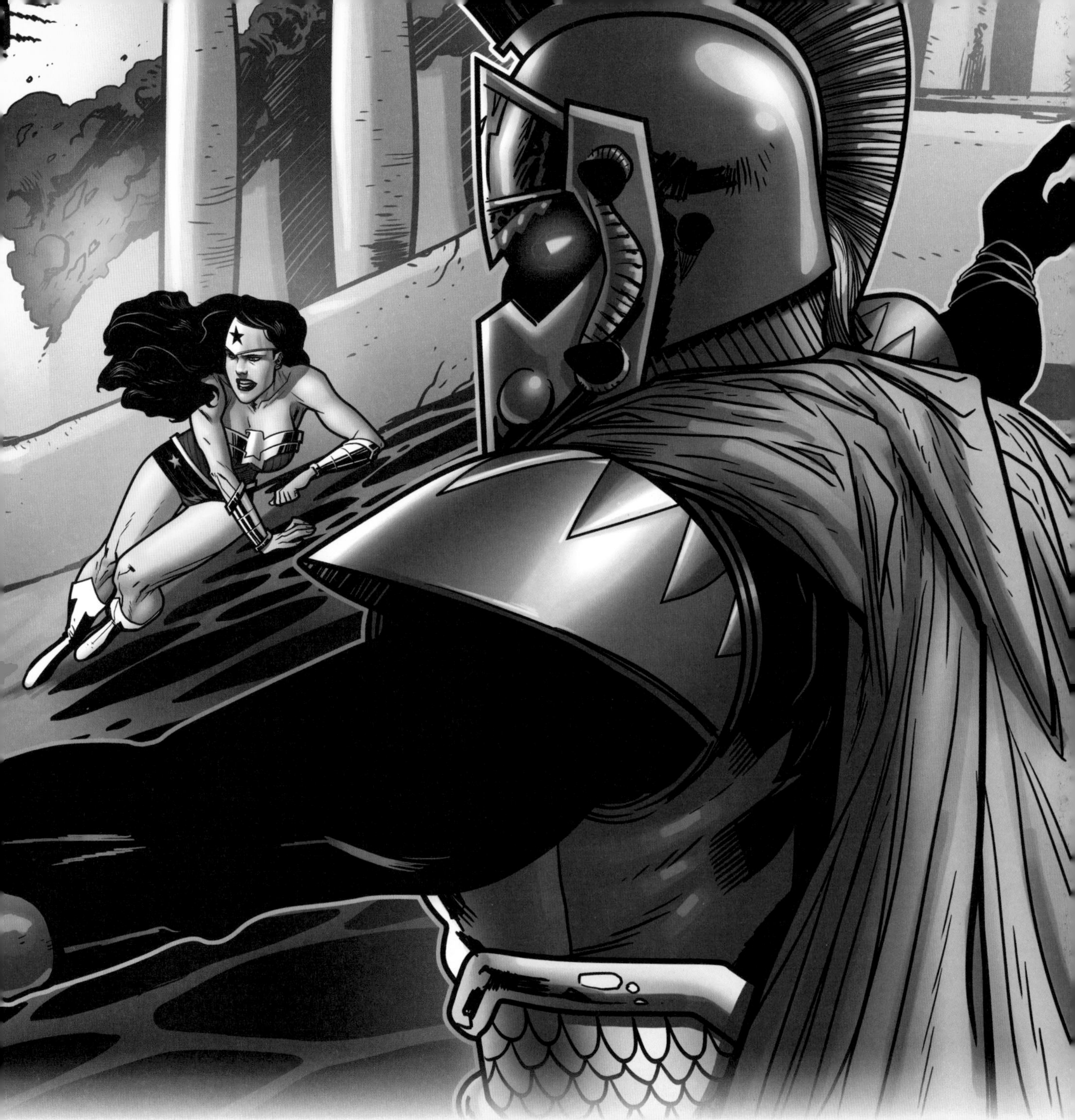

Wonder Woman gasped. Soldiers were fighting as far as she could see. The battle sounds were deafening.

"But *why* have you brought me here?" she asked.

"You love peace," said Ares. "But I feed off war. And this ancient battle will give me the strength I need to defeat you!"

"I do believe in peace," Wonder Woman replied. "However, if I have to fight a bully like you so that others can live peacefully, then so be it."

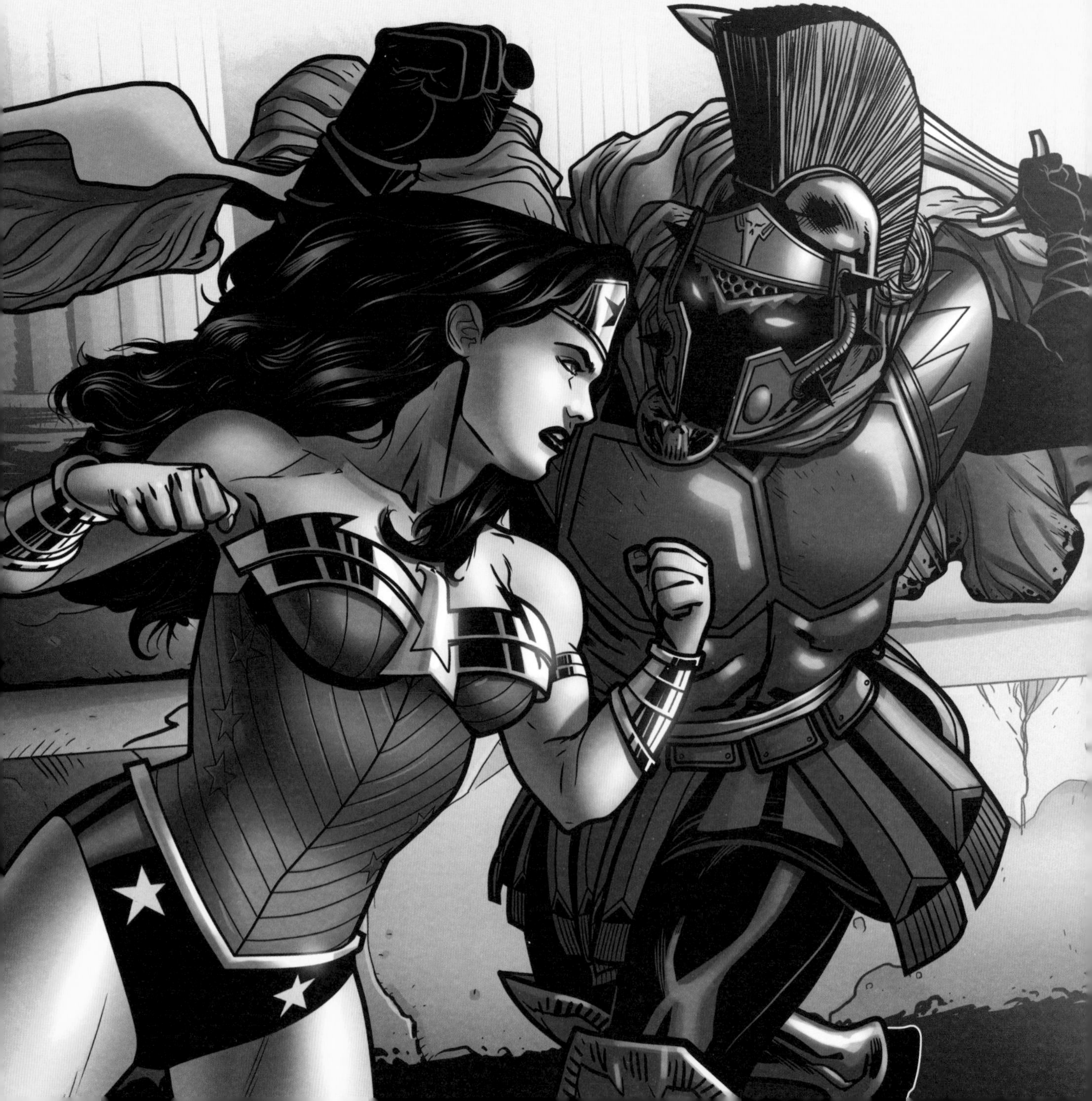

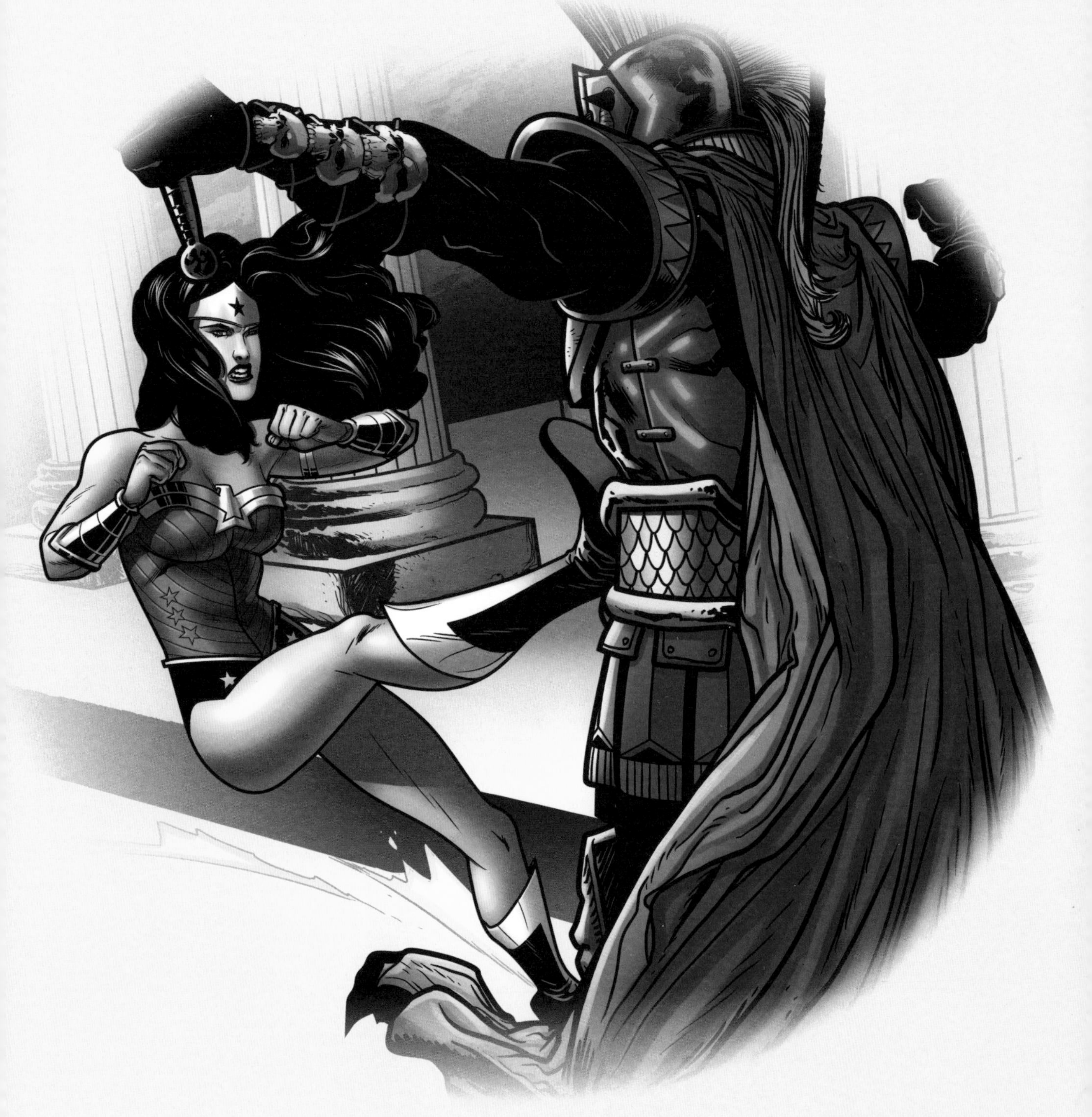

As Wonder Woman fought with Ares, she slowly realized she needed a better strategy. Kicks and punches would not defeat him. In fact, they seemed to make the Greek god more powerful. Fighting only fueled him!

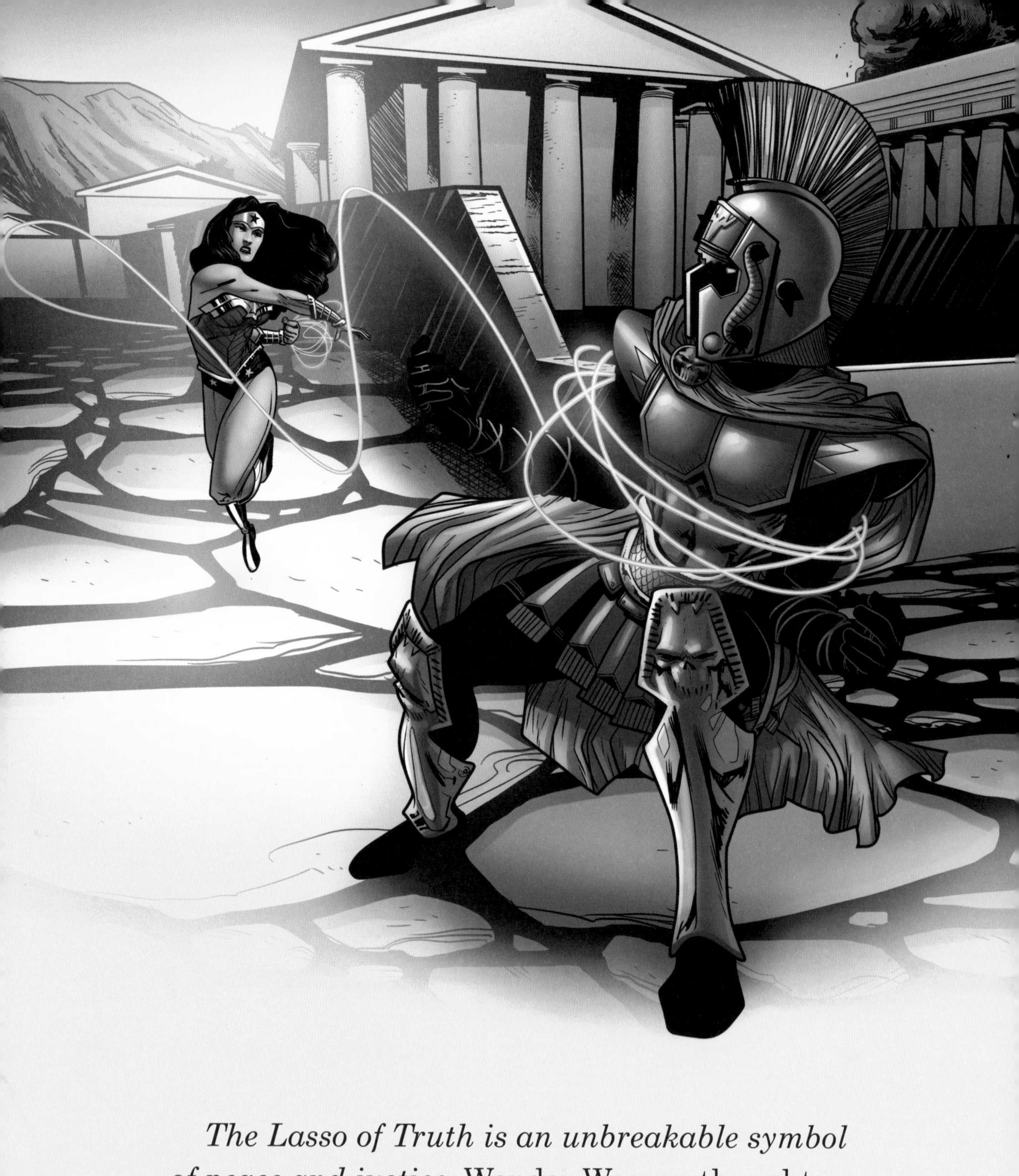

The Lasso of Truth is an unbreakable symbol of peace and justice, Wonder Woman thought. *And maybe it's what will stop this fight.*

Twirling the brightly glowing lasso, she threw it over Ares's head.

Bound tightly by the golden lasso, Ares became powerless. Without his terrible influence, the battle raging behind them ceased. Seeing the god of war defeated, the soldiers threw down their swords.

"Looks like peace has won the day," Wonder Woman said. "Now release me from this spell."

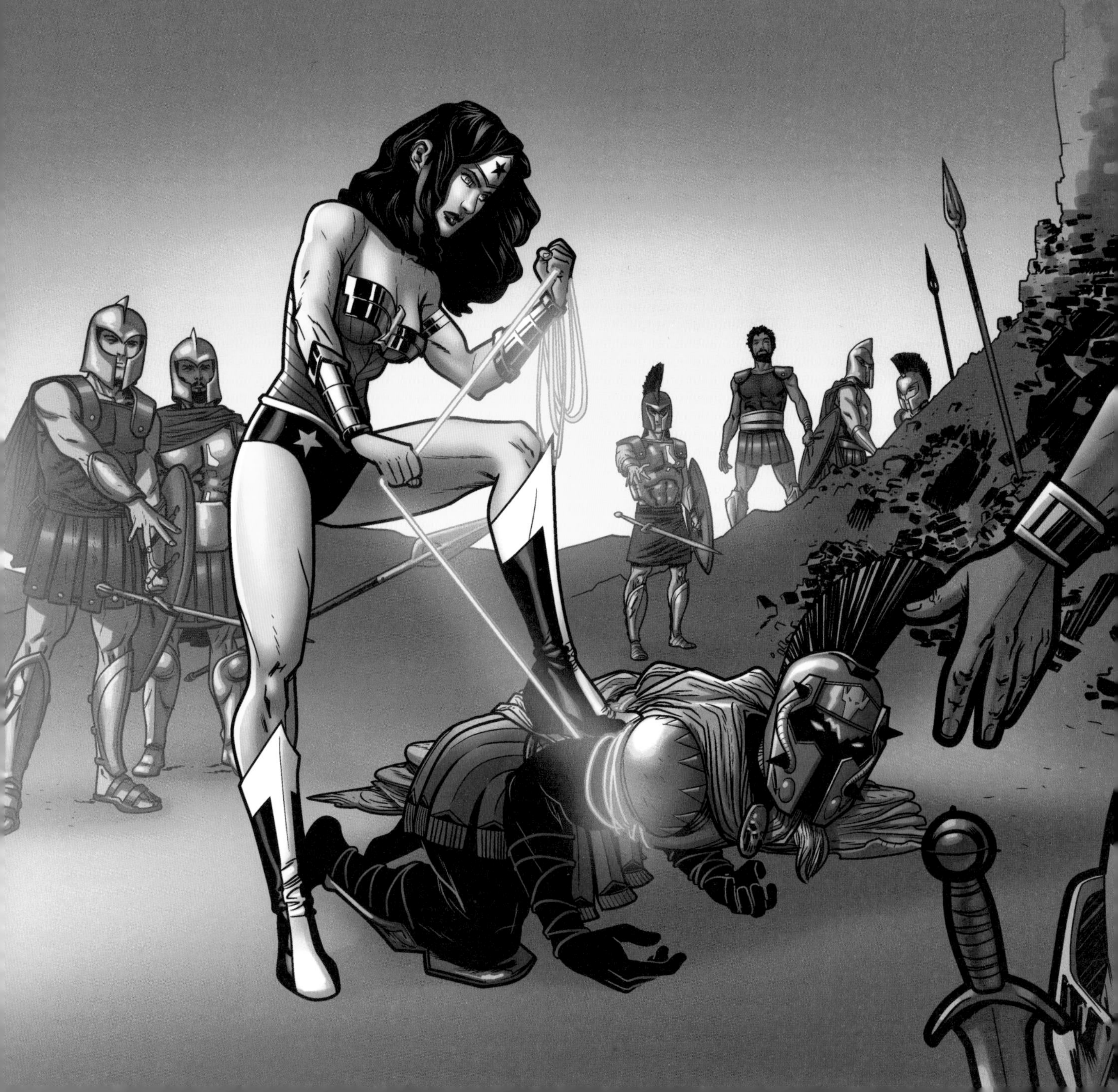

Back in the present, Wonder Woman was glad to see that things had returned to normal.

This is not the last I'll see of Ares, Wonder Woman thought as she looked around at the ruins of Troy. *And I'll be here to stop him when he reappears.*

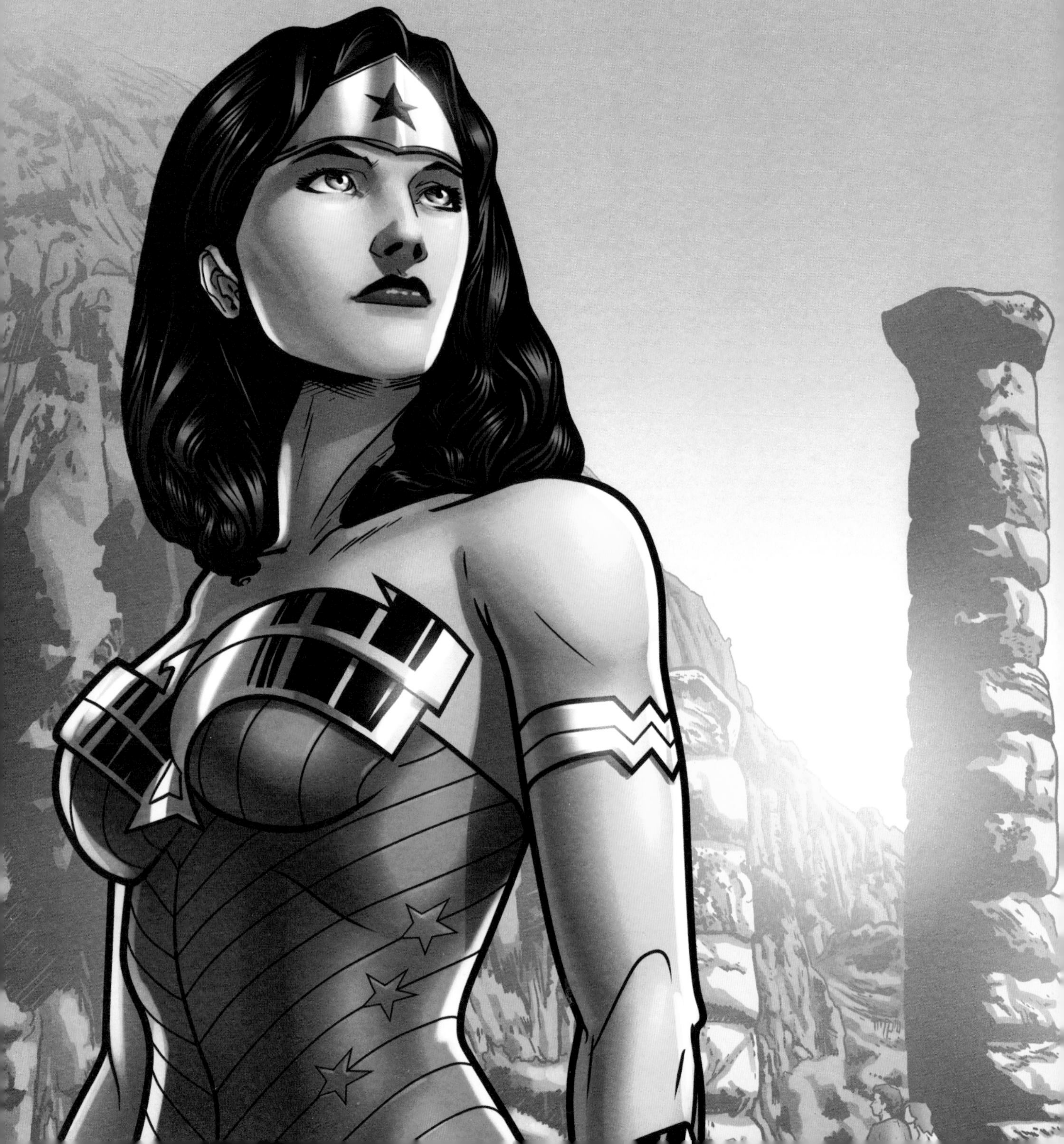

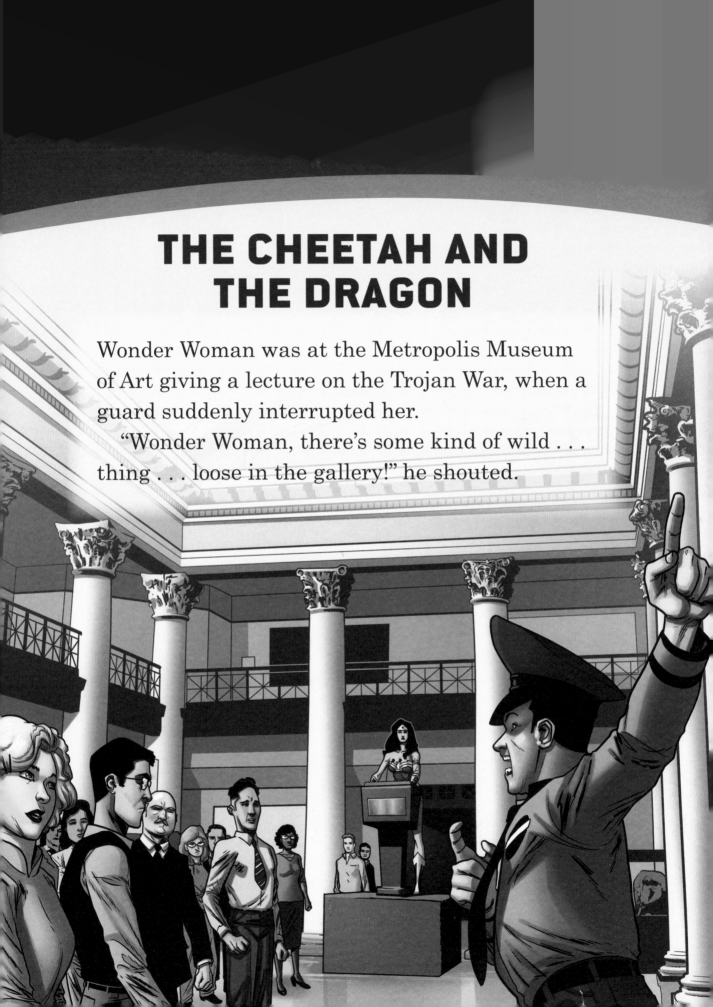

THE CHEETAH AND THE DRAGON

Wonder Woman was at the Metropolis Museum of Art giving a lecture on the Trojan War, when a guard suddenly interrupted her.

"Wonder Woman, there's some kind of wild . . . thing . . . loose in the gallery!" he shouted.

The Amazon warrior ran at super-speed in the direction that the guard had pointed. She reached the gallery in no time. When she arrived, she recognized the villain instantly.

"Cheetah!"

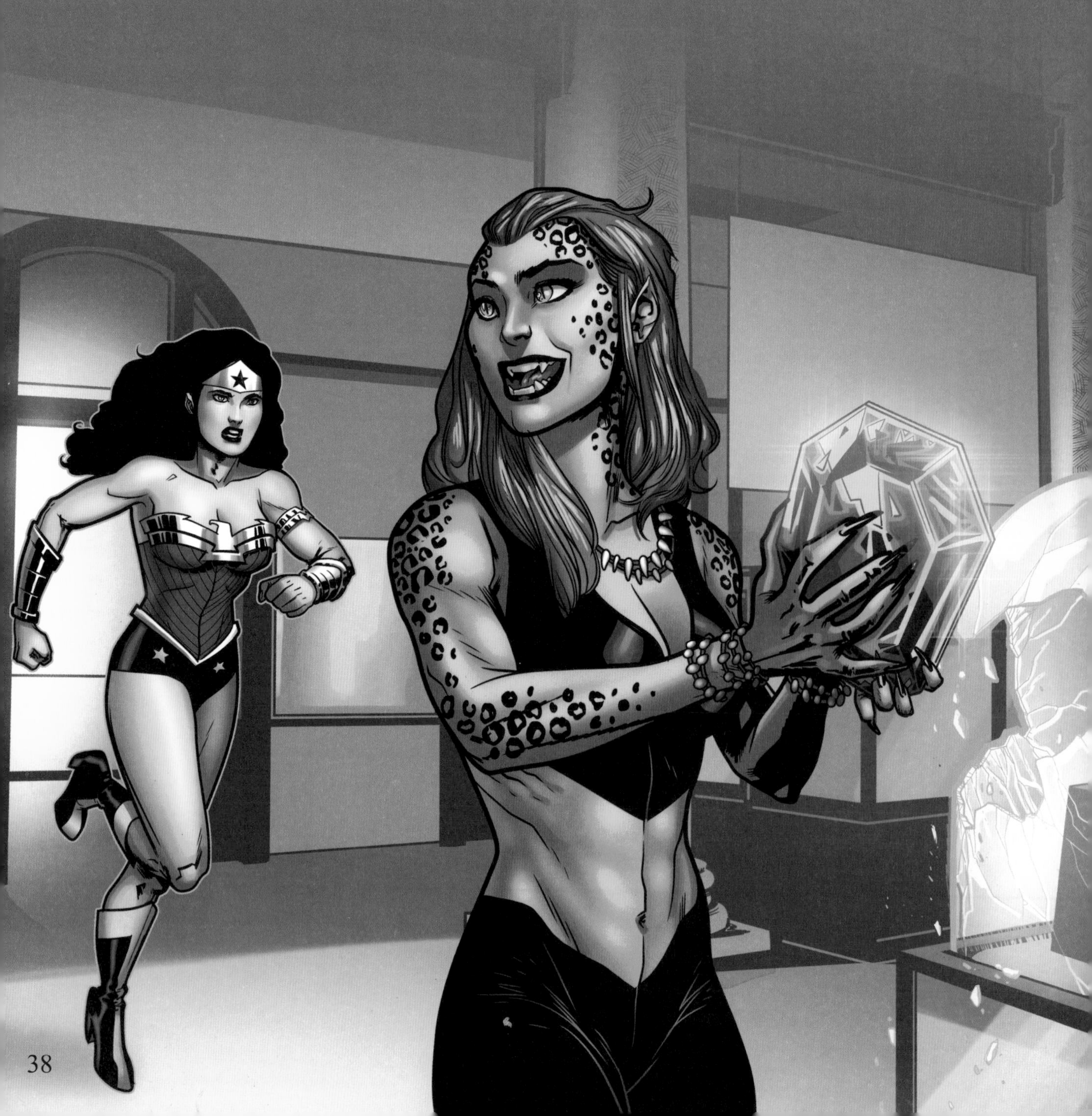

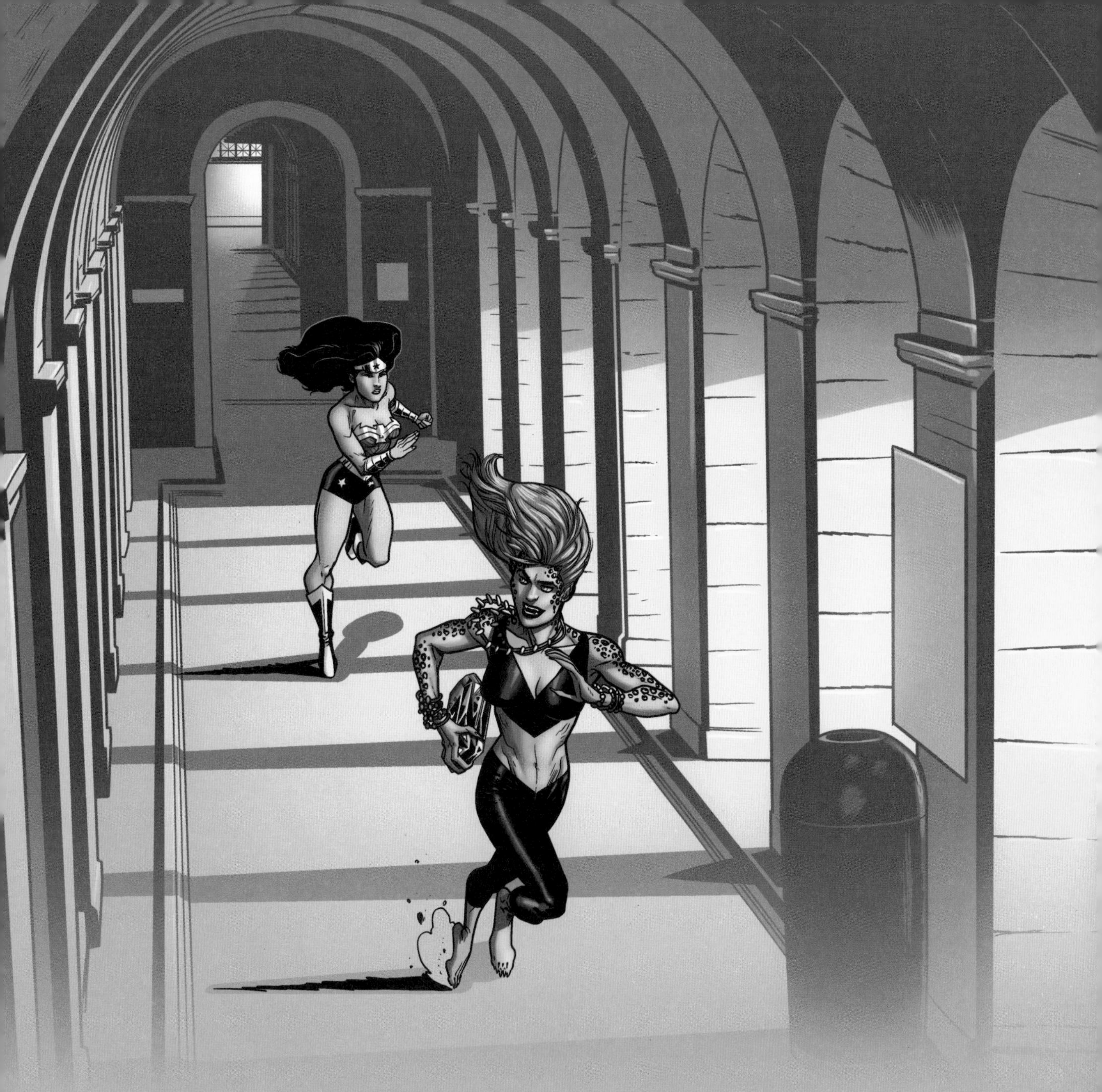

"Catch me if you can," The Cheetah taunted as she ran off with a very large red ruby. "If you can't, this beautiful gem is mine, *all mine*."

Wonder Woman chased the villain, but The Cheetah was fast.

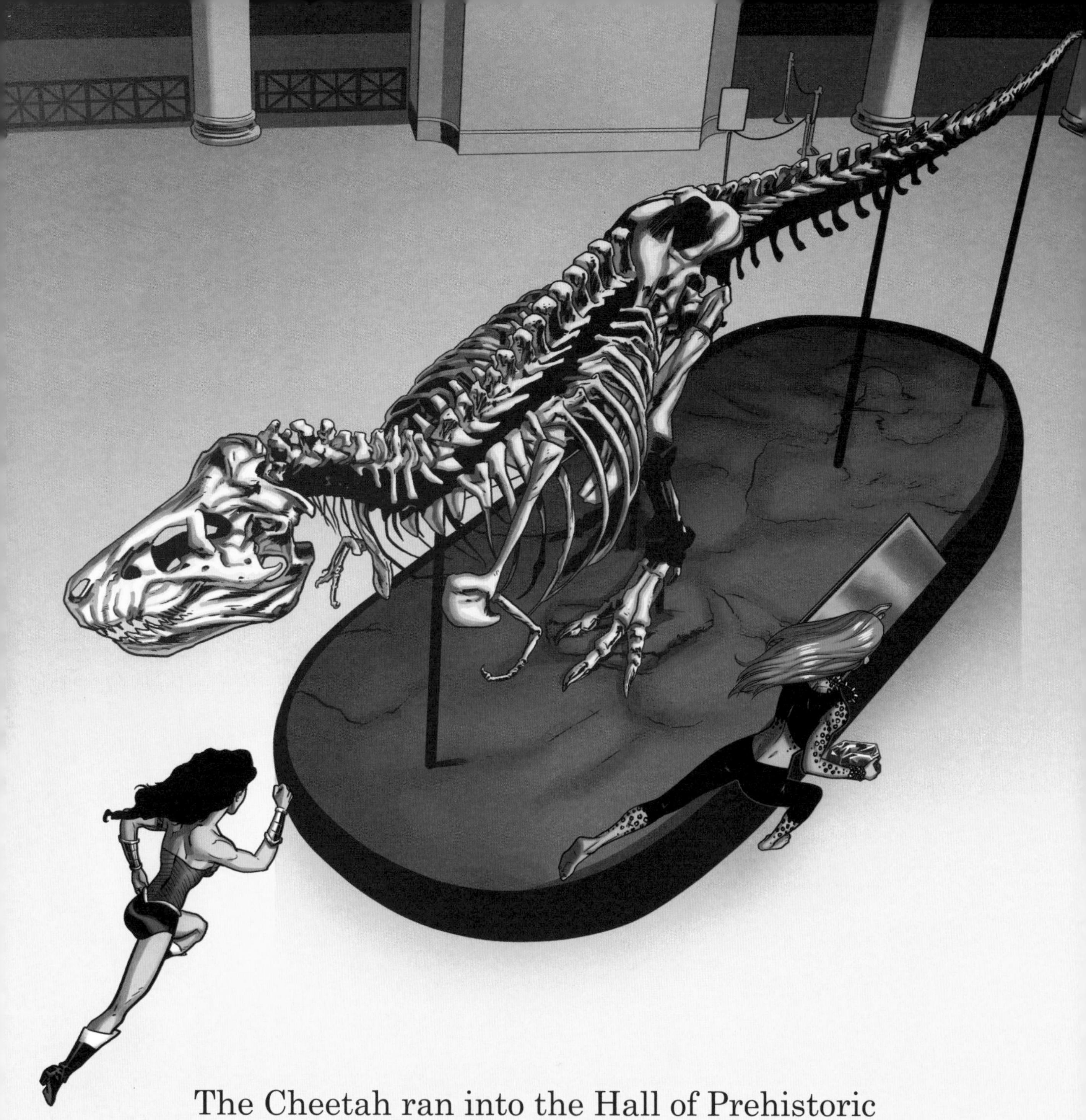

The Cheetah ran into the Hall of Prehistoric Animals. It looked like a dead end, but the fleet-footed feline wasn't about to give up.

"You can't have that gem," Wonder Woman called, still in pursuit. "It's not just valuable—it's an important historic artifact."

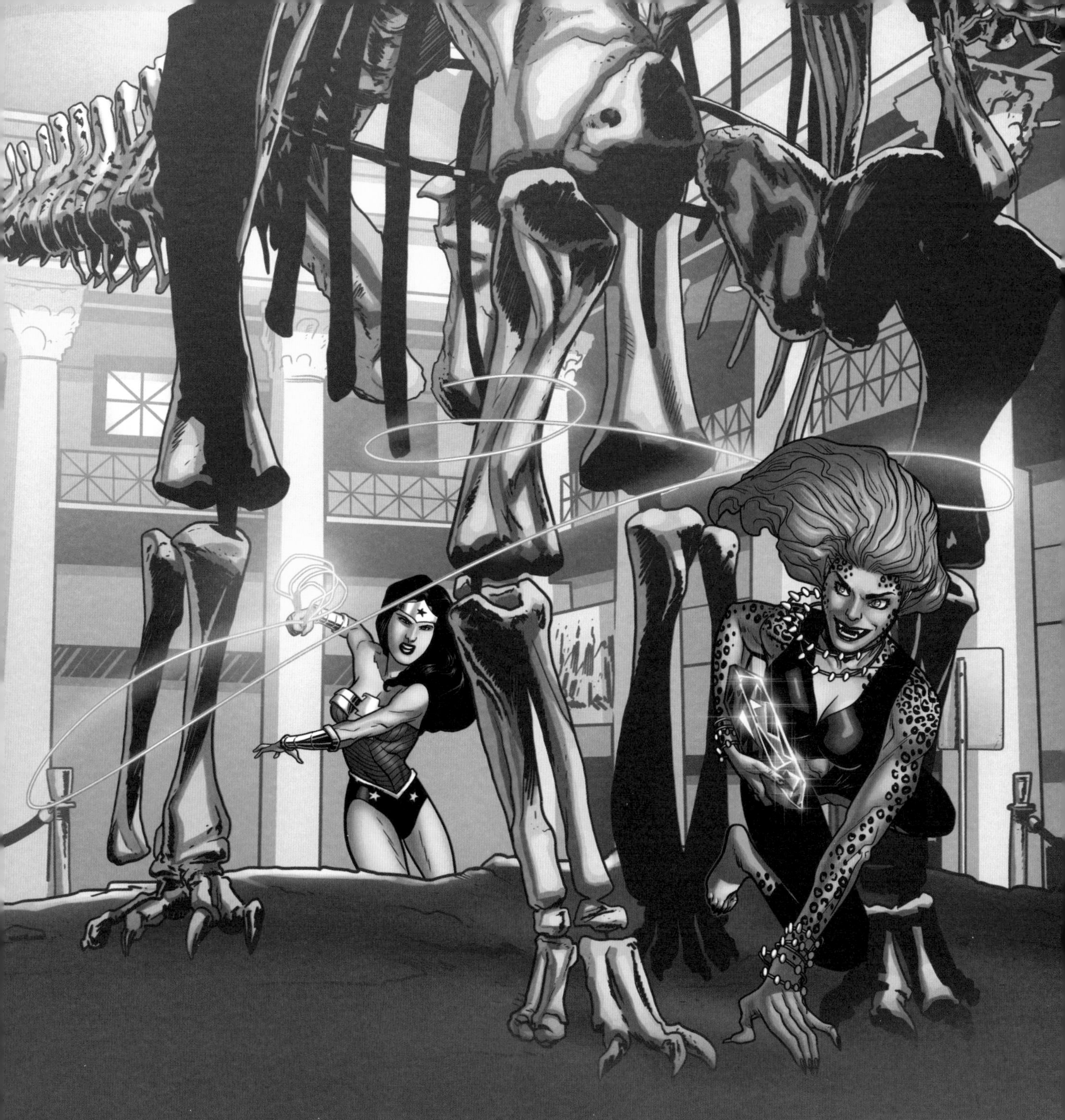

Wonder Woman tried to snag The Cheetah with her magic lasso, but again, the villain was too quick.

"Ha! You'll have to do better than that to catch me," The Cheetah purred.

"Good idea," the super hero said, lunging toward the villain and tackling her just as she tried to leap over the bones of a large dinosaur. The ruby flew from The Cheetah's hands.

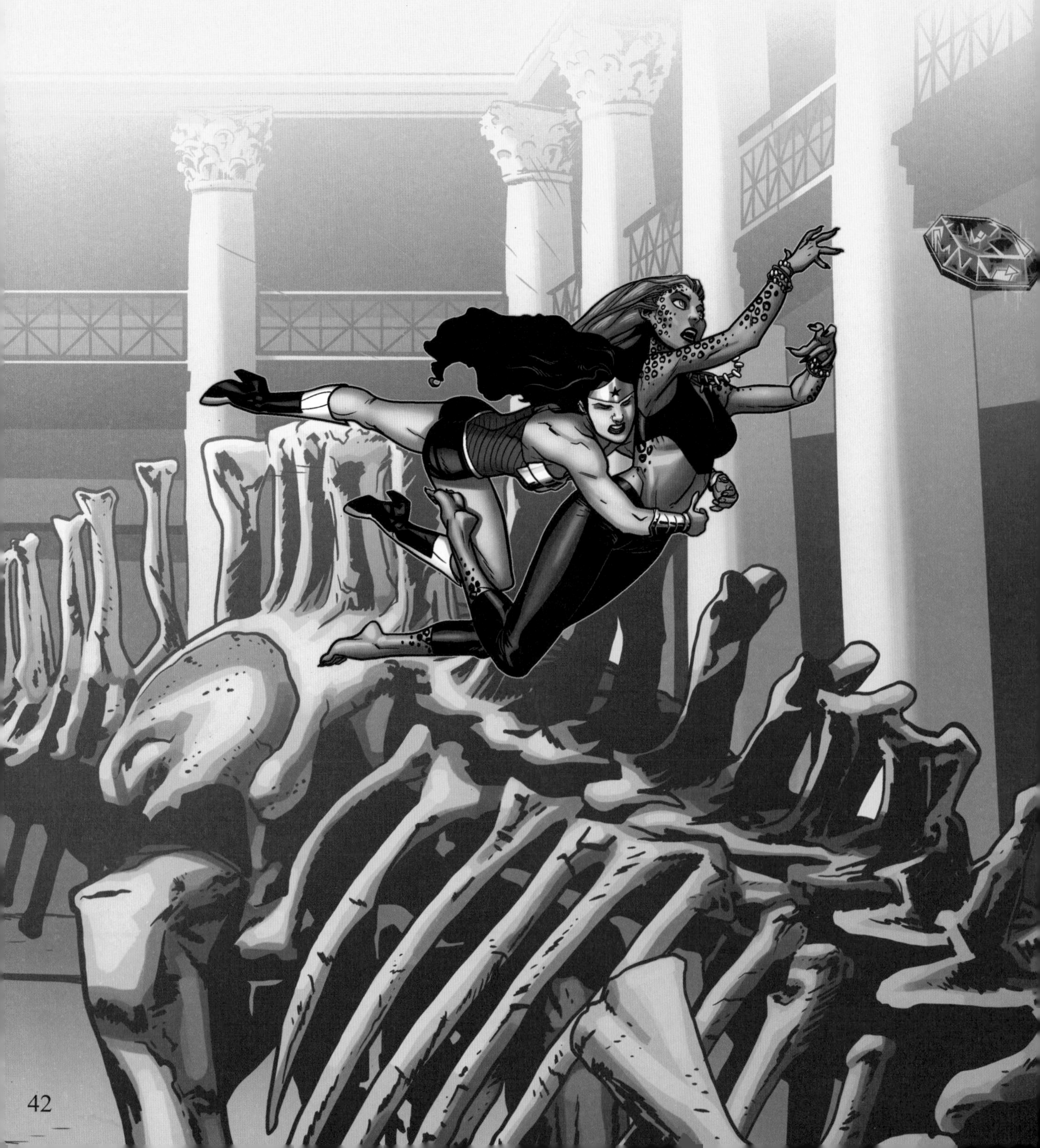

The huge red gem smashed against the
floor and—oh, no!—cracked.

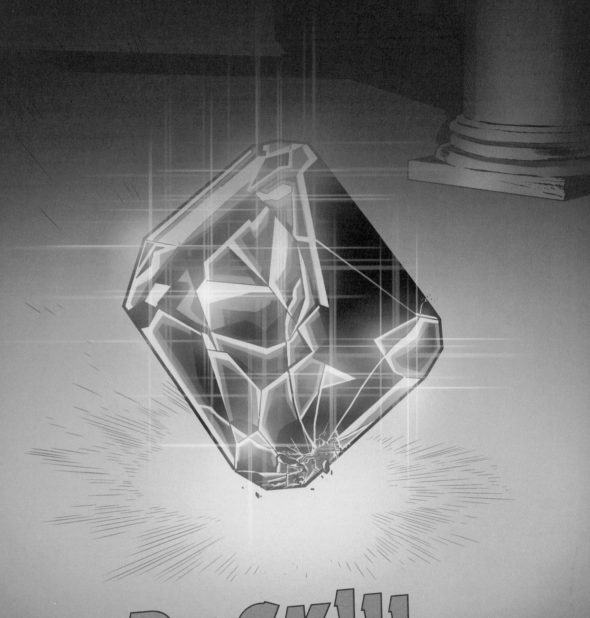

CRACK!!!

Suddenly, a dragon appeared. It crashed through the skylight and

ROARED!!!

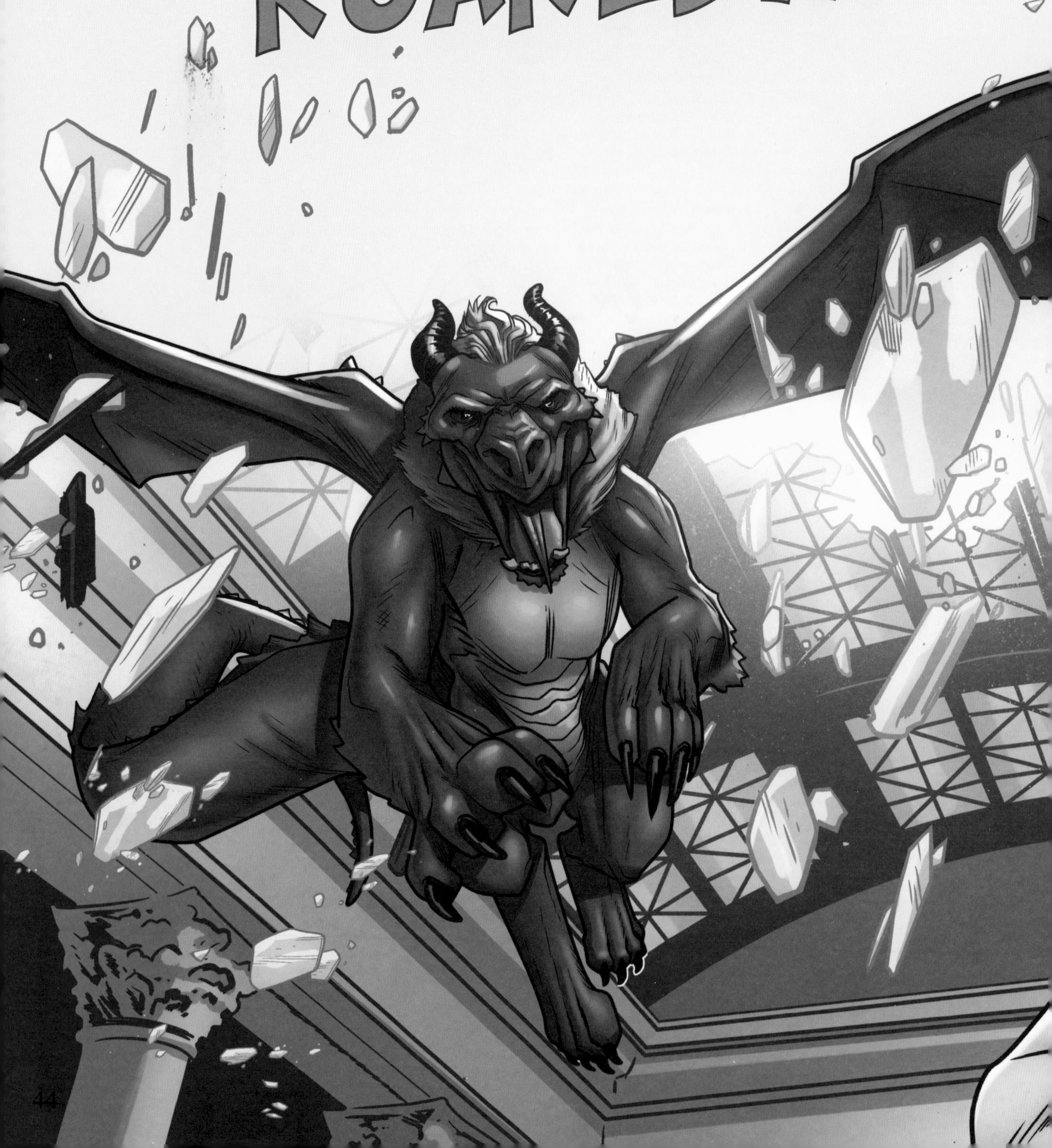

“I think we’ve got trouble,” The Cheetah said, backing away. “And I think I’ll let you be the hero and handle it.”

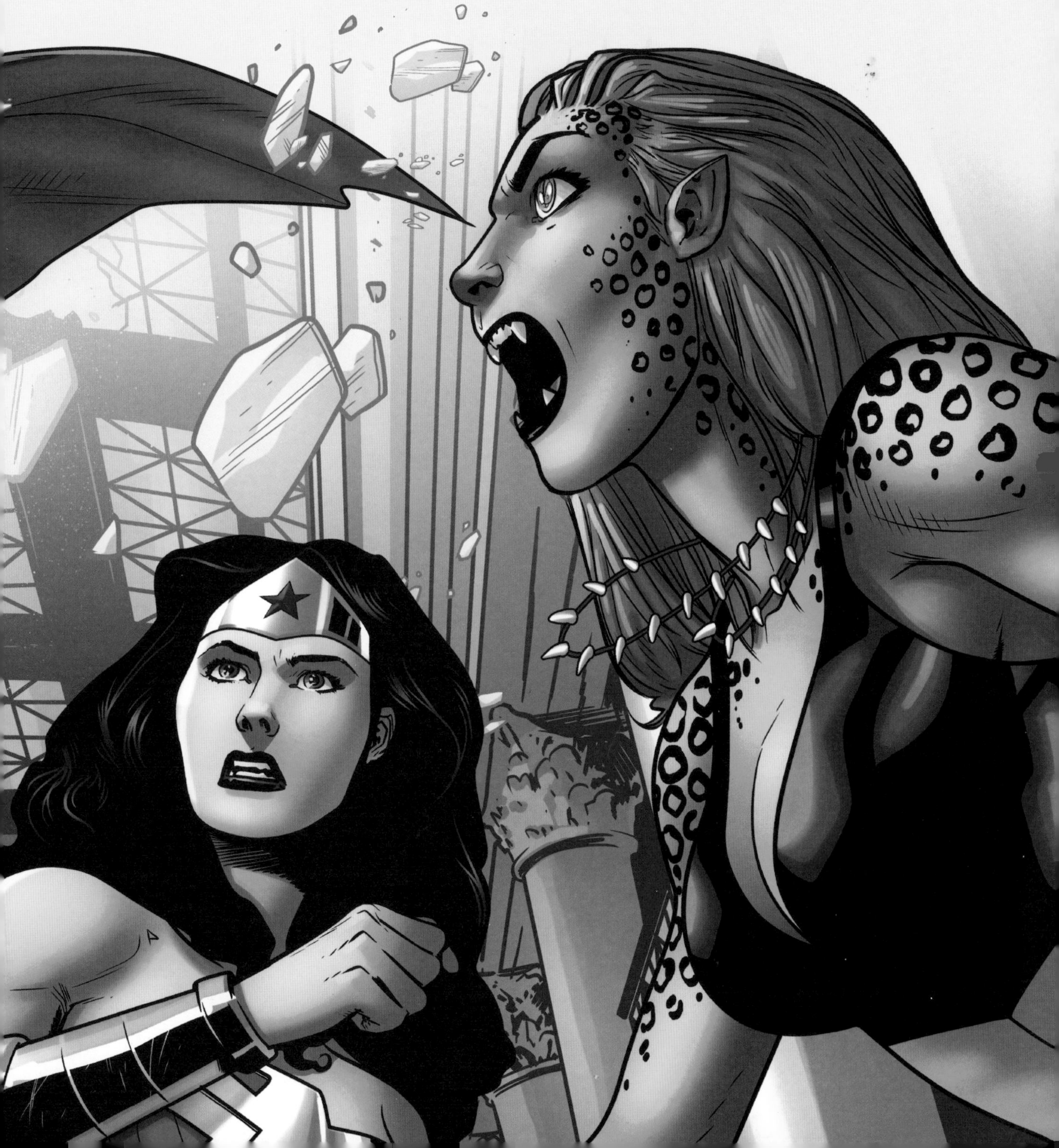

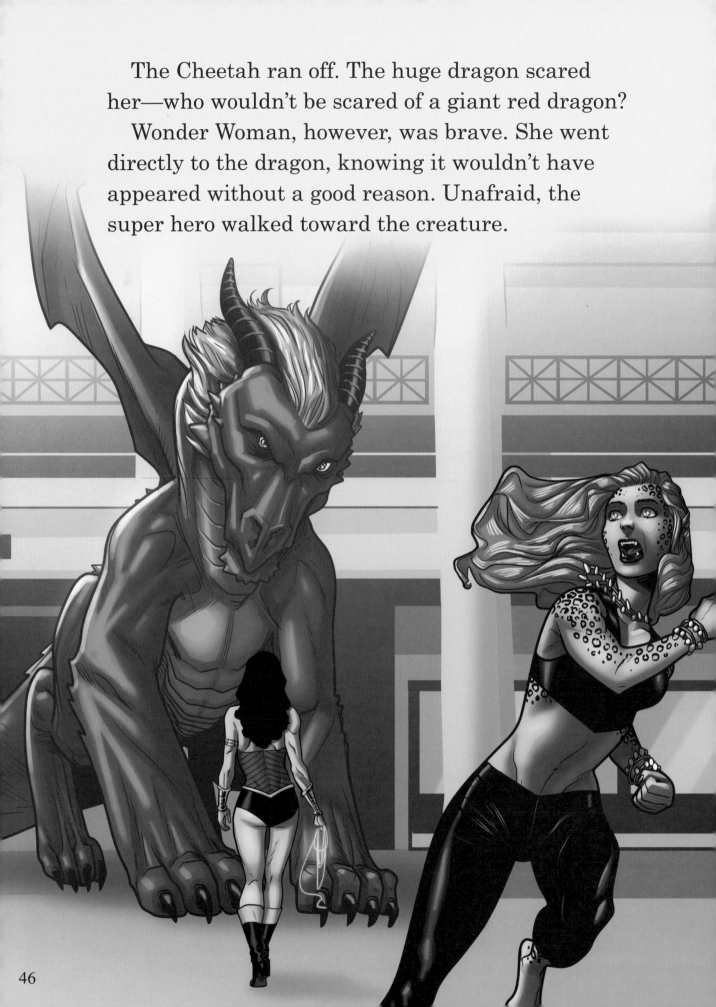

The Cheetah ran off. The huge dragon scared her—who wouldn't be scared of a giant red dragon? Wonder Woman, however, was brave. She went directly to the dragon, knowing it wouldn't have appeared without a good reason. Unafraid, the super hero walked toward the creature.

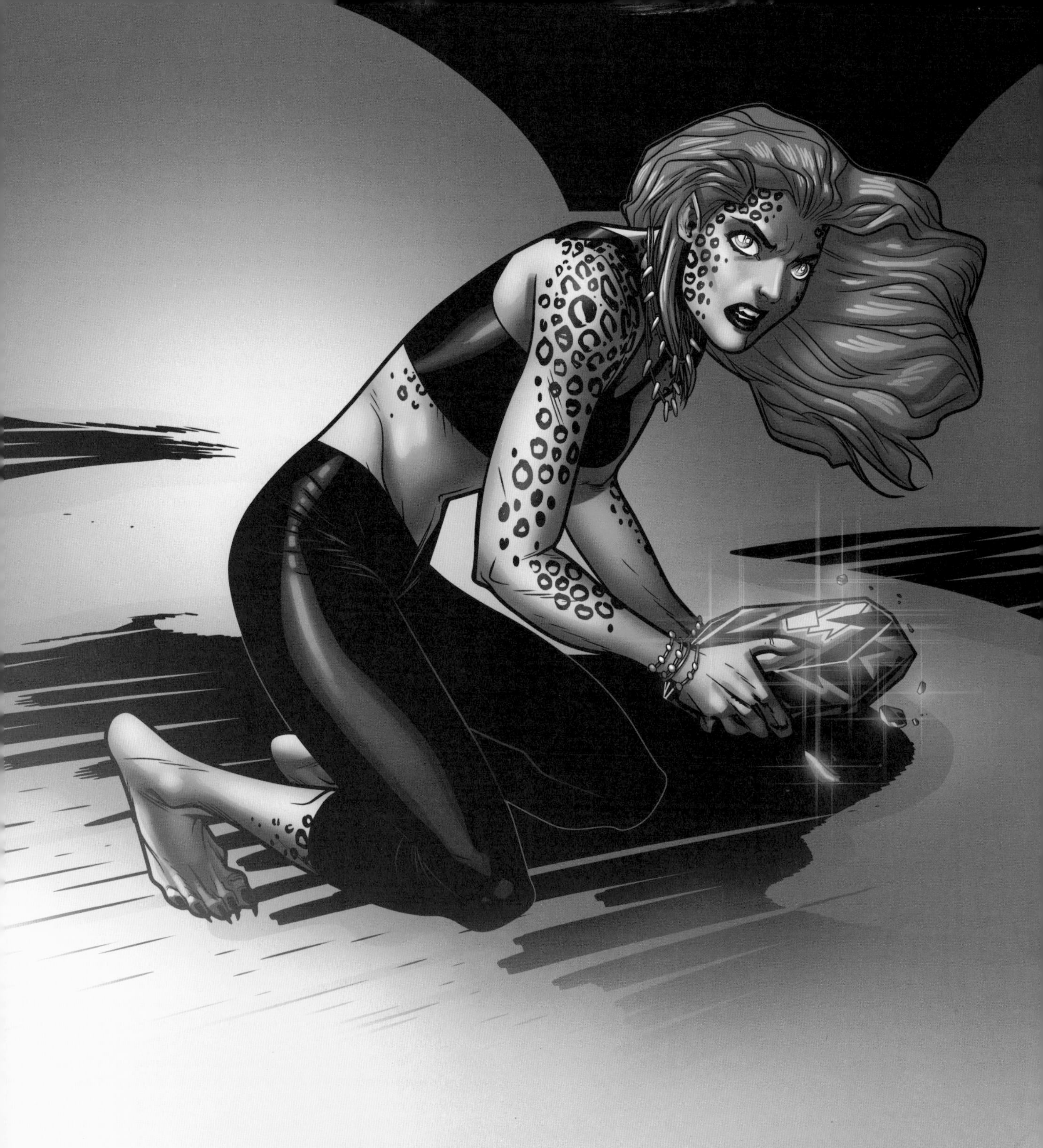

The Cheetah was scared—but not so scared that she was willing to leave a valuable gem behind. "I'm pretty sure a rock this size is still worth something, even if it's cracked," the villain muttered.

But when she picked up the ruby, it began to quiver and splinter in her hands. She couldn't believe her eyes. Something was inside! The gem split open along the crack, and out popped a cute baby dragon.

"YIKES!" shrieked The Cheetah.

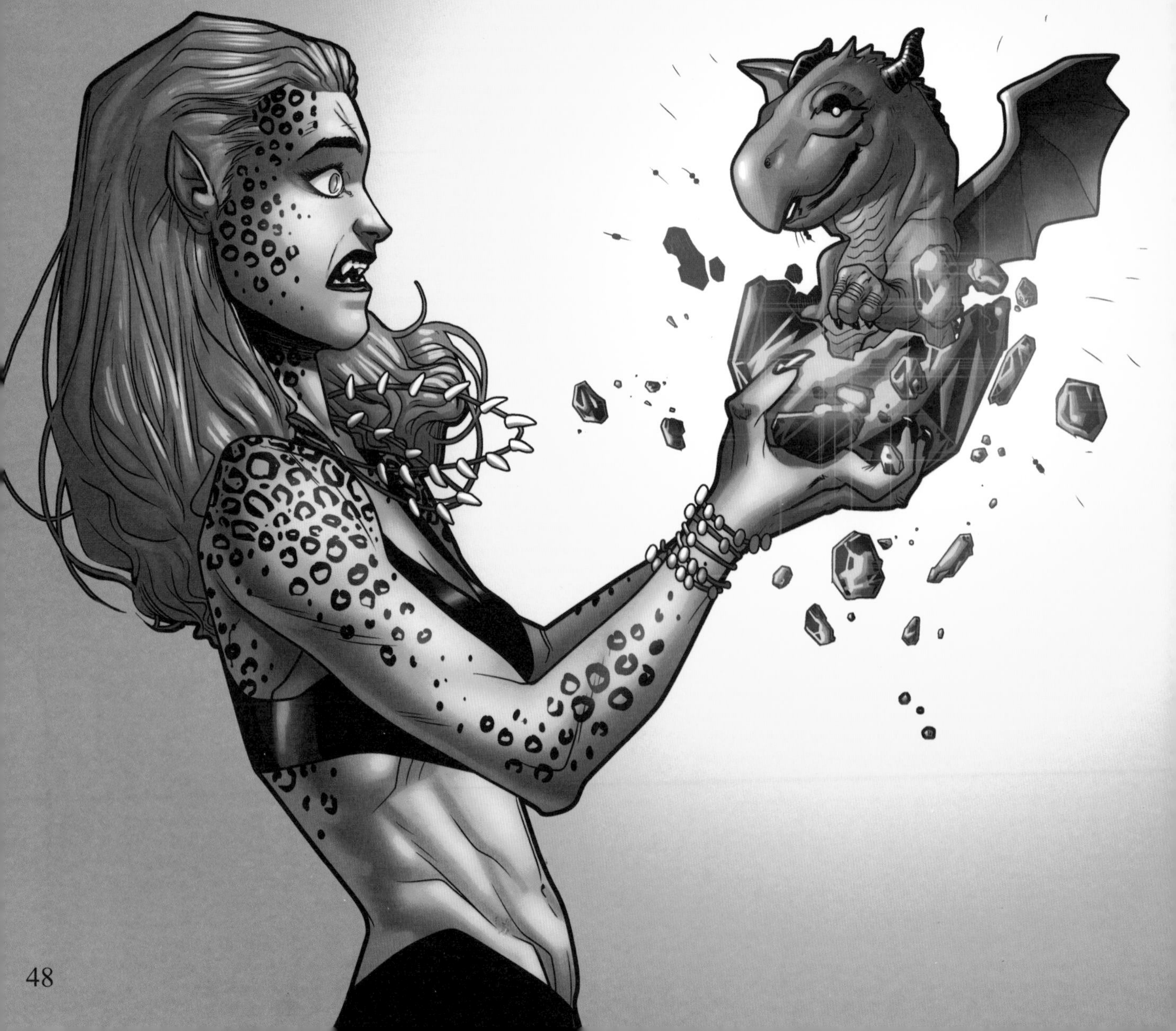

The villain was more surprised by the baby dragon than she had been by the big one. The baby squawked, and The Cheetah shrieked again, throwing the little creature into the air!

"I've got you," said Wonder Woman.

She leapt into the air to catch the baby.

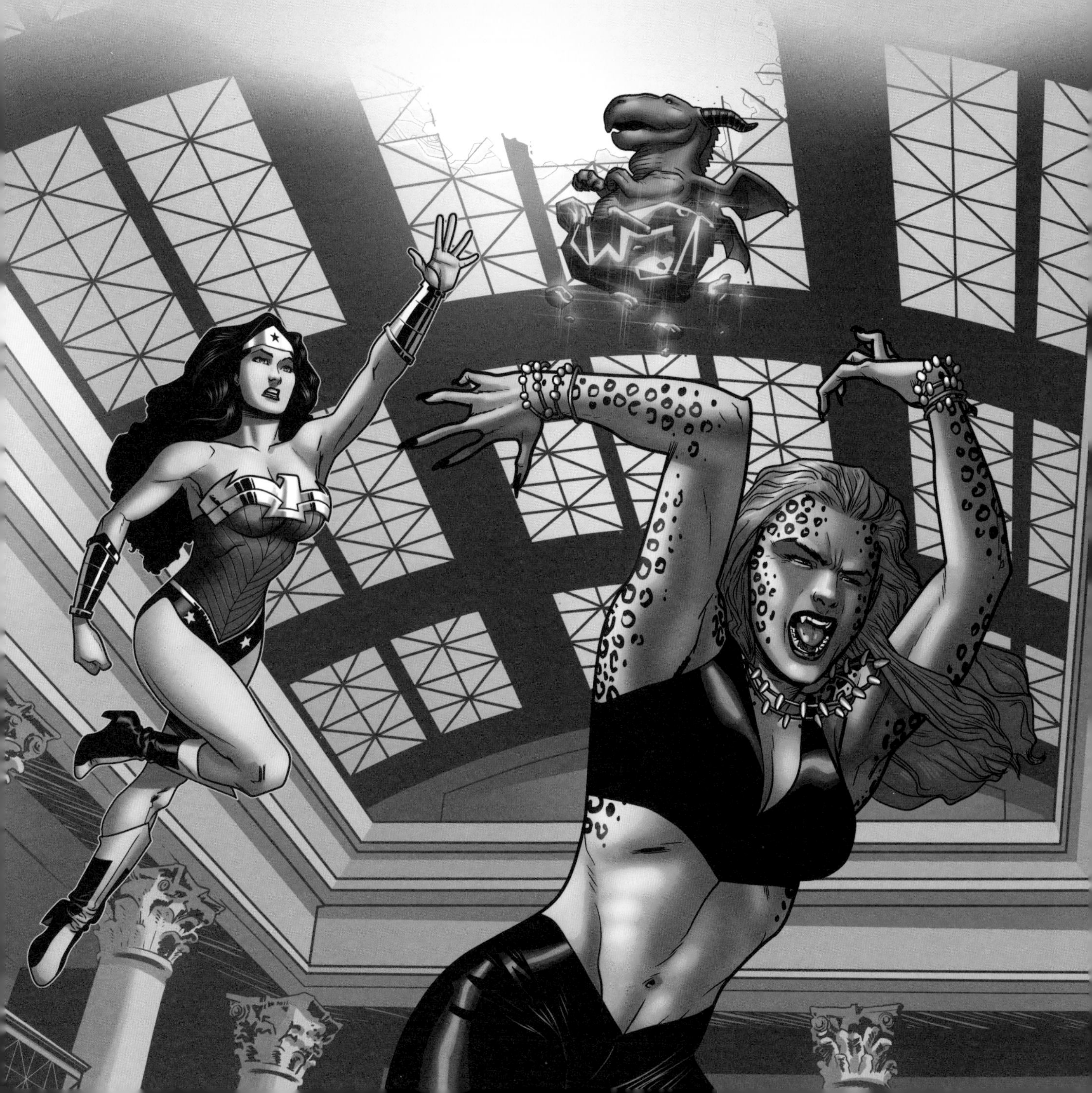

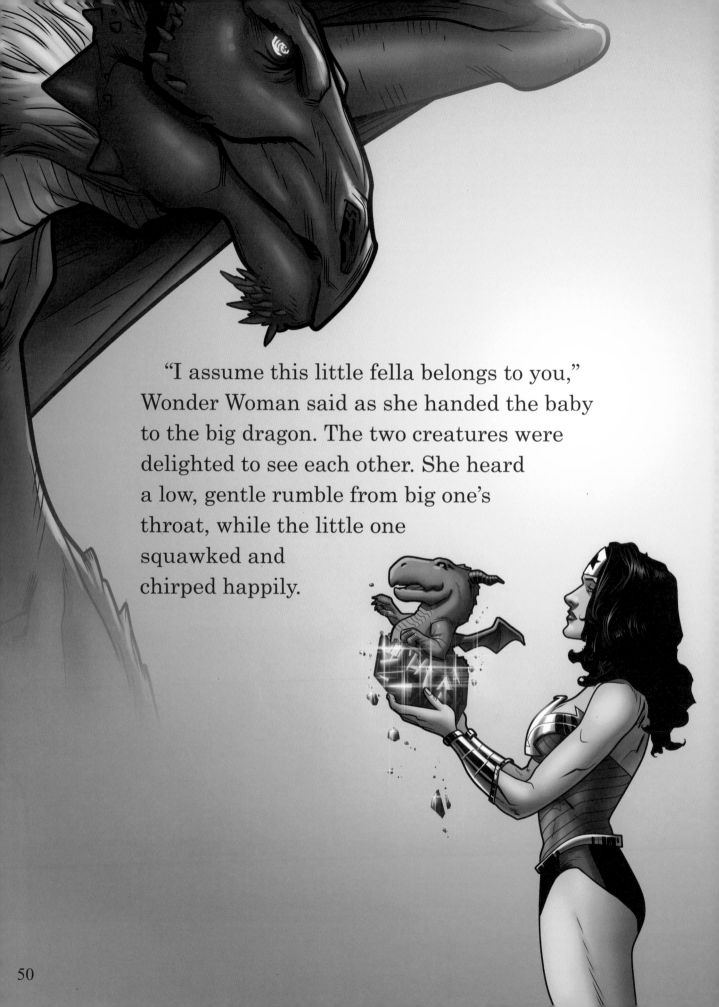

"I assume this little fella belongs to you,"
Wonder Woman said as she handed the baby
to the big dragon. The two creatures were
delighted to see each other. She heard
a low, gentle rumble from big one's
throat, while the little one
squawked and
chirped happily.

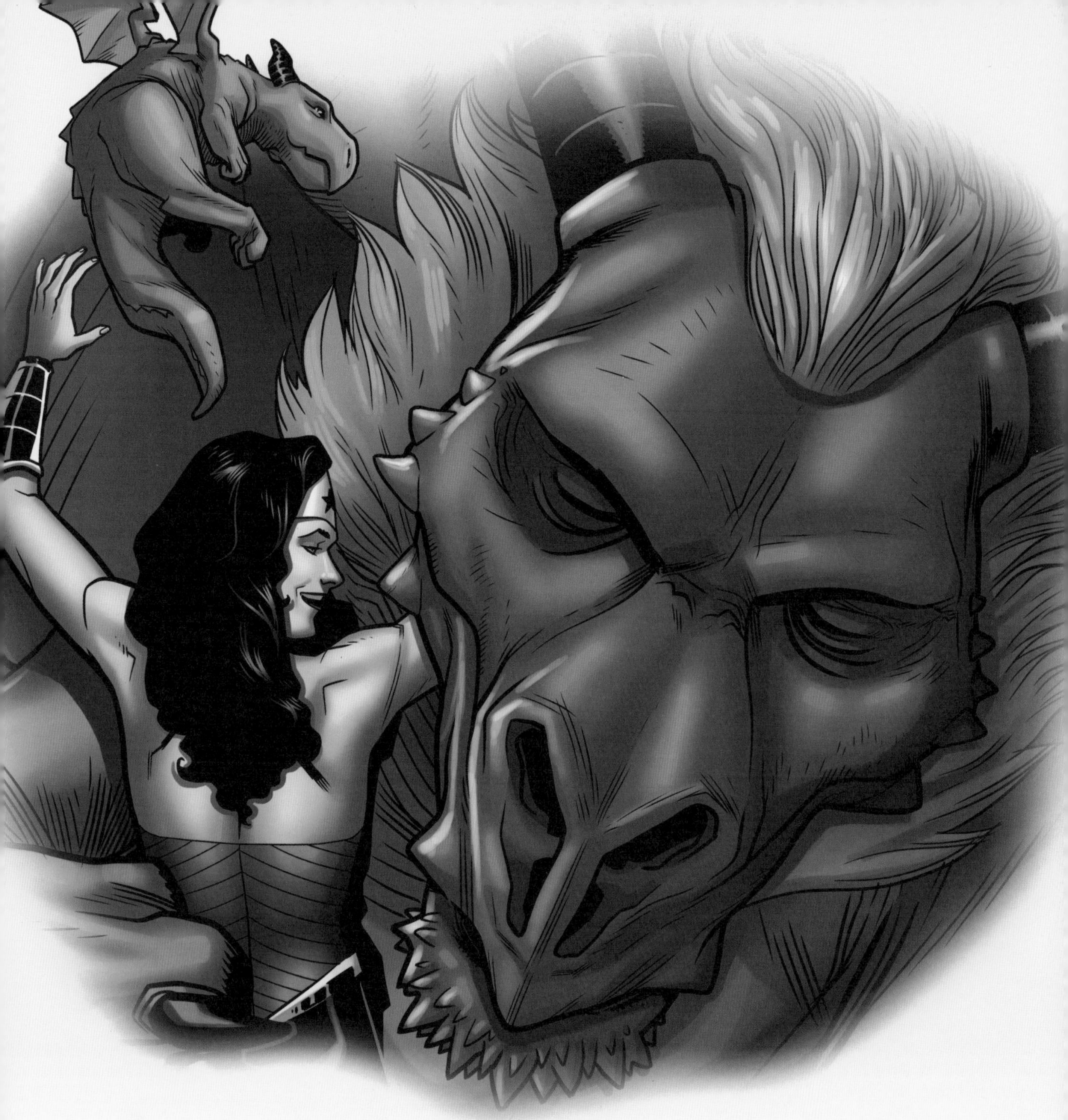

The large dragon wrapped its paws gently around Wonder Woman. It seemed to be thanking her.

"You're welcome," the Amazon replied. "You get going. I've got other business to tend to."

Wonder Woman tied The Cheetah up with the unbreakable Lasso of Truth and led her out of the museum.

"Some things are more precious than gems or treasure," she said to the villain. "And you'll have plenty of time to think about that while you're in prison."

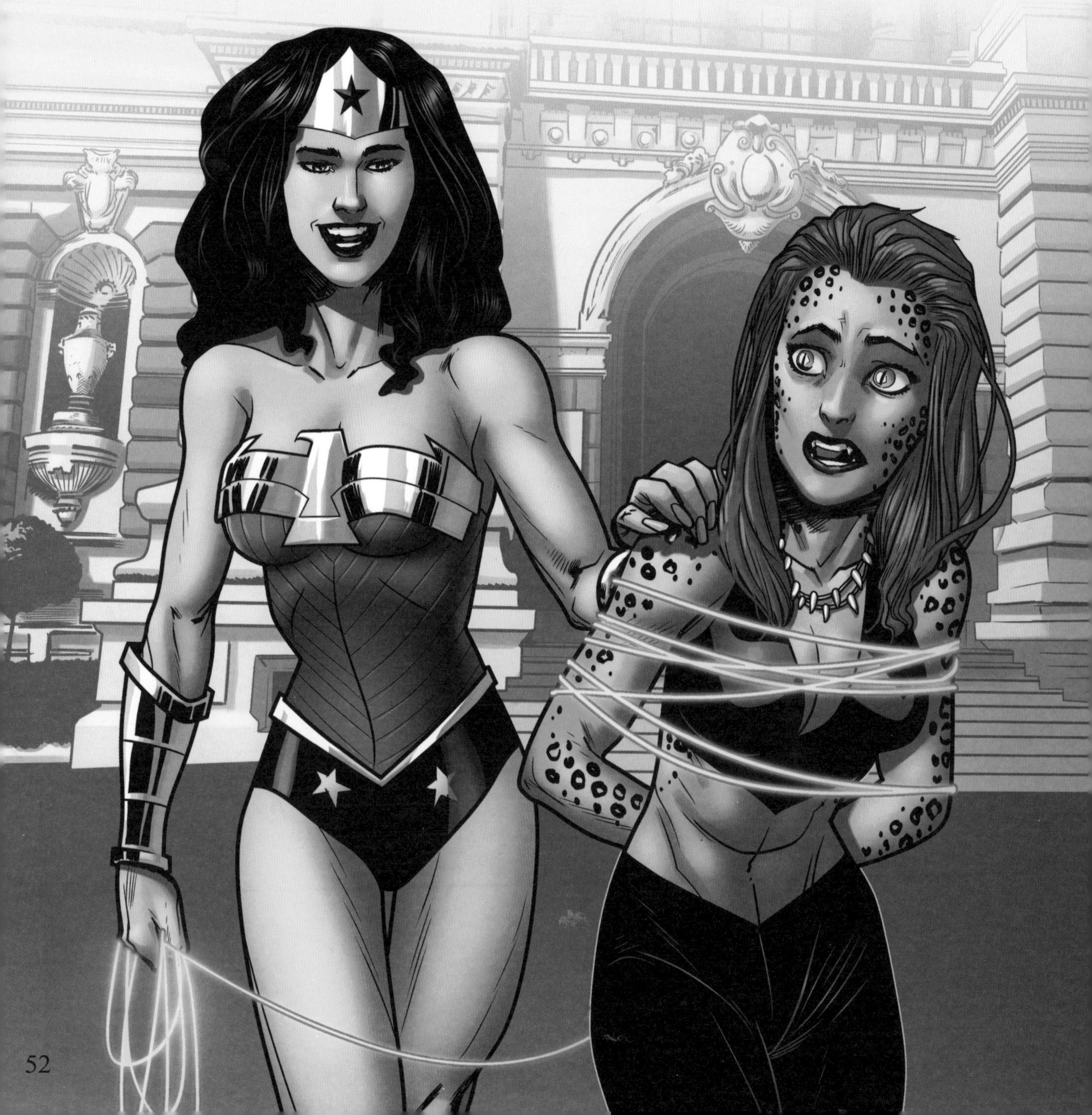

TRIPLE TROUBLE

Wonder Woman roared through the sky in the Invisible Jet. She had received a report that there was trouble at the Metropolis Botanic Garden.

"It looks like all the people got outside to safety," Wonder Woman said. "Now to check out the situation."

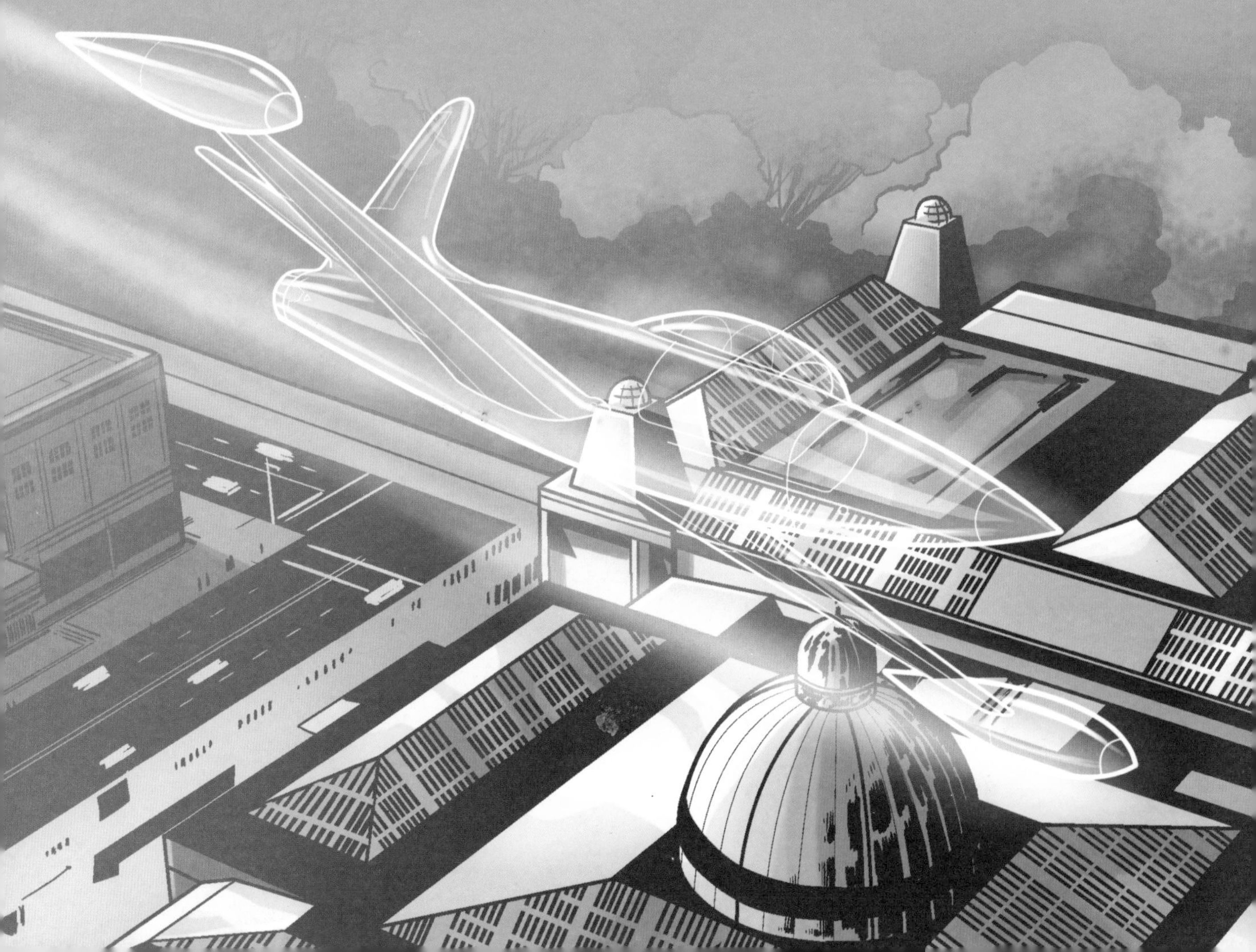

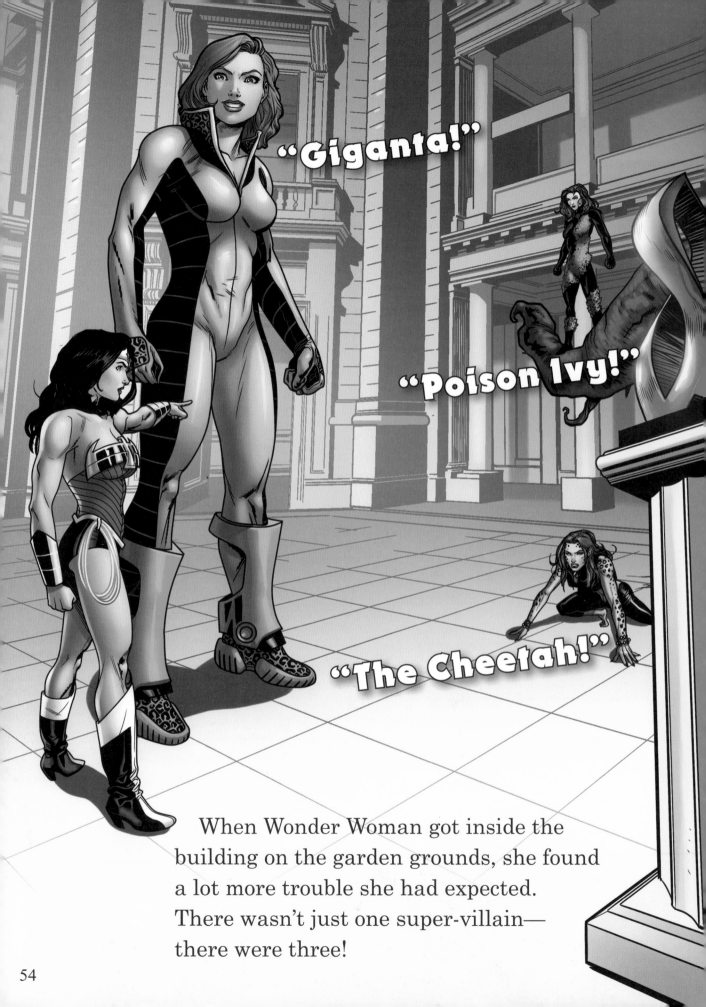

"Giganta!"

"Poison Ivy!"

"The Cheetah!"

When Wonder Woman got inside the building on the garden grounds, she found a lot more trouble she had expected. There wasn't just one super-villain—there were three!

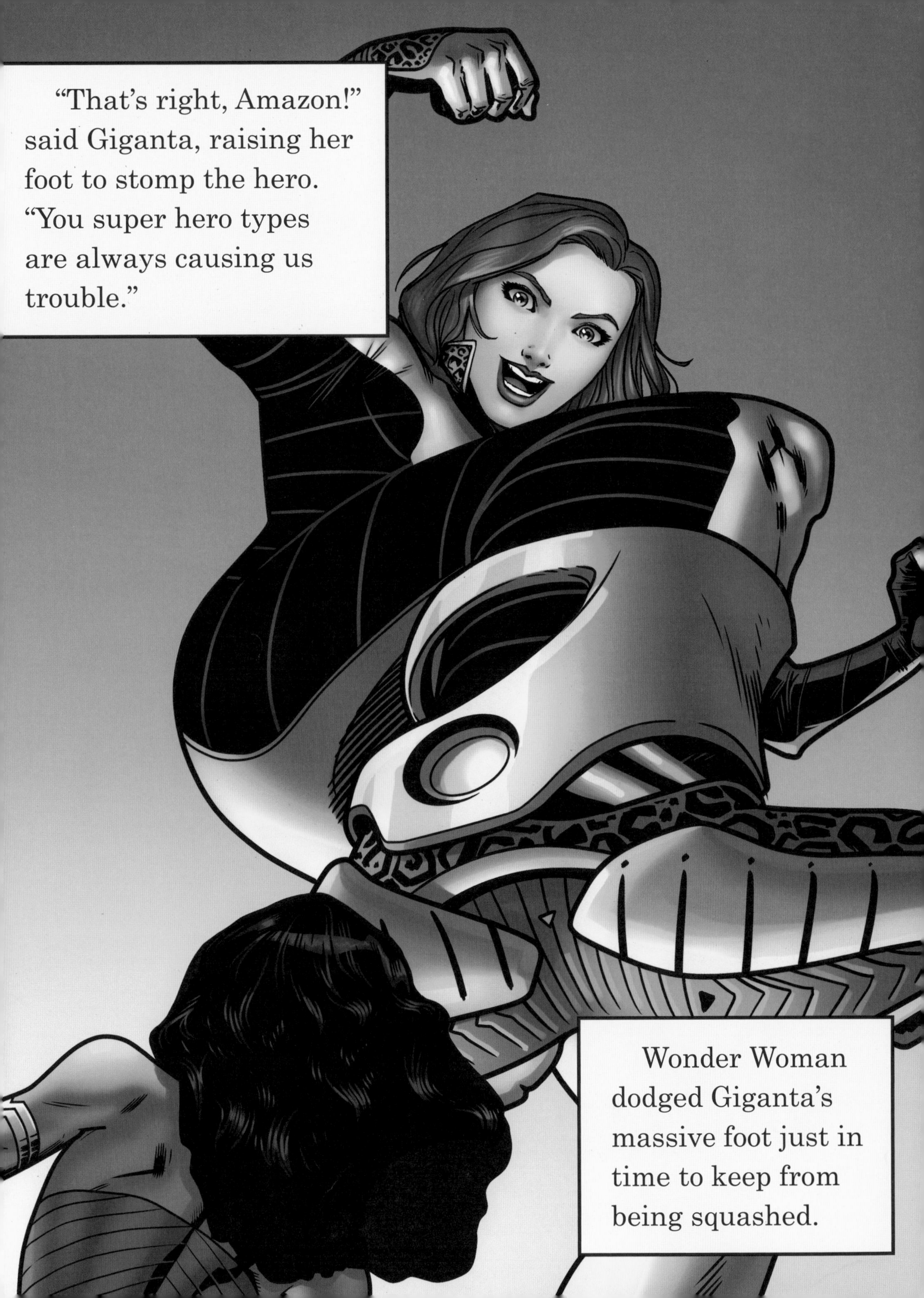

"That's right, Amazon!" said Giganta, raising her foot to stomp the hero. "You super hero types are always causing us trouble."

Wonder Woman dodged Giganta's massive foot just in time to keep from being squashed.

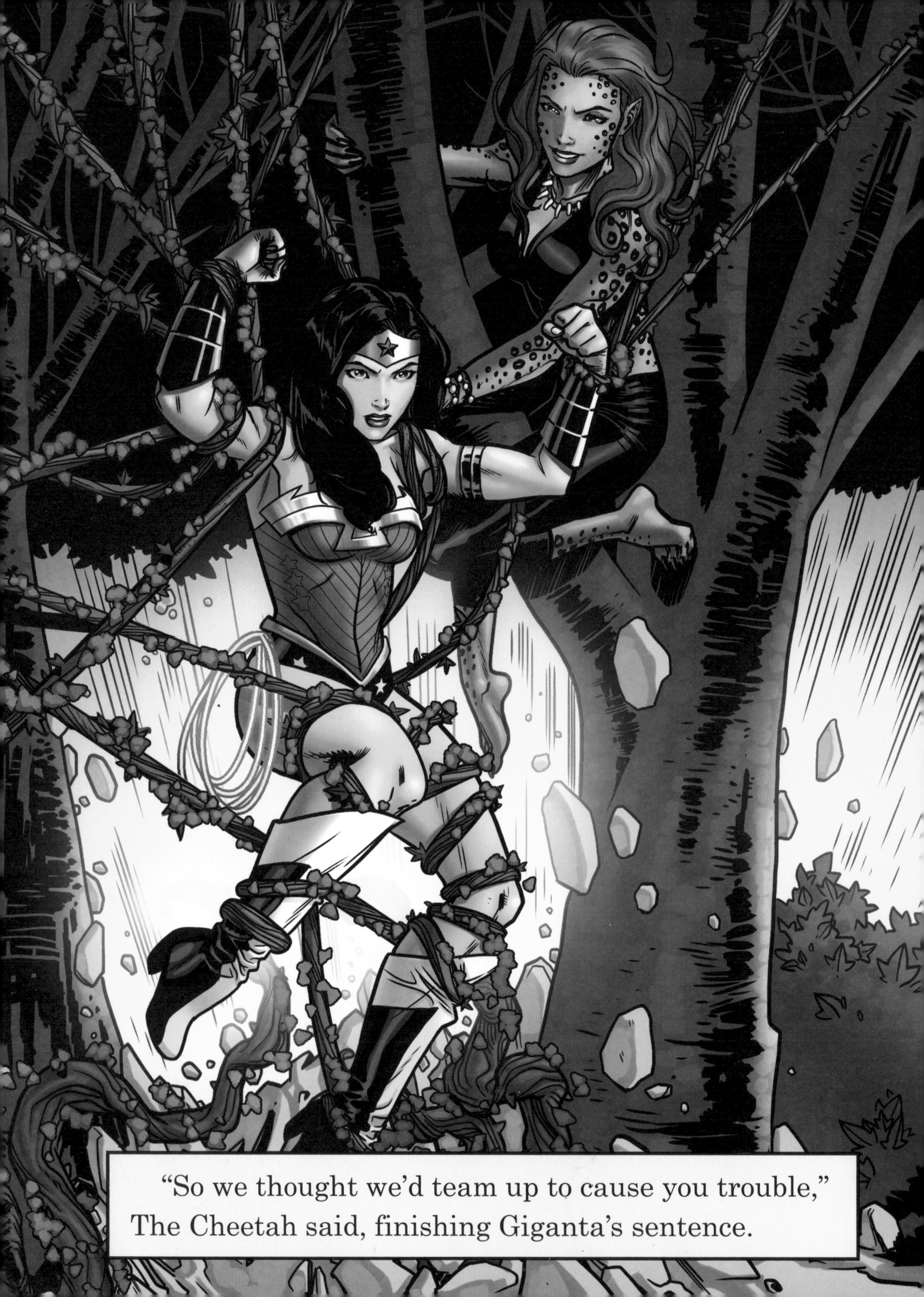

“So we thought we’d team up to cause you trouble,” The Cheetah said, finishing Giganta’s sentence.

Wonder Woman spun around to face the villains, but it was too late. Tough vines slithered up behind the super hero, wrapping tightly around her. The vines were under Poison Ivy's control. She had the power to make plants do her bidding. She chuckled, "Right where I want you . . ."

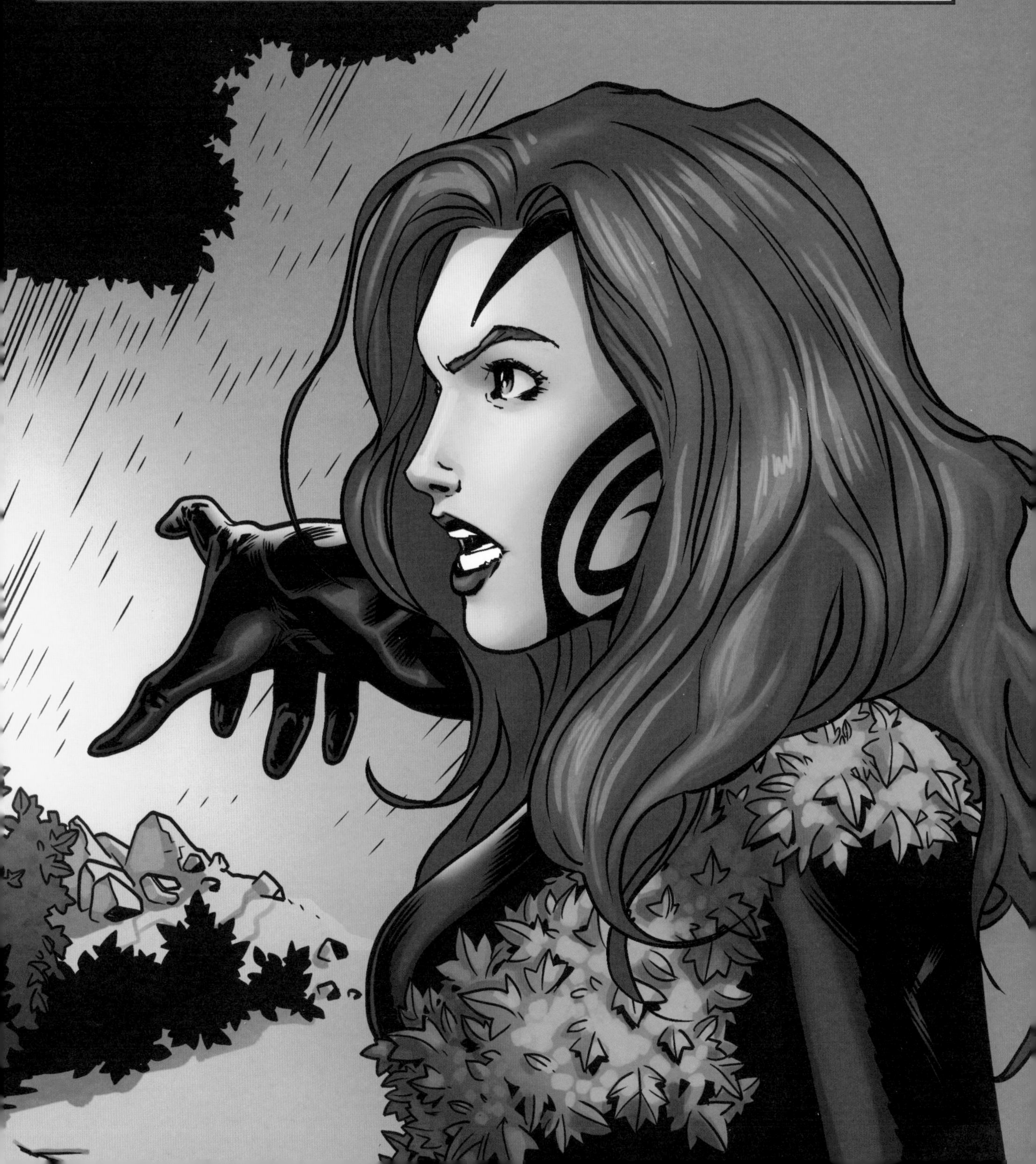

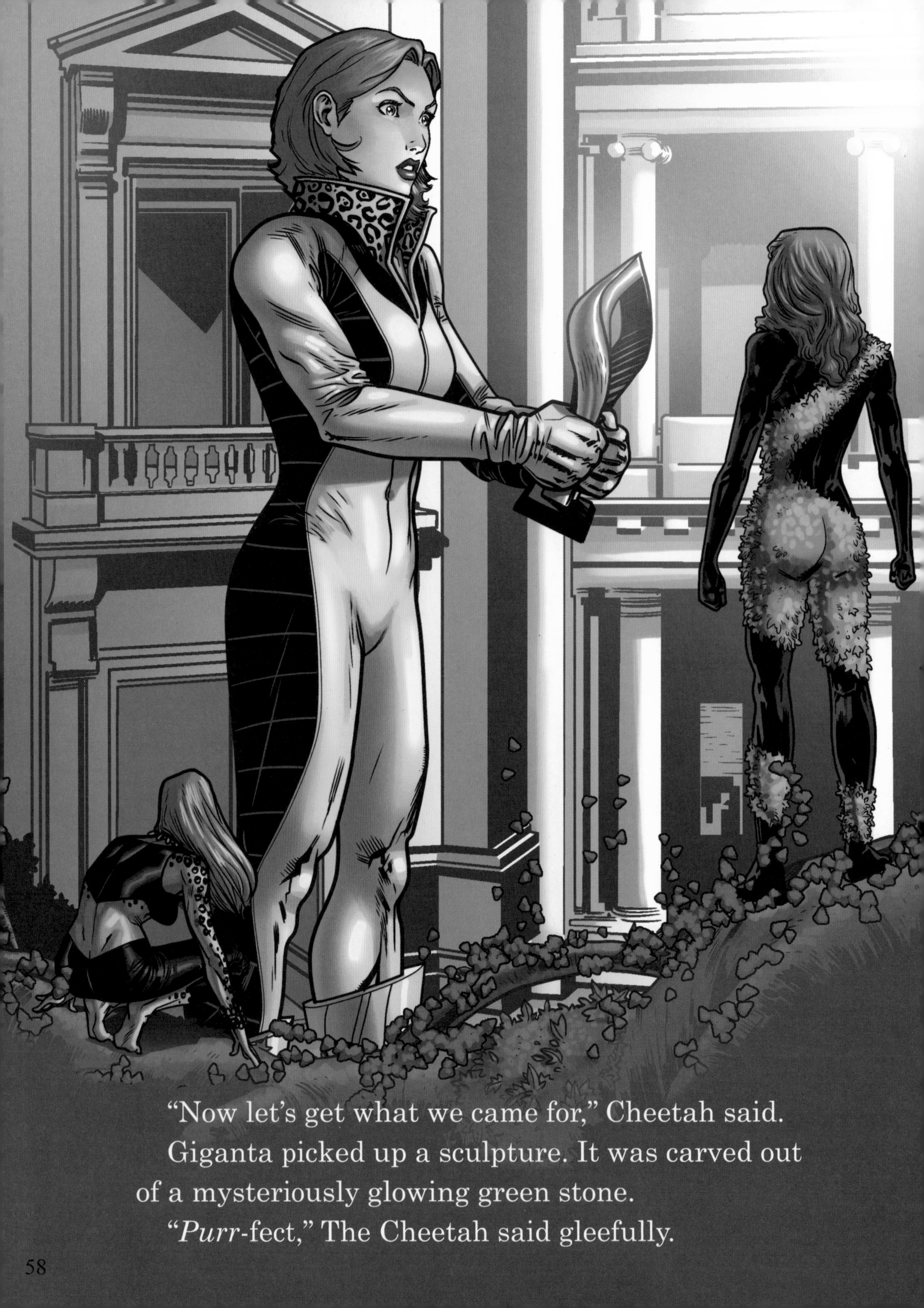

"Now let's get what we came for," Cheetah said.

Giganta picked up a sculpture. It was carved out of a mysteriously glowing green stone.

"*Purr*-fect," The Cheetah said gleefully.

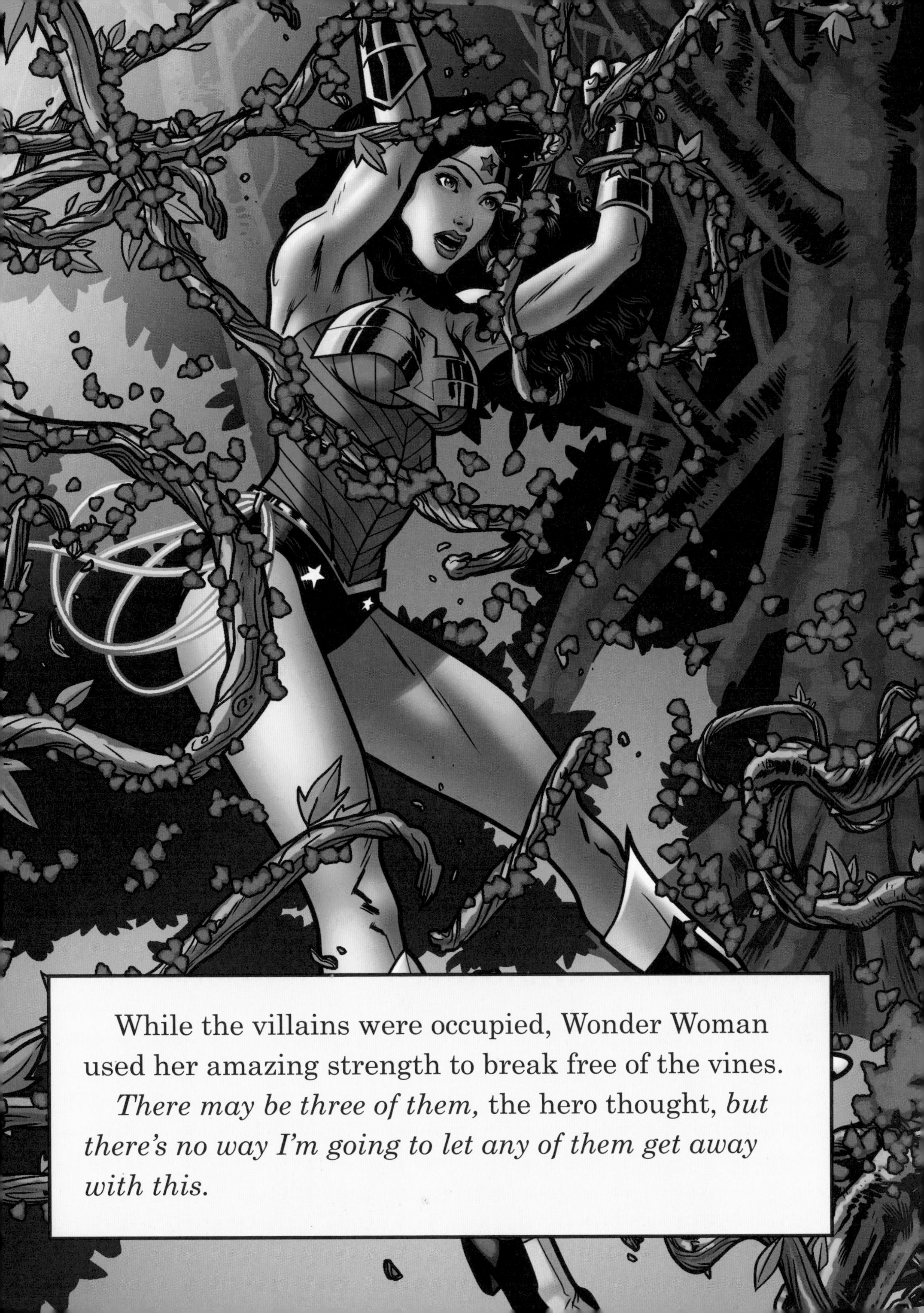

While the villains were occupied, Wonder Woman used her amazing strength to break free of the vines.

There may be three of them, the hero thought, *but there's no way I'm going to let any of them get away with this.*

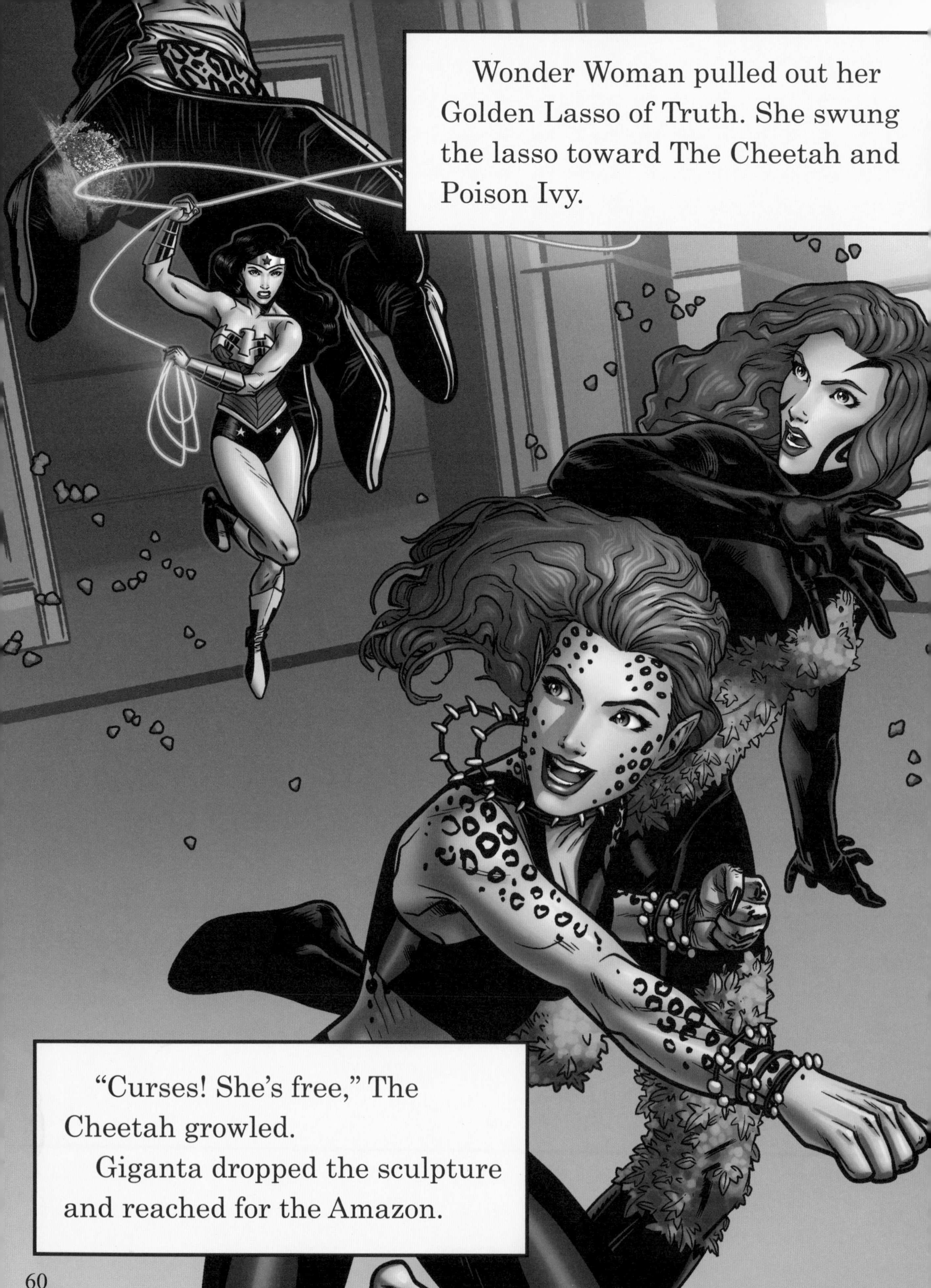

Wonder Woman pulled out her Golden Lasso of Truth. She swung the lasso toward The Cheetah and Poison Ivy.

"Curses! She's free," The Cheetah growled.

Giganta dropped the sculpture and reached for the Amazon.

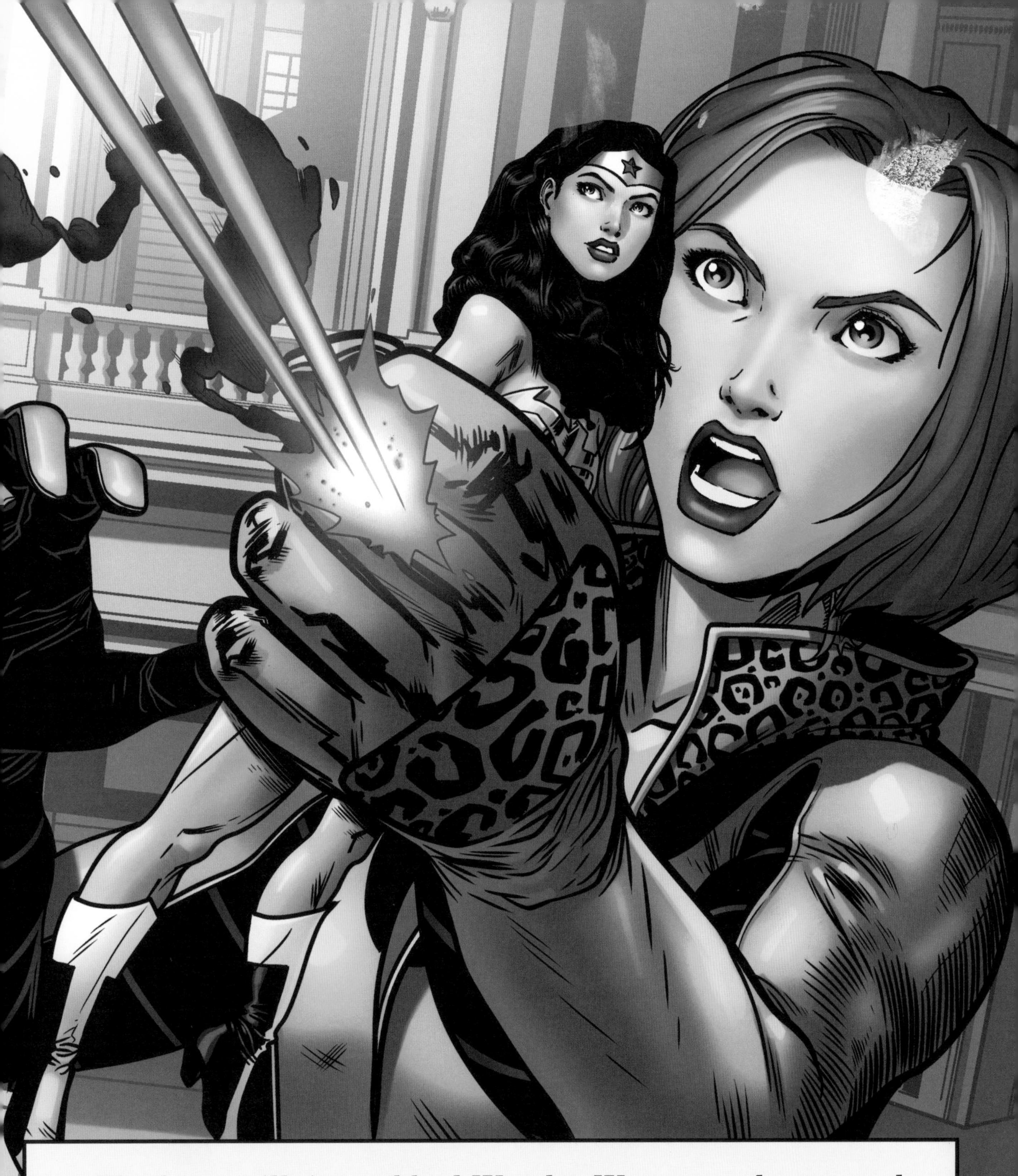

The large villain grabbed Wonder Woman and squeezed her tightly.

"Now I'm gonna— OWWW!" Giganta suddenly howled.

Two red-hot laser beams came from out of the sky zapped her hand!

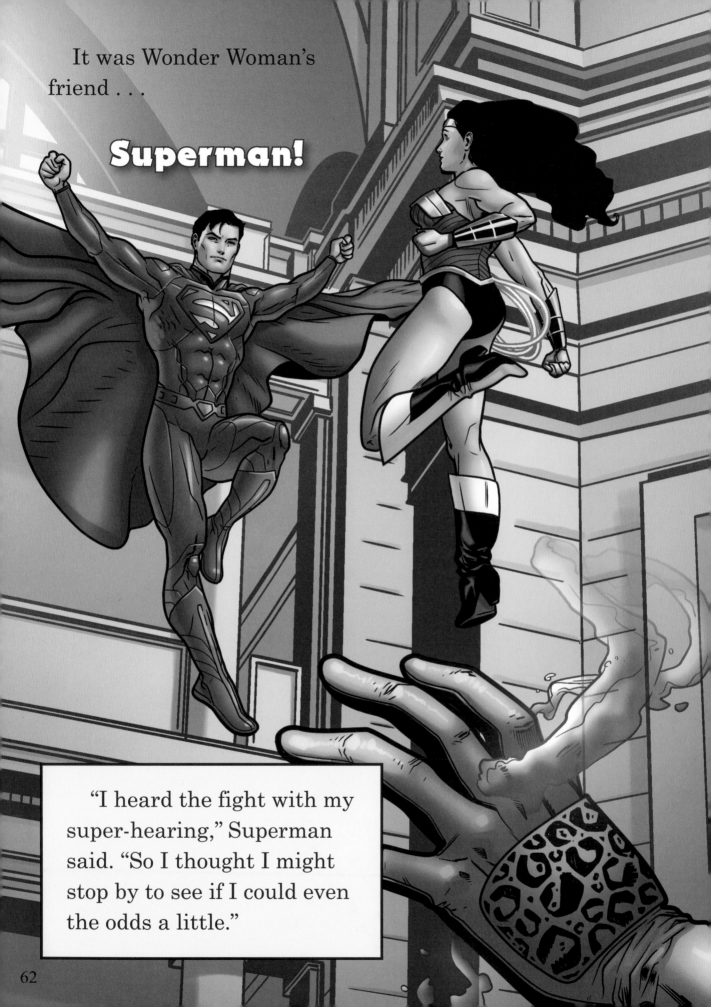

It was Wonder Woman's friend . . .

Superman!

"I heard the fight with my super-hearing," Superman said. "So I thought I might stop by to see if I could even the odds a little."

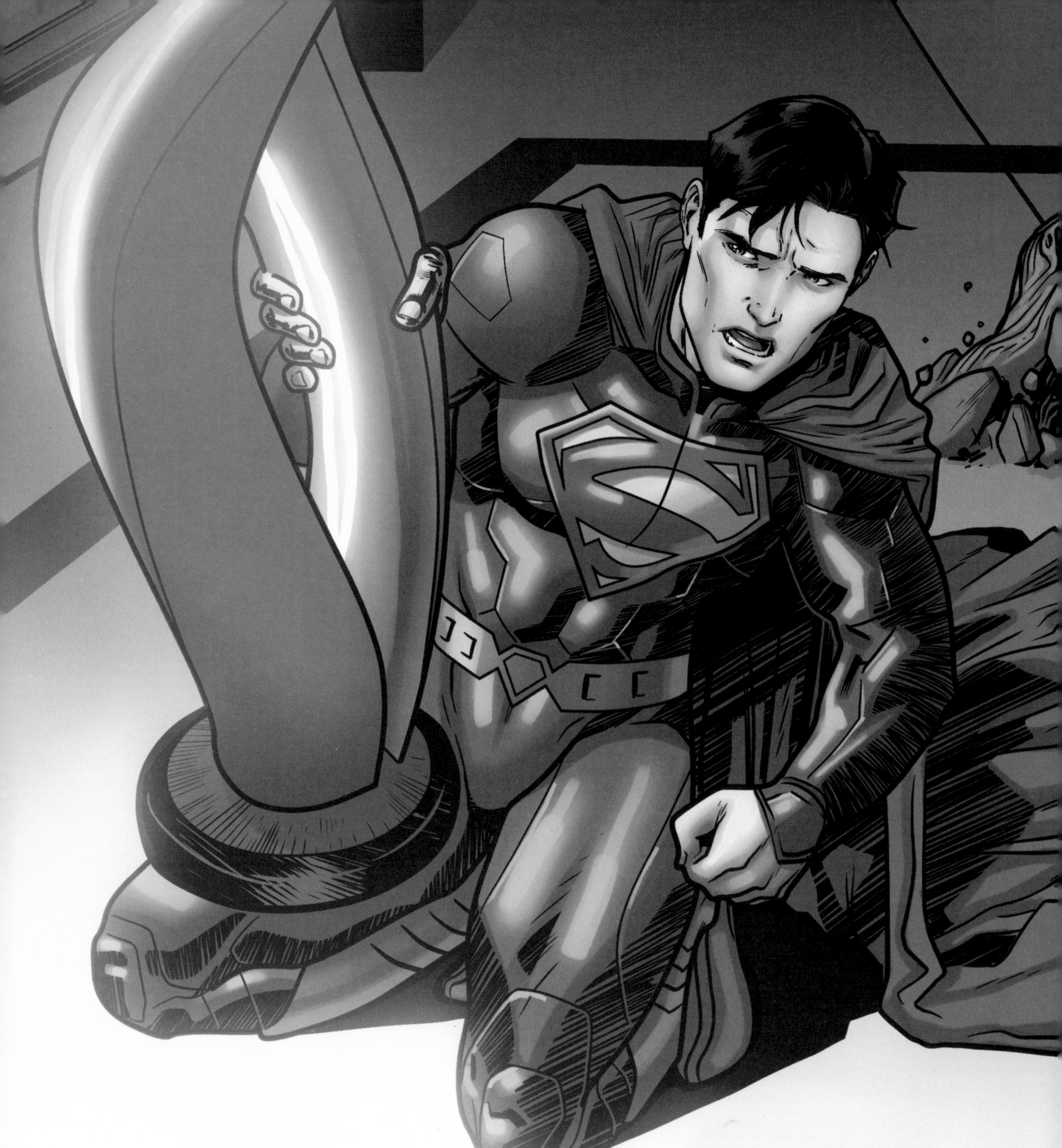

Superman swooped down to get the sculpture away from the three villains, but something strange happened as soon as he touched it. The hero fell to his knees—he was suddenly as weak as a baby.

"Wonder Woman," he gasped. "It's . . .

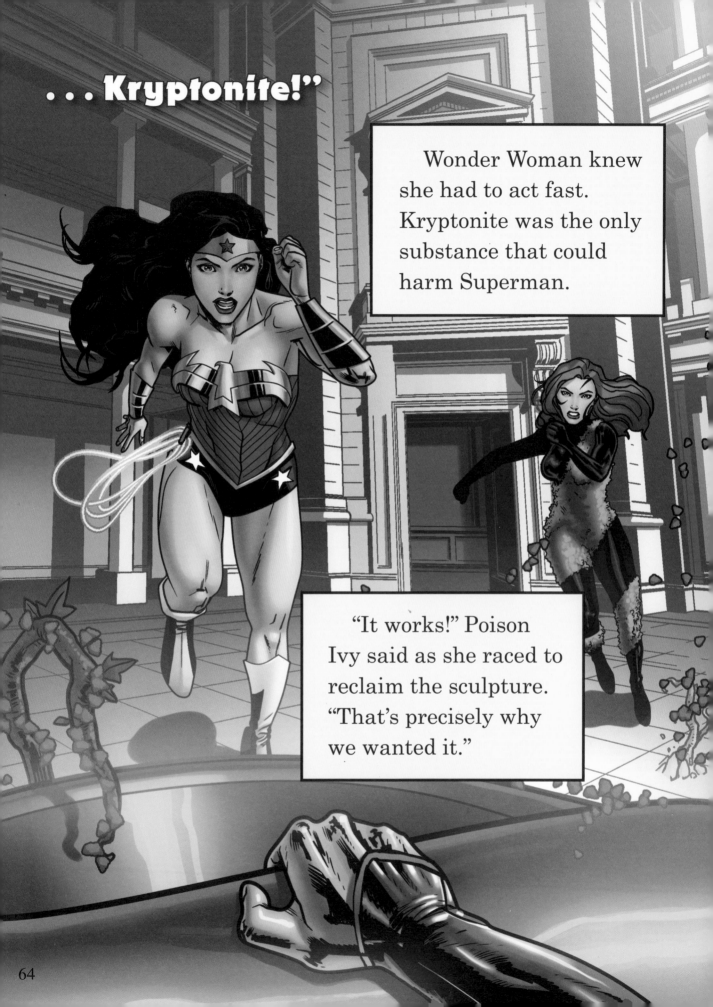

". . . Kryptonite!"

Wonder Woman knew she had to act fast. Kryptonite was the only substance that could harm Superman.

"It works!" Poison Ivy said as she raced to reclaim the sculpture. "That's precisely why we wanted it."

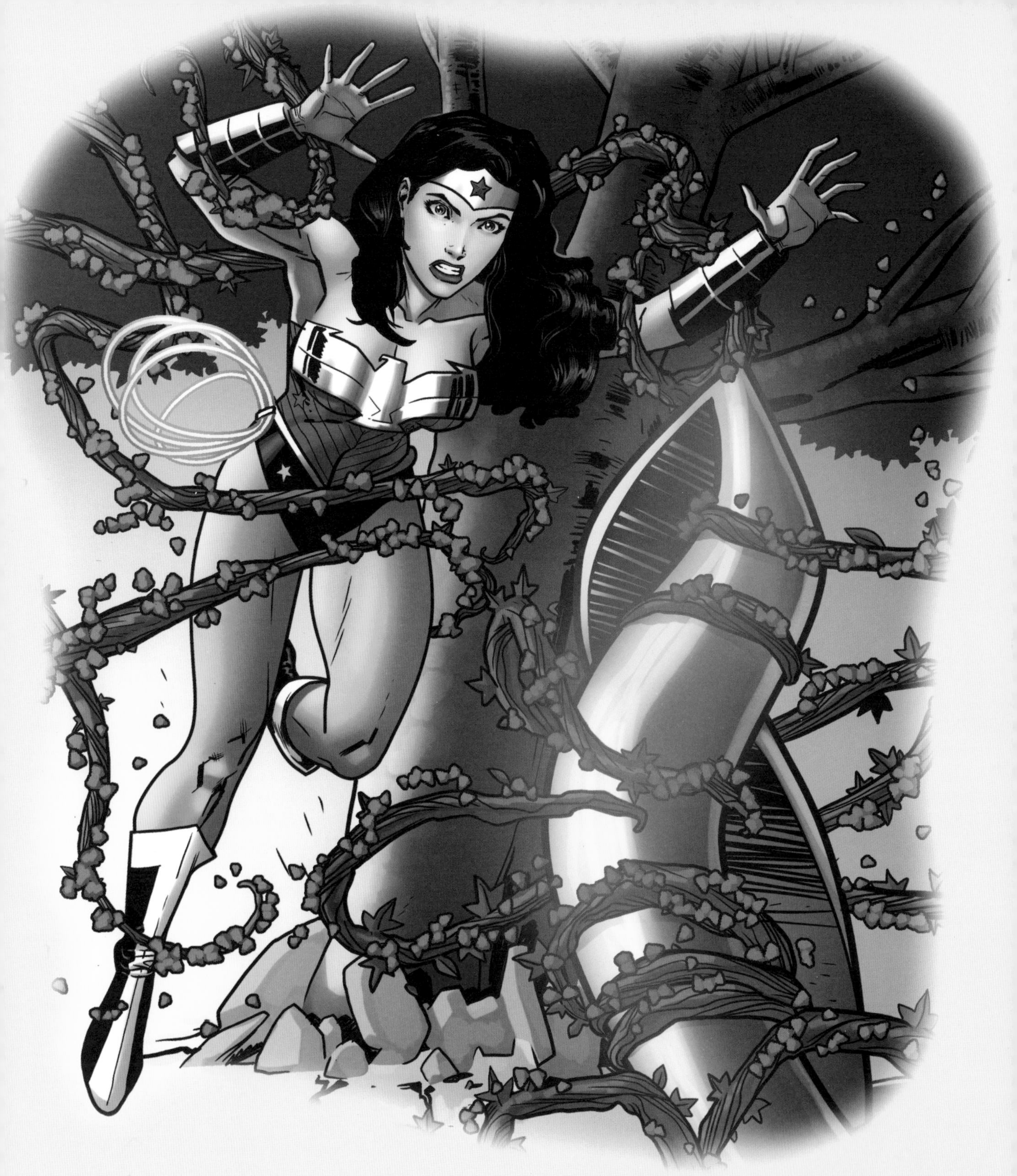

Poison Ivy used her vines to slow Wonder Woman down and grab the sculpture.

"Now, quickly, Giganta!" Poison Ivy ordered. "Before the Amazon gets free again!"

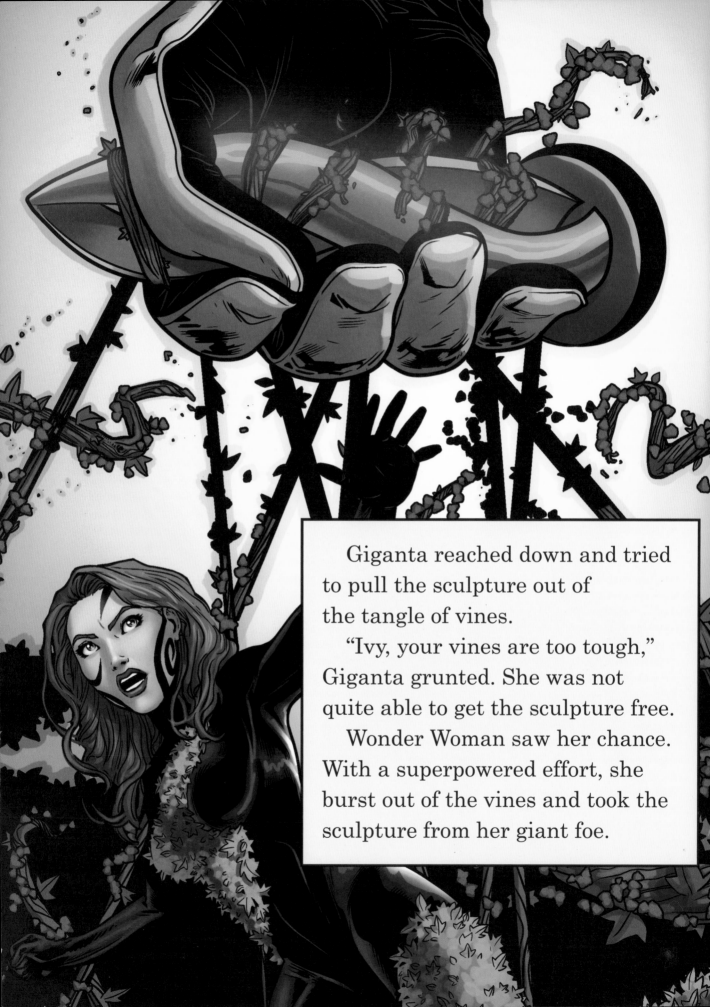

Giganta reached down and tried to pull the sculpture out of the tangle of vines.

"Ivy, your vines are too tough," Giganta grunted. She was not quite able to get the sculpture free.

Wonder Woman saw her chance. With a superpowered effort, she burst out of the vines and took the sculpture from her giant foe.

Wonder Woman raced outside.

"I'll lock the sculpture in the Invisible Jet," Wonder Woman said. "The villains won't be able to find it, and my jet will shield Superman from the Kryptonite."

Behind her, Giganta smashed through the roof of the Botanic Garden. Poison Ivy and The Cheetah were right behind her.

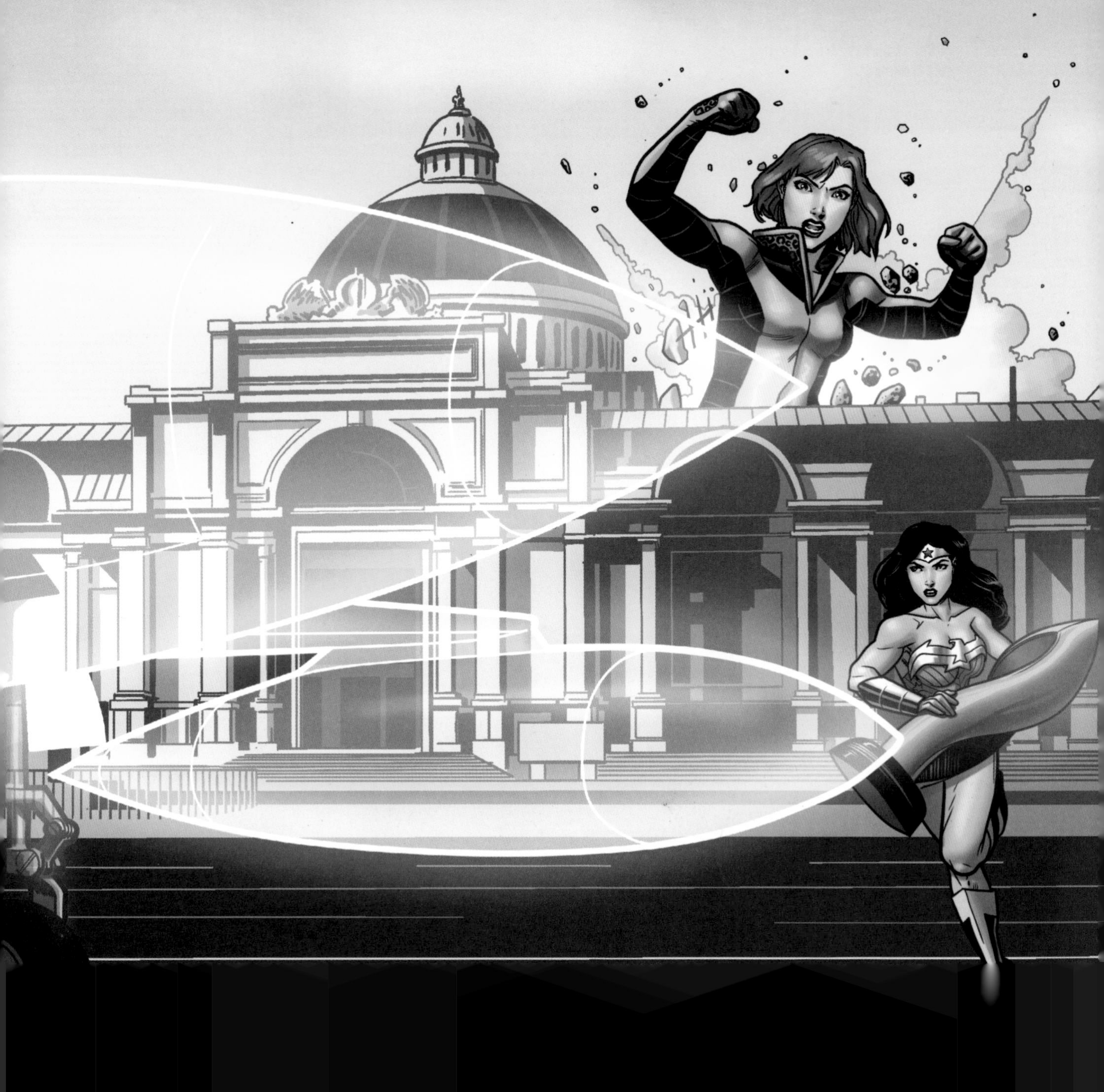

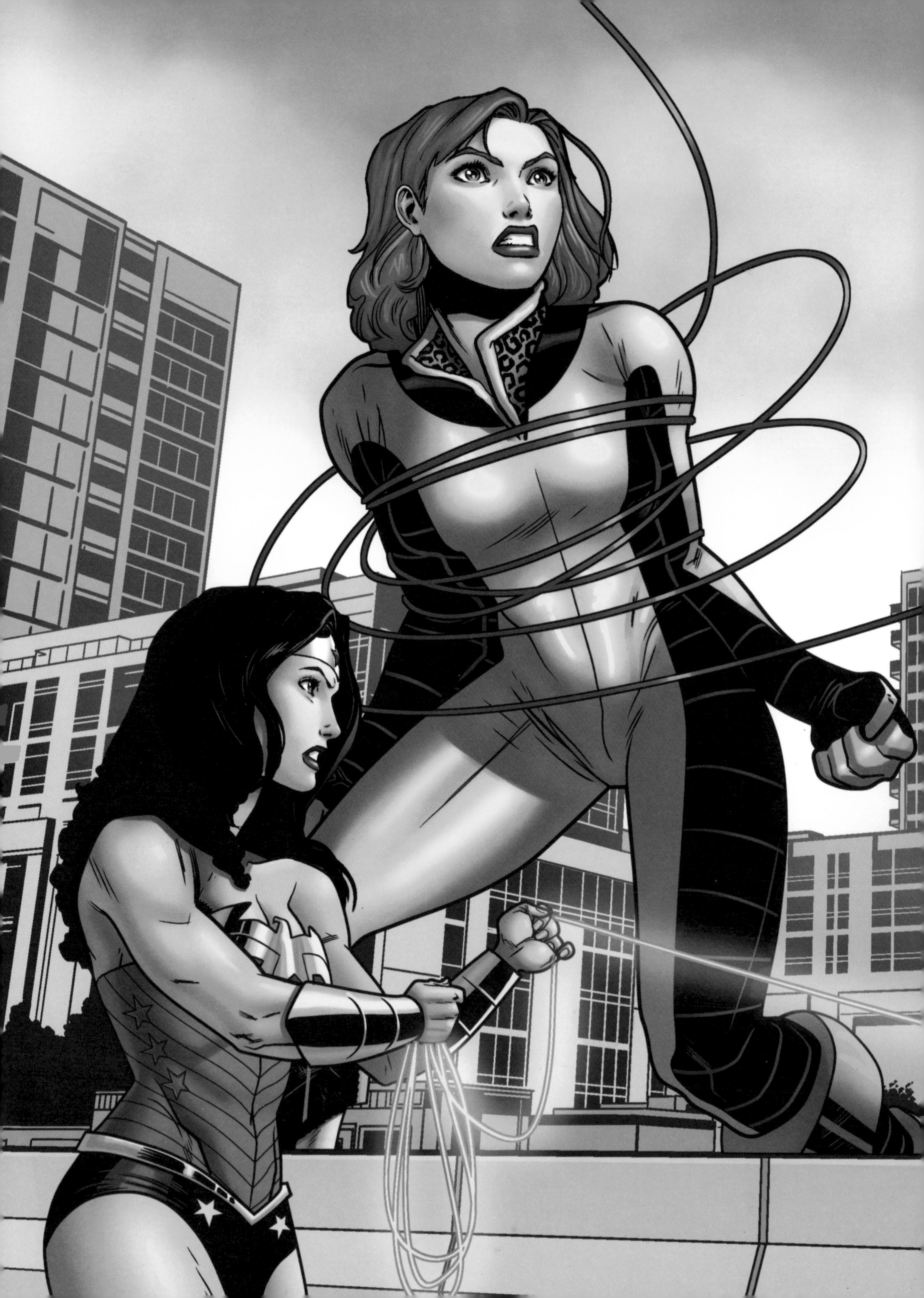

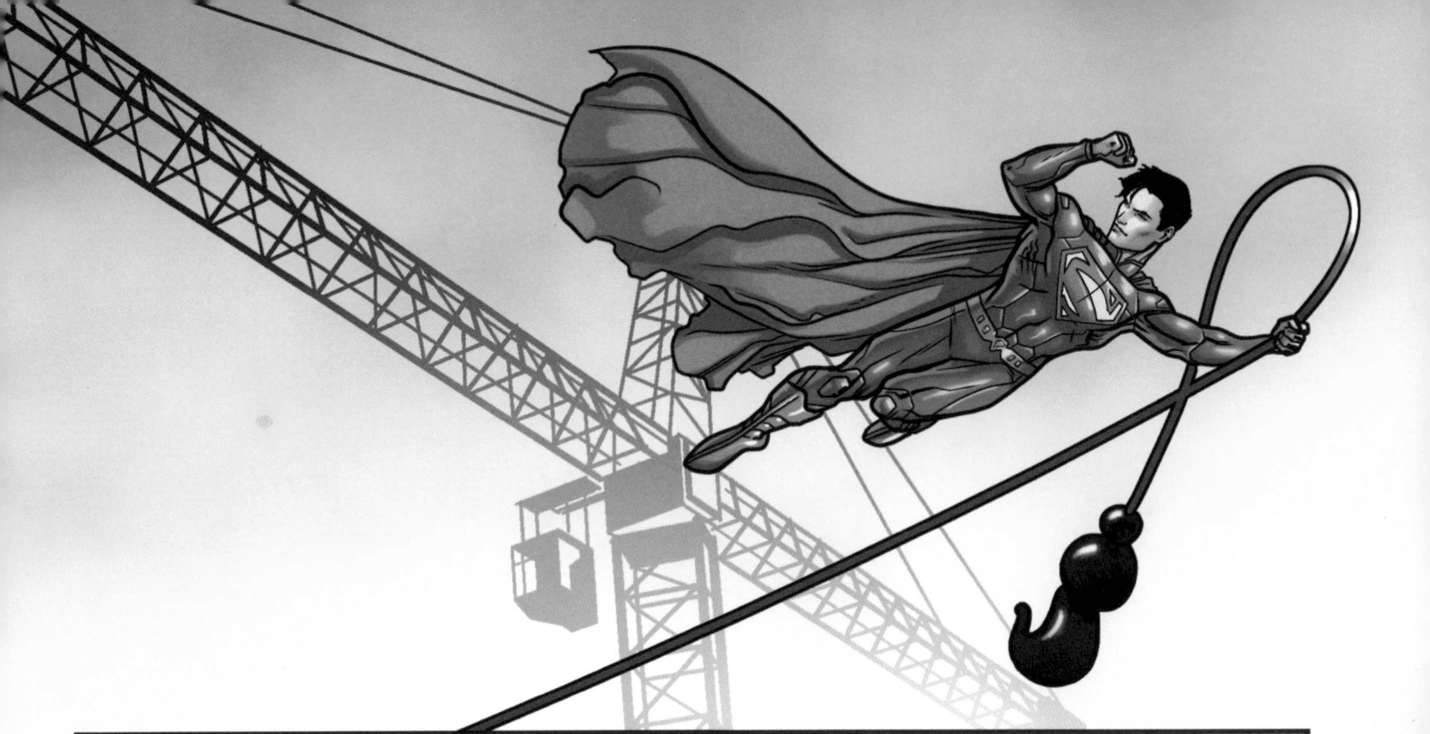

As the villains advanced on Wonder Woman, a blue-and-red blur streaked through the air. It wrapped Giganta up in a steel cable from a construction site.

"Thanks for getting rid of that Kryptonite," Superman said. "I'm feeling much better."

"Thanks for the assist," Wonder Woman replied as she lassoed Poison Ivy and The Cheetah. "I'll take care of the other two."

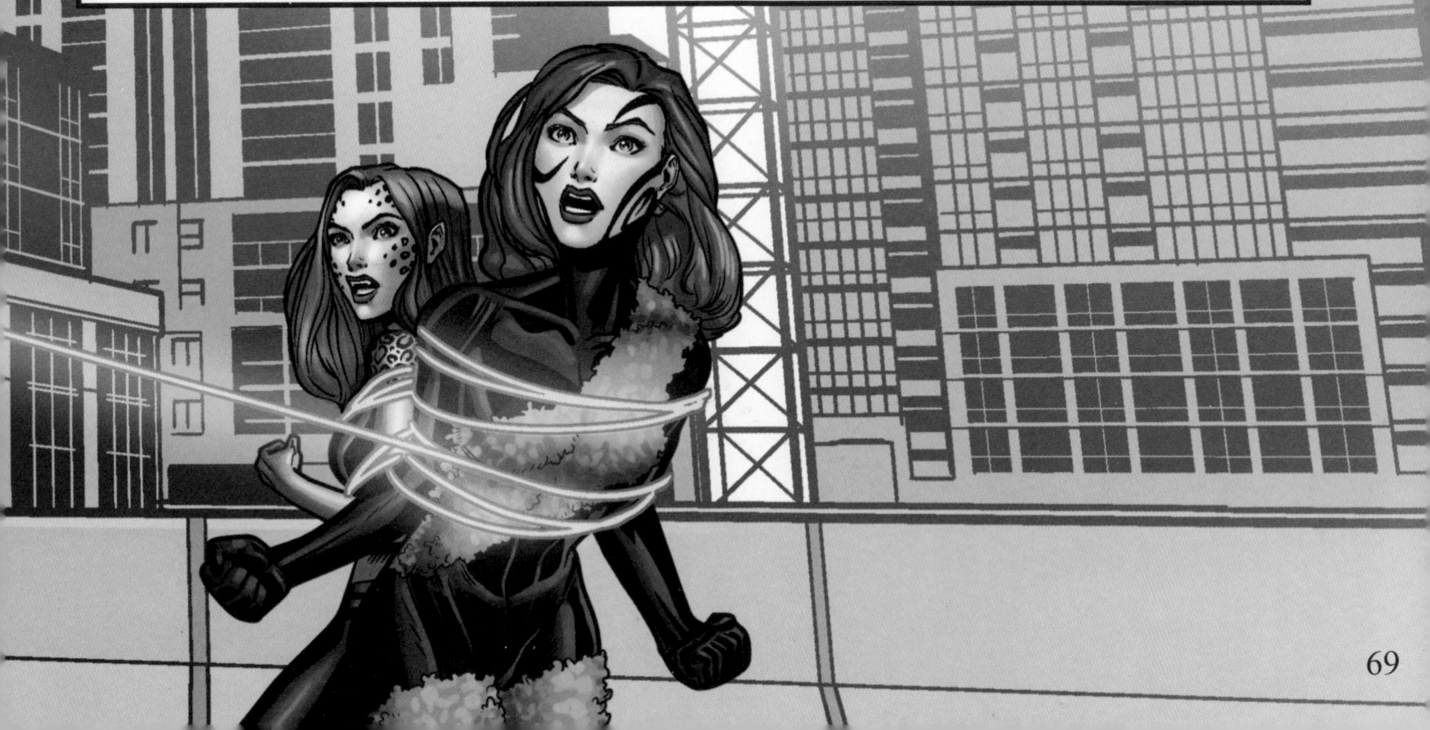

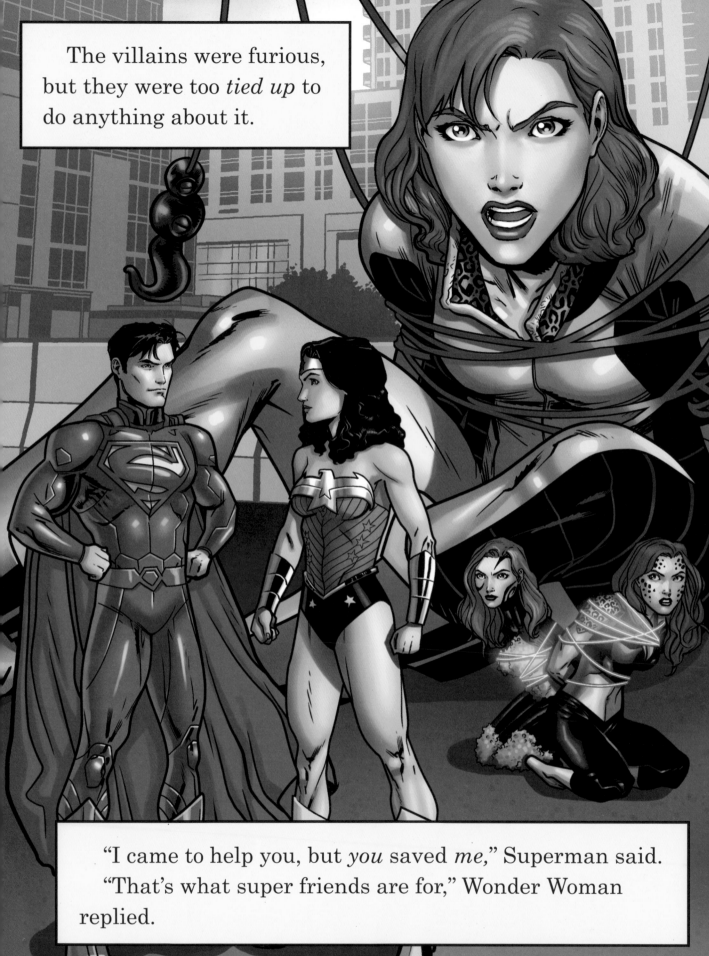

The villains were furious, but they were too *tied up* to do anything about it.

"I came to help you, but *you* saved *me*," Superman said. "That's what super friends are for," Wonder Woman replied.

A MERMAID TALE

The wicked sorceress Circe escaped from her mystical prison in another dimension and returned to Earth. She sought revenge on the Amazons. She blamed them for her being locked away. Now she planned to use her magic to turn humans into an army of sea creatures and invade Paradise Island!

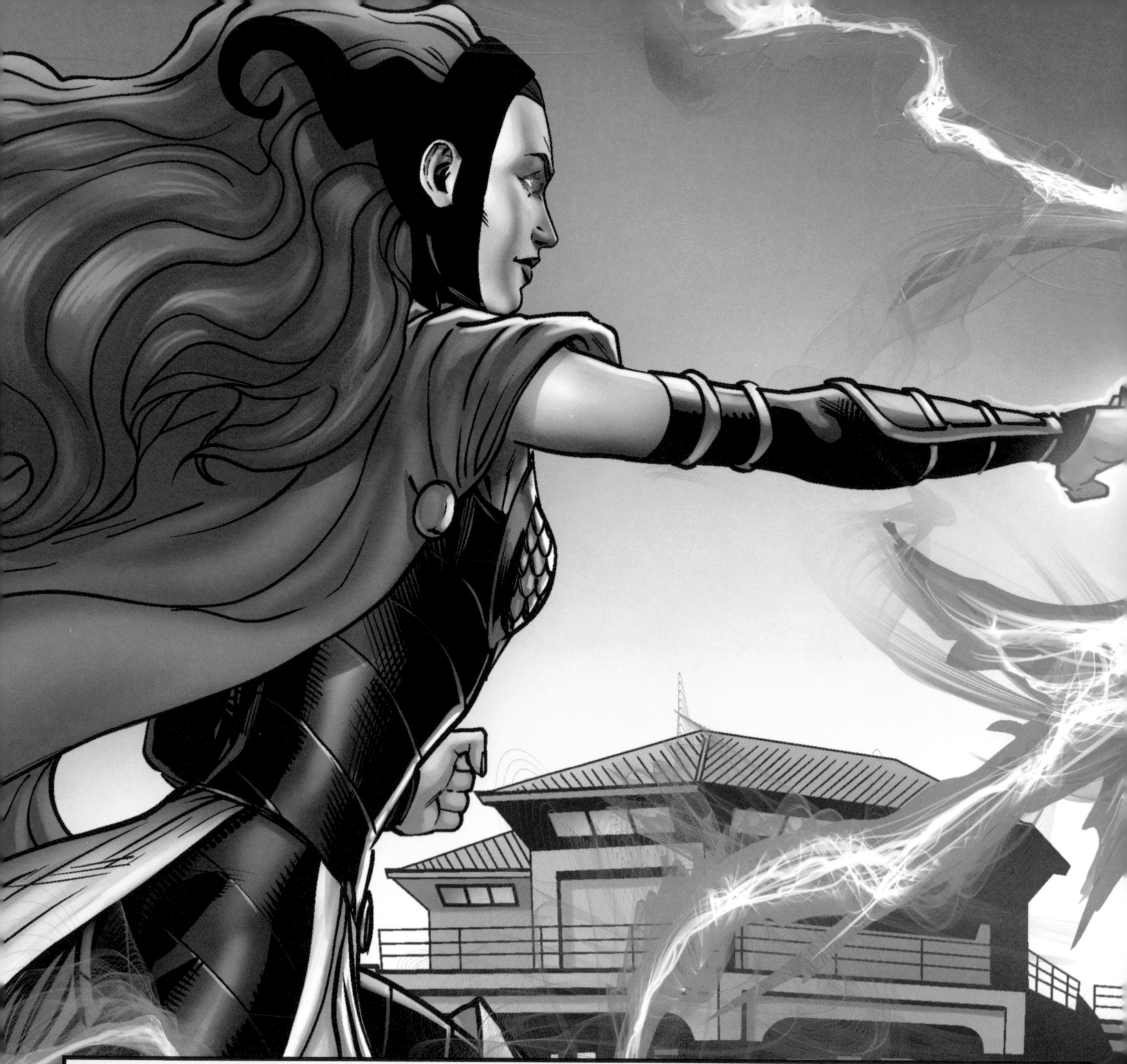

"Free those mortals," Wonder Woman commanded when she arrived on the beach.

"I was hoping you would show up," Circe said. "I want you to be the first Amazon to suffer at the hands of my magical might."

Circe weaved a colorful blast of mystical energy and fired it at Wonder Woman. The Amazon hero blocked the blast with her indestructible bracelets.

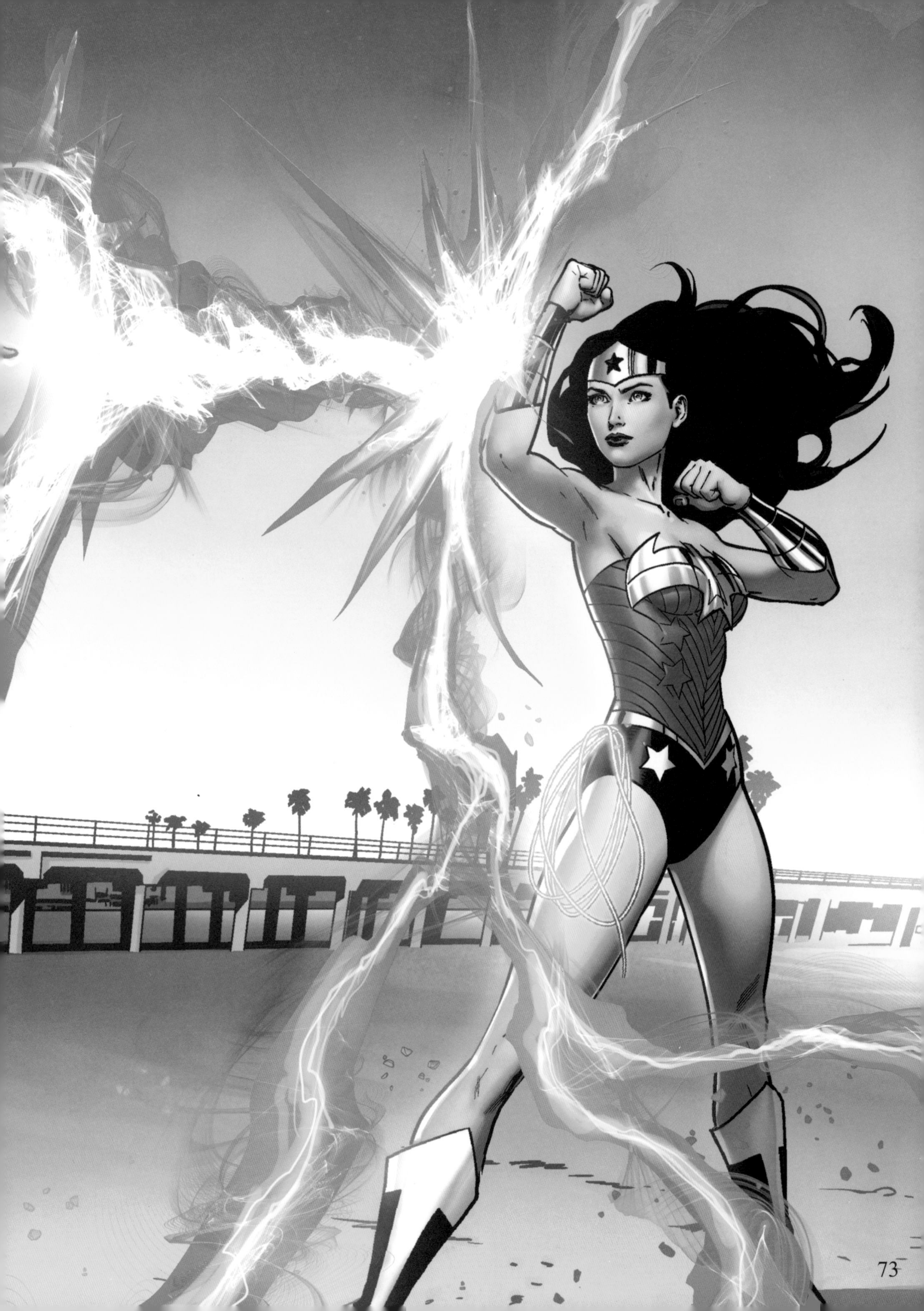

Wonder Woman tried to capture Circe with her Lasso of Truth, but now it was time for the sorceress to block an attack.

Circe used her magic to repel the golden lasso, and it fell away from her. The villain laughed. "You'll find that I am not so easy to trap!

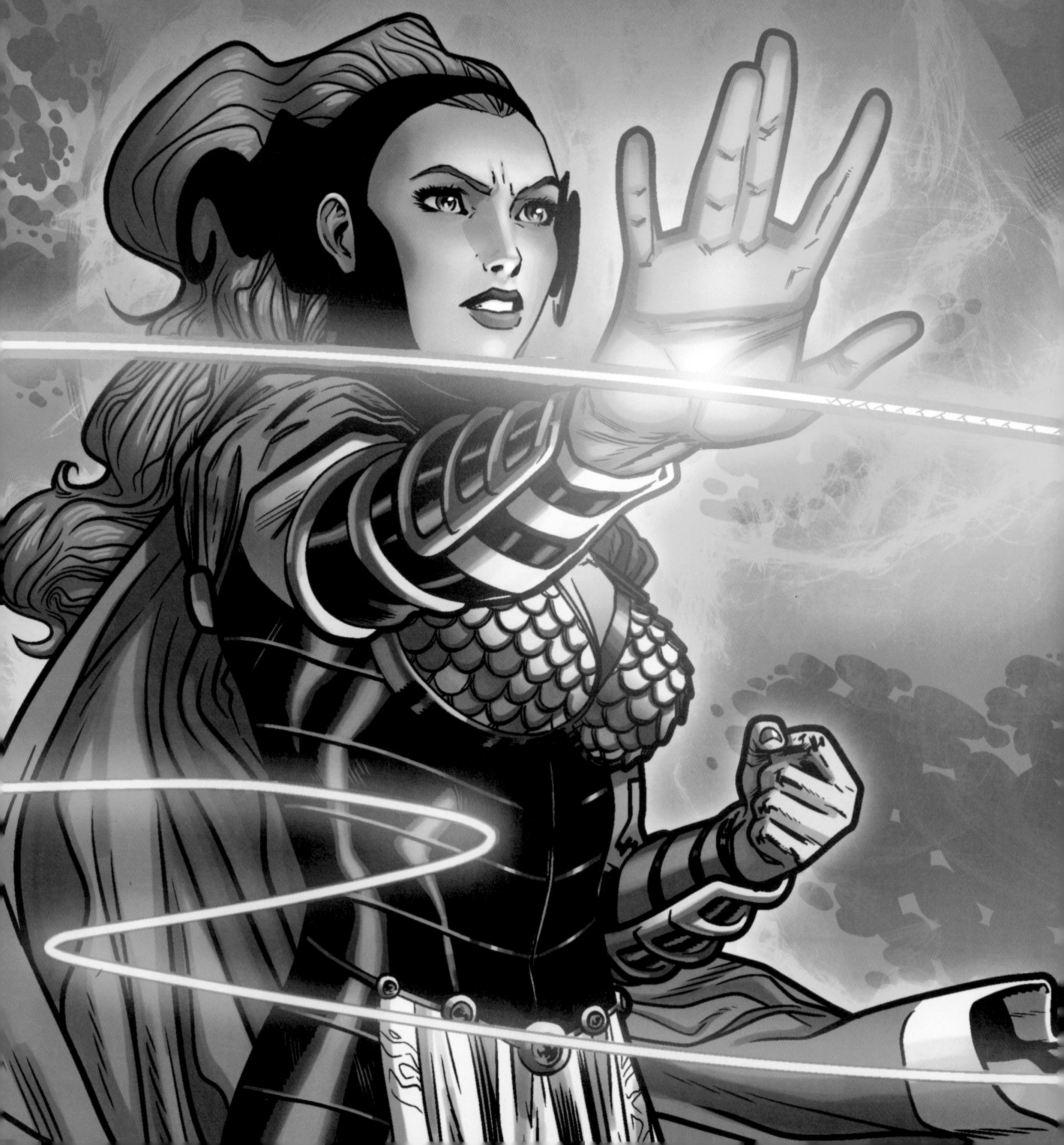

"I will have my revenge on the Amazons," she said, summoning her most powerful magic. "And I will start with you—NOW!"

Circe cast a spell that shot a blinding light at Wonder Woman.

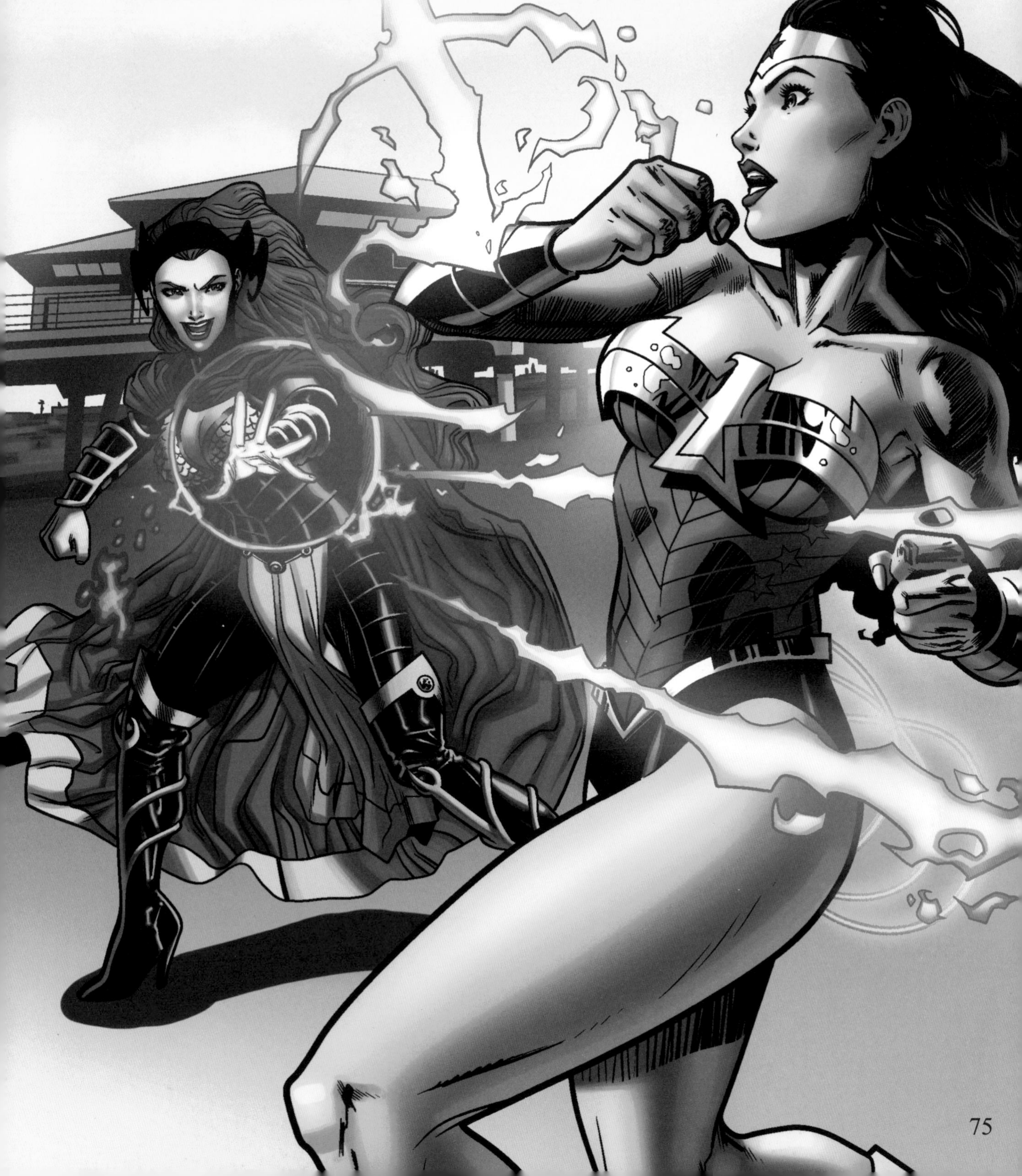

The bright flickering light of Circe's spell surrounded the super hero.

"I feel so strange," said Wonder Woman. When she looked down, she saw that her fingers were becoming webbed. "Oh, my! I'm turning into a . . .

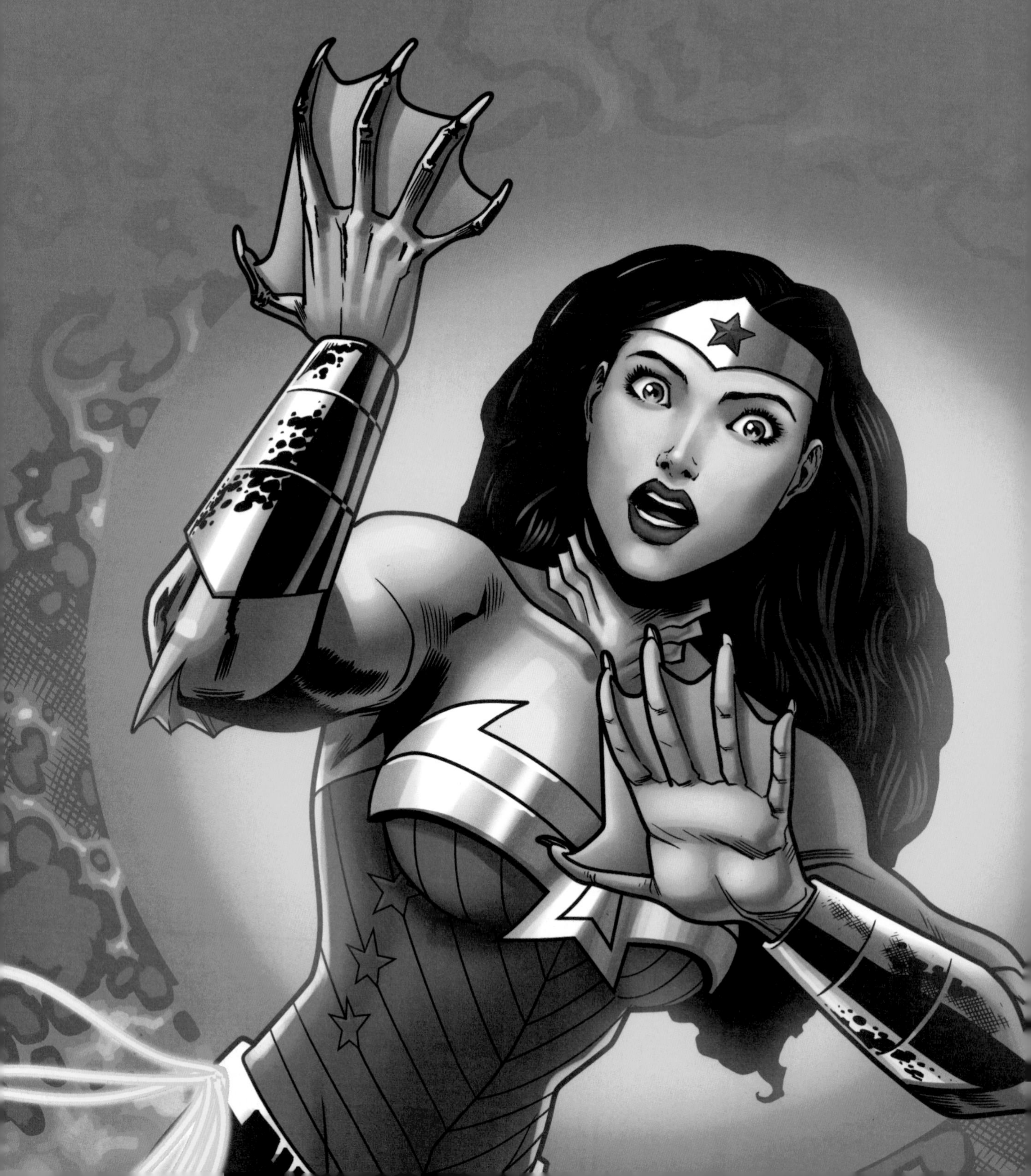

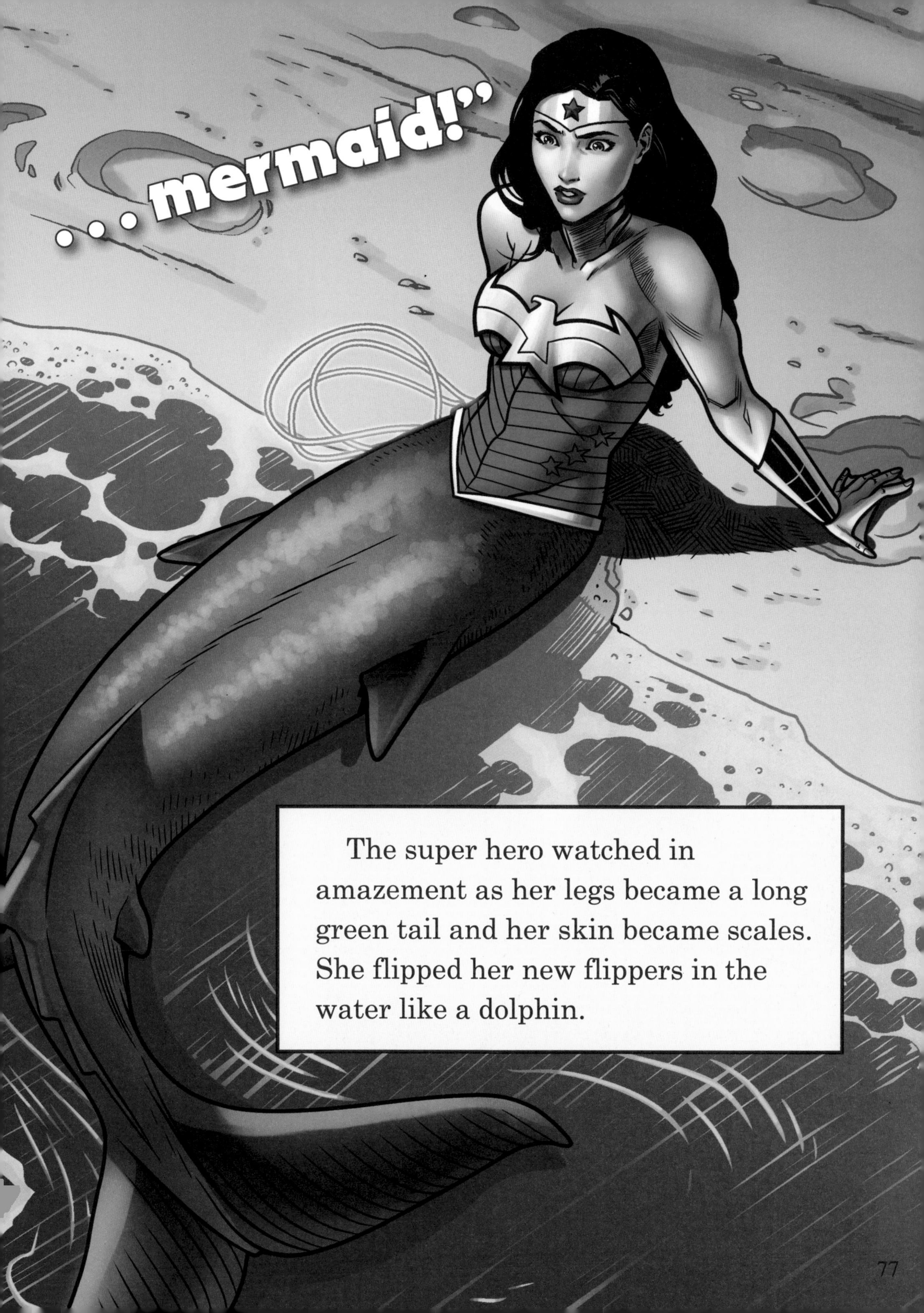
. . . mermaid!”
The super hero watched in amazement as her legs became a long green tail and her skin became scales. She flipped her new flippers in the water like a dolphin.

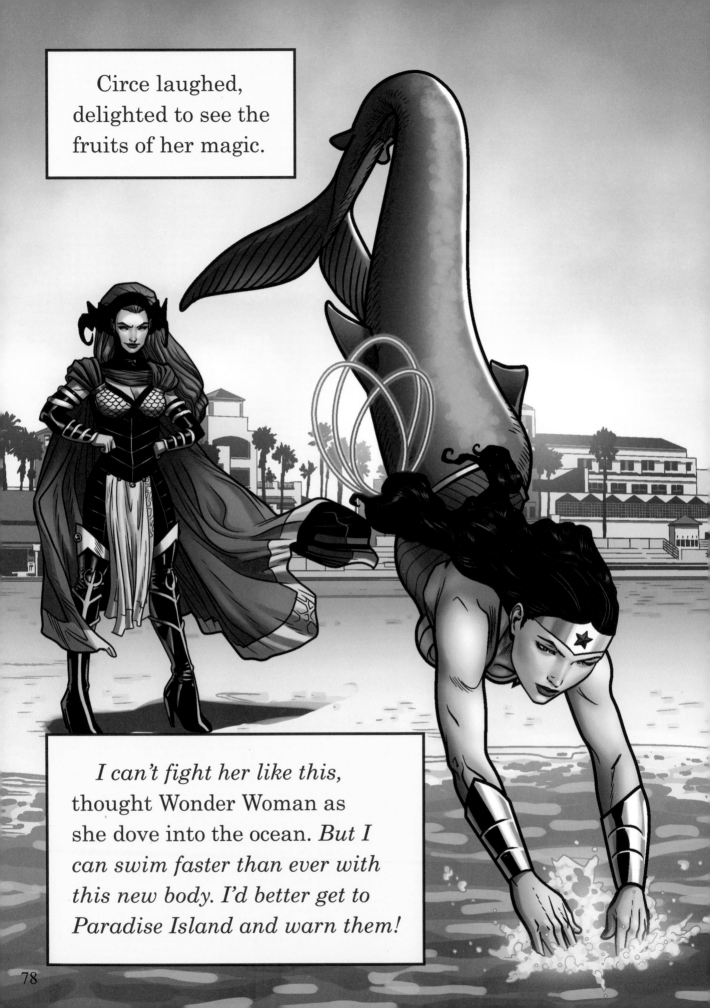

Circe laughed, delighted to see the fruits of her magic.

I can't fight her like this, thought Wonder Woman as she dove into the ocean. *But I can swim faster than ever with this new body. I'd better get to Paradise Island and warn them!*

Wonder Woman swam several miles. *Being a mermaid is fun,* she thought. *It's too bad I don't have time to enjoy it.* Just then, she ran into the friend she needed—

Aquaman!

"I heard about what's going on from the fish," he said. "So I thought I would lend you a hand."

Wonder Woman was glad to see her ocean friend. They zoomed to Paradise Island.

"Circe beat us here!" Aquaman exclaimed when they got there. They could see her working her terrible magic on the Amazons, who were bravely fighting the sorceress.

“Let’s go,” Wonder Woman said, gaining speed. “We can still save the day.”

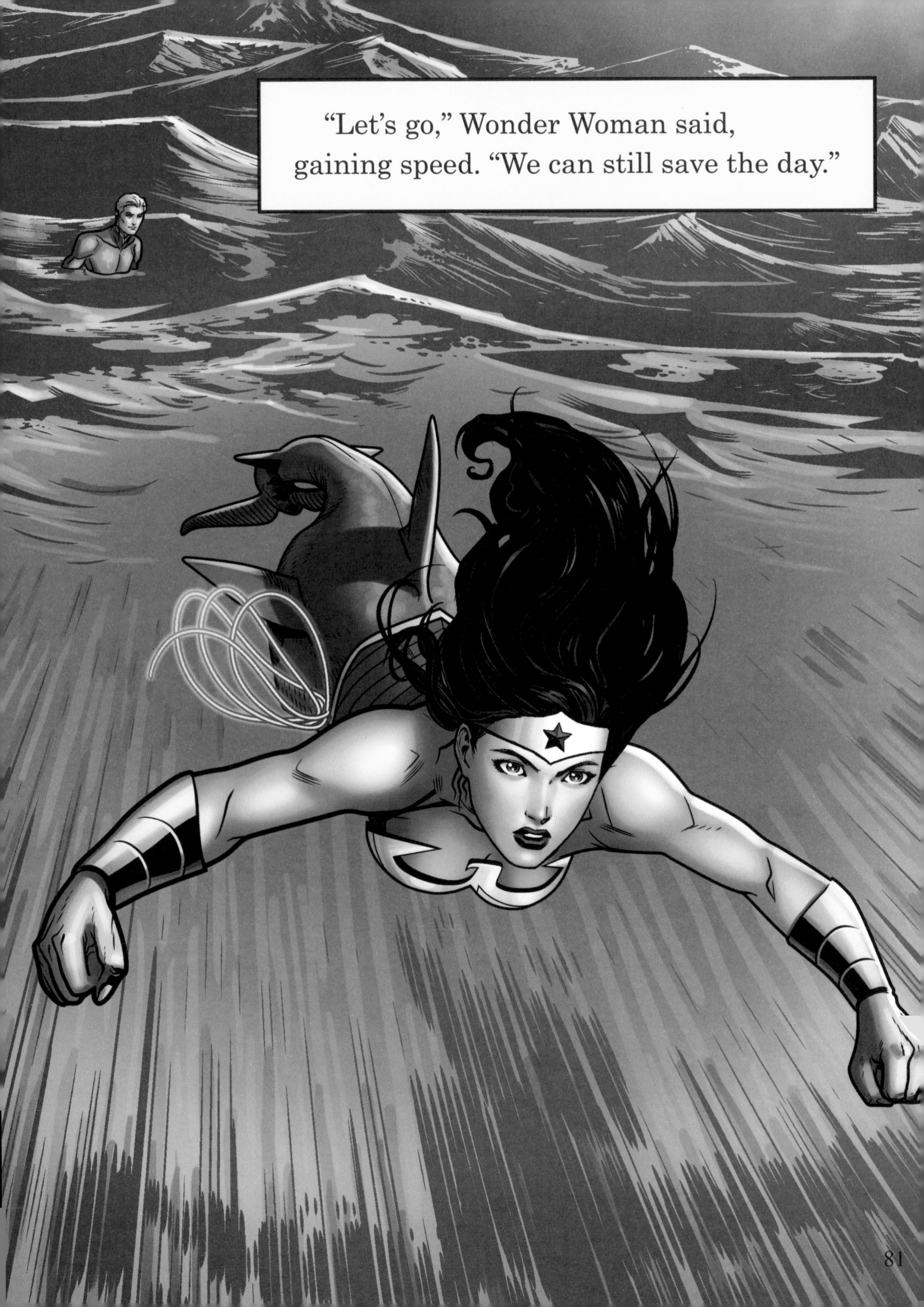

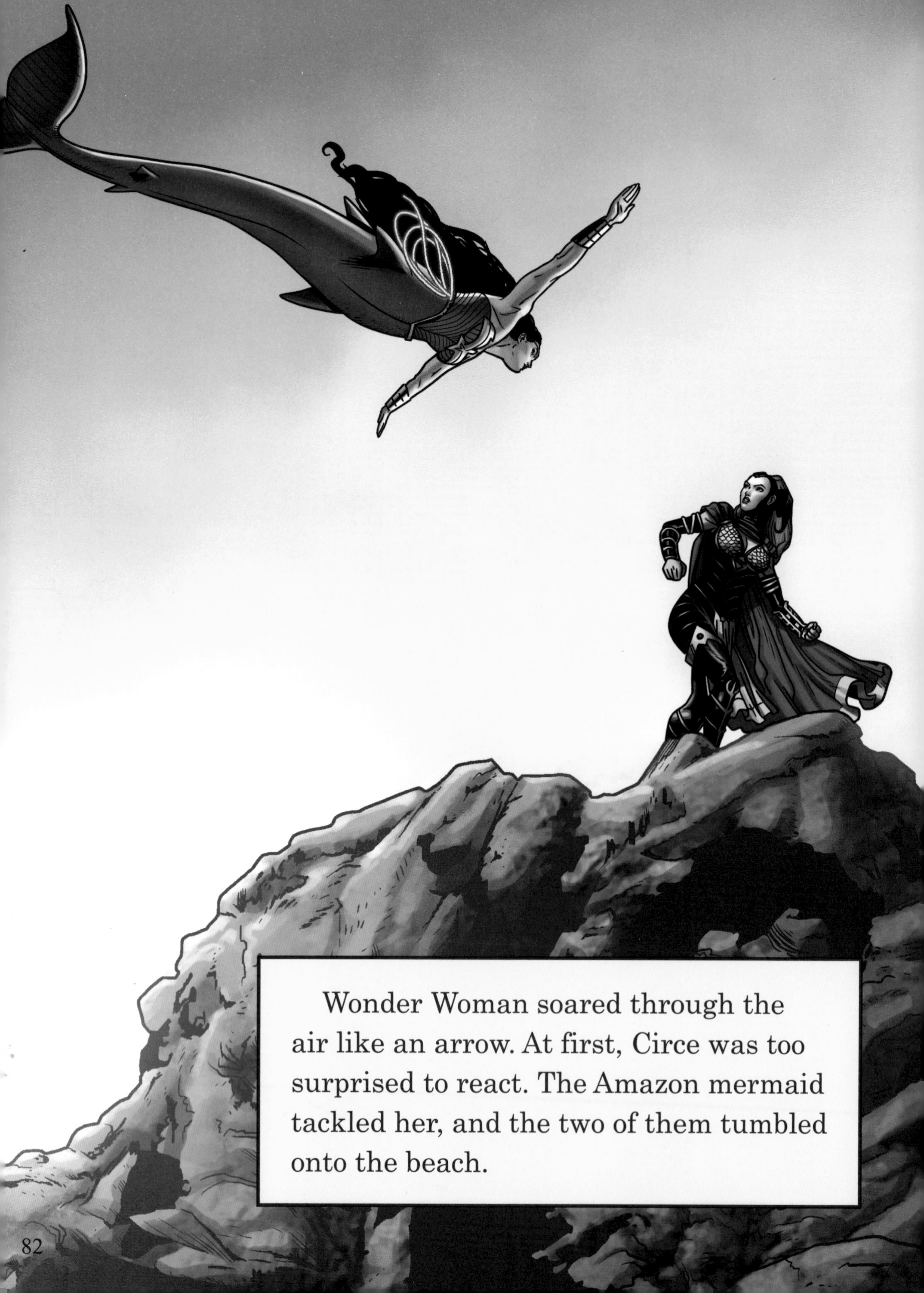

Wonder Woman soared through the air like an arrow. At first, Circe was too surprised to react. The Amazon mermaid tackled her, and the two of them tumbled onto the beach.

"I won't let you stop me!" Circe shouted. She started to weave another spell. "This time, I will make you hideous. I will make you as monstrous as the Medusa of legend!"

Wonder Woman knew she couldn't let the spell overtake her, so she leapt toward the villain. With her bracelets, Wonder Woman was able to reflect Circe's magic right back at her.

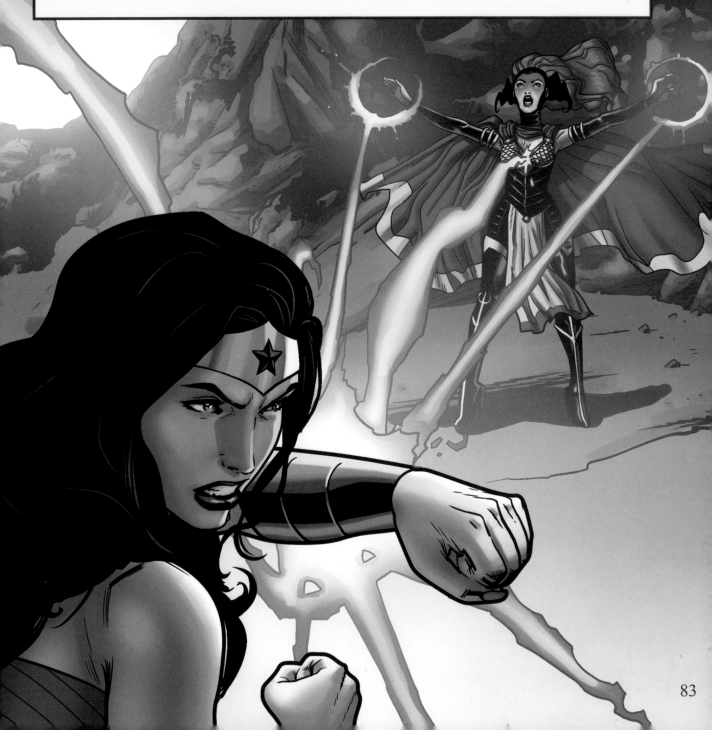

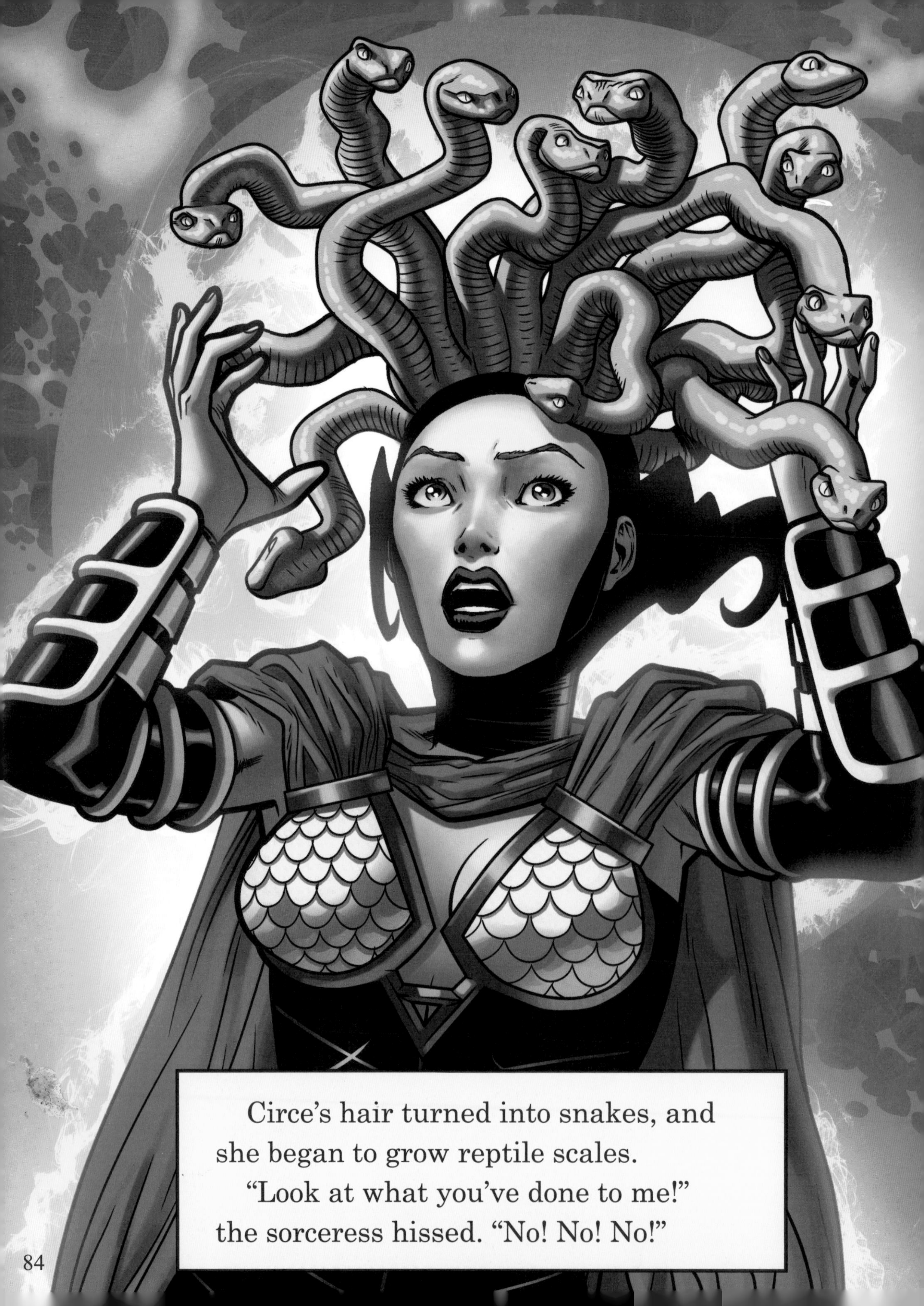

Circe's hair turned into snakes, and she began to grow reptile scales.

"Look at what you've done to me!" the sorceress hissed. "No! No! No!"

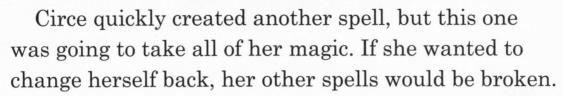

Circe quickly created another spell, but this one was going to take all of her magic. If she wanted to change herself back, her other spells would be broken.

Moments after Circe unleashed her powerful magic, she, Wonder Woman, and everyone else returned to their original forms. Circe's plans were foiled.

Wonder Woman quickly lassoed the villain. The last spell had drained the sorceress of her magic . . . at least for a little while. It would be no trouble to put her back in prison.

"This is quite a fish *tale* that we have to tell," Aquaman said.

"I'm just glad Circe isn't *the one that got away,*" Wonder Woman added with a laugh.

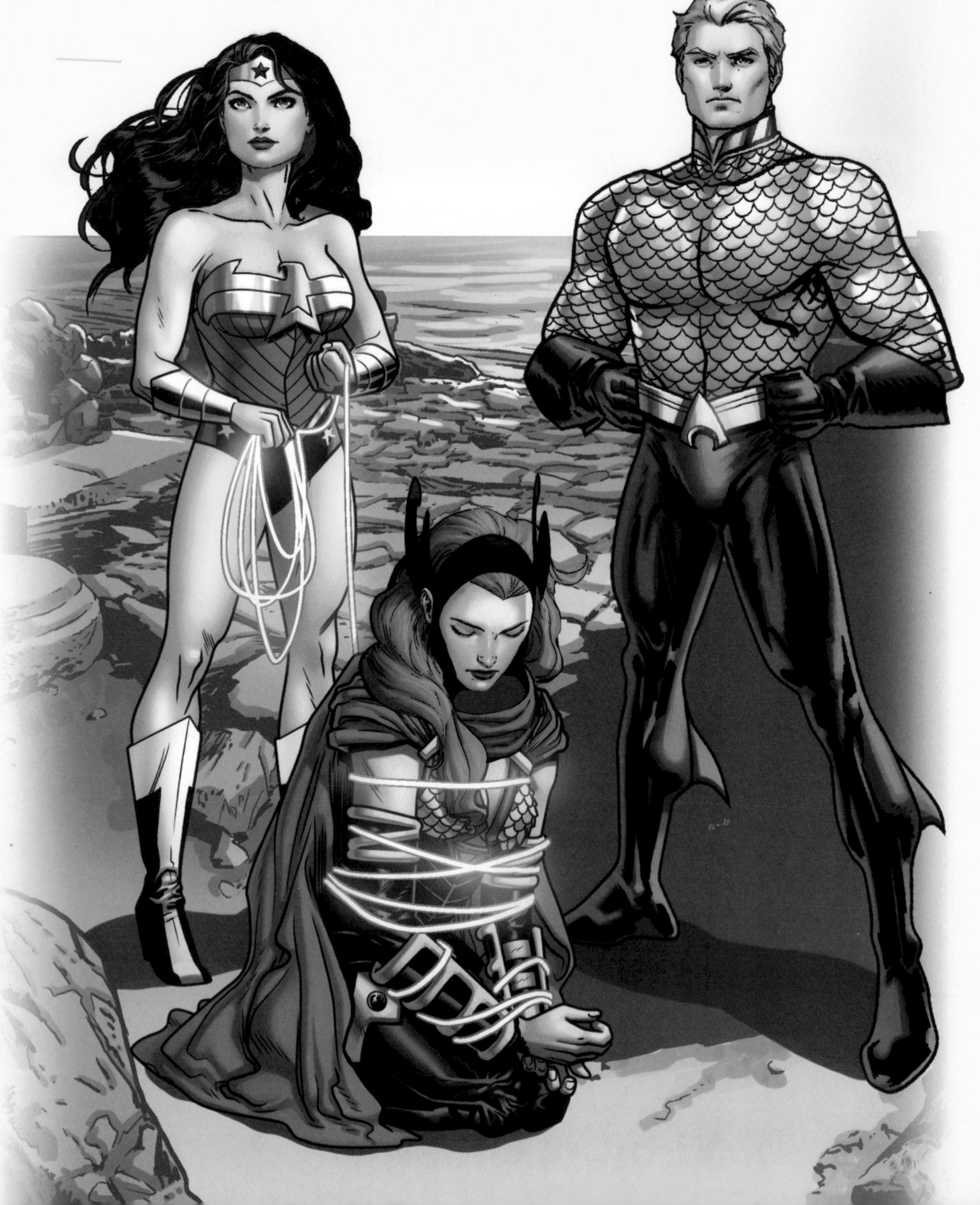

MIGHTY MAGIC!

In Egypt, several guards stood near an ancient pyramid. Legend had it that a book of powerful magic was hidden in the tomb, and the guards were protecting it.

CRACKLE! ZZZAP!

Suddenly, a bold of lightning hit the top of the pyramid!

"Call Wonder Woman!" one of the guards yelled.

Wonder Woman was meeting with her friends in the Justice League. They were at the group's high-tech headquarters. Trouble seemed to be brewing around the globe.

"Magical objects have been stolen all over the world," Batman said, pointing to places on a globe marked with Xs.

"Magical objects can be bad news in the wrong hands," Wonder Woman said.

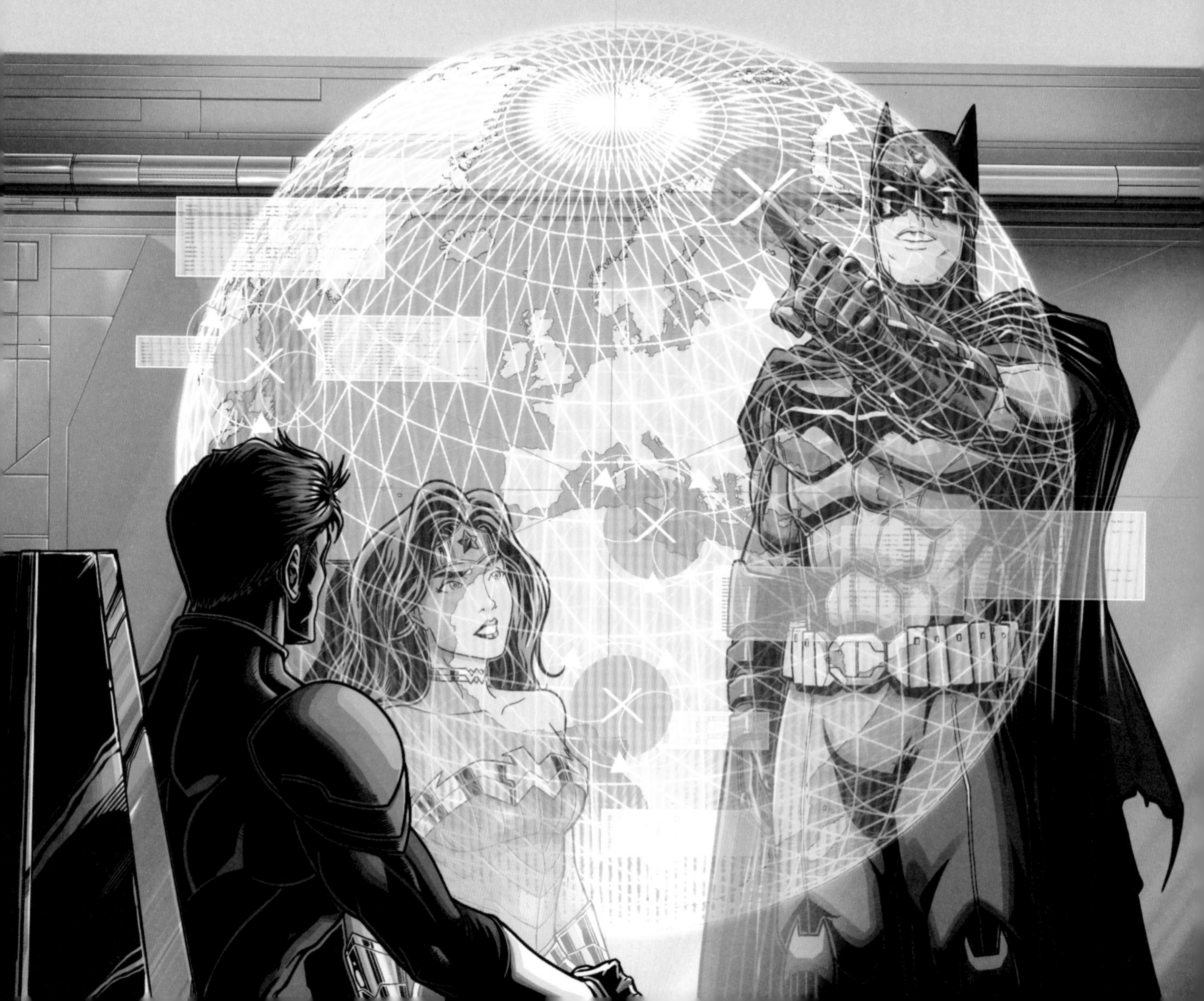

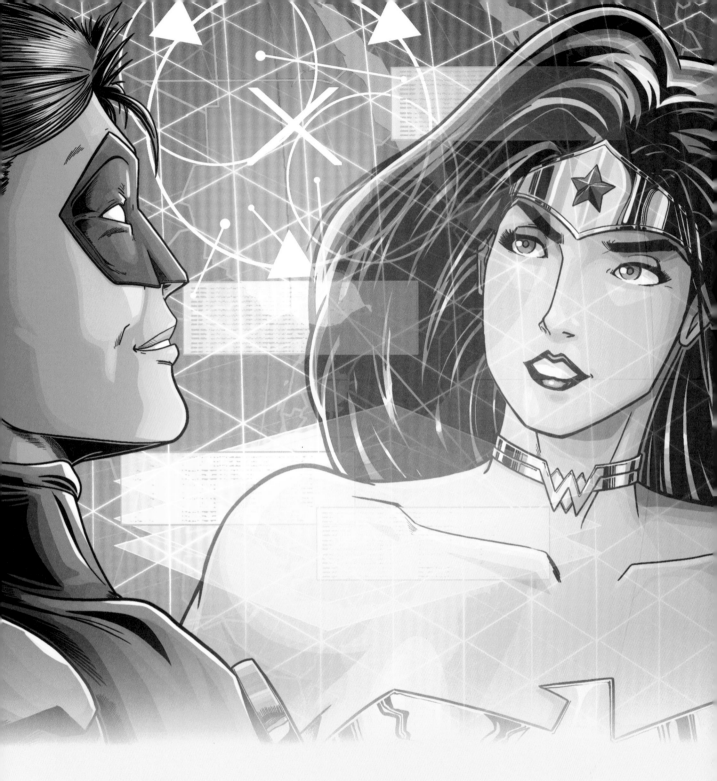

An X on the globe lit up just then.

"We're getting a call from Egypt," Wonder Woman said, eyeing the new emergency signal. "If we move fast, we might get there in time to catch the culprit. Let's go!"

The Amazon and her two friends leapt into action.

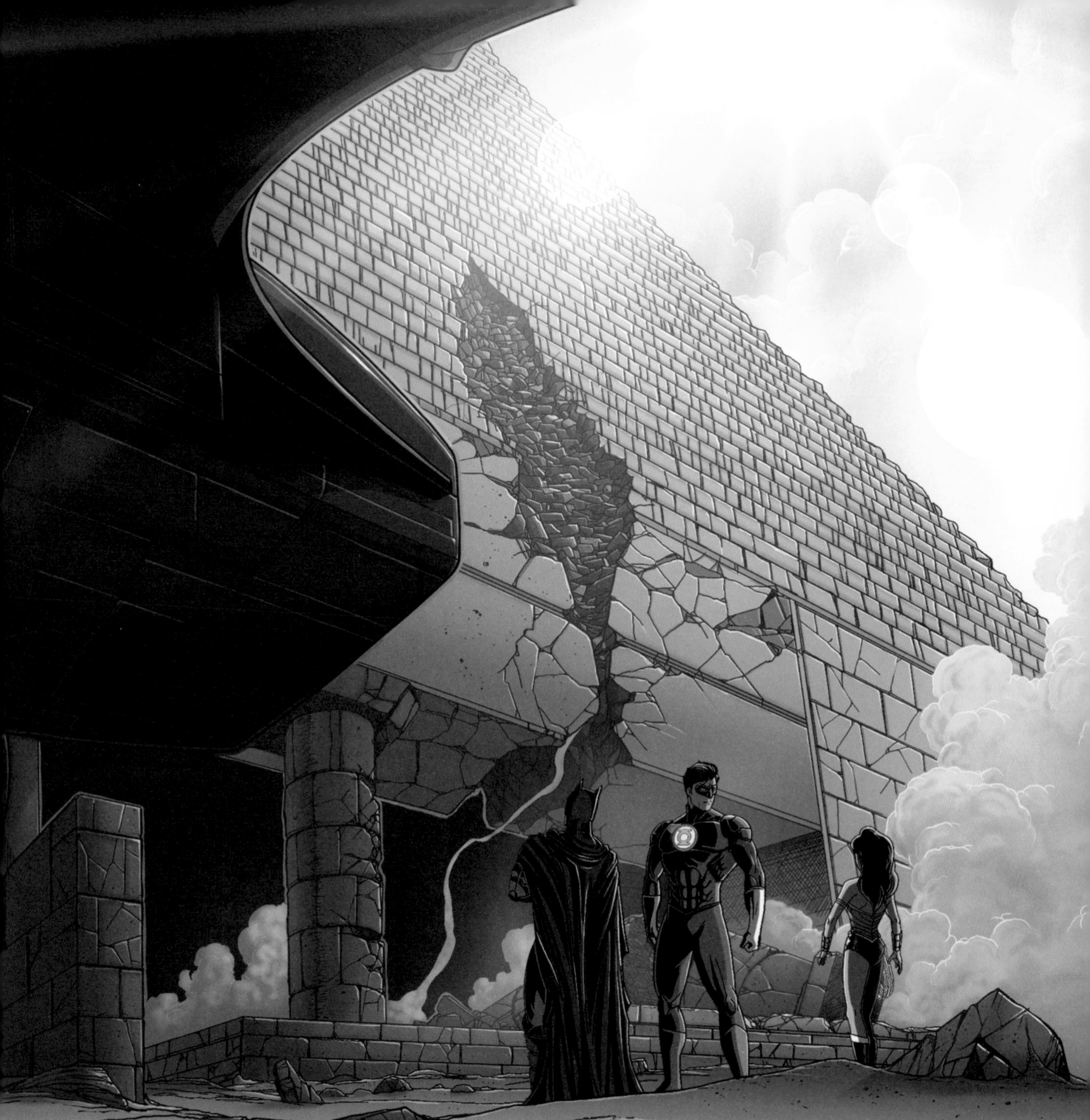

Using the Batplane, the heroes reached Egypt in record time, but they were too late to catch the thief. The pyramid was badly damaged, and gold, jewels, and ancient artifacts were scattered in the sand.

"Who would do this and not take all this valuable stuff?" Green Lantern asked.

“Maybe that’s the clue,” Wonder Woman said. “Perhaps the rumors and legends about a book of magic were true. That would be more valuable than gold or jewels.” She bent down to examine some of the rubble and added, “I’m beginning to think some sort of battle took place here.”

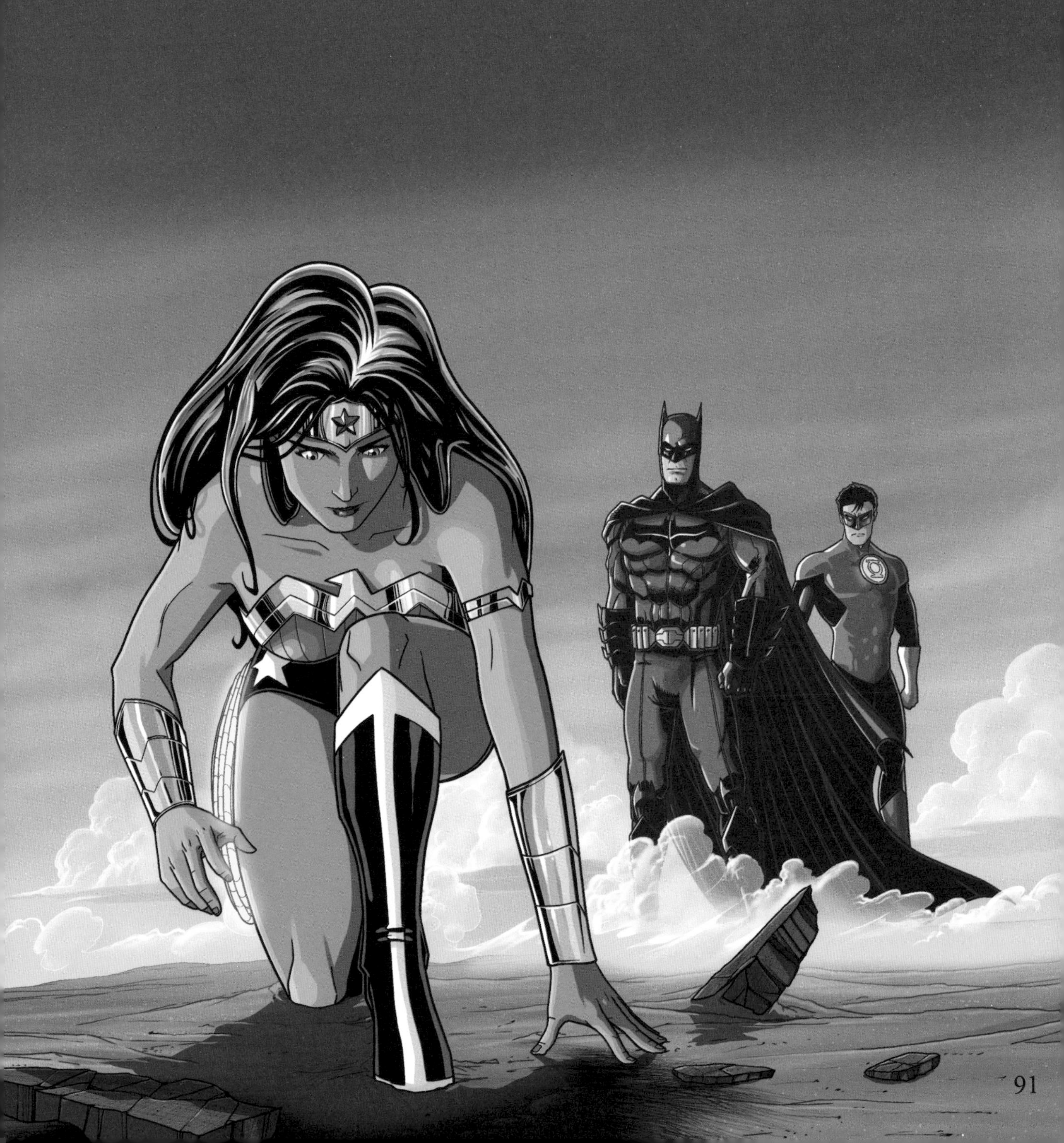

The heroes took off in the Batplane, and Wonder Woman spotted something they had missed before. There were letters spelled out in the sand.

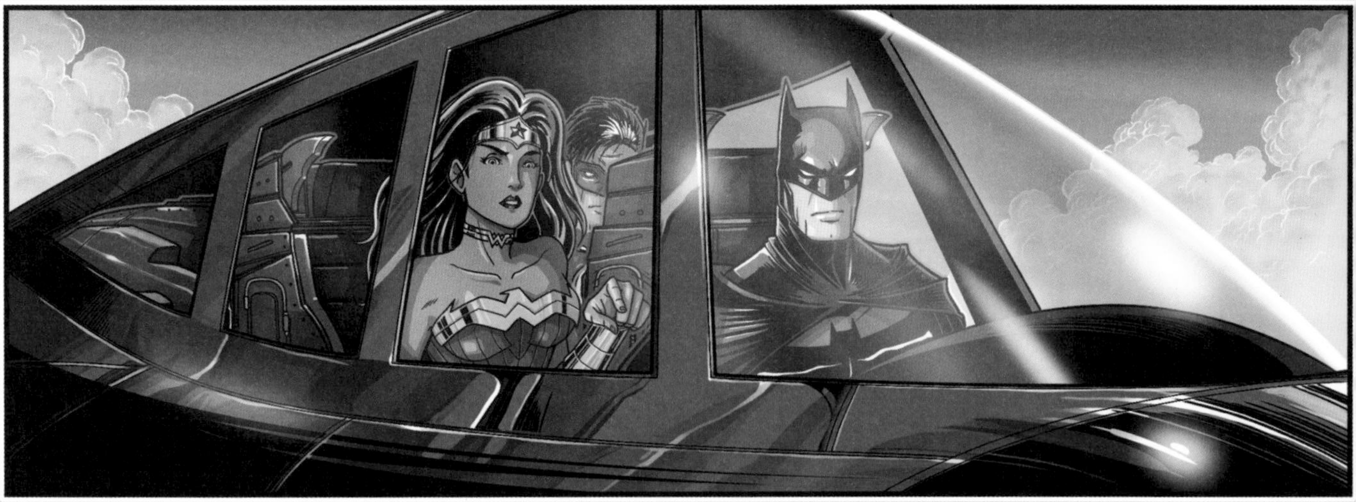

"What does K-A-H-N-D-A-Q mean?" Green Lantern asked.

"It spells trouble," Batman said.

"That's the home of the hero Shazam's mightiest enemy," Wonder Woman replied. "And that means we're dealing with . . .

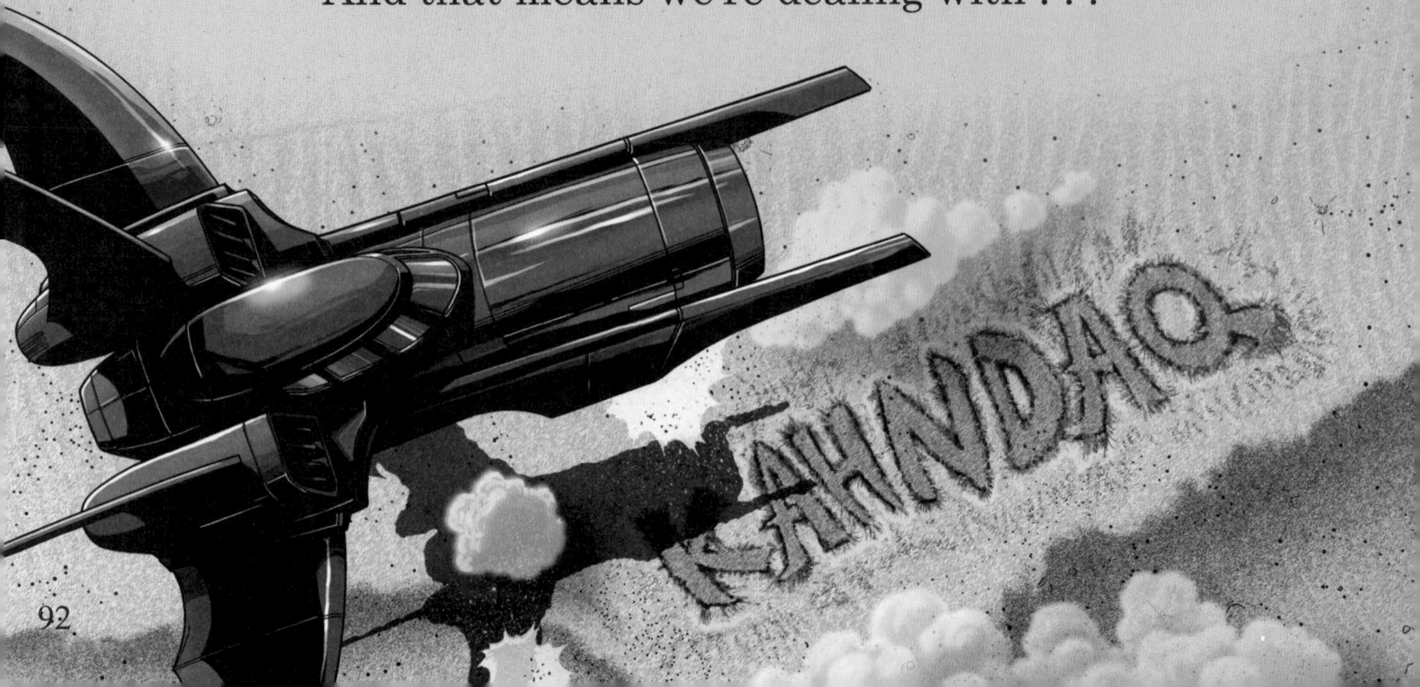
KAHNDAQ

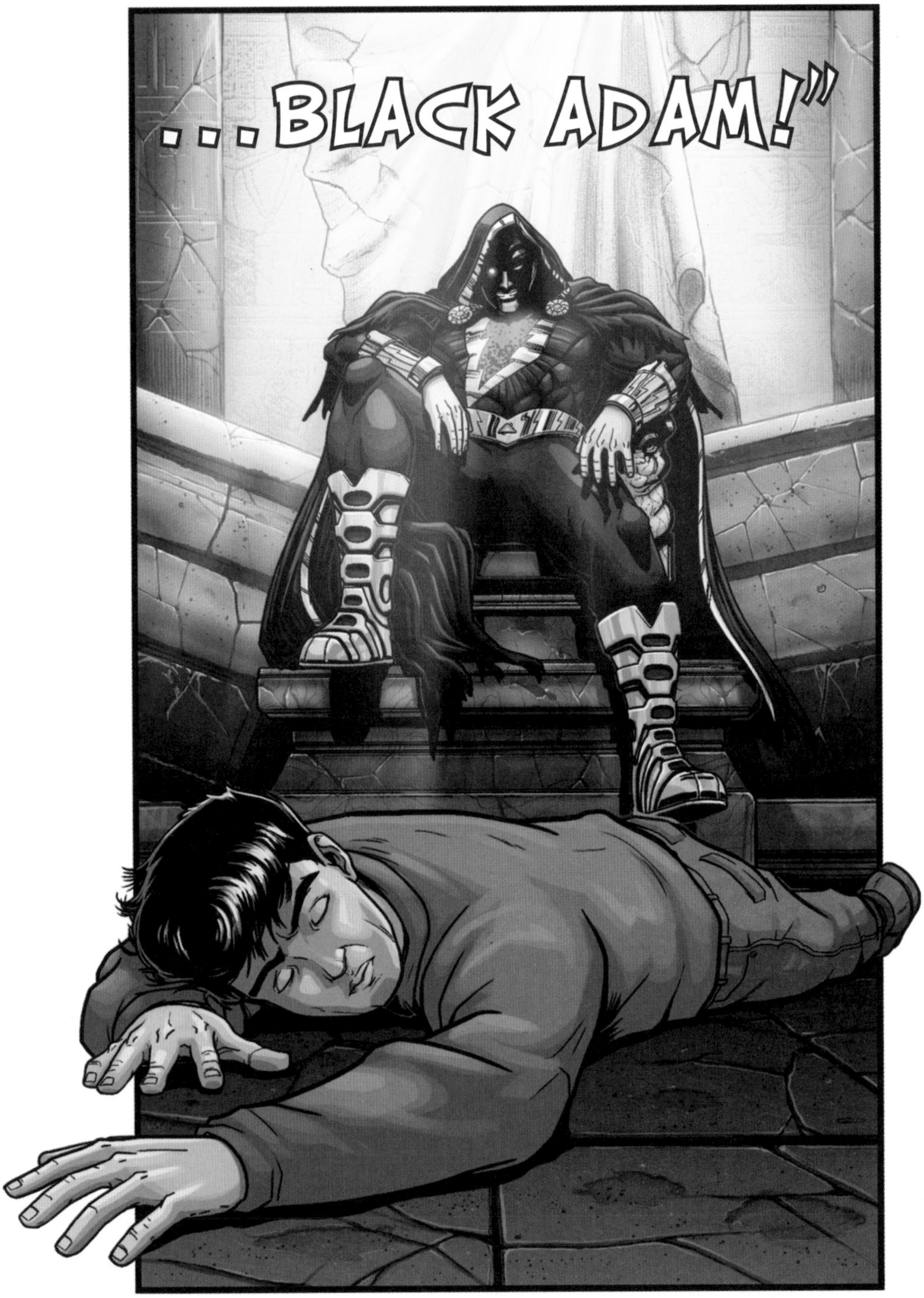
". . . BLACK ADAM!"

At the moment, it appeared that Black Adam was holding Billy Batson as his prisoner. Billy was a young boy whose alter ego was actually the World's Mightiest Mortal—SHAZAM!

"With a simple spell, I am keeping him fast asleep," the villain gloated. "My greatest foe is now no trouble at all.

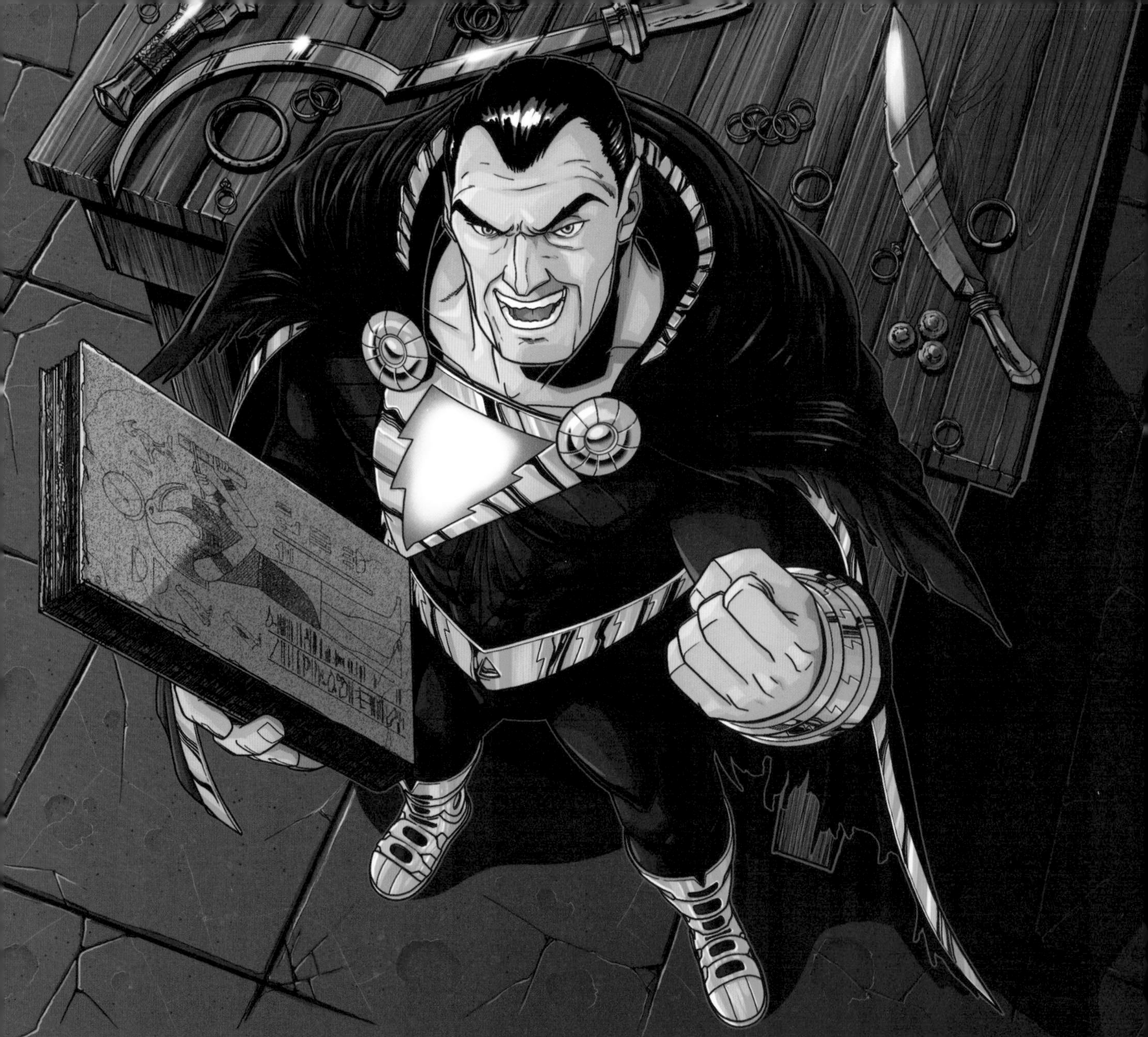

"Not so mighty anymore," Black Adam said, reveling in his triumph. "With the power I have gained from the magical objects I stole and this book of magic, I am now far more powerful than you! And once I get rid of you, I will take over the world!"

"Except one thing stands in your way," Batman said as the super heroes entered the room.

"Make that *three* things," Green Lantern added.

"And we're not going to let you harm Shazam or take over the world," Wonder Woman said.

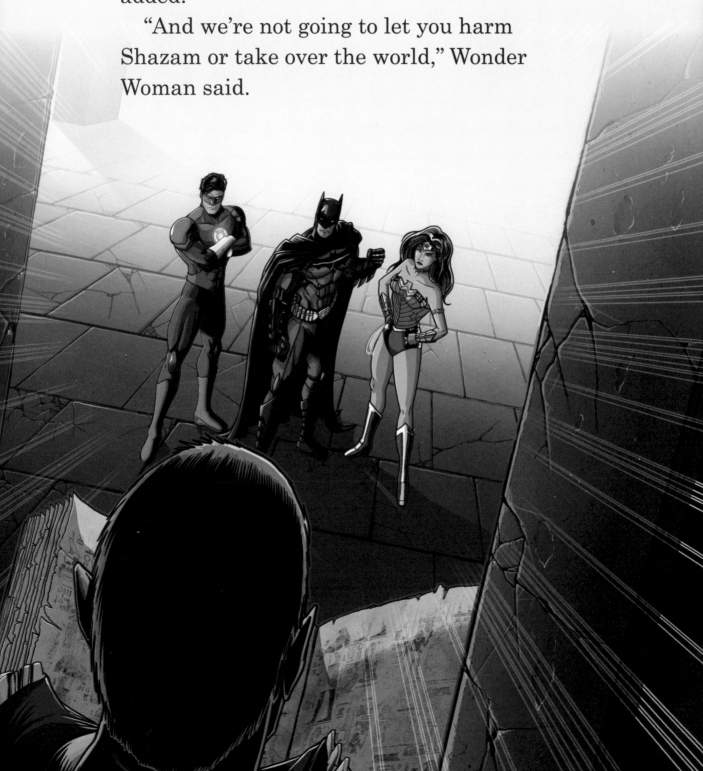

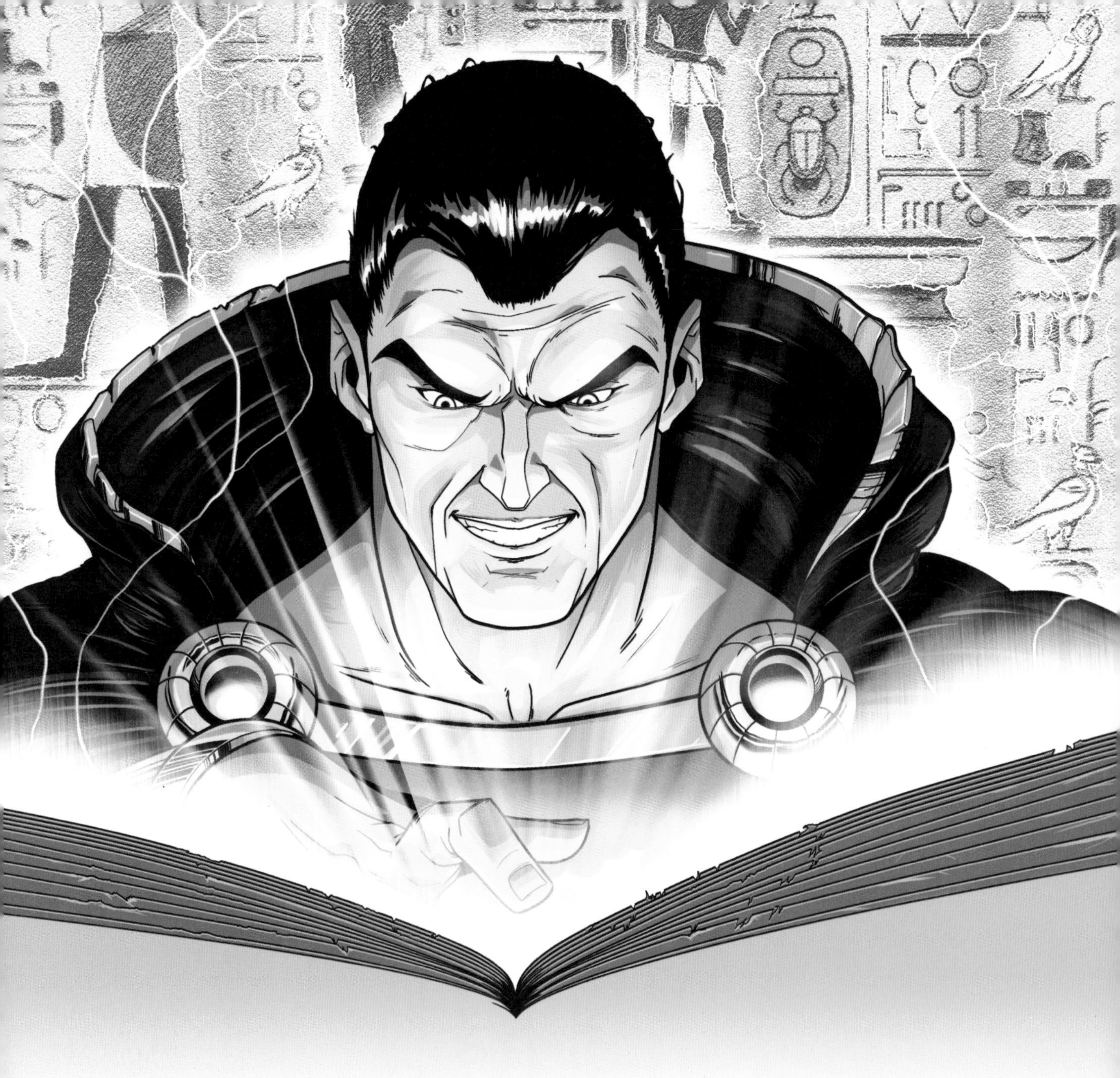

The villain laughed and opened the book of magic. "I think my newfound powers will be more than a match for you and your friends, Wonder Woman," he said.

He began to read a spell and draw power from the book.

As the ancient book began to glow, so did Black Adam's eyes. Energy crackled in the room. The villain released a powerful mystical bolt at the heroes.

"Green Lantern, protect Batman!" Wonder Woman shouted. "I can handle his attack."

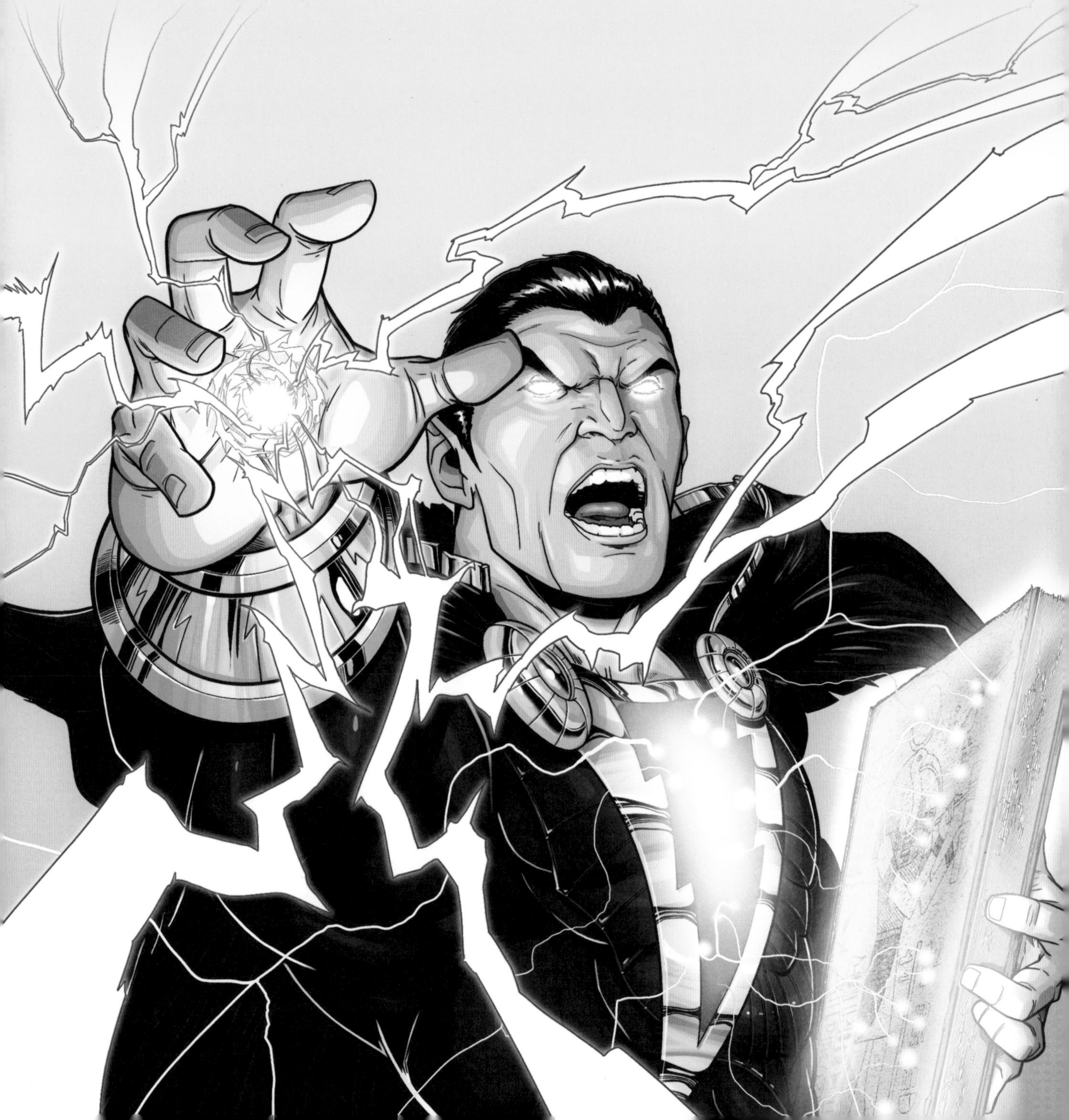

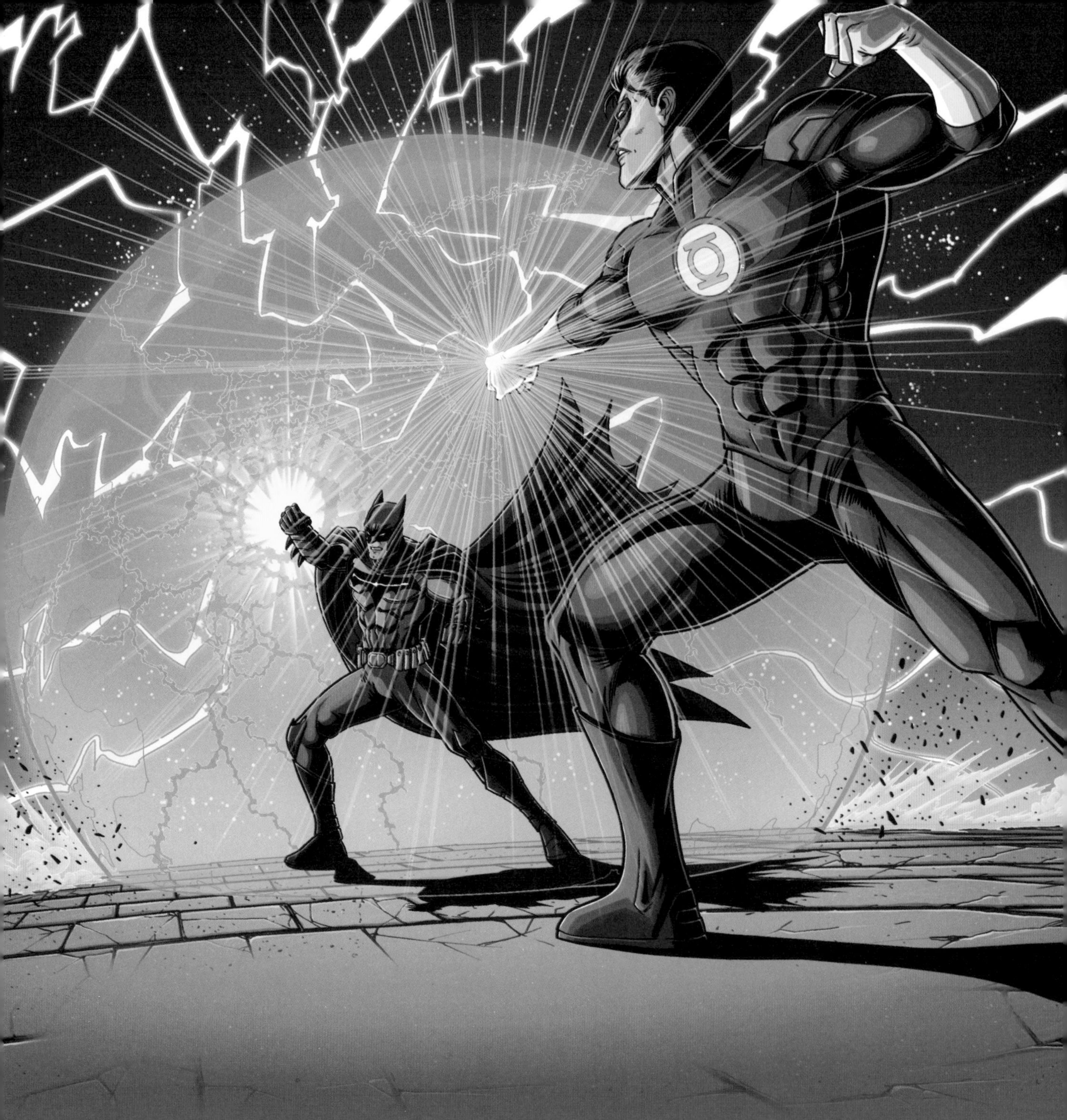

Green Lantern used his power ring to project a force field around the Caped Crusader. The ring's energy absorbed the first round of Black Adam's attack, but Green Lantern wasn't sure if it could stand up to another.

"Whatever we're going to do, let's do it quick," Green Lantern said.

"You got it, Green Lantern," Wonder Woman said, leaping into action. She pulled out her unbreakable Lasso of Truth and began to twirl it over her head.

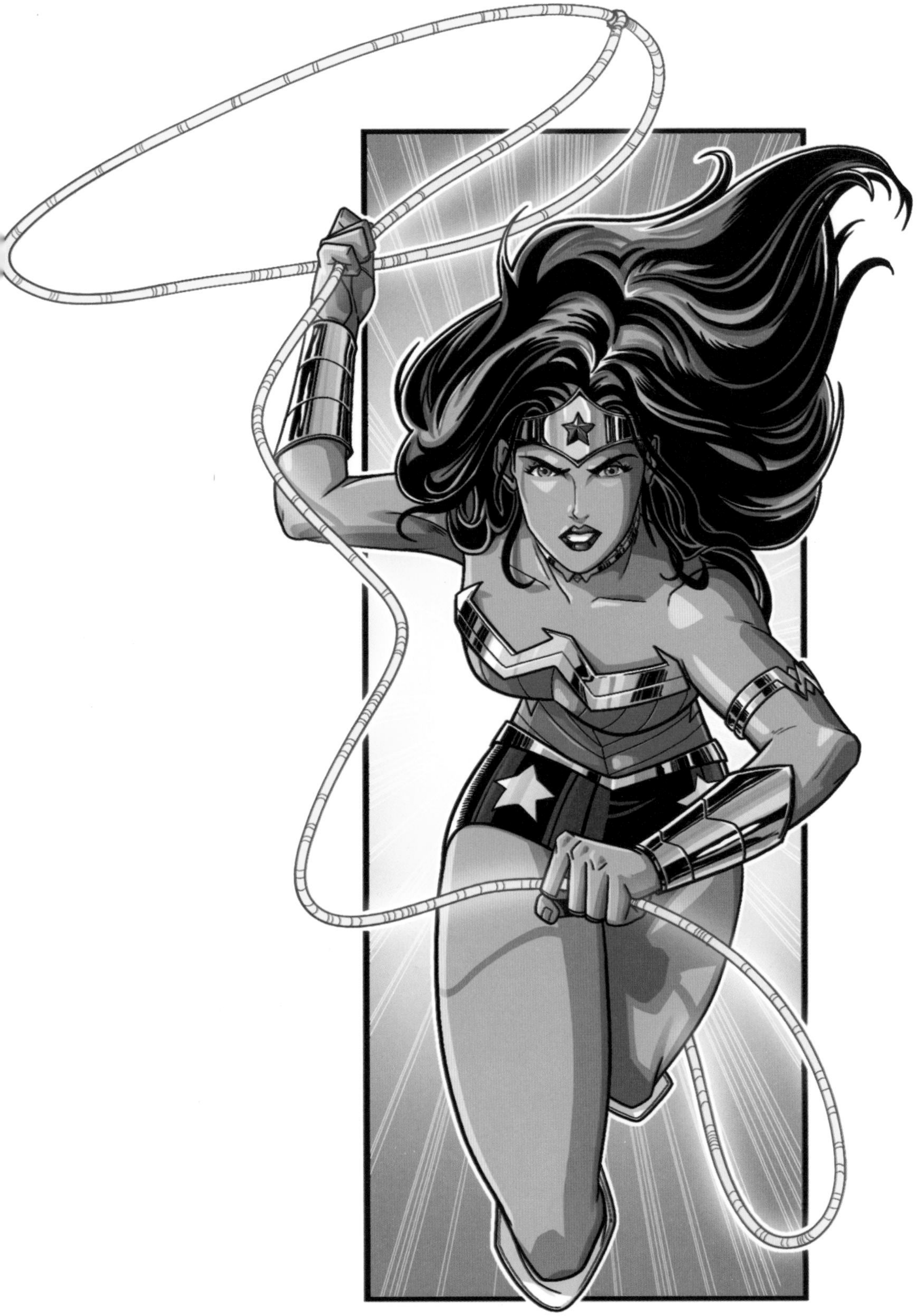

Wonder Woman lassoed the book and pulled it from Black Adam.

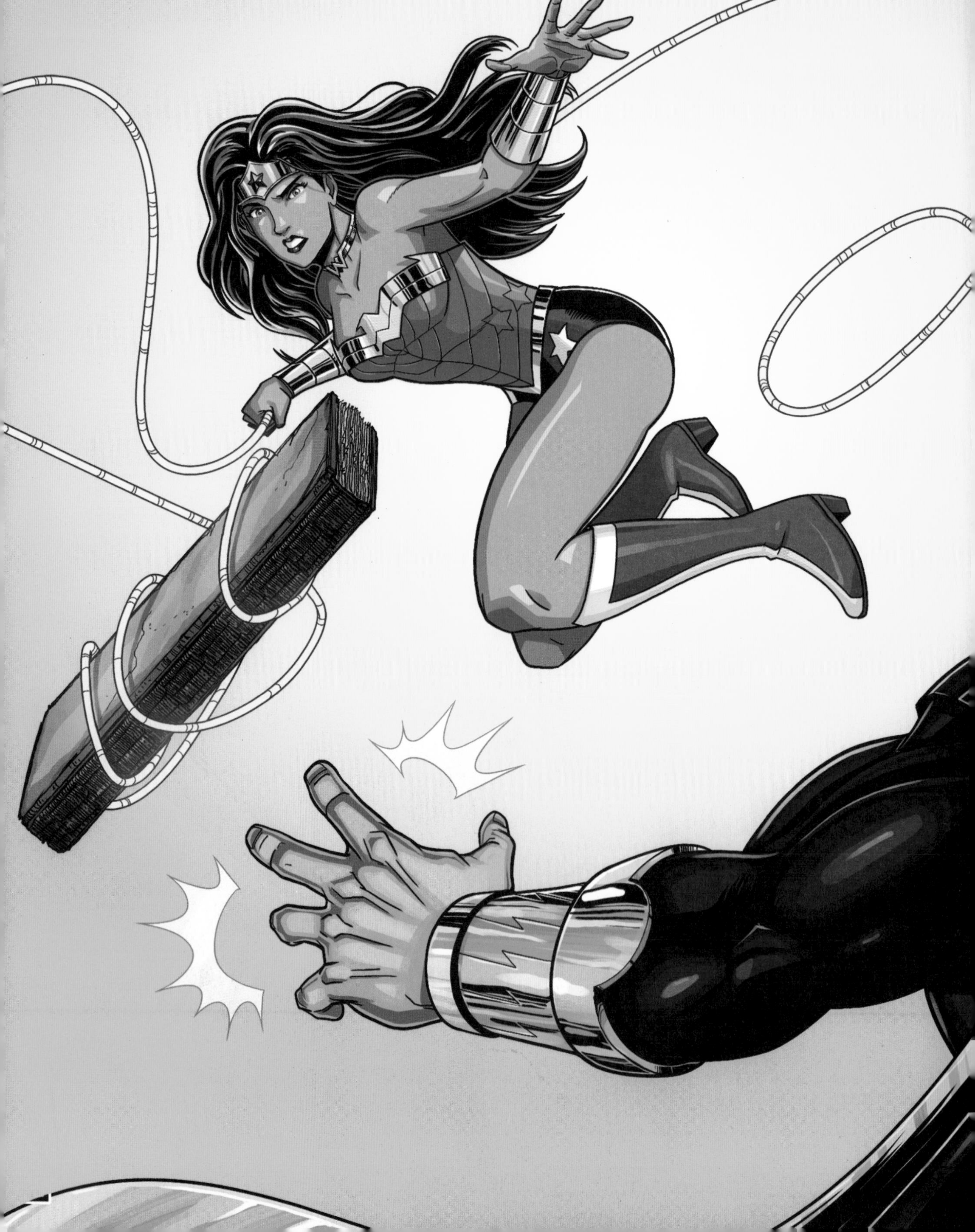

"NO!" the villain screamed. "Its power is mine!"

With Black Adam distracted, the spell he was using to keep Billy asleep was broken. In seconds, Billy was on his feet. He ran at the villain and tackled him, shouting . . .

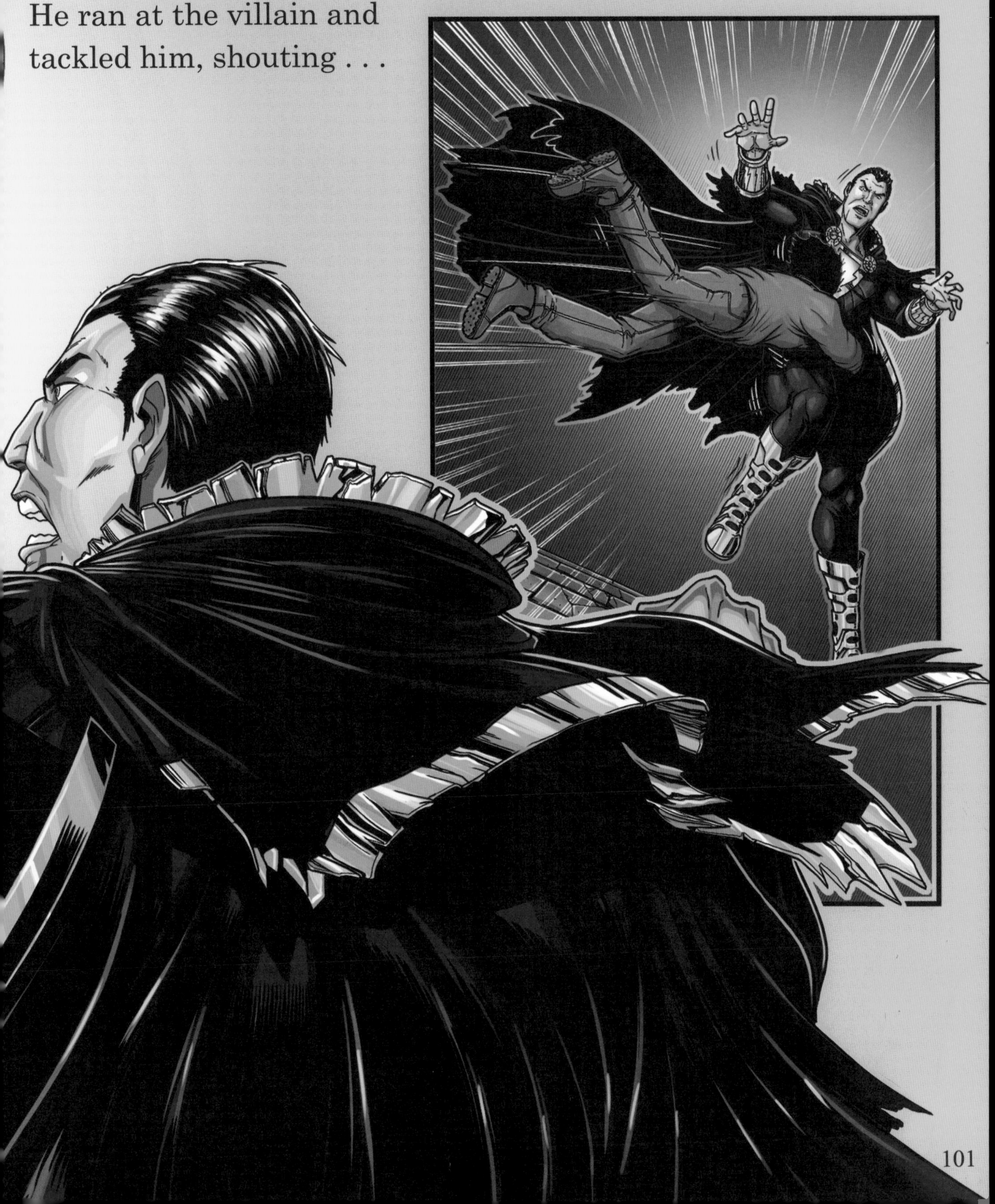

"SHAZAM!"

The magic word that was the hero's name called a powerful bolt of lightning from the sky. It struck Billy and Black Adam!

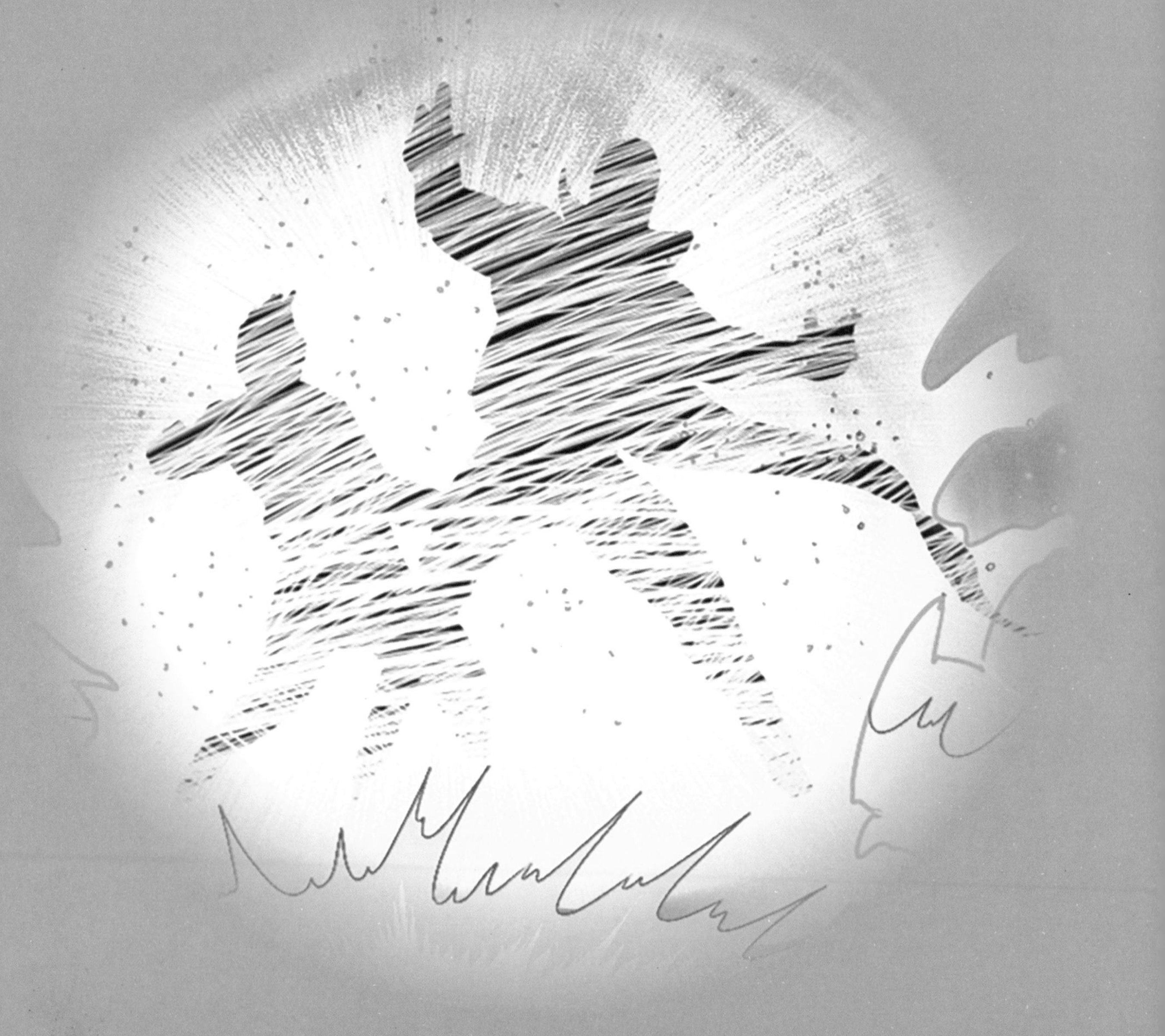

The bolt knocked Black Adam off his feet and transformed Billy in a mighty super hero! Without the added power of the book, Black Adam knew he was no match for Shazam—especially if he was teamed up with members of the Justice League.

"Thanks, friends," Shazam said.

"You're welcome," Wonder Woman replied. "While you gentlemen get Black Adam to a jail that's strong enough to hold him . . .

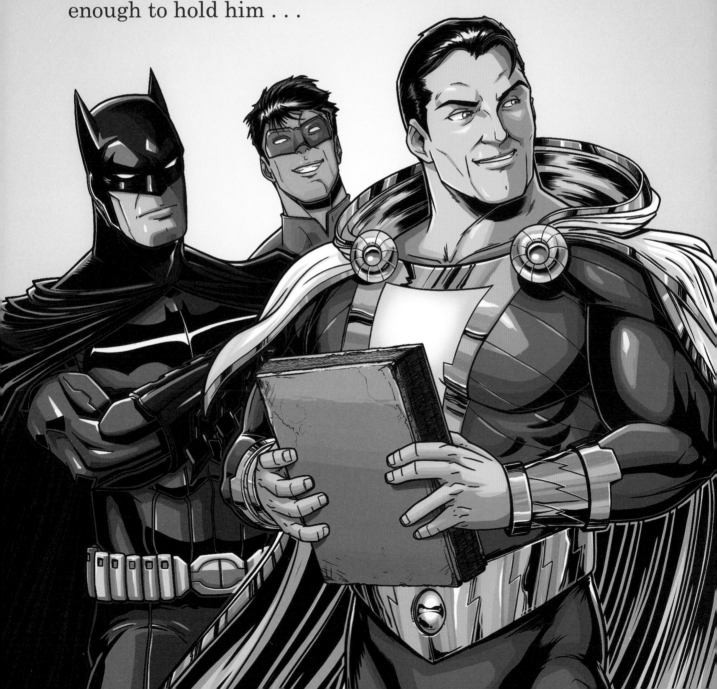

"... I'll take this book and the other magical objects that he stole someplace where their power can never be used for wrongdoing again." And then Wonder Woman flew off, with the ancient book under her arm for safekeeping.

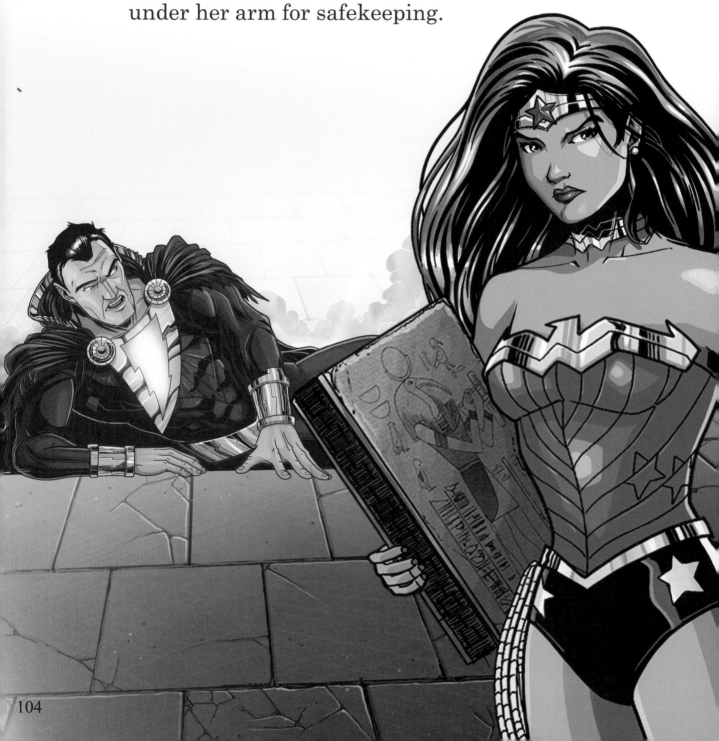

THE TERRIBLE TEAM-UP!

Lex Luthor was a rich and very powerful businessman. He was also secretly a super-villain. And he had become *very* tired of super heroes like Wonder Woman, Superman, Batman, and the rest of the Justice League always foiling his plans.

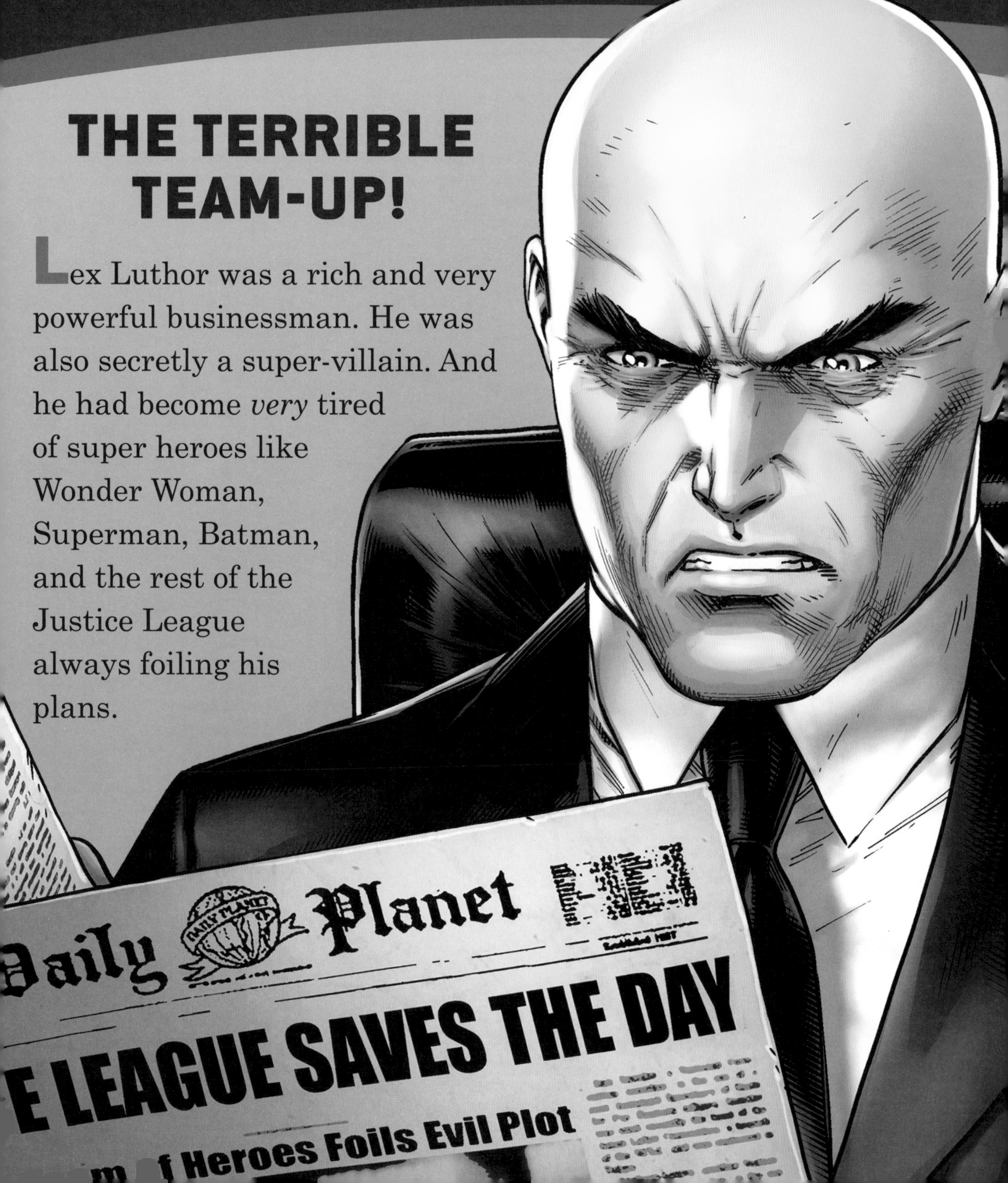

Daily Planet
E LEAGUE SAVES THE DAY
f Heroes Foils Evil Plot

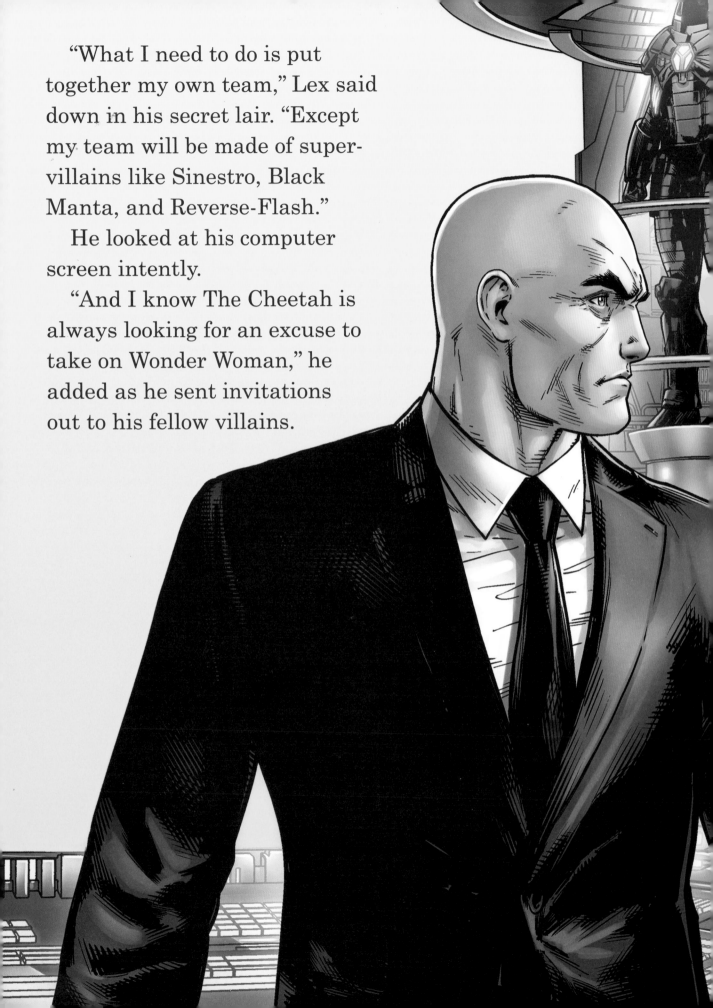

"What I need to do is put together my own team," Lex said down in his secret lair. "Except my team will be made of super-villains like Sinestro, Black Manta, and Reverse-Flash."

He looked at his computer screen intently.

"And I know The Cheetah is always looking for an excuse to take on Wonder Woman," he added as he sent invitations out to his fellow villains.

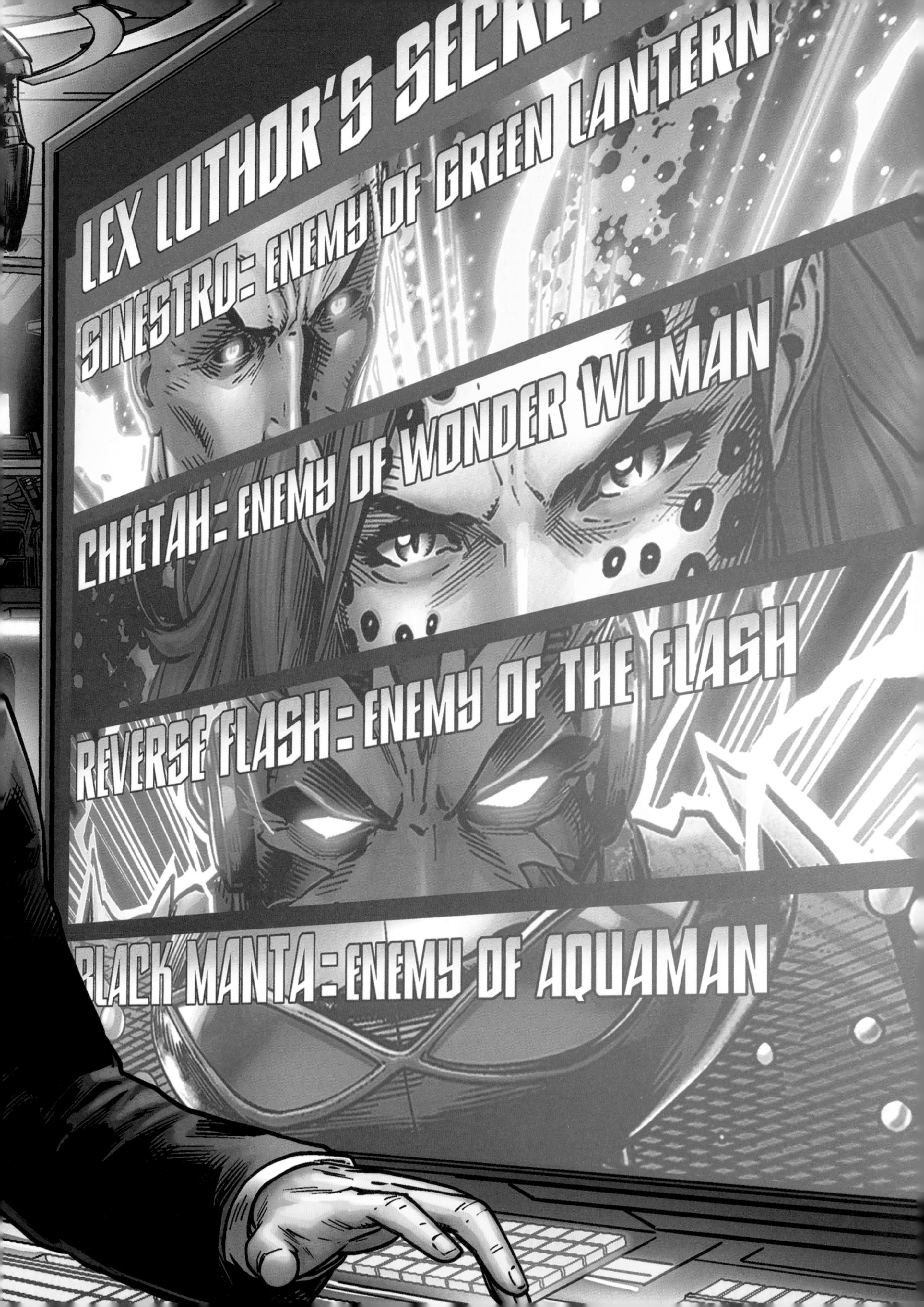
LEX LUTHOR'S SECRE
SINESTRO: ENEMY OF GREEN LANTERN
CHEETAH: ENEMY OF WONDER WOMAN
REVERSE FLASH: ENEMY OF THE FLASH
BLACK MANTA: ENEMY OF AQUAMAN

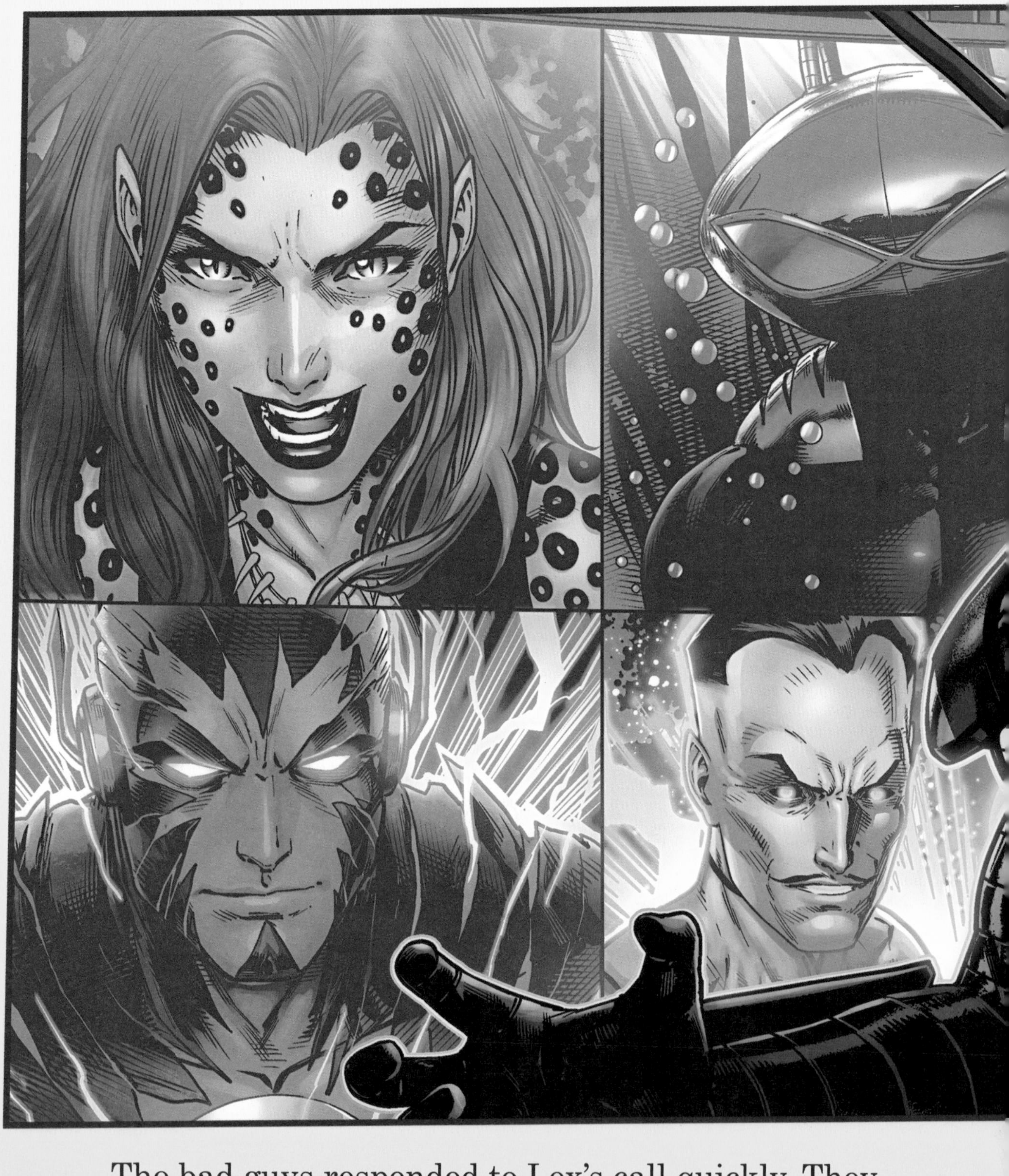

The bad guys responded to Lex's call quickly. They were eager to fight.

"Your plan is *purr*-fectly, wonderfully awful," The Cheetah purred. "Wonder Woman won't know what hit her when I have you four backing me up."

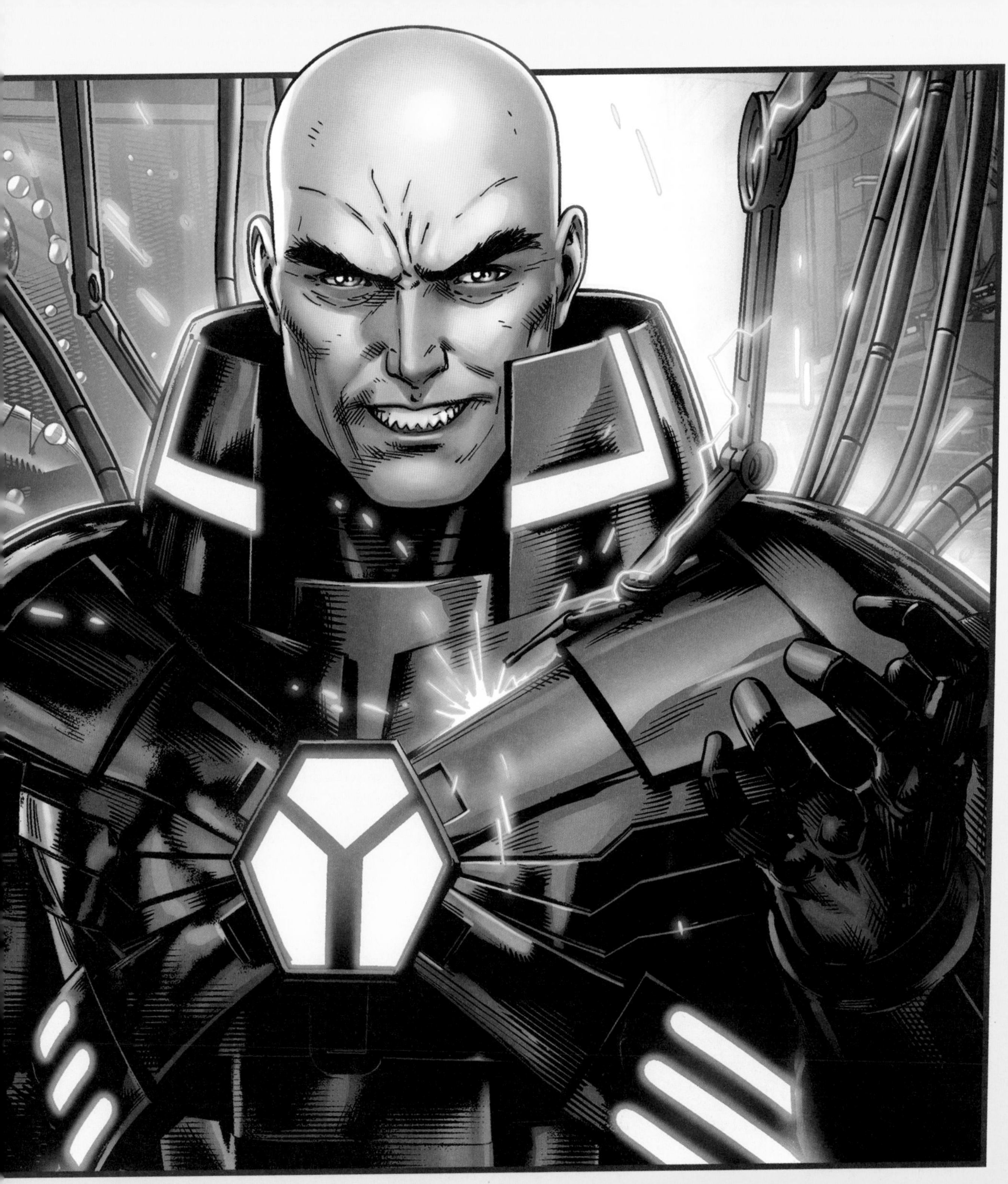

"Remember, this is about putting a stop to the whole Justice League," Lex said, putting on his superpowered high-tech armor, "not just settling old scores. With our combined might, there is no way those goody-goodies can stop us! Agreed?"

"AGREED!" the villains cheered in unison.

The villains attacked downtown Metropolis, causing chaos and damage everywhere they went. They knew the Justice League would would take action as soon as they learned of the threats. And they were right!

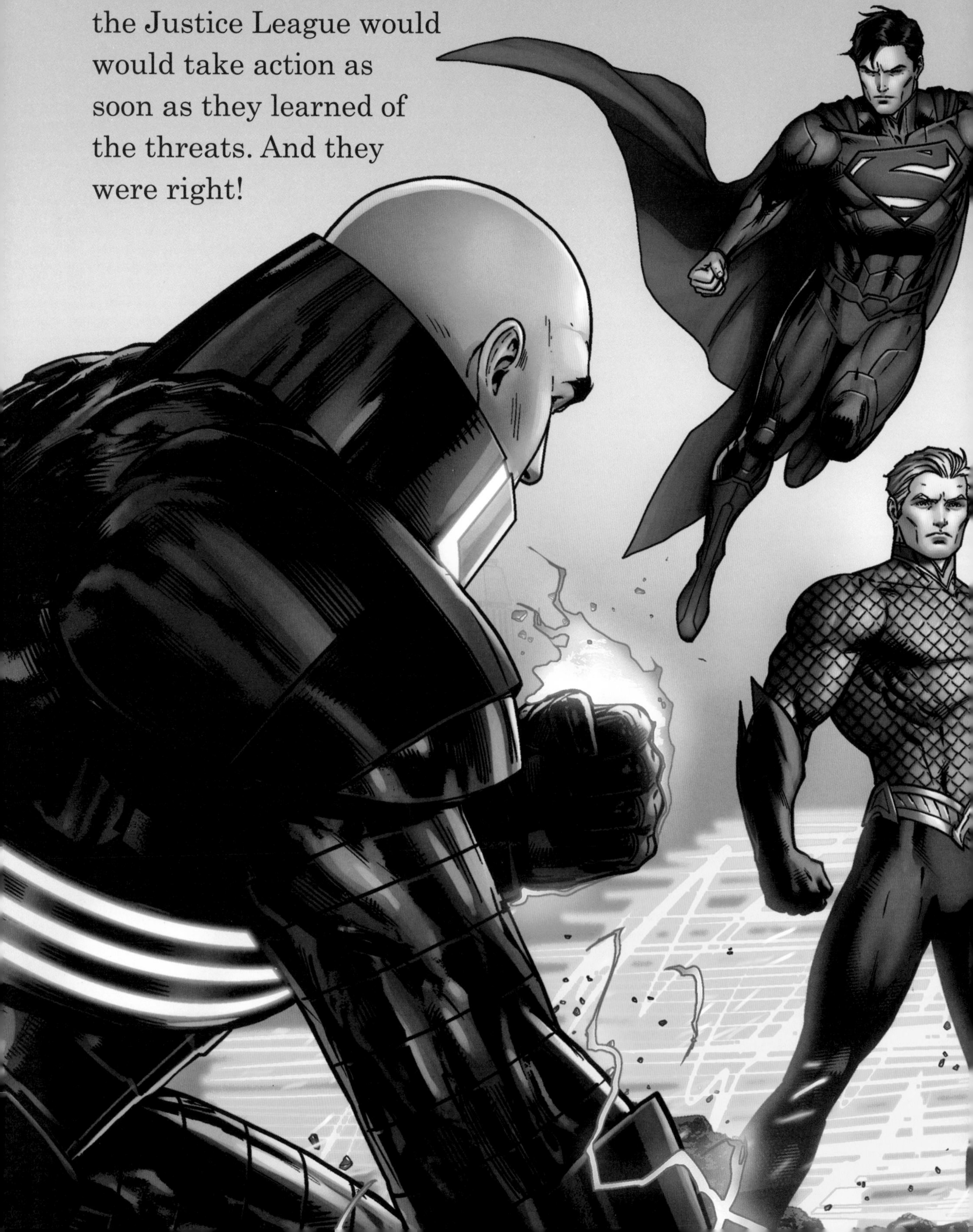

“Stop right there!” Wonder Woman shouted at the villains. “I don’t know what you think you’re up to, but my friends and I are about to put a stop to it.”

“Remember what we planned,” Lex whispered to his criminal cohorts. “Let’s stop Superman first. . . .

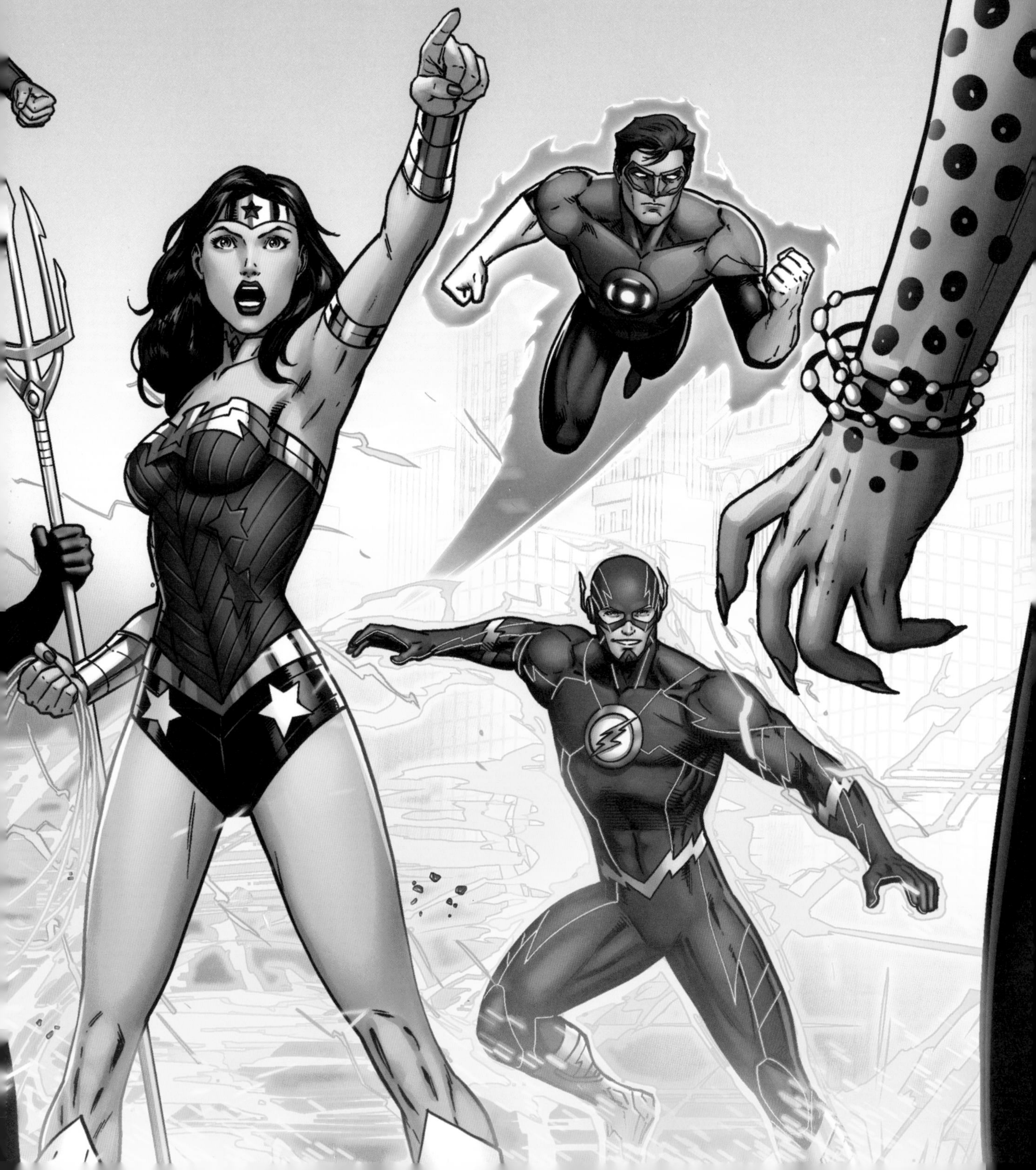

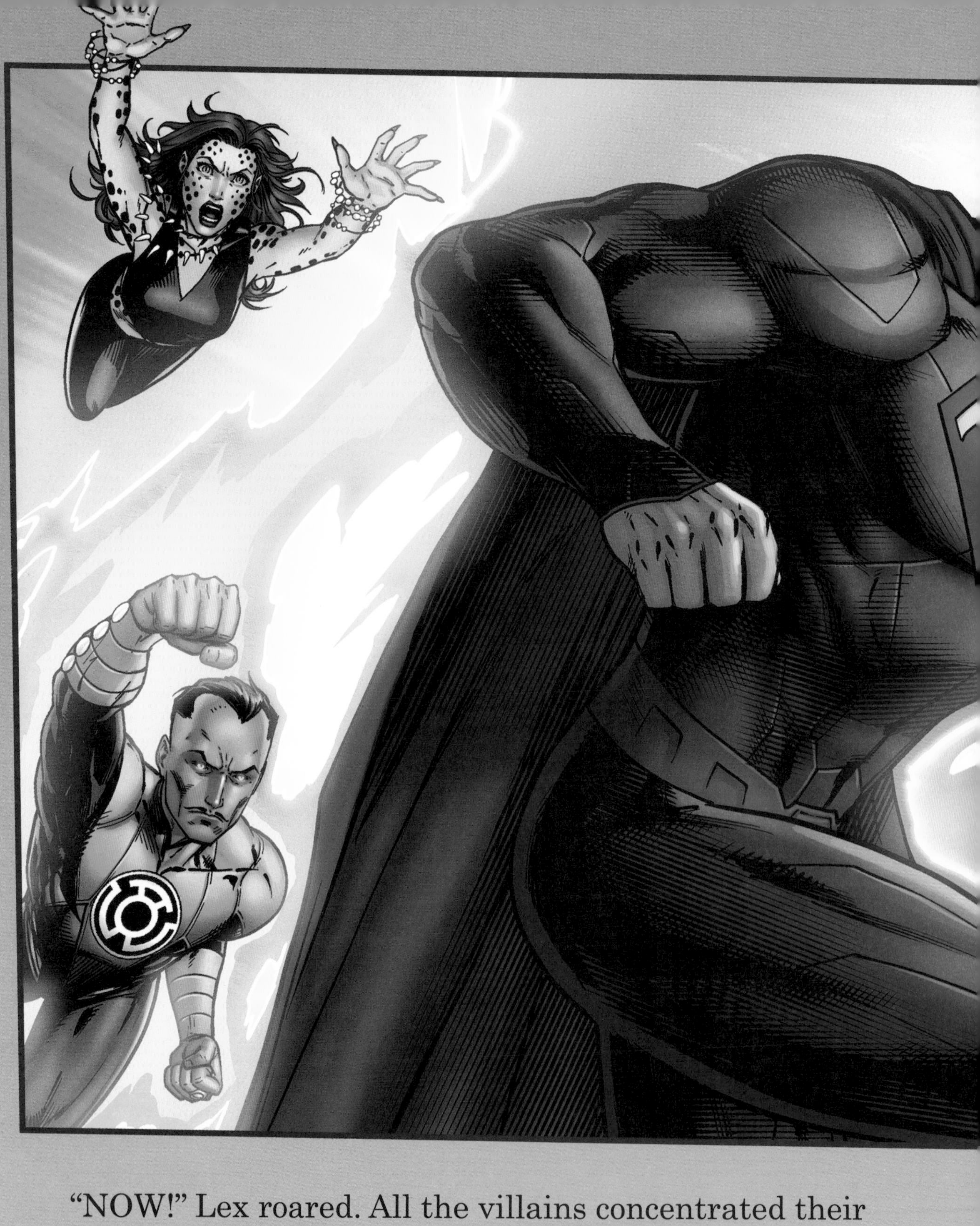

"NOW!" Lex roared. All the villains concentrated their powers on Superman.

"Even though there are five of you, I can still take you all on," Superman said confidently. But the super hero found his strength fading under their ruthless attack.

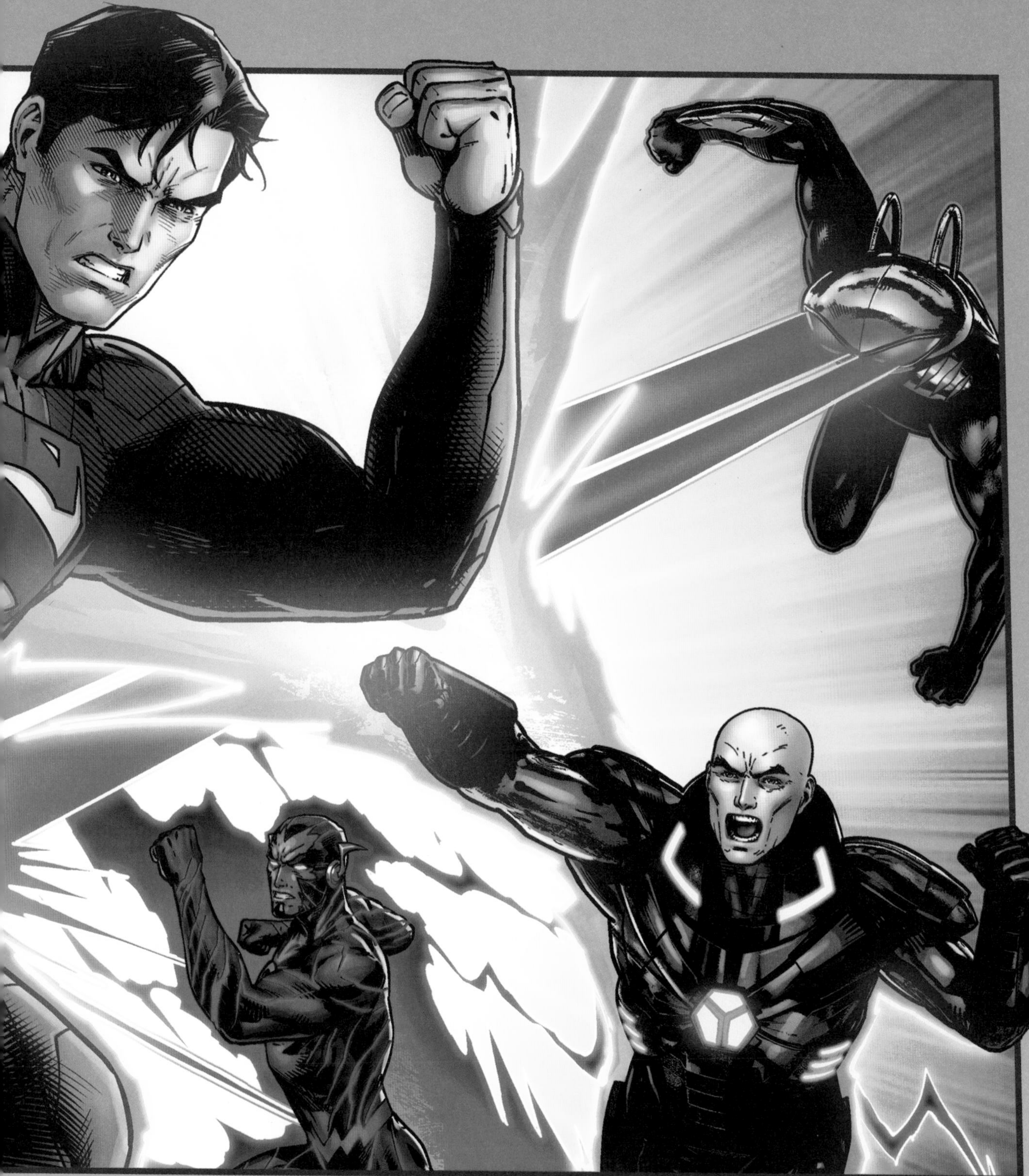

"I have a surprise for you, Superman," Lex said with villainous glee. "My armor is powered by a small piece of Kryptonite. That's not enough for me to stop you by myself, but combined with my friends' powers, it can crush you—and then the rest of the Justice League!"

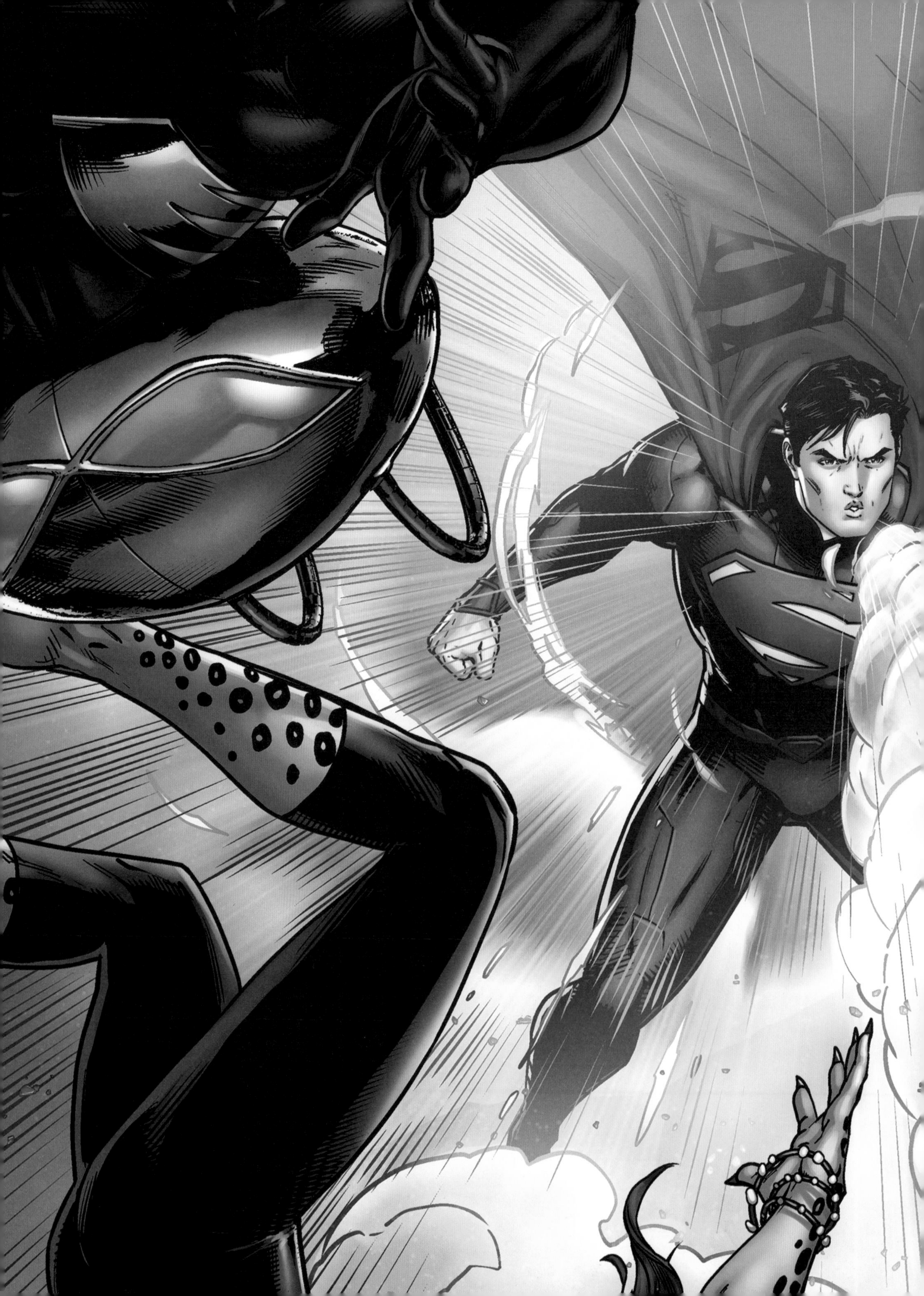

With his last ounce of strength, Superman used his super-breath to blow the villains back. The fight had lasted only seconds, but Superman could not go on until he got away from the Kryptonite for a little while.

"Pull yourselves together," Lex growled at his teammates as they tumbled around in the air current created by the Man of Steel.

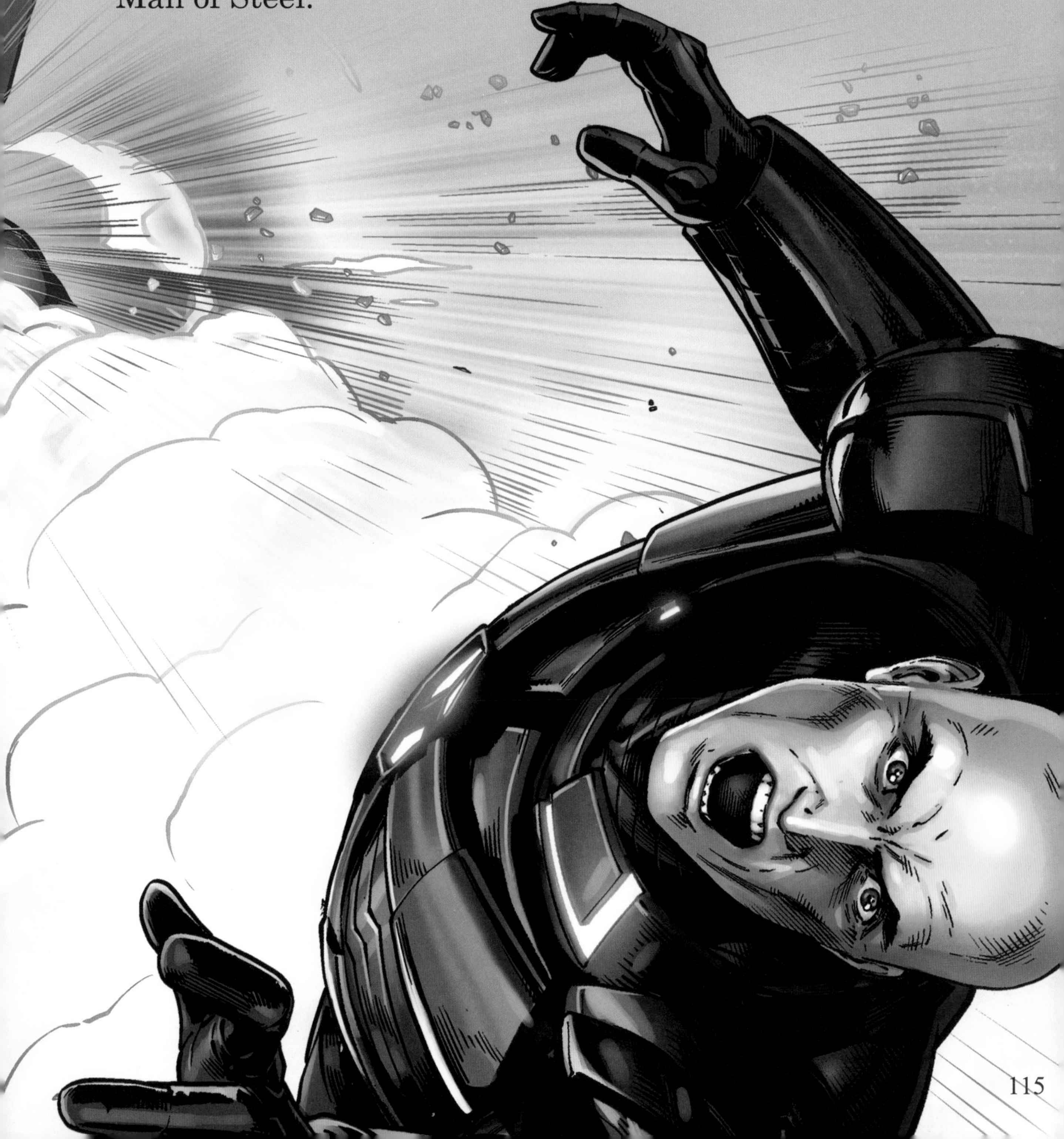

“Quickly! There’s not a moment to spare,” Wonder Woman said to Green Lantern. “Pull Superman out of there and put a force field around him until the effects of the Kryptonite wear off.”

“Gotcha,” Green Lantern replied, and he flew into action.

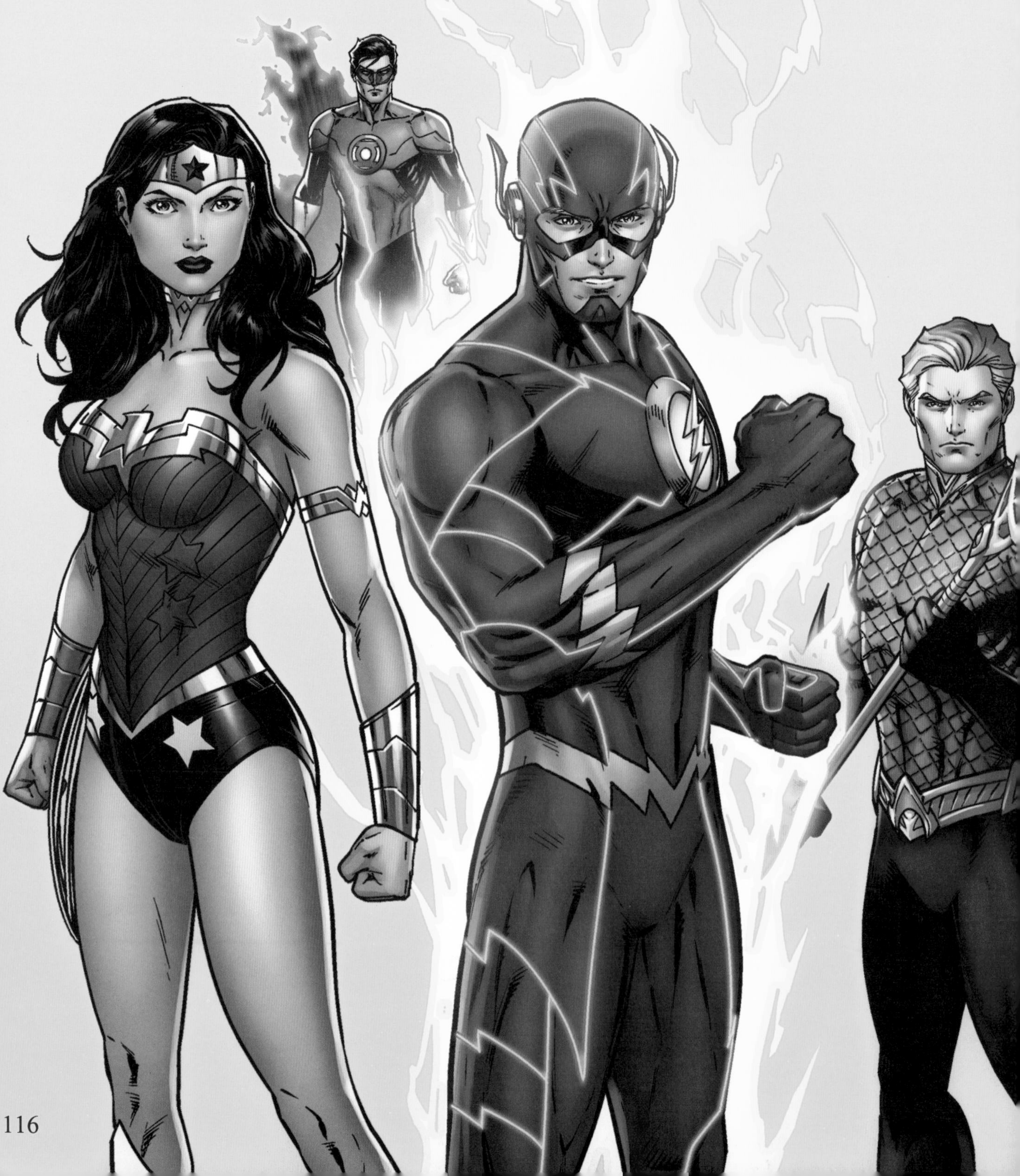

“As for the rest of them,” the Amazon added while Green Lantern rescued Superman, “they’ll expect the same old fight we always give them. Let’s each fight a villain we haven’t fought before. I’ll take on Black Manta.”

“Great idea!” The Flash responded. “The Cheetah’s fast, but wait till she gets a load of my speed.”

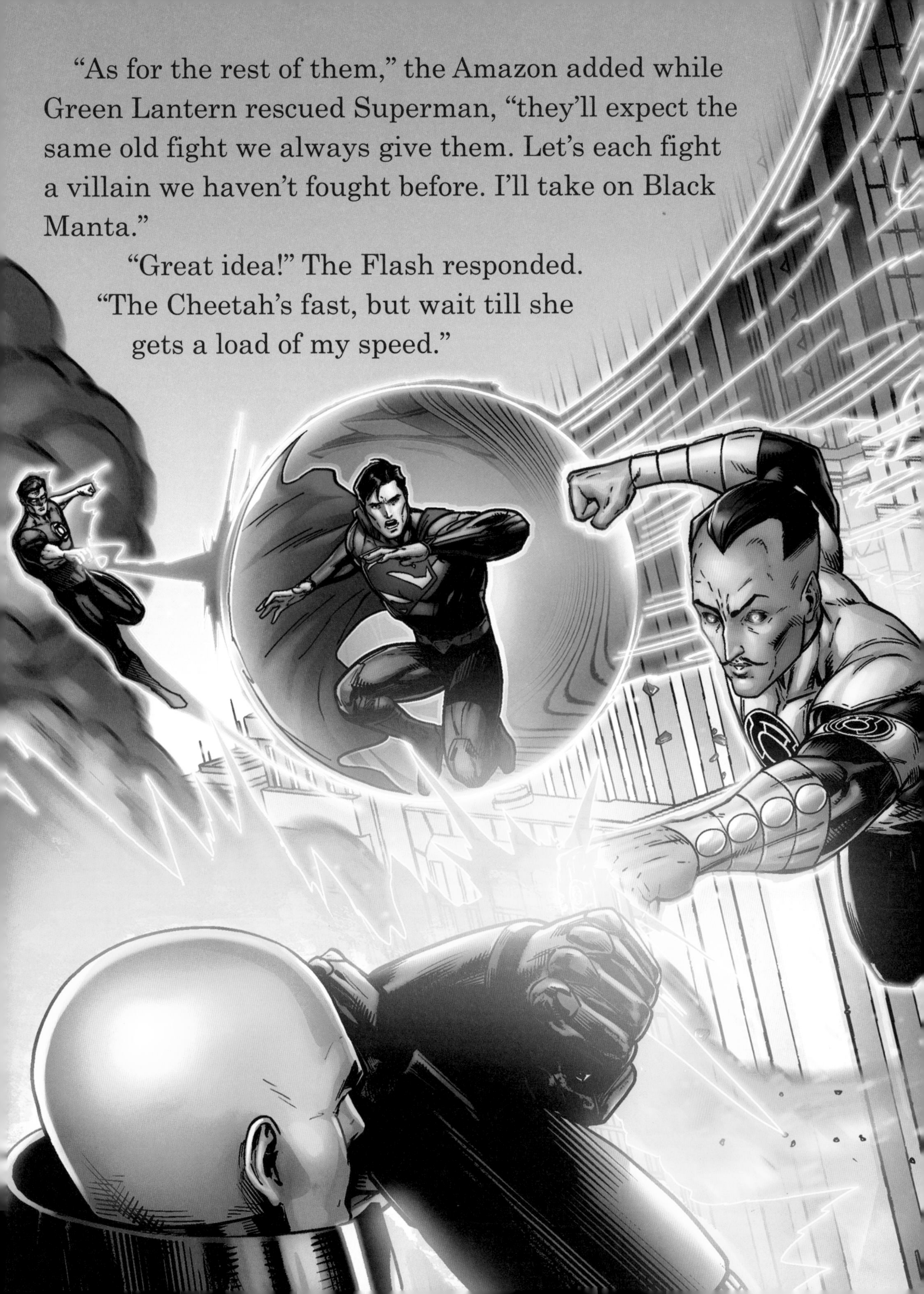

Wonder Woman jumped into battle. She used her unbreakable Lasso of Truth to capture Aquaman's nemesis, Black Manta.

"Wha—?" Black Manta cried as Wonder Woman pulled the lasso tight.

As the hero reeled in the villain, she said, "Looks like I made an unexpected catch."

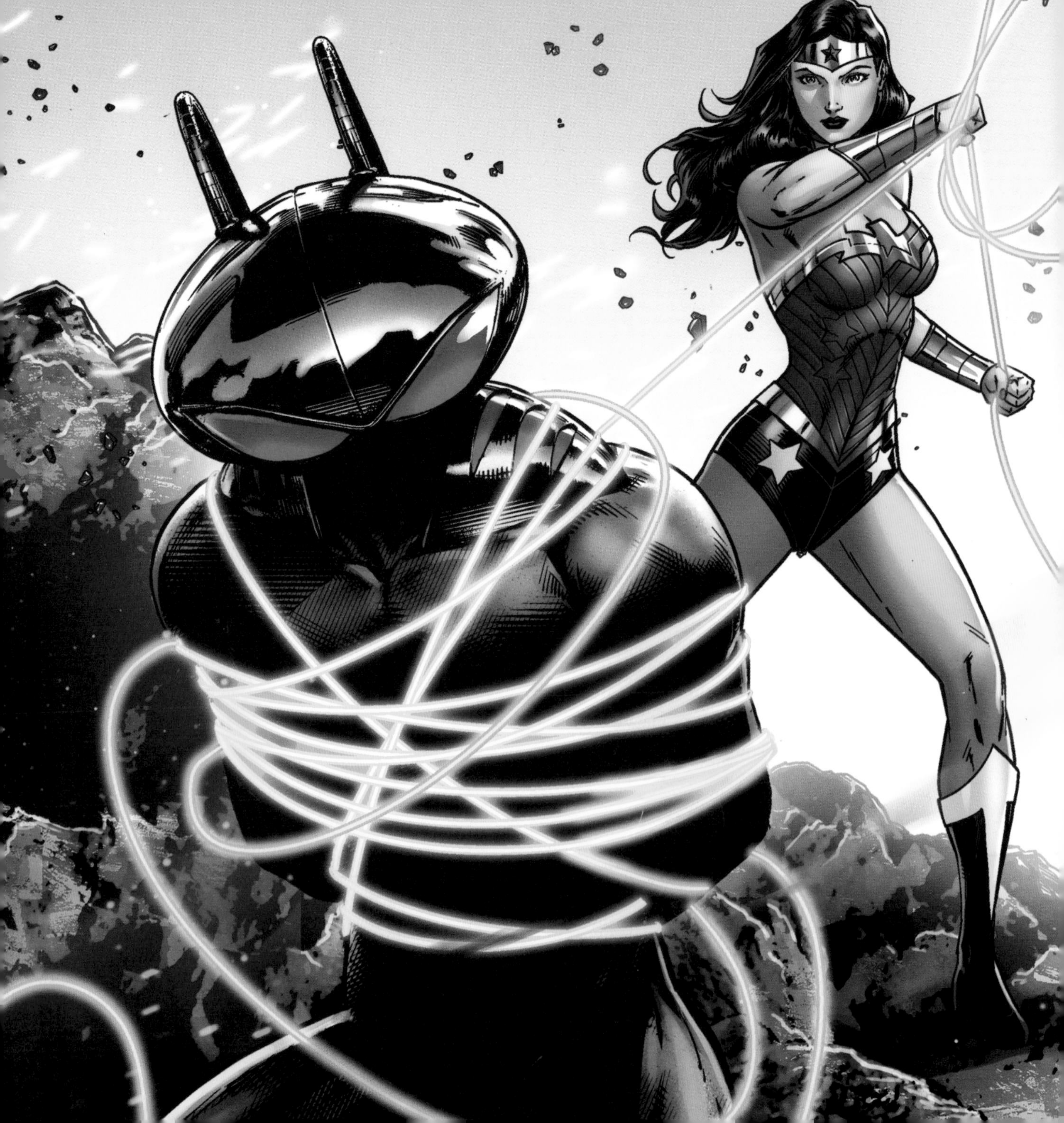

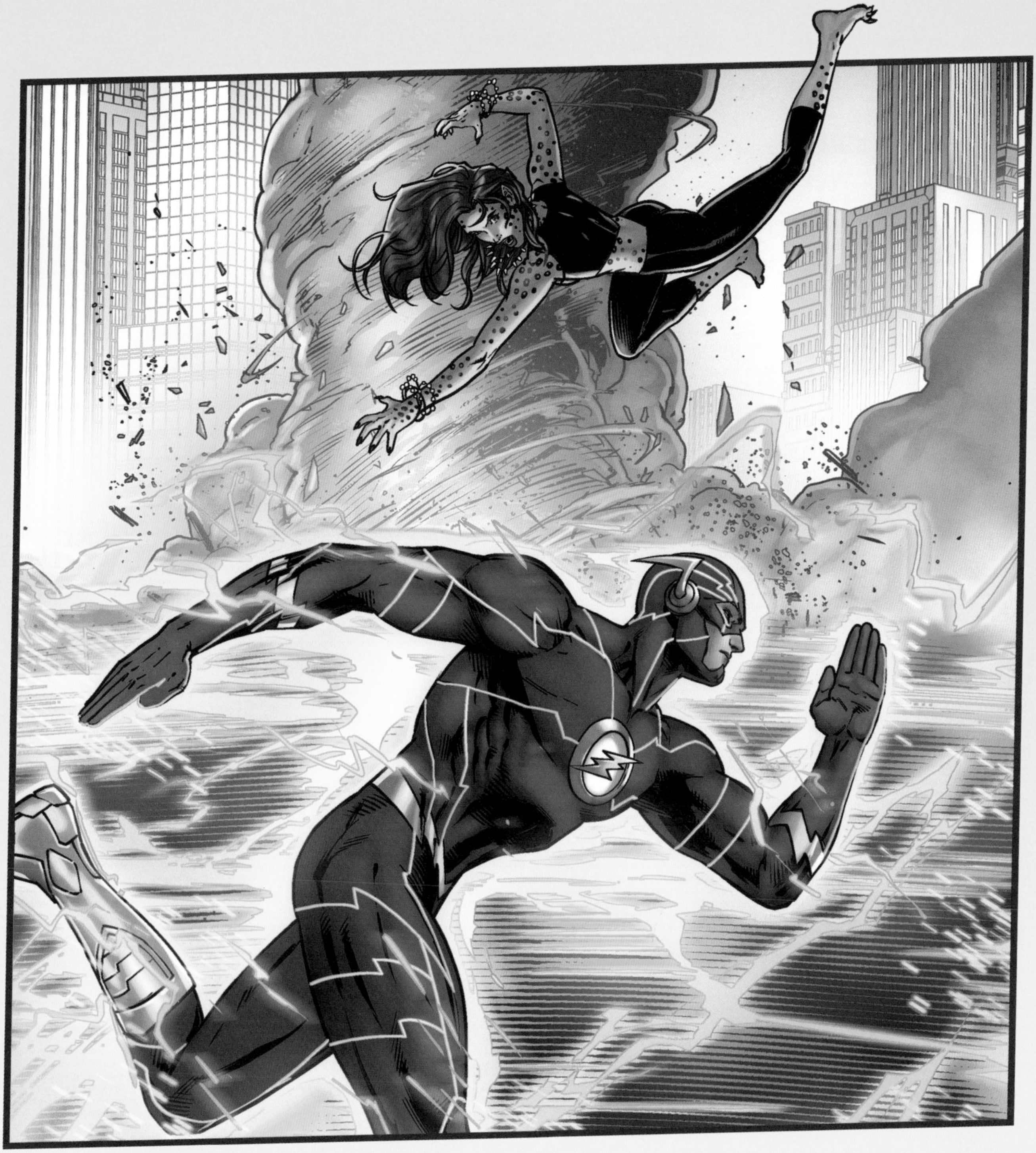

"Hey, Cheetah, I know I'm not your usual scratching post," The Flash said with a laugh. "But let's see if you're fast enough catch me."

The Flash ran so fast, he created a whirlwind that lifted The Cheetah right up off the ground.

"RRROWR!" the feline meowed as she spun around and around, getting dizzier and dizzier.

"Well, this isn't going as planned," Reverse-Flash said. "I'd better get out of here!"

"Not so fast," Green Lantern said as Reverse-Flash started to run away. The hero grabbed the villain with a giant, glowing green fist and held on with a firm grip.

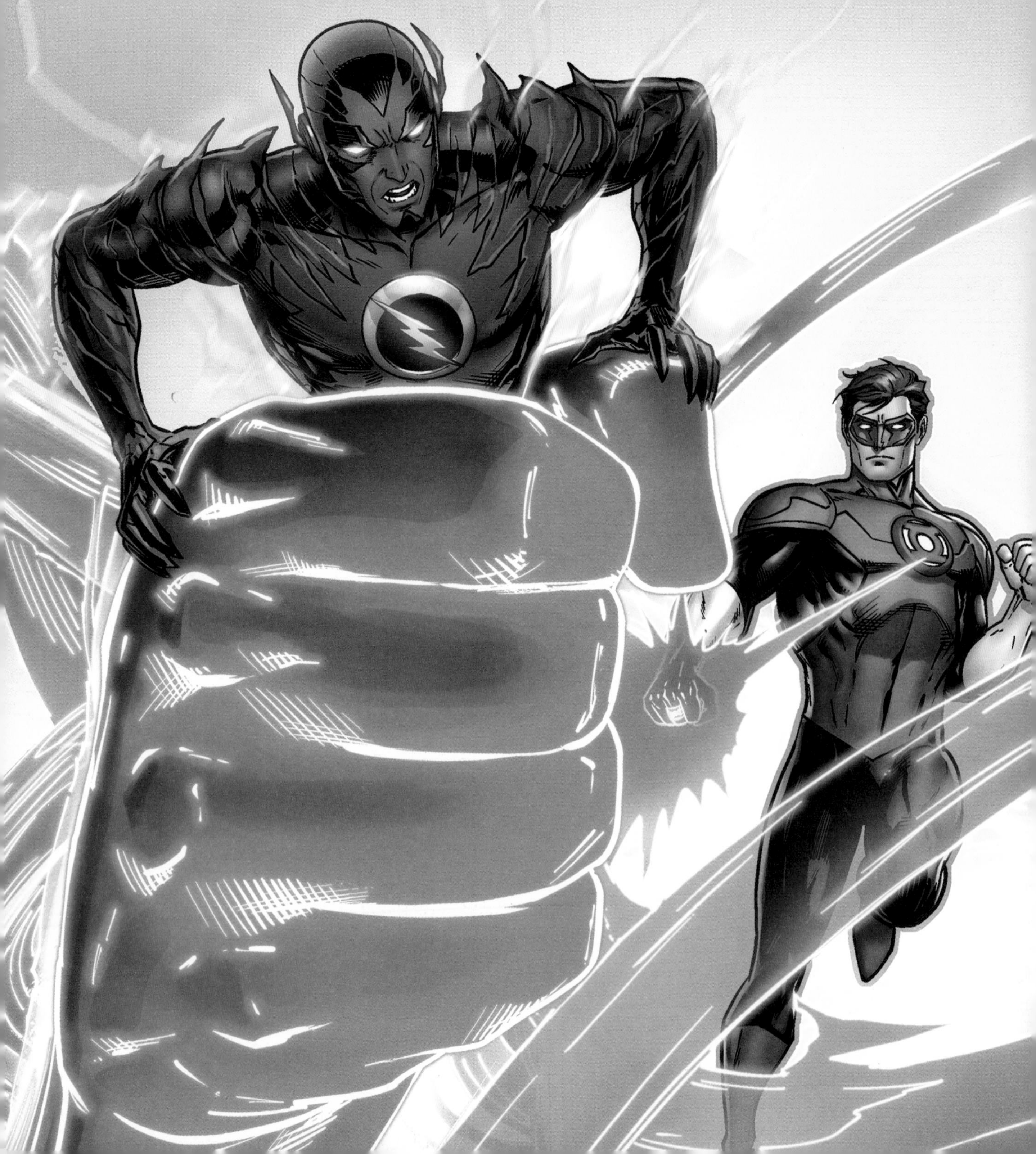

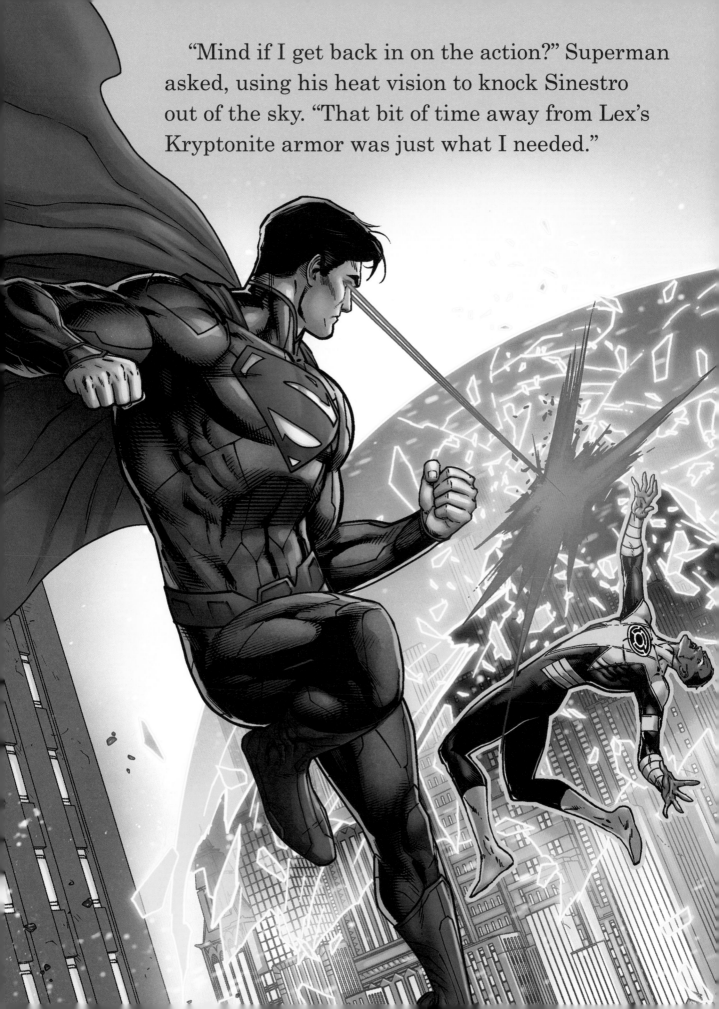

"Mind if I get back in on the action?" Superman asked, using his heat vision to knock Sinestro out of the sky. "That bit of time away from Lex's Kryptonite armor was just what I needed."

"We can still defeat them if I just can get close enough to blast Superman again," Lex said as he powered up his armor to fire another blast at the Man of Steel.

"Not so fast," Aquaman said, using his mighty trident to unleash a jet of water at the villain. "I don't think you realize that your team of baddies is all washed up—just like you!"

"Arghhh!" Lex yelled as the water short-circuited his armor.

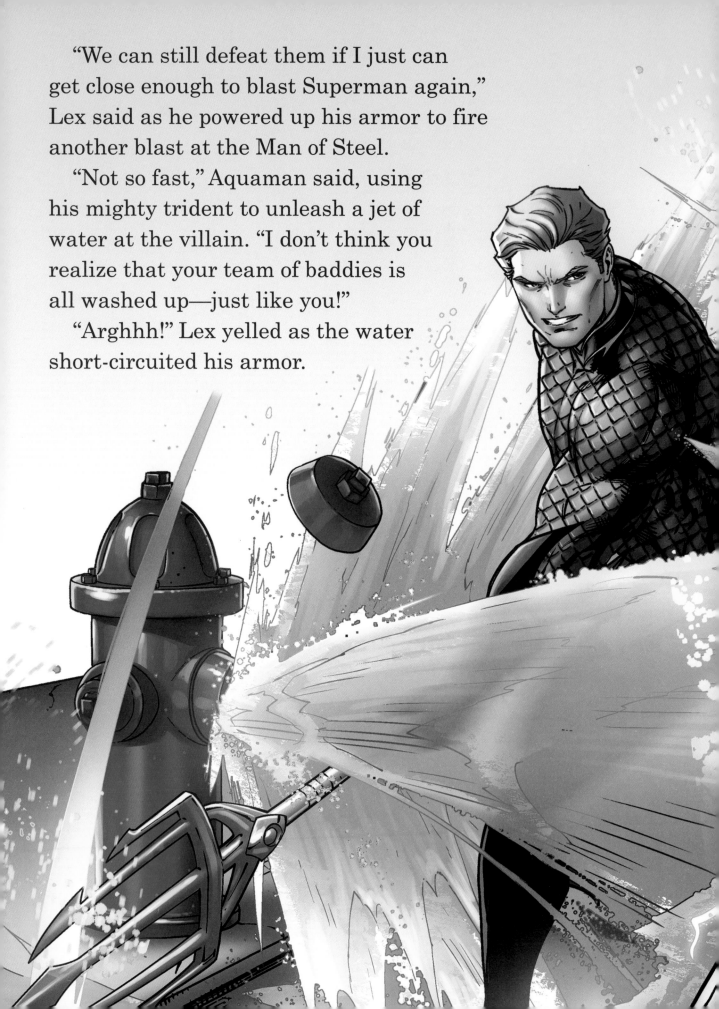

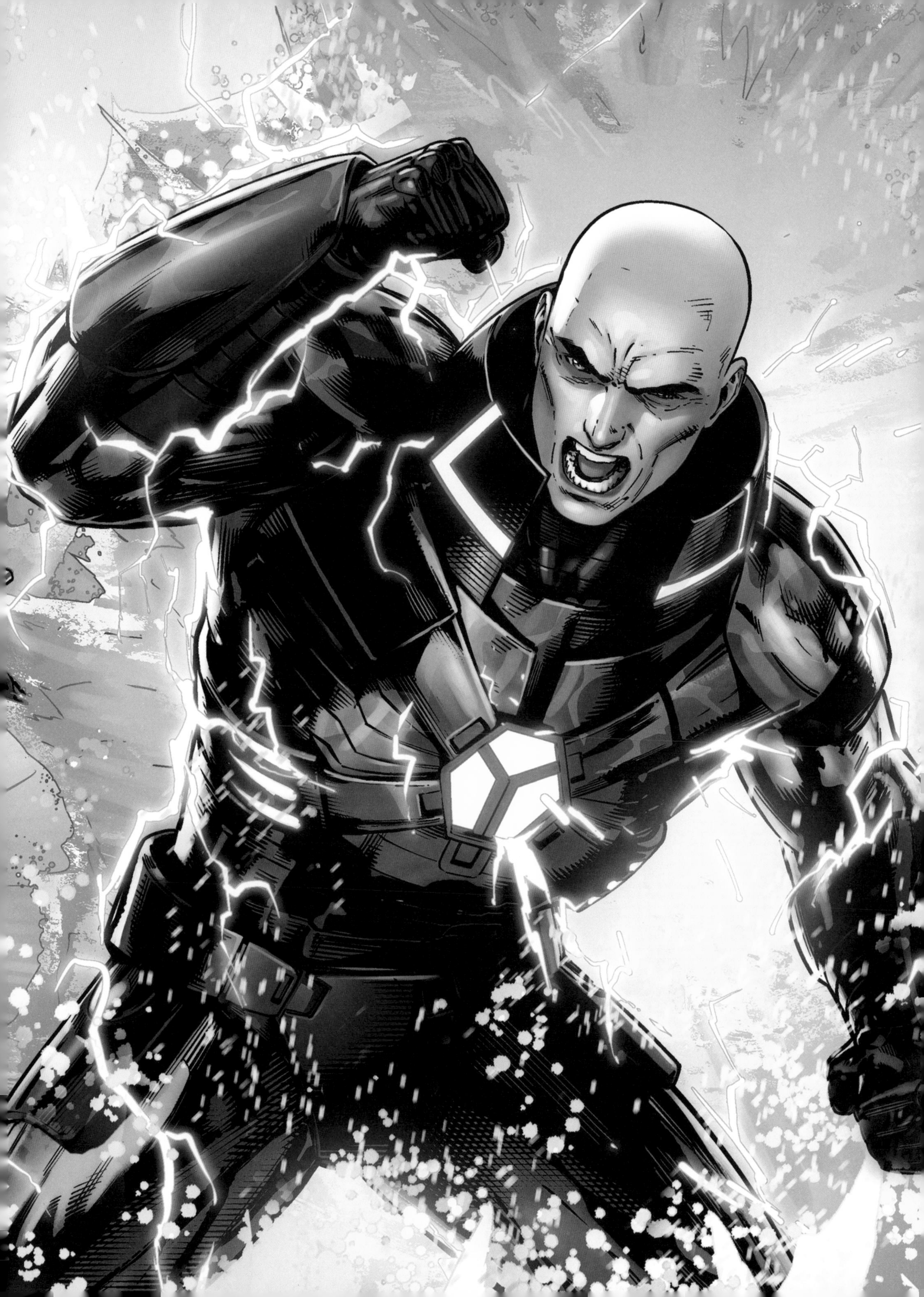

Green Lantern created an unbreakable force field of light with his power ring to hold the villains. They all hissed and growled at the heroes, but they could not escape.

"We'll get you!" Lex yelled. "One day!"

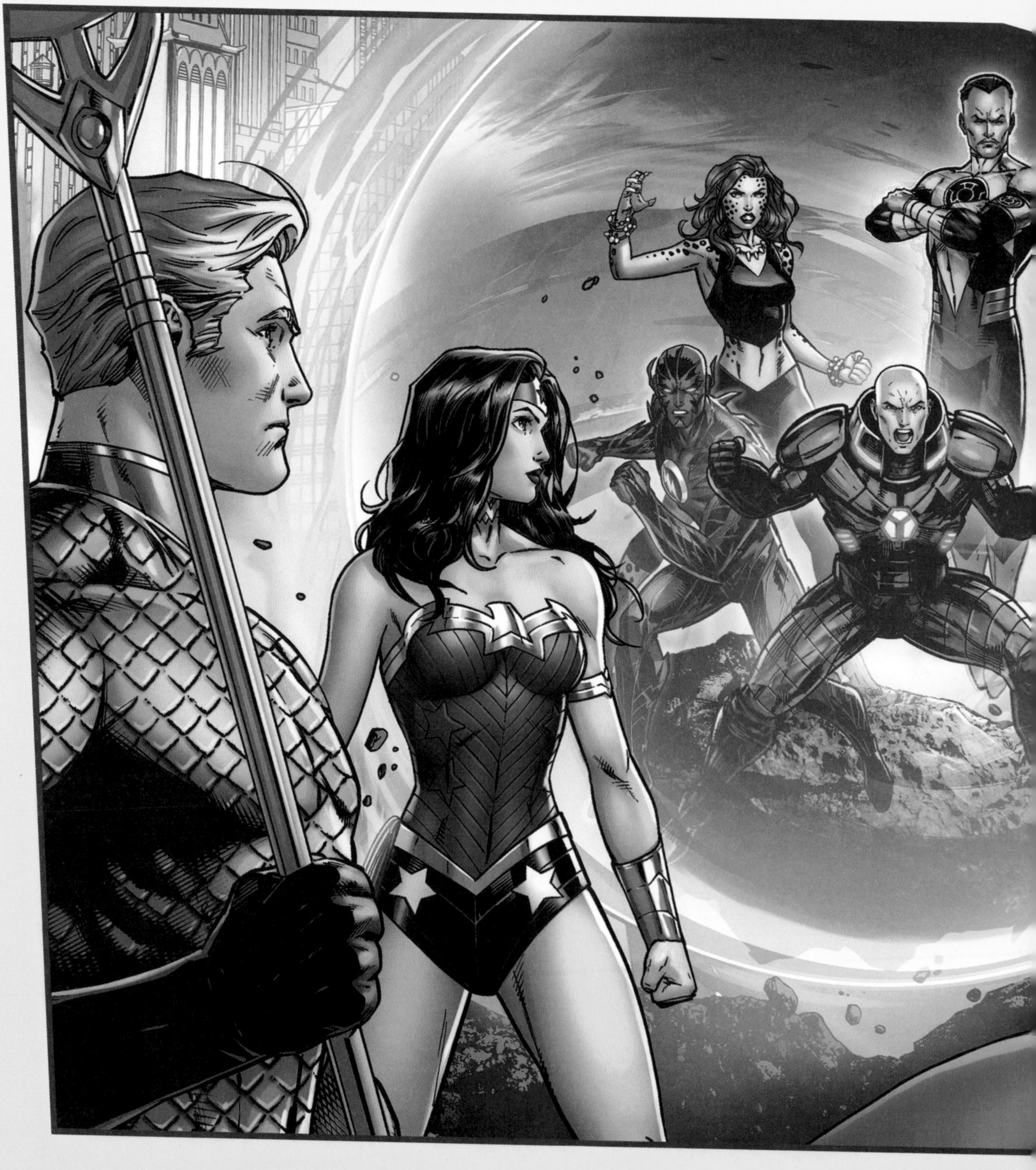

"But not today," said Wonder Woman. "One thing you don't understand about being a super hero is that we win by working together, adapting our abilities to the situation and helping one another."

"And if there's one thing we have plenty of," Superman added, "it's . . ."

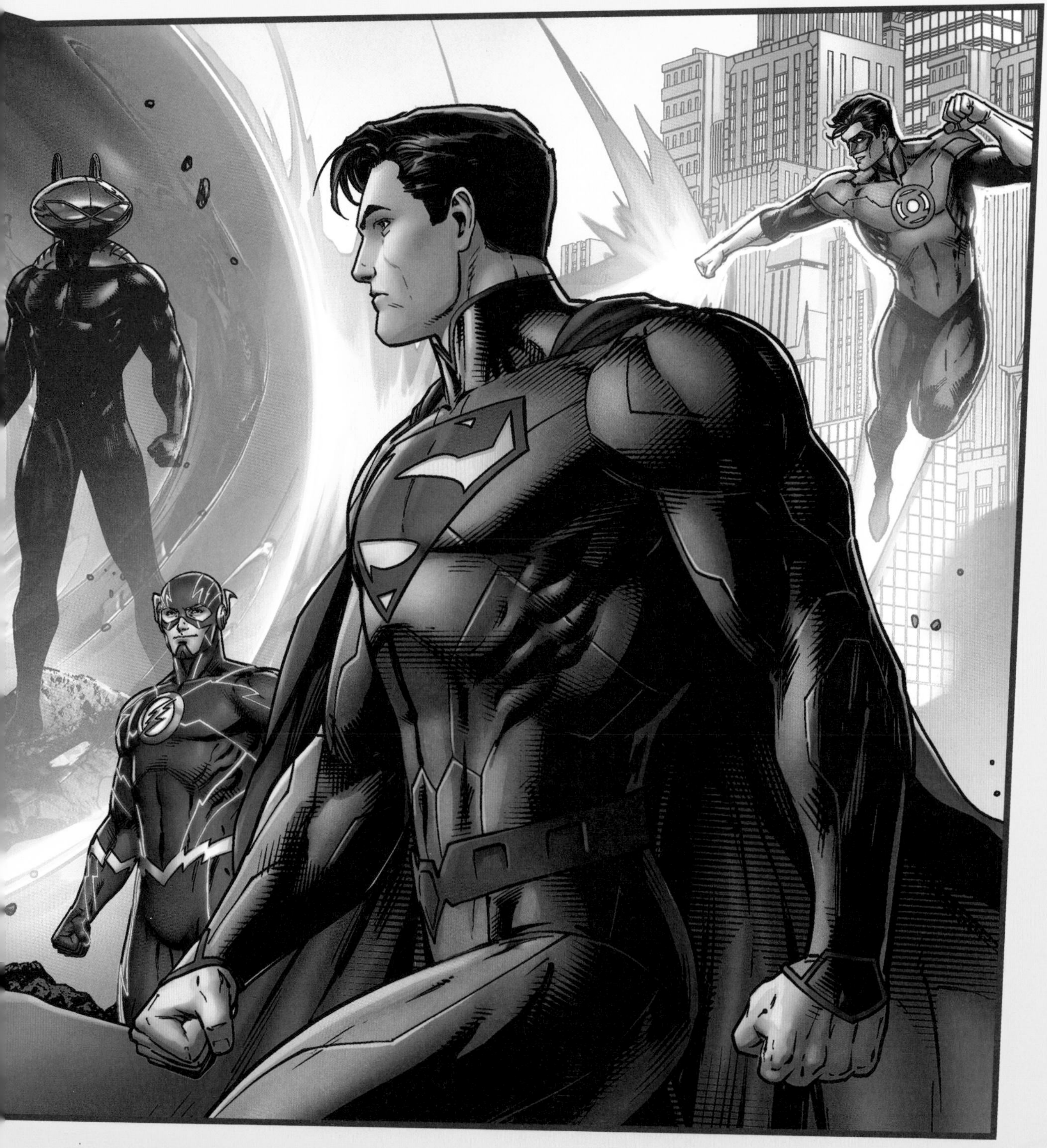

“Teamwork,” Wonder Woman finished. “And that’s how the Justice League always saves the day!”

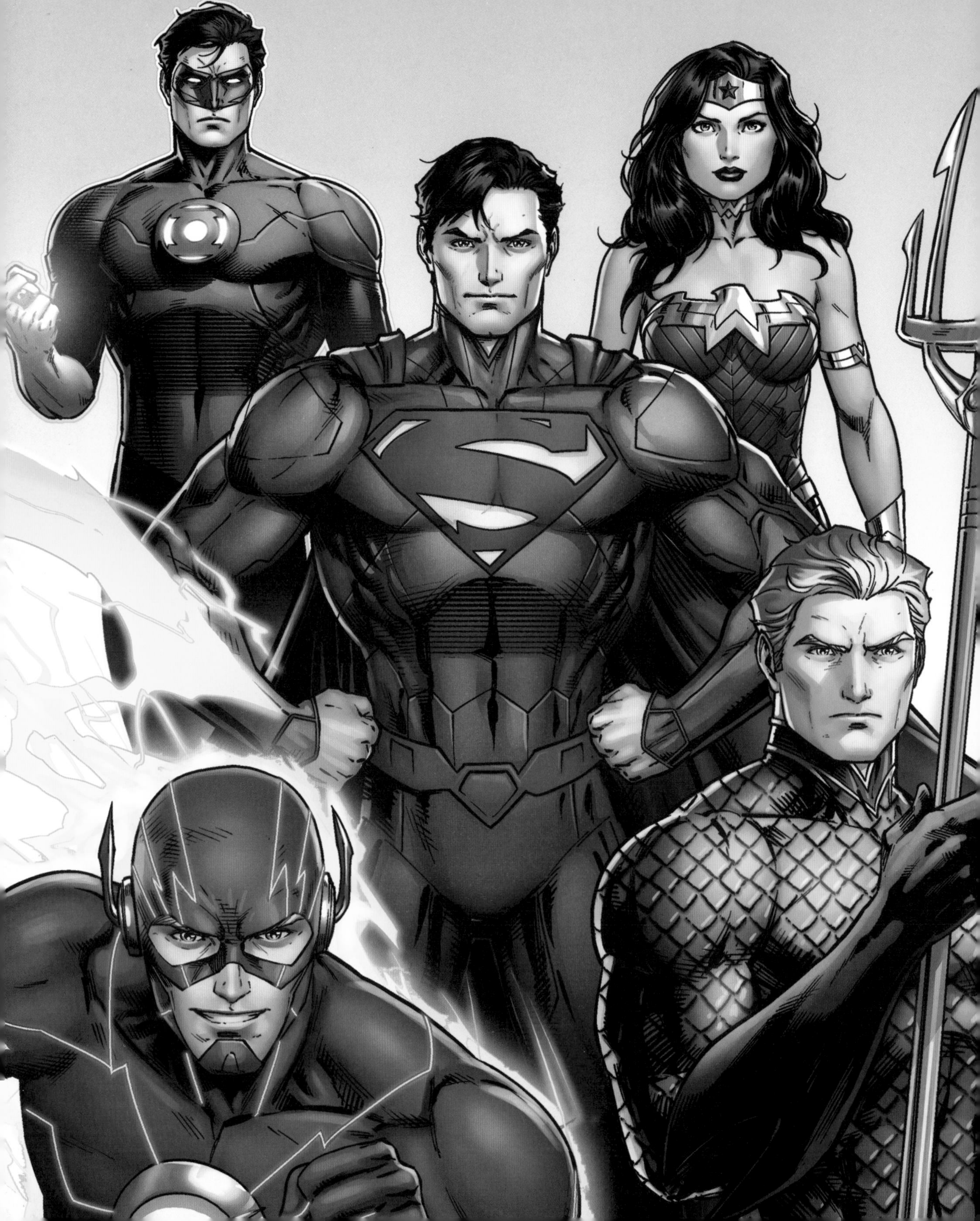

MEDUSA'S MAZE

Wonder Woman was returning from her home on the Island of Themyscira when her flight took her over some of the sights and wonders of ancient Greece that tourists loved to visit.

She suddenly heard a strange voice in her head. *Come to me,* the voice seemed to say. *There are many in danger, and only you can rescue them . . . if you dare.*

"I don't who you are," Wonder Woman said. "But I will come to the rescue of anyone who needs my help."

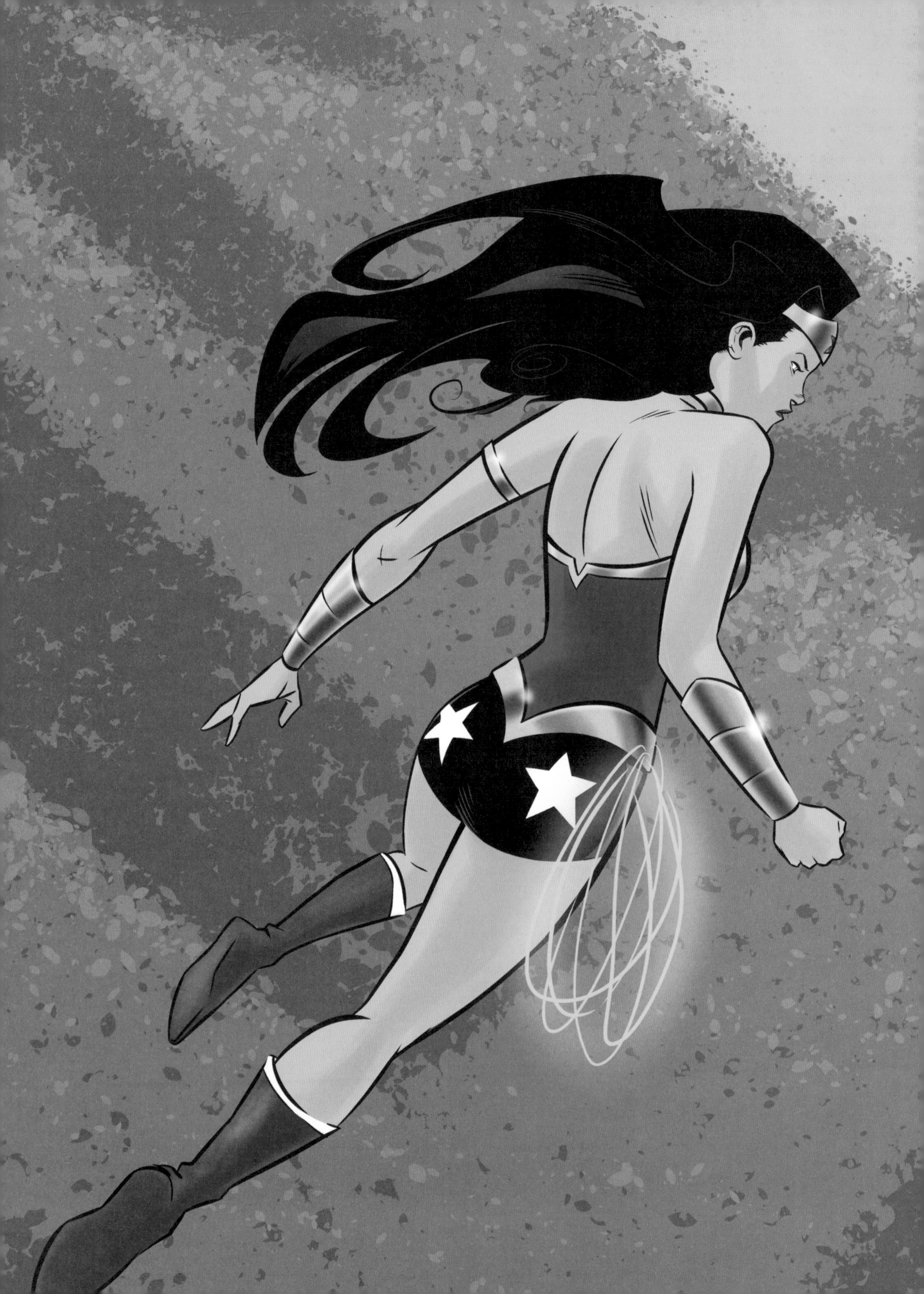

Oh, I'm counting on that, the voice said.

In the distance, the Amazon spotted a huge stone column that seemed to be at the center of a huge garden maze carved out of the plants and bushes of a very old garden.

"This is strange," Wonder Woman said. "But I had better investigate, in case someone is in trouble."

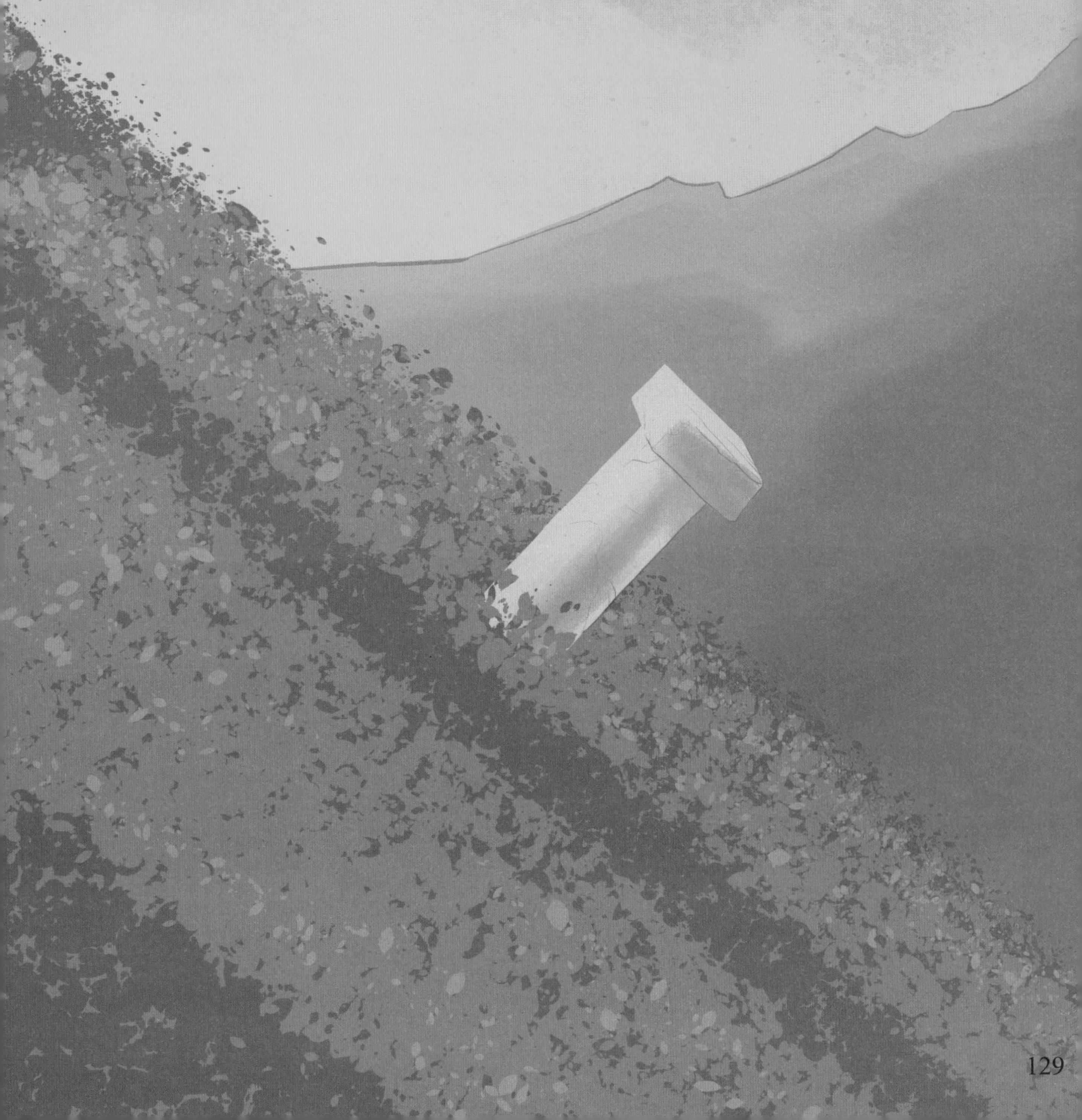

Wonder Woman cautiously made her way through the maze. The deeper she went, the more complex the maze became. And then she noticed something really out of the ordinary. She saw statues of animals.

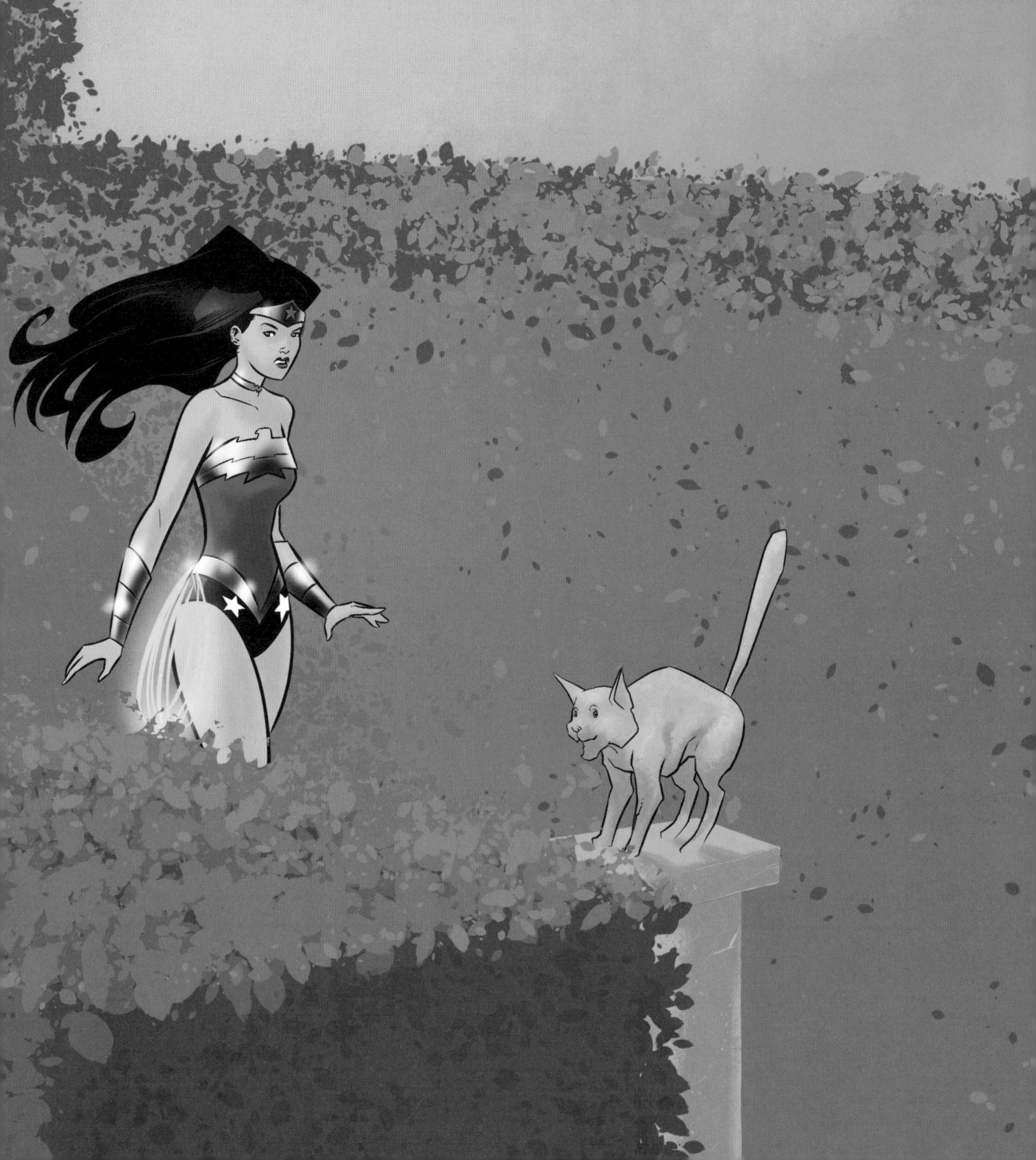

"Cats. Dogs. Other creatures," Wonder Woman said, examining them closely one by one. "They look so real—and so frightened. I get the feeling that there's more here than meets the eye."

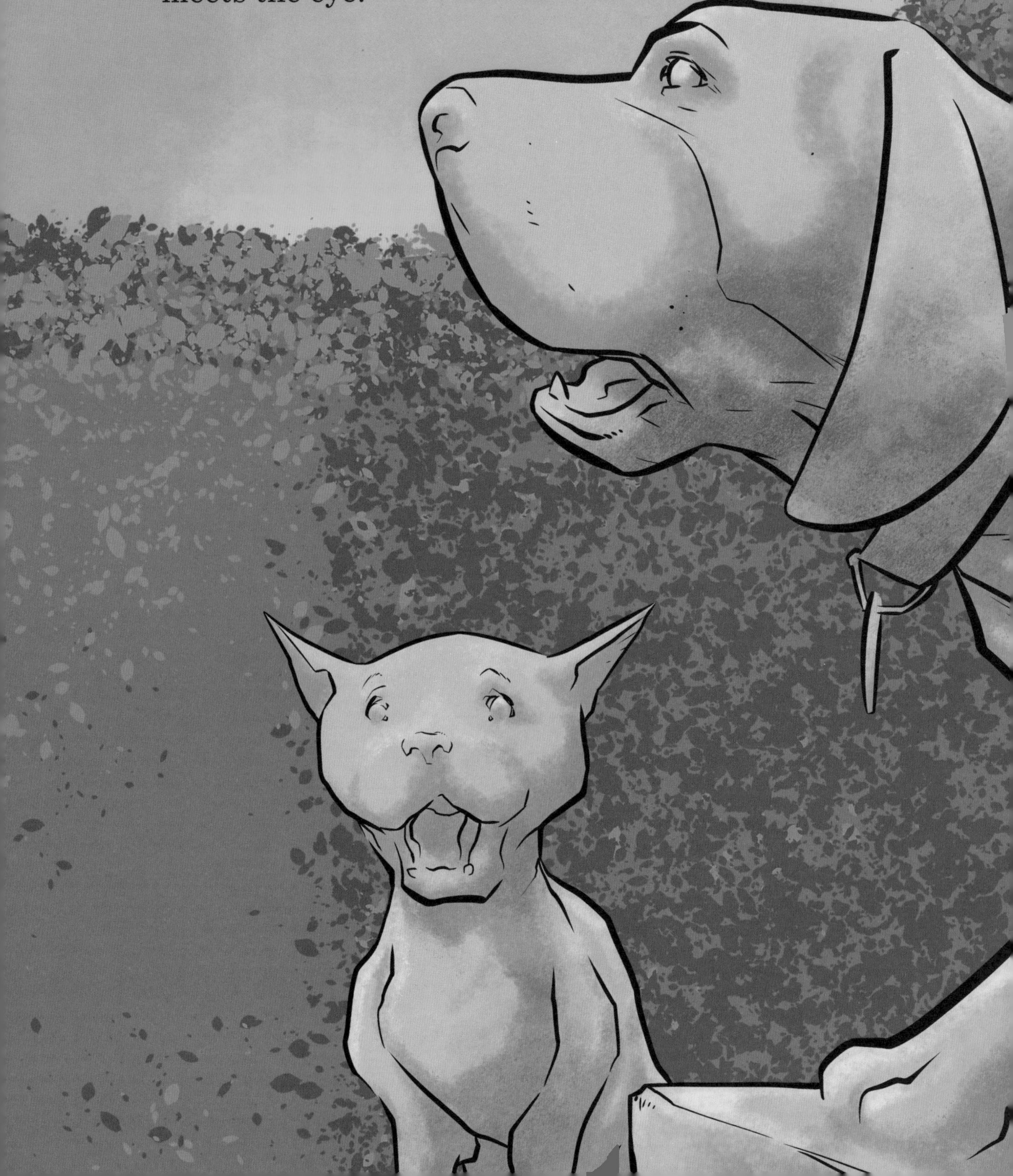

When the hero turned the next corner, she found another statue and gasped. It was a big stone reproduction of the famed winged horse from mythology named Pegasus.

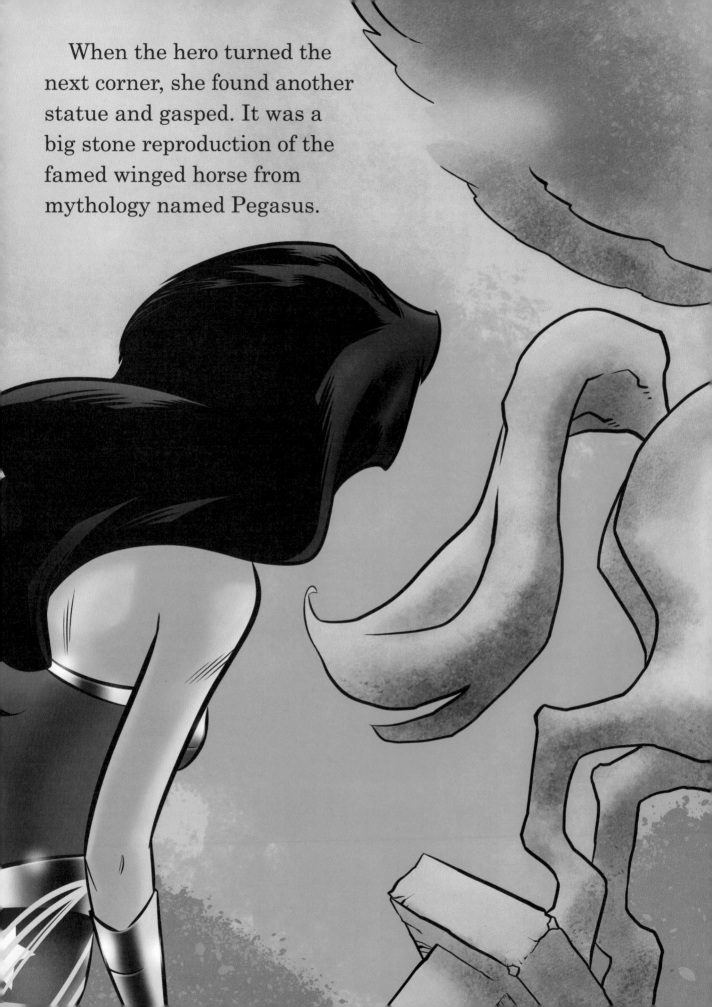

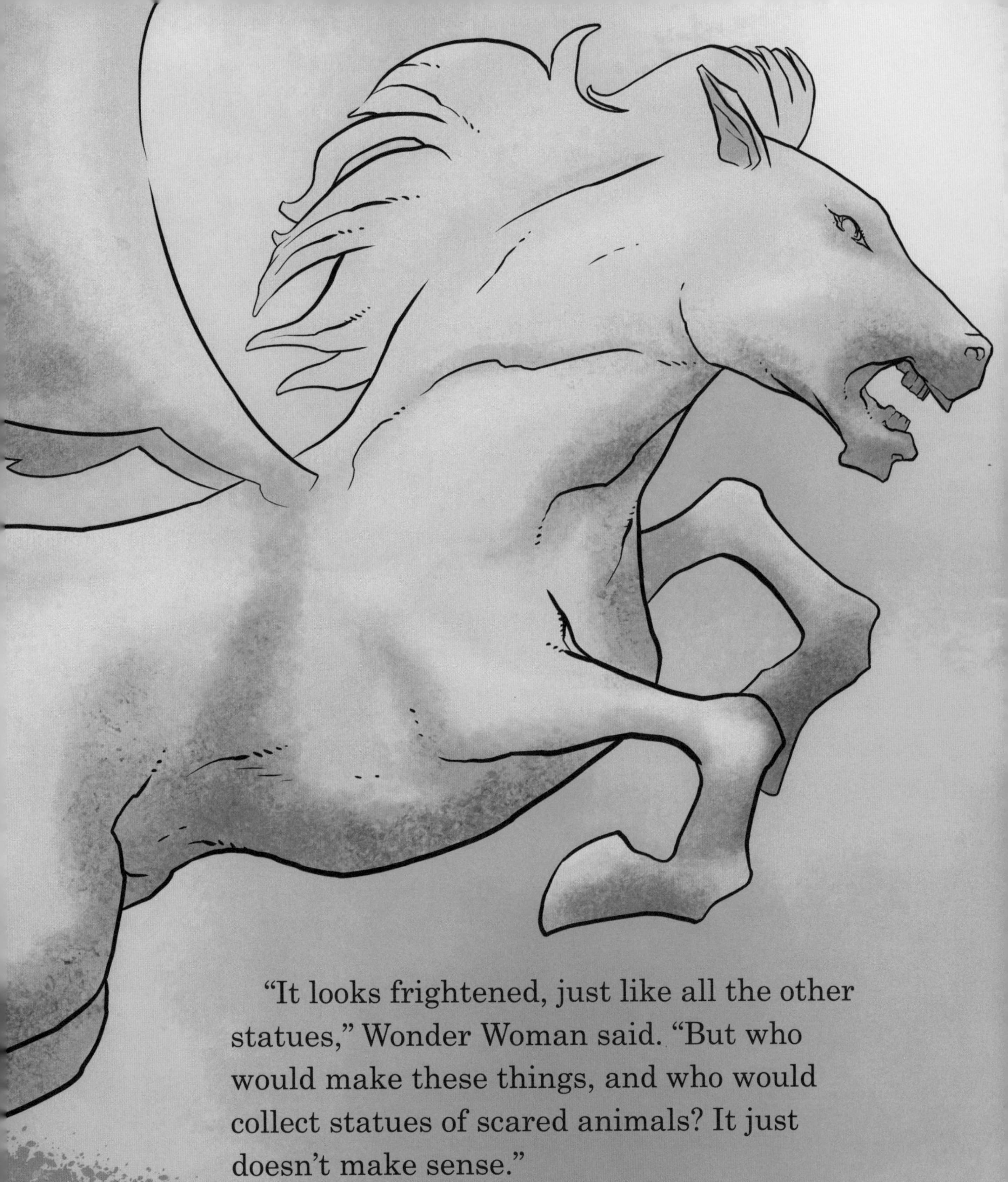

"It looks frightened, just like all the other statues," Wonder Woman said. "But who would make these things, and who would collect statues of scared animals? It just doesn't make sense."

"Oh, no!" Wonder Woman cried out as she went even farther into the maze and saw more statues. "These statues look like frightened *people*! In fact, I think they're actually real people! And the animals are real, too. Who would do this?"

Heh-heh-heh. I told you there was danger, the voice said in her head. *You'll have to look deeper into the maze if you want to solve this mystery.*

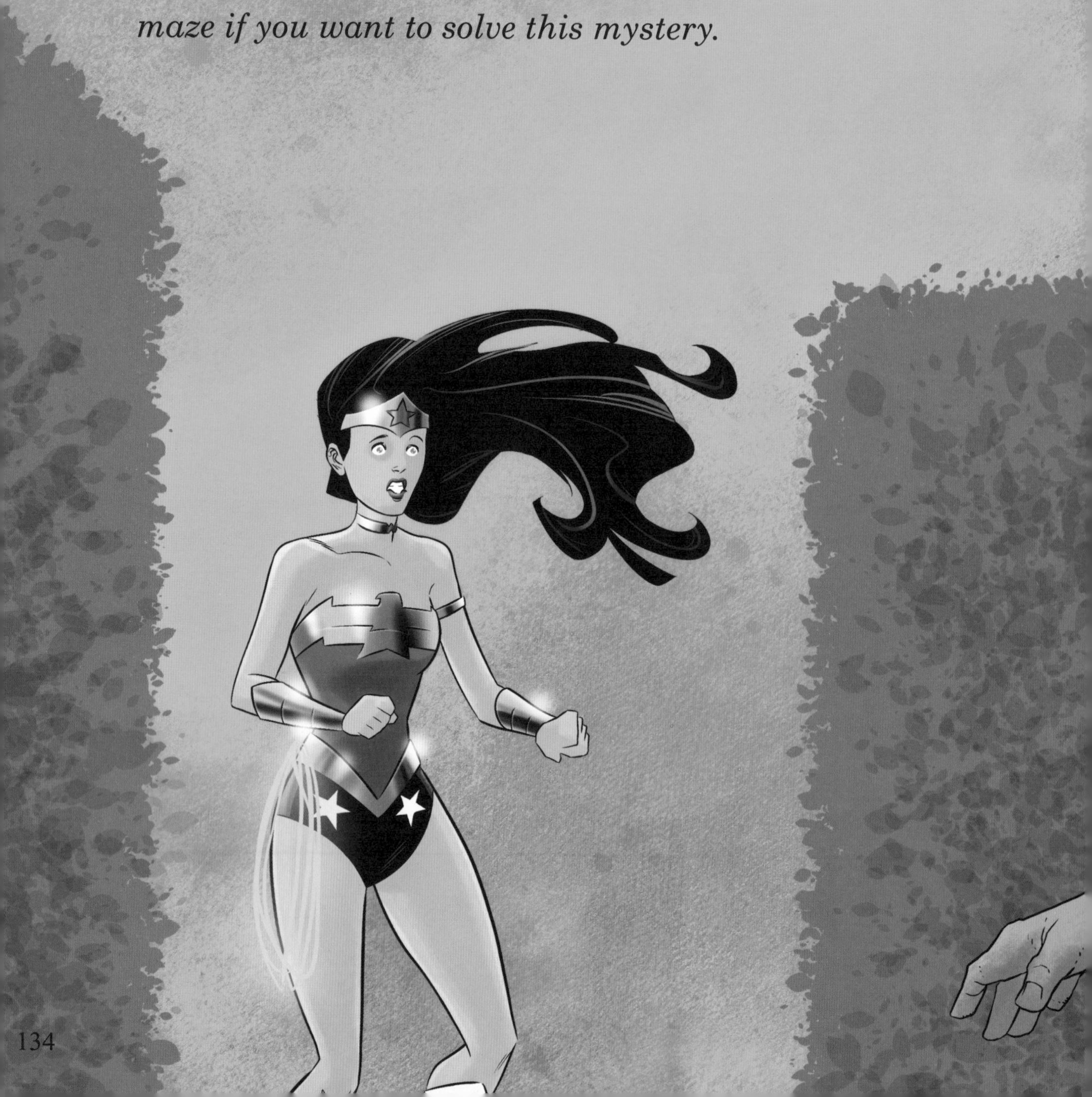

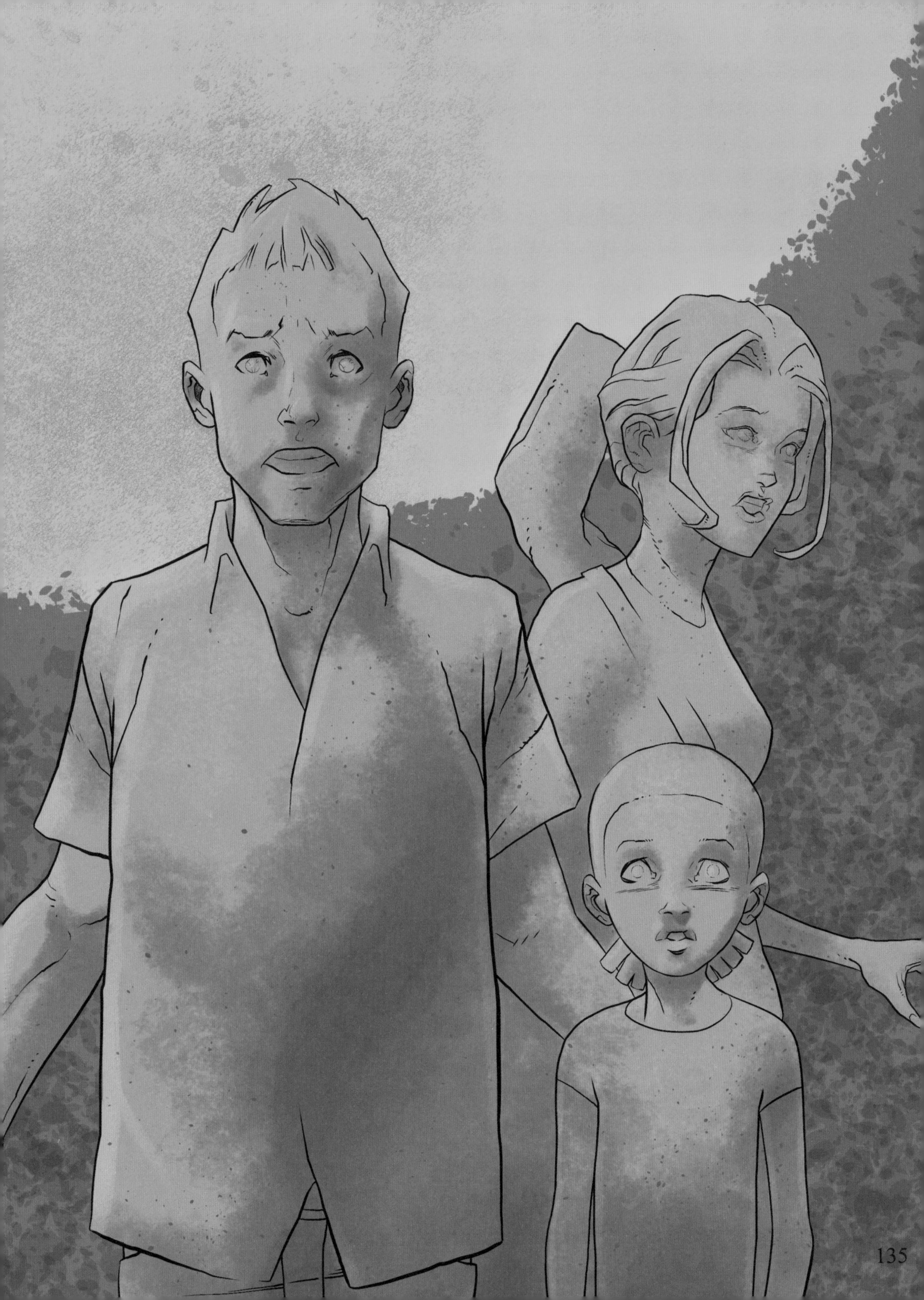

Wonder Woman tilted her head when she heard faint footsteps somewhere nearby. And there was another sound.

Hisssssssss . . .

"That's the sound of snakes," Wonder Woman whispered to herself. "And that can only mean one thing. . . .

IT'S MEDUSA!"

Wonder Woman remembered her lessons from when she was a little girl.

"Medusa was a Gorgon. A monster from classical mythology," she said. "She had a head covered with writhing snakes. And she could turn living creatures to stone with her terrible stare."

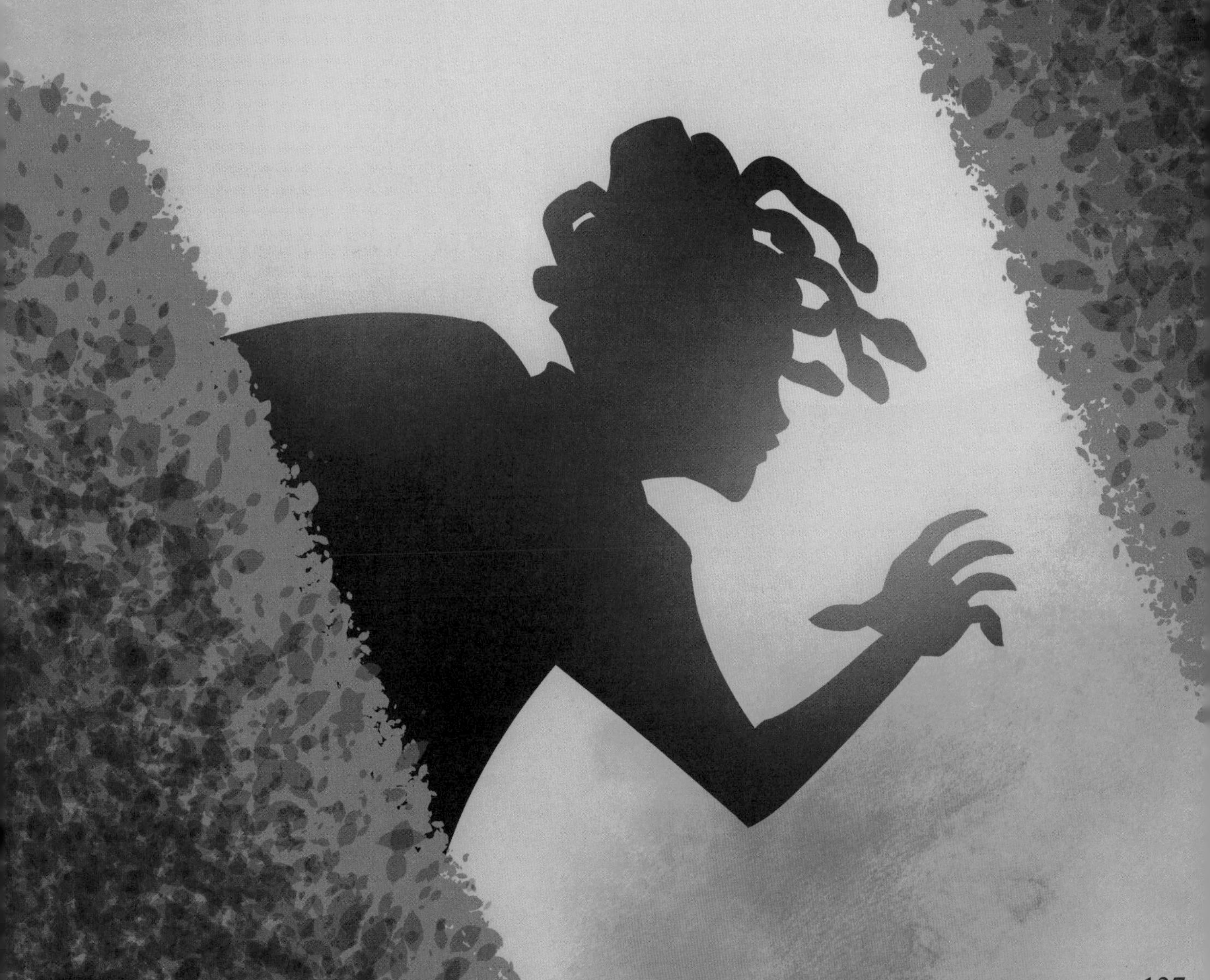

Wonder Woman continued through the maze.

"I'd better not let her sneak up on me," she said. "I'm going to find her first."

The Amazon slipped silently through the bushes. She listened for the sound of the snakes in Medusa's hair.

Where are you? hissed the voice in the hero's head. *I can sense you near.*

"I'm right here!" Wonder Woman jumped out of the bushes with her eyes closed and her indestructible bracelets up and ready. She always kept them so finely polished that the bracelets were like mirrors.

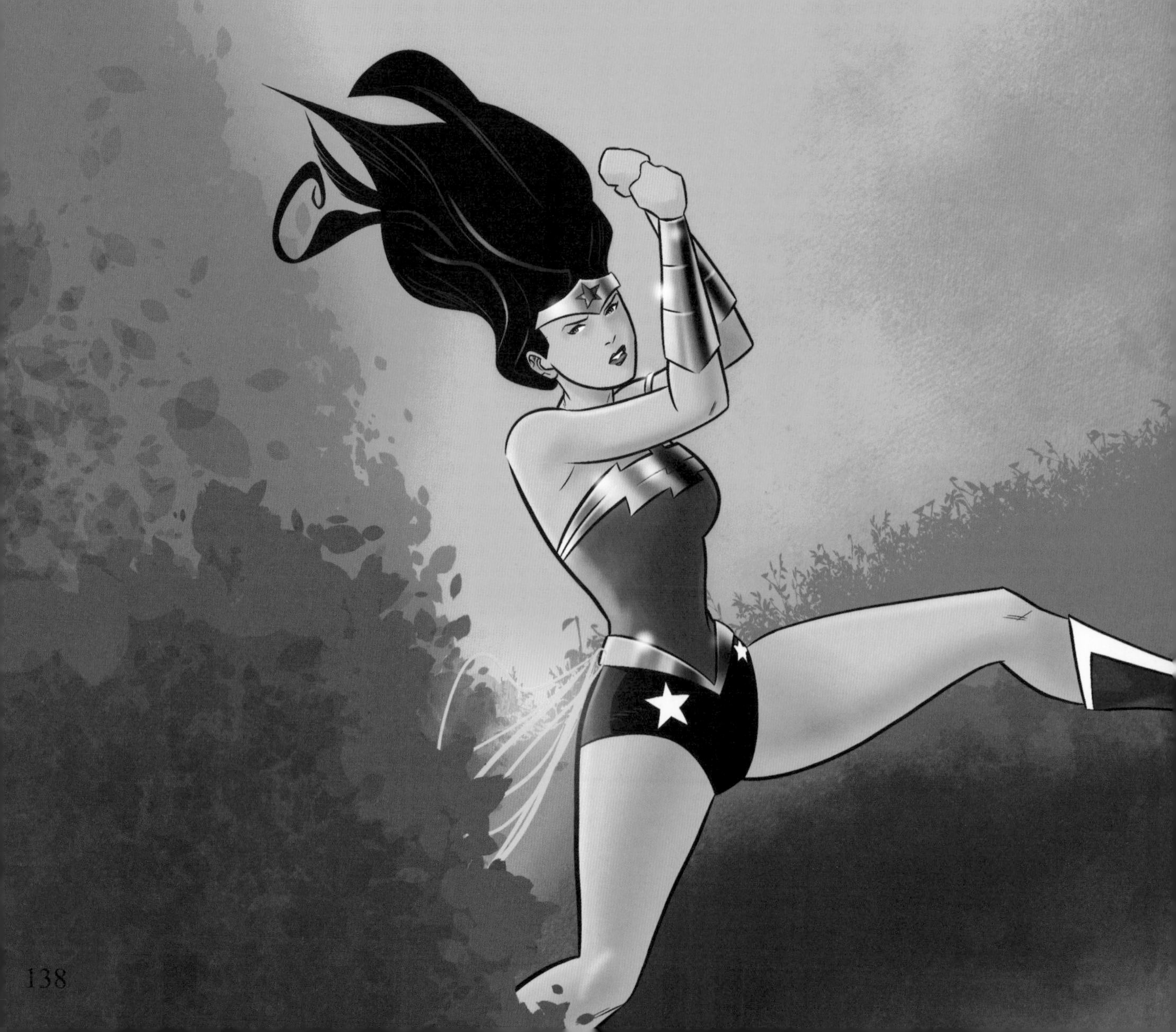

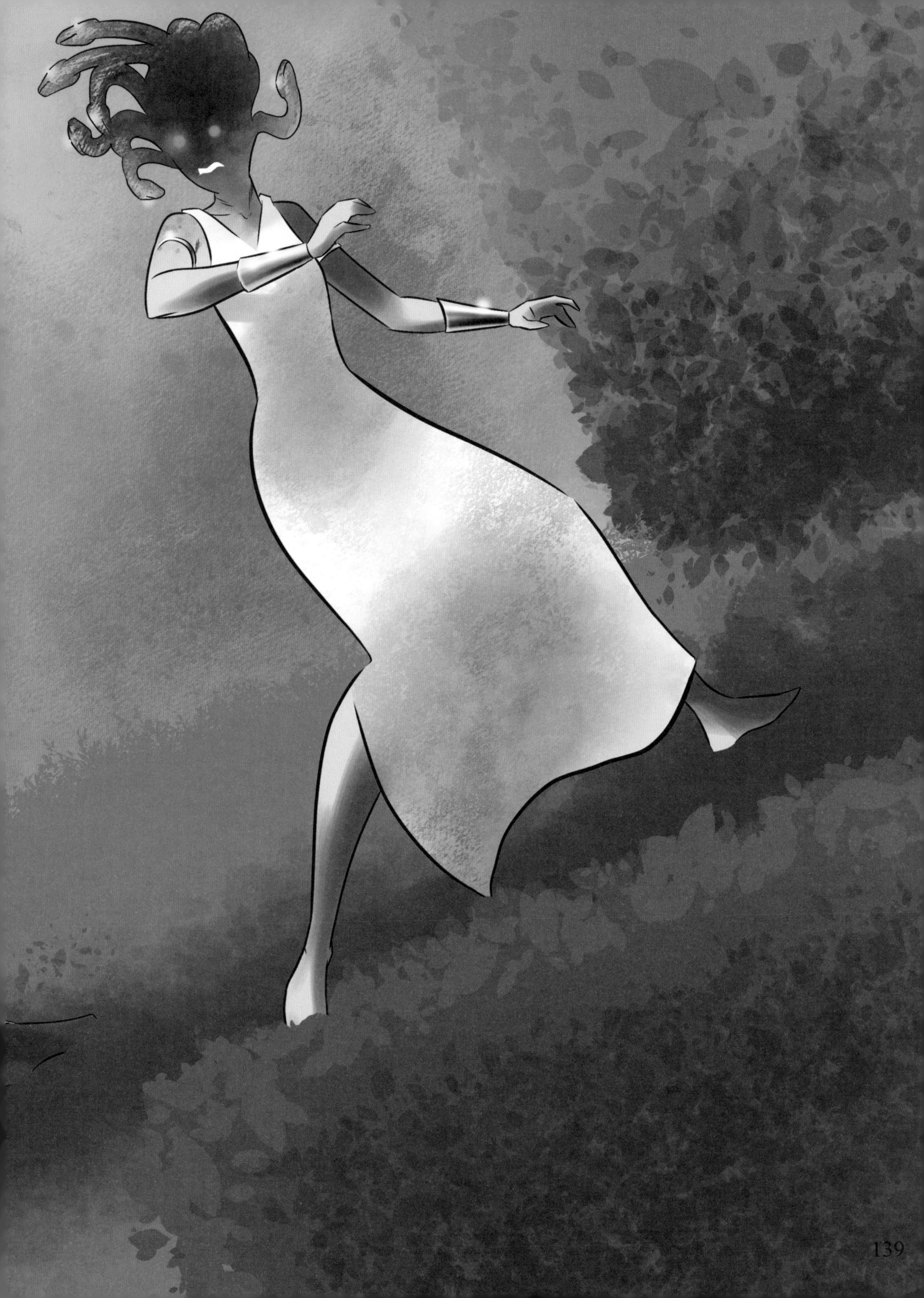

Medusa finally found Wonder Woman. The villain turned to her, hoping to catch the hero with her monstrous stare and make the Amazon her next victim. Instead, she saw herself in Wonder Woman's bracelets. It was the first time Medusa had ever seen herself! She gasped.

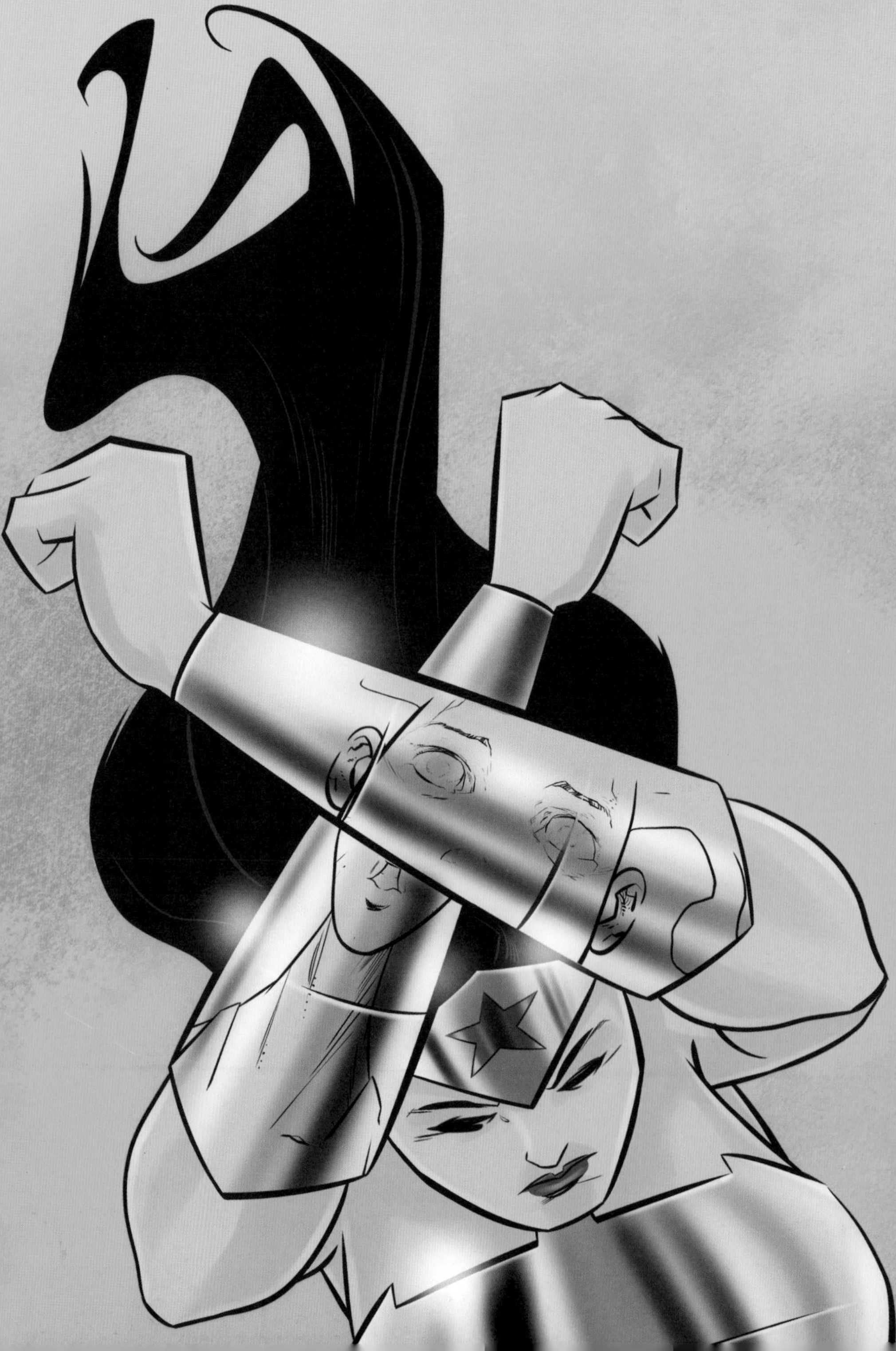

"Oh, no. No. No. No," the Gorgon hissed. She tried to look away, but she had already seen her own terrible reflection, and the magic could not be undone.

Instead of turning Wonder Woman to stone, Medusa turned *herself* into a statue.

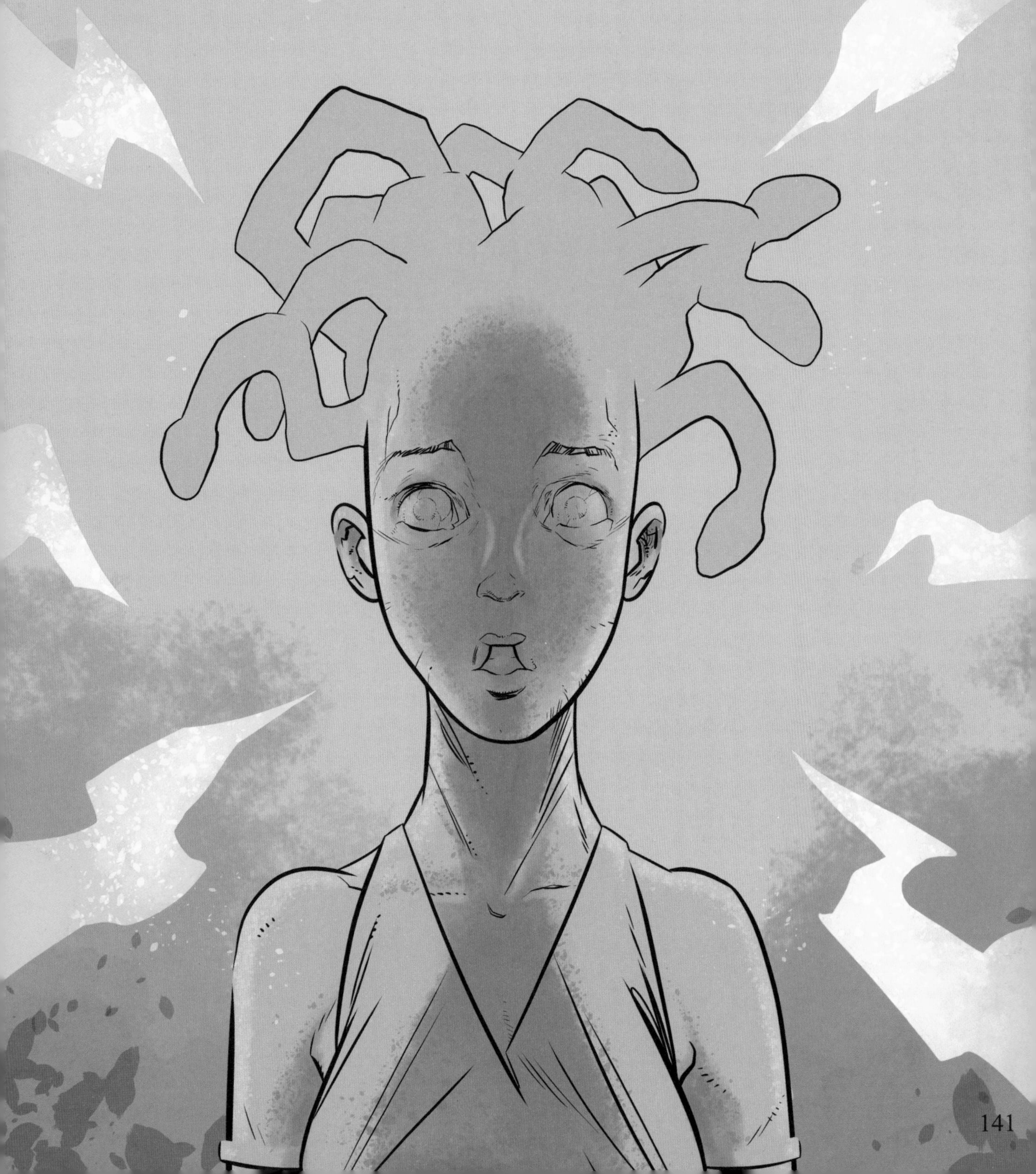

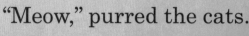

Once the Gorgon turned to stone,
her magic began to fade from the maze.
Slowly, all the animals came back to life.
"Woof!" barked the dogs.
"Meow," purred the cats.

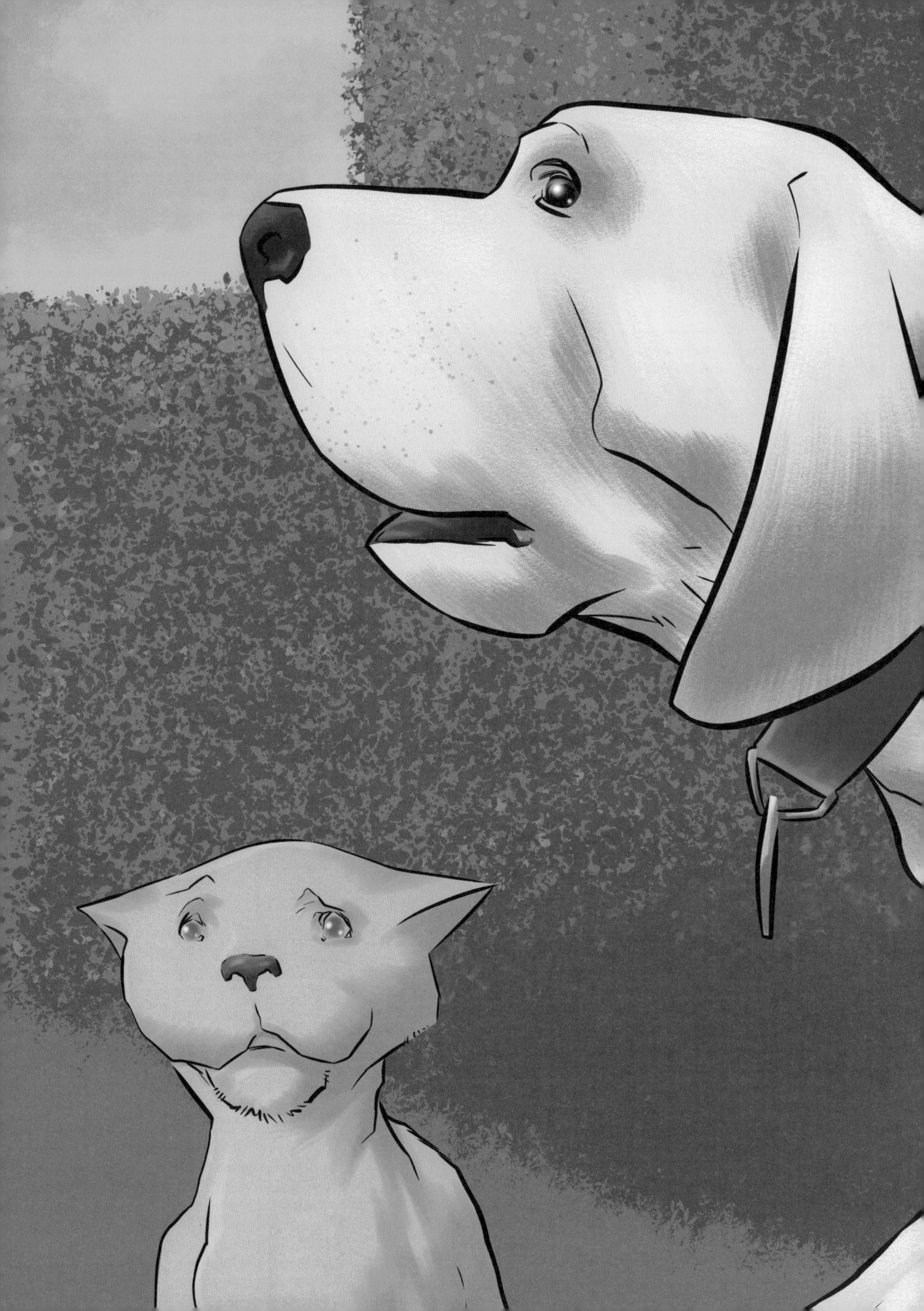

The humans were next. A little girl raced over to Wonder Woman.

"Thank you," she cried, throwing her arms around the hero. "You're so brave."

"Being brave is just doing what you know is right," Wonder Woman replied.

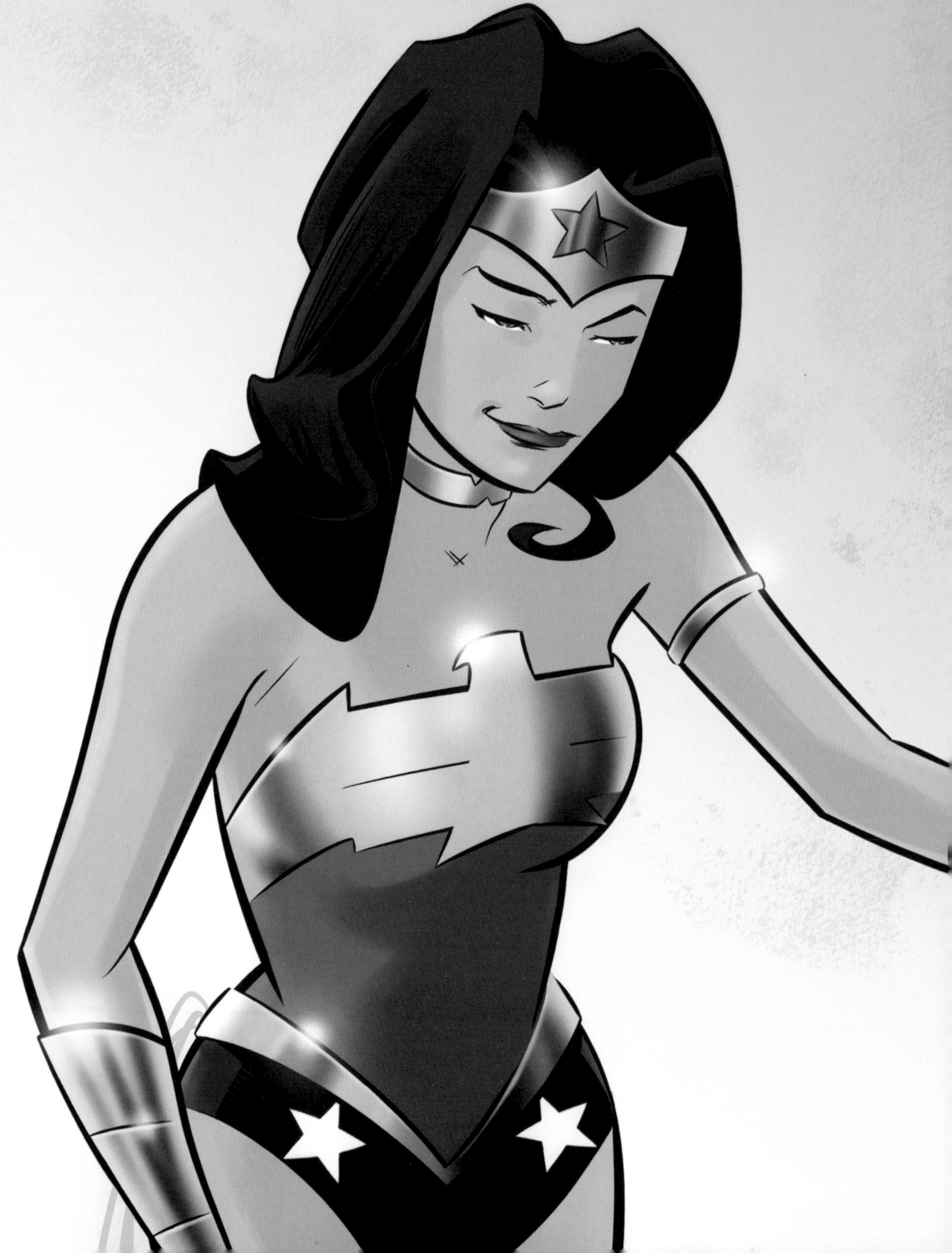

“Even when there are snakes?” the little girl asked.

“Yes, even when there are snakes,” Wonder Woman said with a laugh.

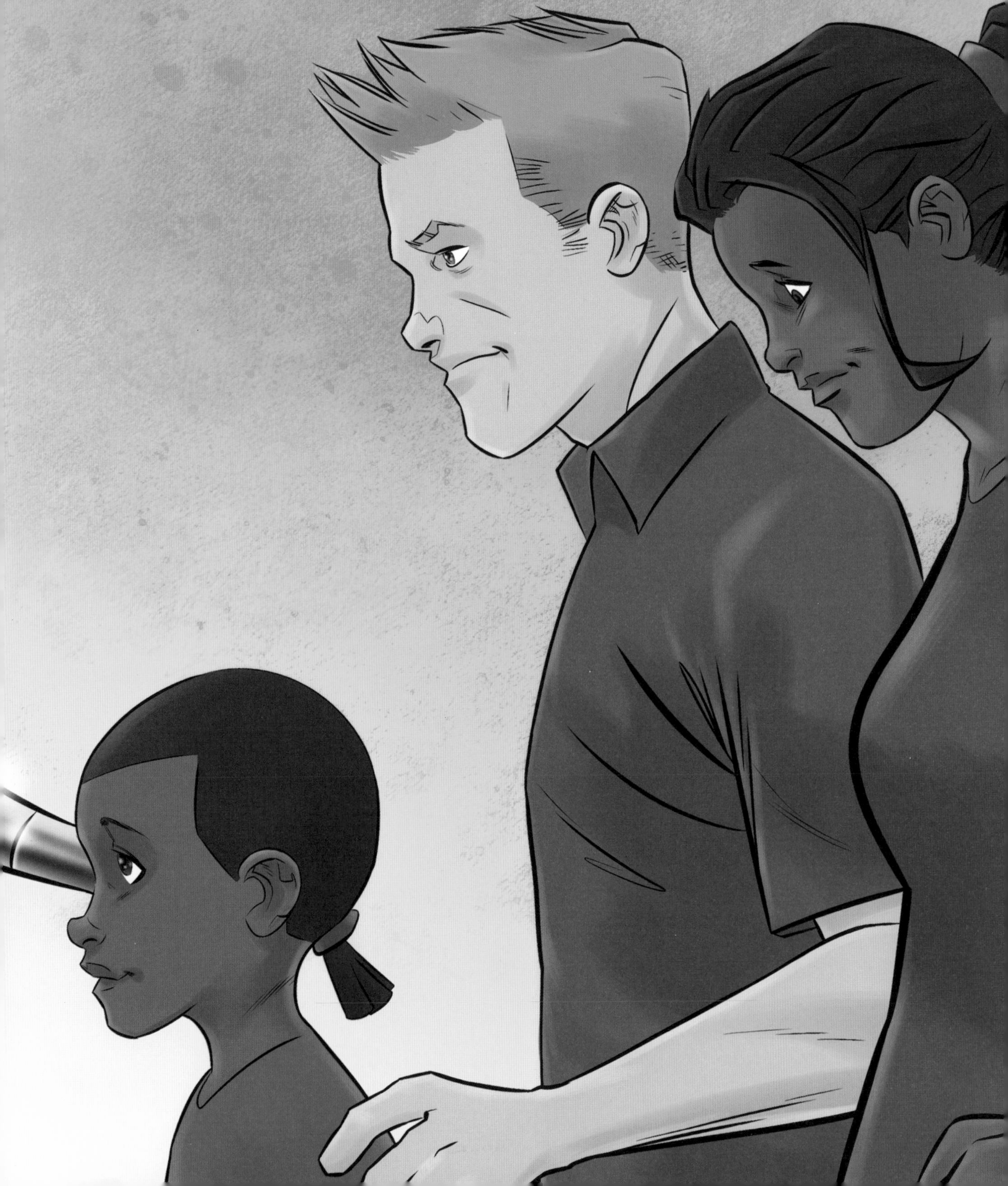

"You've already done so much," said the girl's father. "But . . ."

"How do we get home?" the girl's mother finished.

"I know! I know!" the little girl squealed. "Can we ride Pegasus home?"

"That's up to him," Wonder Woman said. "Let's go ask."

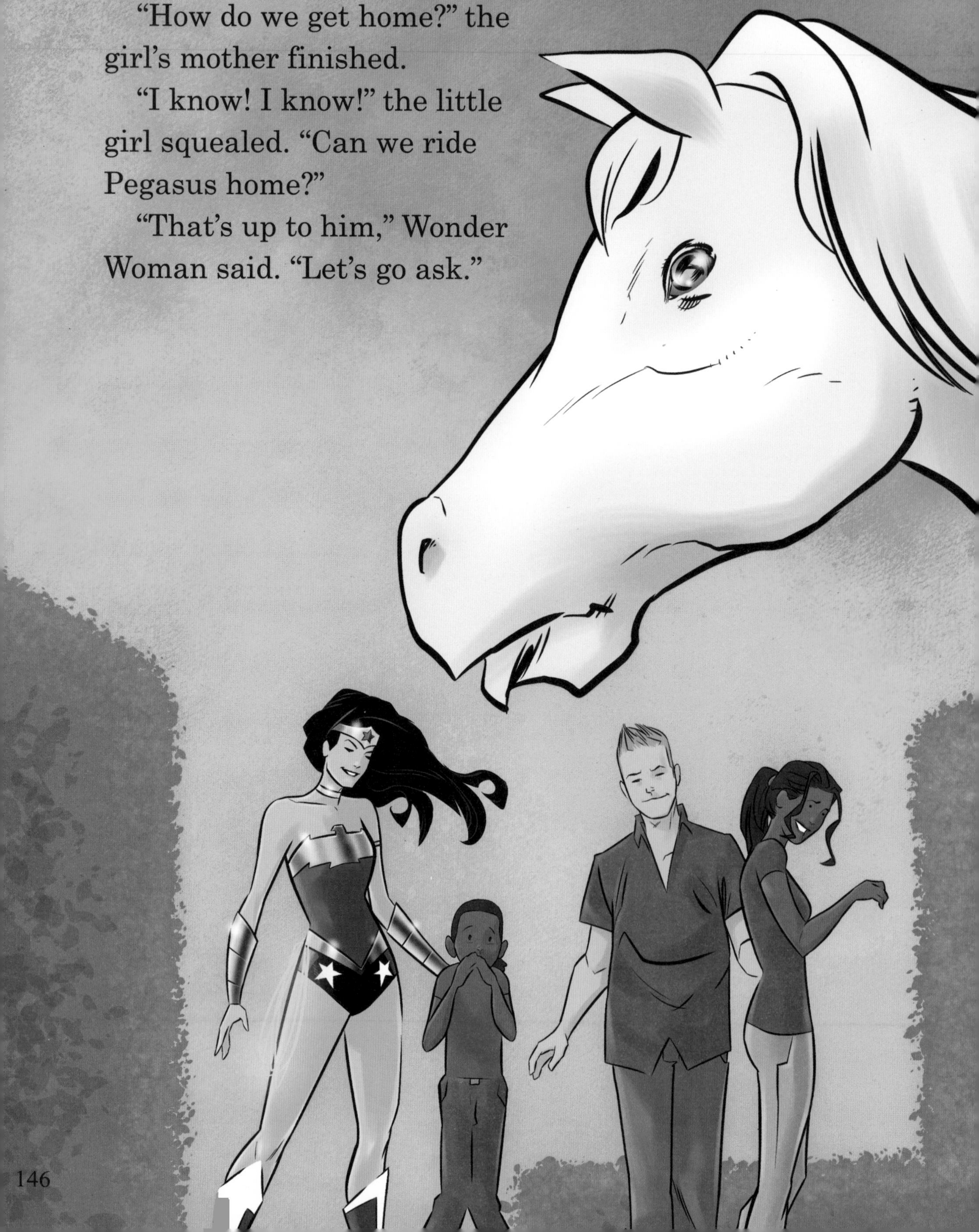

The girl's parents looked at each other nervously. Riding a magnificent winged horse was not something most people ever got to do.

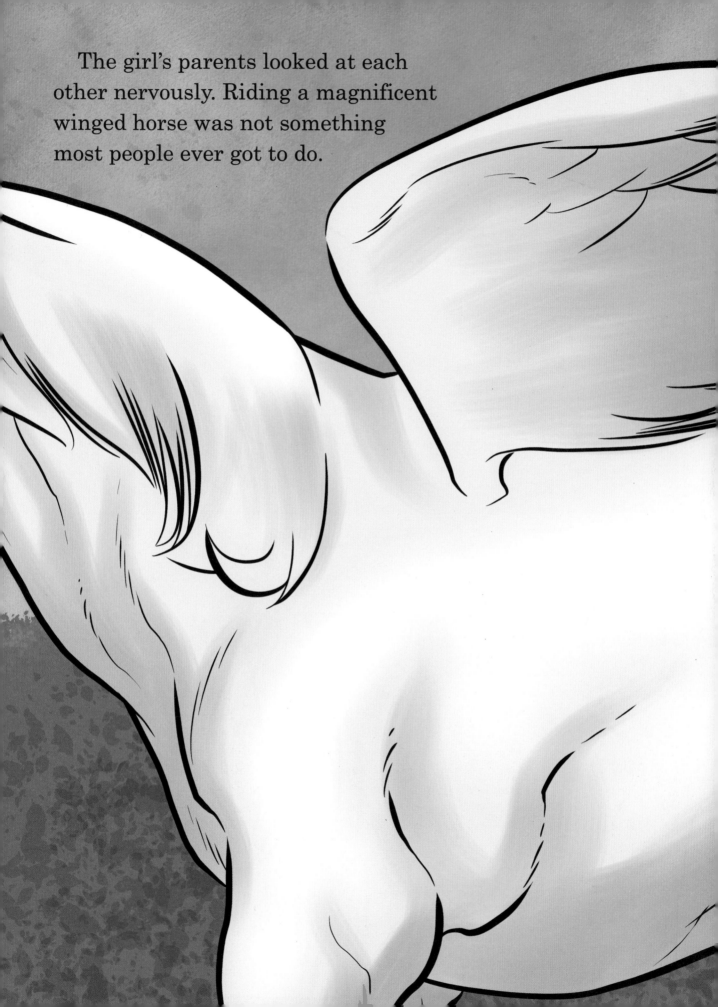

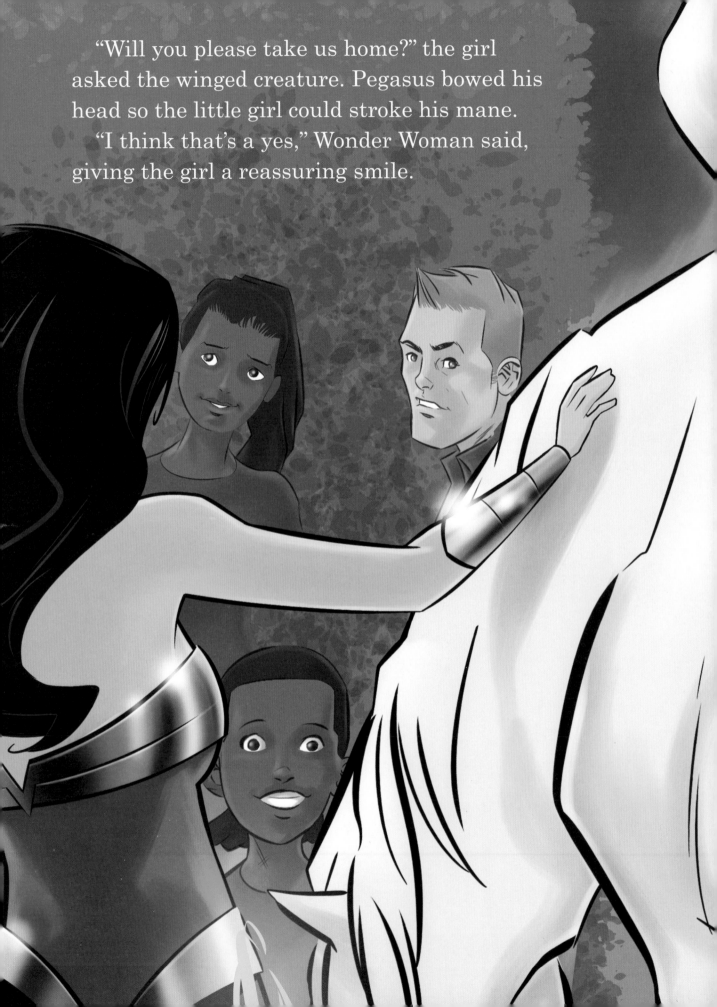

"Will you please take us home?" the girl
asked the winged creature. Pegasus bowed his
head so the little girl could stroke his mane.
   "I think that's a yes," Wonder Woman said,
giving the girl a reassuring smile.

The family climbed onto the horse. Pegasus stretched her mighty wings and soared into the air.

"Whee!" the girl shrieked. Her parents held on tight and tried not to look down.

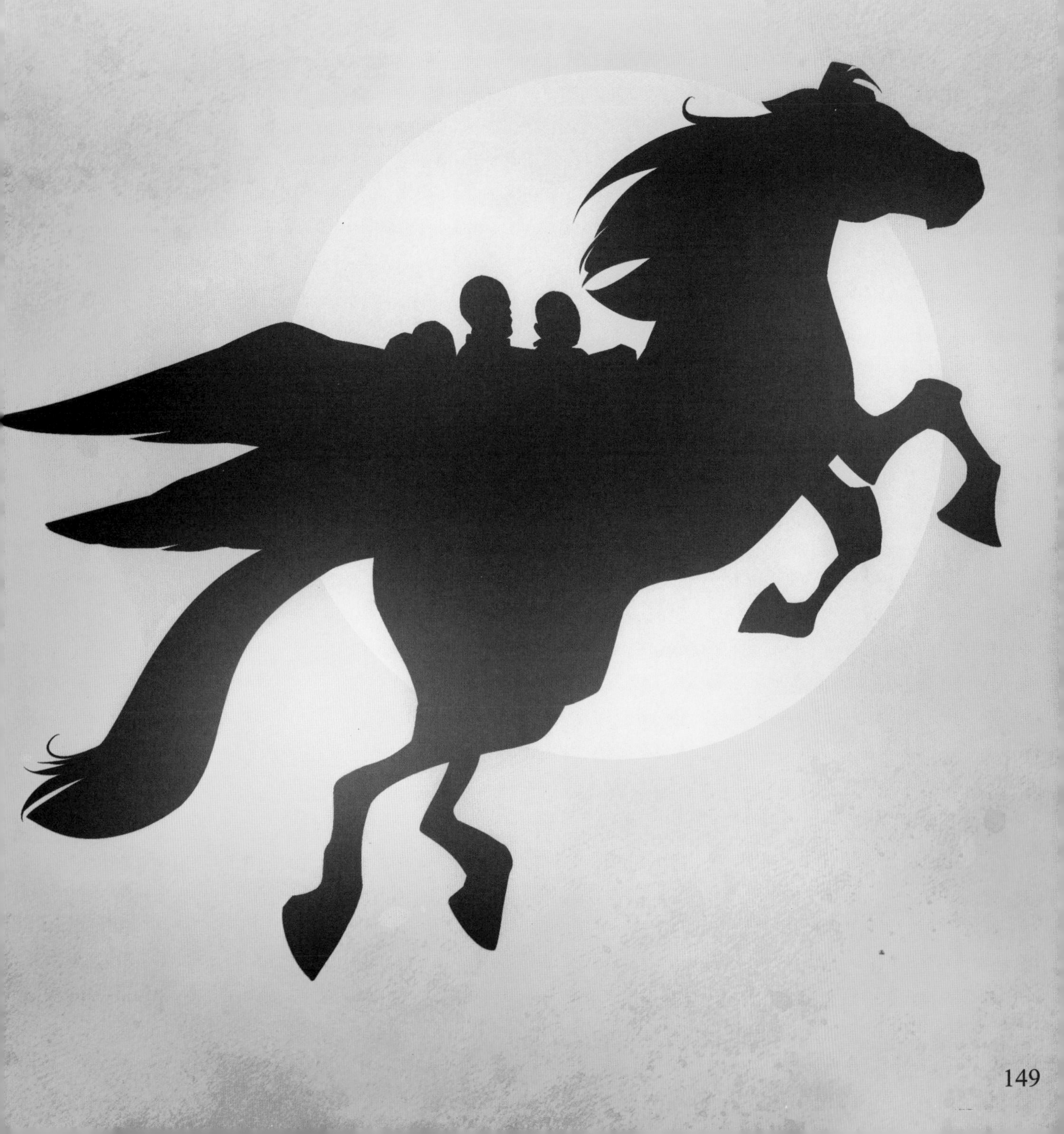

Wonder Woman soared next to them. She would lead the way home.

The amazing Amazon had saved the day again.

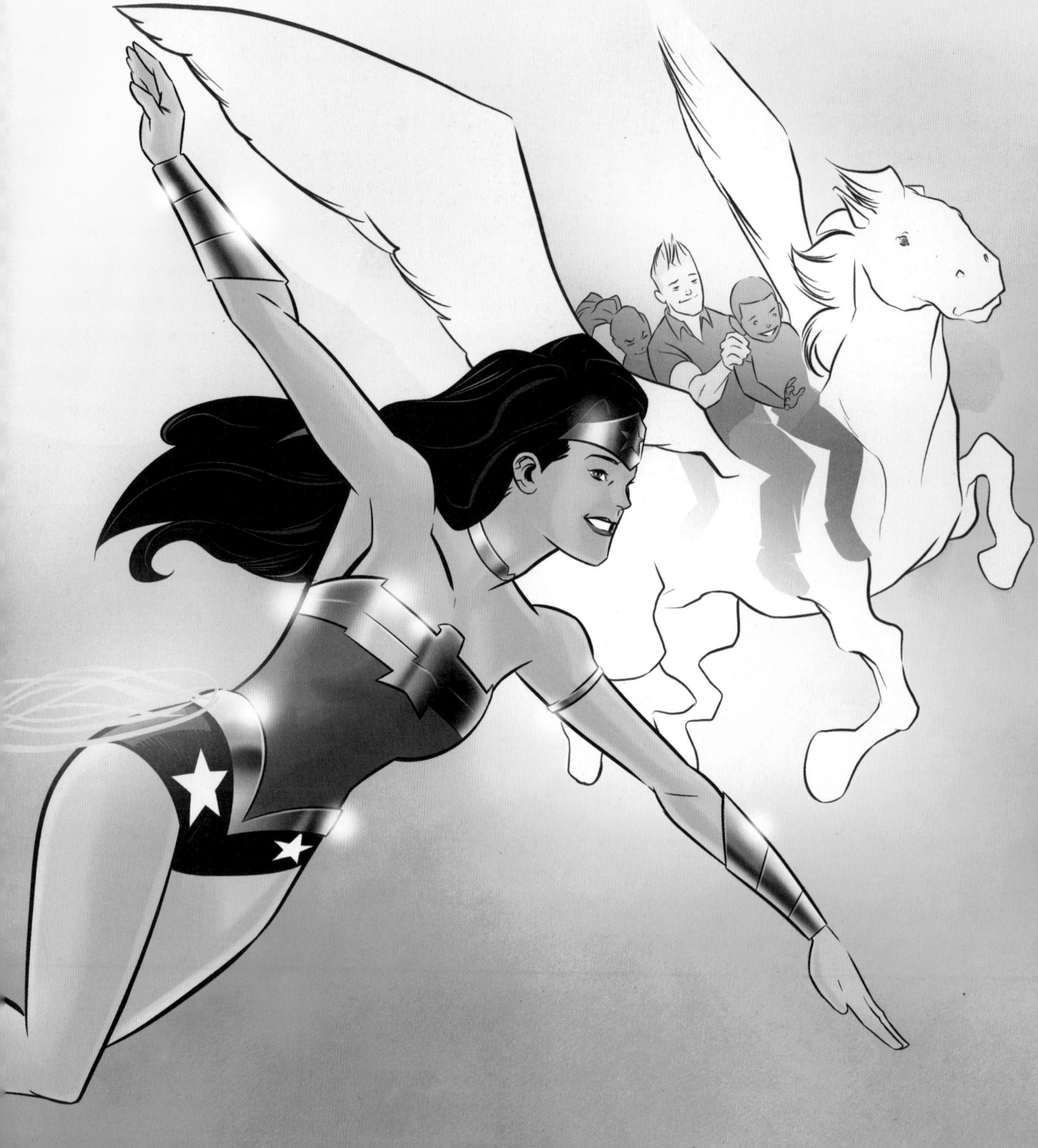